STAR TREK®
MYRIAD UNIVERSES
SHATTERED LIGHT

STAR TREK®
MYRIAD UNIVERSES
SHATTERED LIGHT

David R. George III
Steve Mollmann & Michael Schuster
Scott Pearson

Based upon *Star Trek* and *Star Trek: The Next Generation*®
created by Gene Roddenberry

Star Trek: Deep Space Nine®
created by Rick Berman & Michael Piller

and *Star Trek: Enterprise*®
created by Rick Berman & Brannon Braga

GALLERY BOOKS
New York   London   Toronto   Sydney   Galor IV

Gallery Books
A Division of Simon & Schuster, Inc.
1230 Avenue of the Americas
New York, NY 10020

First Pocket Books trade paperback edition December 2010

GALLERY BOOKS and colophon are registered trademarks of Simon & Schuster, Inc.

For information about special discounts for bulk purchases, please contact Simon & Schuster Special Sales at 1-866-506-1949 or business@simonandschuster.com.

The Simon & Schuster Speakers Bureau can bring authors to your live event. For more information or to book an event, contact the Simon & Schuster Speakers Bureau at 1-866-248-3049 or visit our website at www.simonspeakers.com.

Manufactured in the United States of America

10   9   8   7   6   5   4   3   2   1

Library of Congress Cataloging-in-Publication Data

Shattered light / David R. George III . . . [et al.].—1st Gallery Books trade paperback ed.
    p. cm.—(Star Trek. Myriad universes)
    1. Star Trek fiction. 2. Science fiction, American. I. George, David R., III.
II. Star trek, the next generation (Television program)
    PS648.S3S455 2010
    813.087620806—dc22   2010022986

ISBN 978-1-4391-4841-9
ISBN 978-1-4516-0590-7 (ebook)

The Embrace of Cold Architects

David R. George III

To Steven H. Pilchik,
The first stranger I met in a strange land,
Who turned out to be a fine man and a lifelong friend,
One of the few who always understood and who always believed,
And whose presence in my life has enriched it greatly.

Until the long march of seasons
Brought an empty, treacherous night
That drew her into hollow depths.
I journeyed out, seeking reune
With the soul that lighted my own,
To wrest her from the cold embrace
  Of remorseless winter.

—PHINEAS TARBOLDE,
  "THE LOST CHILD"

Picard: There are times, sir, when men of good conscience cannot
  blindly follow orders.

—"THE OFFSPRING"

I

Like the waters of a vast ocean, the voices threatened to drown him. They surrounded him, weighed him down, pulled him inexorably into their midst. As uncountable as sea waves and as unsympathetic, they battered him from all sides.

Captain Jean-Luc Picard lay on his back, the metal table beneath him once cold and hard, but now beyond his ability to feel. He stared blindly upward, no longer seeing the complex equipment pervading the alien vessel. Numbness suffused his body, a welcome release from the thousand natural shocks to which his flesh had been heir.

A glimmer of recognition darted through Picard's awareness. *Shakespeare*, he thought, grasping for the paraphrased fragment of dialogue, desperate to latch onto something—anything—familiar. *Shakespeare*, The Tragedy . . . The Tragedy of . . .

William Shakespeare, The Tragedy of Hamlet, Prince of Denmark, said a voice in his head—said *all* the voices, knit together as one. Hundreds of Borg—perhaps a thousand or more—spoke in unison, a chorus of unremitting pressure. Until now, their refrain had articulated only pronouncements of conquest: *Strength is irrelevant. Resistance is futile. We will add your biological and technological distinctiveness to our own.*

A single voice loosed itself from the whole and spoke to him through the continued din of the aggregate. *To die, to sleep—no more; and by a sleep to say we end the heartache and the thousand natural shocks that flesh is heir to.* The words came in flat tones, devoid of emotion, the cadence robotic. *Act Three, Scene One, of* Hamlet.

How do they know that? Picard wondered. Had they extracted the information from his brain, or had they gleaned it from some other source? Even as he posed the question, he understood the answer. Though he and the *Enterprise* crew had discovered from their first encounter with the Borg that the physically augmented humanoids procreated, it had grown clear just how they added the "biological distinctiveness" of other species to their own: by brute force. The restraints that bound Picard prevented him from peering down at himself, but earlier he'd heard the awful sound of a drill penetrating the side of his skull, he'd felt the strange sensation of tubes pushing into newly opened holes in his torso, he'd watched a dark, plated mechanism being secured to the right half of his face.

And he had begun to hear their voices, no longer without, but within, side by side with his own thoughts. As he resisted, they continued to tell him that he had been chosen to speak for the Borg in all communications, in order to facilitate their introduction into Federation societies. The Borg would make him one of their own, both physically and mentally—just as they had with so many others. Their knowledge of Shakespeare had not come from him, but from some other individuals they had incorporated into their hive.

When did you learn Shakespeare? came another lone voice, barely distinguishable from that of the Borg mass, yet divergent enough to impose a primacy of attention.

Where did you learn Shakespeare? asked a second.

Why did you learn Shakespeare? demanded a third.

Picard did not intend to respond in any way, but his mind's eye conjured the image of a classroom. He saw himself in school at the age of fourteen, listening to Ms. DeGiglio, his literature instructor. He knew at once that the Borg had in that moment ascertained the answers they'd just sought, and more: the appearance and name of his teacher. The mere act of hearing their questions had amounted to an irresistible interrogation.

More voices peeled away from the ongoing swell of Borg thought rushing through Picard's mind.

What else did you learn?

What scientific concepts did you learn?

What scientific applications did you learn?

Though he made no conscious effort to do so, Picard thought about the warp-field effect, about the equations he'd studied during his years at Starfleet Academy. He envisioned the classroom, the campus in San Francisco, diagrams in textbooks, and schematics he'd seen in *Enterprise*'s engineering section. Distressed by the idea of the Borg gathering any information at all about Starfleet and its abilities, Picard attempted to blank his mind. He understood that the human brain did not function as a computer did, or even as Data's positronic brain did. The Borg could not simply download his organic intelligence and memory, so that they could then scour the data for useful information, but after connecting their collective mind to his psyche, they could "see" and "hear" his waking thoughts. If they could compel him to think of some particular detail, then they could incorporate that detail into their own body of knowledge.

Despair washed over Picard like the tide, carried along by the unrelenting voices of the Borg. They had already exhausted his body and his mind, leaving him with a faltering resolve that he knew he couldn't maintain for much longer. He had promised to resist the Borg with his last ounce of strength, but once they had worn him down, what then? It required no guesswork to determine the information they wanted most—information he retained as the captain of *Enterprise*.

No! Picard cried without opening his mouth. He would not think of his starship. Instead, he struggled to envisage the night sky above his childhood home in La Barre. As a boy, he'd often stood out in his family's vineyard, gazing upward and identifying the constellations and stars that so fascinated him. He'd spent more than a few nights imagining himself aboard a starship, warping through space.

Your vessel possesses warp capabilities, stated a Borg voice. *What other technologies does it employ?*

Cepheus, the constellation of the King, Picard forced himself to think. He recalled the formation of stars from memory. *Ursa Minor, the Little Bear*, he thought next. *Draco, the Dragon.*

What are your vessel's armaments?

Alderamin and Errai in Cepheus, Picard recited to himself—to himself and to the Borg. *Polaris and Kochab in Ursa Minor. Eltanin and—*

What are your vessel's newest technological developments?

Newest, Picard echoed, the word shining in his mind bright as a nova. *Newest*, he thought again. *The newest technological developments aboard* Enterprise.

His thoughts drifted backward to—when? Hours ago, perhaps? Or had days passed? The perception of time had slipped away from him beneath the constant assault of the Borg intelligence. Still, whenever he had last been aboard *Enterprise,* he'd witnessed firsthand his crew's most recent technological achievement. In a flash, related sights and sounds, thoughts and feelings, emerged from his memory.

The Borg saw everything.

The turbolift glided to a stop, its doors easing open with a whisper. Captain Picard stepped out onto deck twelve and strode purposefully down the corridor, headed for one of *Enterprise*'s numerous science laboratories. His presence there had been requested by Commander Riker, who had just contacted him about a highly unusual—and wholly unauthorized—project undertaken by Lieutenant Commander Data. Unclear as to precisely what he would find in the lab, the captain feared the worst-case scenario, already rehearsing what he would say to Starfleet Command in such a circumstance.

Picard approached Room 5103 and reached for the door control. The panels parted before him to reveal Riker standing beside Data and Counselor Troi at the periphery of the raised octagonal platform that dominated the space. Lieutenant Commander La Forge and Ensign Crusher stood off to one side. Each of the officers faced the experiment chamber at the center of the room, though they all peered over at Picard as he entered. Whatever conversation they might have been having immediately ceased.

Gesturing toward the chamber as Picard mounted the platform, Riker said, "Captain, this is Data's—" He hesitated, seeming to search for the appropriate word. "—creation," he finished.

Picard regarded the humanoid figure. Slight of form, perhaps a meter and a half tall, it projected a neutral, unfinished appearance. It wore no clothing, and its bronze skinlike covering showed neither hair nor sexual characteristics. Its nose had no nares. Narrow slits formed its eye sockets and mouth.

"Lal," Data said, "say hello to Captain Jean-Luc Picard."

The android looked first to Data, then to Picard. Its head did not turn smoothly, but incrementally, much as Data's often did. "Hello, Captain Jean-Luc Picard," it said, its voice possessed of a vaguely electronic quality, not really masculine, not really feminine.

Picard did not reply. Of Data, he asked, "How similar is this android to you?"

"Lal is very similar to me," Data said, "though I have attempted to improve those design elements I could."

Any hope Picard nurtured for an uncomplicated resolution to the situation vanished. He studied the android, and began slowly working his way around the experiment chamber to examine it further. It had not been so long ago that Picard had fought Starfleet to establish Data's own rights as an individual. While a reasonable argument could be made to apply that decision to Data's new creation, the captain doubted that Command would agree so readily.

"Lal has a positronic brain much like my own," Data continued. "I began programming it during my time at the cybernetics conference on Galtinor Prime." Data had attended the conference more than a month earlier.

"Nobody's ever been able to do that," said La Forge. "Not since Doctor Soong programmed you, anyway." Soong had constructed Data three decades earlier, not long before the doctor's death.

"That is true," Data agreed, "but at the conference, I learned of a new sub-micron matrix-transfer technology. The process intrigued me. As I studied it, I discovered that it could be utilized to set up complex neural-net pathways."

"So you used your brain as a template," Ensign Crusher said, "and transferred the setup to Lal's brain."

"That is correct, Wesley," Data said. "With this advance, I realized that it would be possible to continue Doctor Soong's work. The initial transfers proved promising, and so I brought Lal's brain back to the *Enterprise* with me. Several more transfers will be required in order to complete the process."

As Picard completed his circuit around the new android, Riker asked, "Data, why didn't you tell anybody about this?" The question bespoke the captain's own thoughts.

"It was a personal experience," Data said. "I have not observed members of the crew involving others in their attempts at procreation."

Riker's eyebrows arched as he glanced over at Picard. Data's characterization of his building the android as an act of reproduction signaled an added complexity to what Picard had already assumed would develop into a difficult situation. The captain needed to understand everything he could about Data's invention before the inevitable inquiries from Starfleet Command. "Commander Data, I would like to speak with you in my ready room in one hour."

"Aye, sir."

"Commander Riker," Picard said, bidding his first officer to follow him. "Counselor." The captain exited, headed back to the bridge, his two officers in tow. Once in the corridor, Picard asked, "Why did we not know about this?"

"Technically, Data hasn't done anything wrong," Riker said. "He may have conducted his efforts privately, but he didn't violate any regulations about personal, off-duty use of the ship's facilities."

"Even so," Picard said, "his operating in secret precluded the possibility of us preventing this from happening."

"I don't think he meant to deceive anybody," Troi said. "You heard him: he views Lal not as his invention, but as his child."

"An outlook we must discourage," Picard said. "This android *is* an invention, *not* a child."

"I'm not so sure," Troi said. "Is biology necessarily a determining factor in what is and what isn't a child? Data has created an offspring, a separate life based at least partly on his own being. That suggests to me that Lal *is* his child."

"A child that can perform sixty trillion calculations a second and could lift me over its head with one arm," Riker observed wryly.

"An exceptional child, perhaps," Troi said, "but a child nonetheless."

The trio arrived at a turbolift and entered. The captain specified their destination, and the car started upward. Thinking beyond the new android's capabilities, it occurred to Picard that Data's motivations might help inform the situation. "Counselor, I'm recollecting Data's experiences during the past couple of months. Could his decision to do this be a reaction to what happened on the *Jovis*?"

"You mean his abduction by Kivas Fajo?" Troi asked.

"And the faking of his death," Picard said. Fajo, a Zibalian trader and a collector of rare and valuable items, had staged a shuttle accident in order to cover his kidnapping and detention of

Data. "Could his facing indefinite confinement have contributed to his desire to construct another of his own kind? Or could his potentially having to kill his captor in order to escape captivity have contributed?"

"It's possible," Troi allowed, though with a tone of skepticism. "Post-traumatic stress can sometimes drive individuals to life-affirming actions, such as having a child. But I think such circumstances imply the presence of emotion, so I'm not sure this would explain Data's behavior."

"The conference was postponed a few months because of severe weather around the cybernetics center on Galtinor Prime," Riker said. "Do you think if it had taken place as originally scheduled, prior to the incident with Fajo, that Data still would have constructed Lal?"

"Provided that the technology he learned about was available at that time," Troi said, "yes, I do."

The turbolift reached the bridge, depositing Picard and his officers on the lower level, beside the door to the captain's ready room. "Counselor," Picard said, "I'd like you to look into that more. See if there's any basis for post-traumatic stress and related actions without an emotional component."

"Yes, sir," Troi said. She padded across to her position.

"Number One," Picard said, and entered his ready room. Riker followed. Inside, the captain crossed to his desk and took his chair. His first officer sat down opposite.

"Will, do you still have whatever research you conducted for the hearing on Starbase One-Seven-Three?" Picard asked. A year and a half earlier, Commander Bruce Maddox, a cyberneticist attached to the Daystrom Technological Institute, had moved to dismantle and reverse-engineer Data. Maddox hoped thereby to complete his own research so that he could then manufacture Soong-type androids for Starfleet. Data refused, causing the judge advocate general in the sector to decide on his legal status. When the JAG declared Data property of Starfleet, Picard challenged the ruling. The captain argued on Data's behalf, and because the judge advocate general's office in Sector 23 had just been set up and had yet to be fully staffed, it fell upon Riker to prosecute the case against Data's freedom. Picard and Data had prevailed, but Riker—unwillingly, but with little choice in the matter—had made the case for the opposing viewpoint quite convincingly.

Riker sighed. "That's not information I made any effort to keep, but I'm sure it's still in my files," he said. "Do you think we're going to have to wage this battle again?"

"I don't know," Picard said, "but I want to be prepared if we do."

The door chime sounded precisely on time, exactly one hour after Picard had asked Data to report to the ready room. The captain reached forward and blanked the display on his computer interface, on which he had been reviewing the transcript of the hearing at Starbase 173. "Come," he said, and the panels retracted into the bulkhead to admit Data. "Have a seat, Commander."

Data sat down across the desk from Picard. "I perceive that you are upset with me, Captain."

"I am not upset with you, Mister Data," Picard said, "so much as I am surprised and concerned. I had no notion at all that you were even considering such a venture, much less actually embarking on one."

Data's eyes shifted, and he turned his head slightly to one side, just as Picard had seen the new android do earlier. When Data looked back over at the captain, he appeared to have reached a conclusion. "Since you have always known me to aspire to truly understand what it means to be human, of which procreation is frequently a part, I gather that your surprise must originate from you being unaware before today of the sub-micron matrix-transfer technology and its application." He paused, then added, "And I presume that your concern mirrors what you feel for other crewmembers who welcome a new child into their families."

"No, Data. I am surprised—I am in fact dismayed—because you told no one of what you were doing," Picard said. "Your creation of an android like yourself—your creation of a sentient being—will have serious repercussions."

"I am sorry, Captain," Data said. "I did not anticipate your objections. Do you wish me to deactivate Lal?"

"Data, we're talking about a living being," Picard said, his voice rising with his frustration. "It can't simply be deactivated." In truth, Picard wished that the complications sure to arise from Data's deed could be avoided by way of such an effortless solution. "What you have done, Data, is of serious moment. Have you considered how Starfleet will react when they learn of this?"

"Captain, I have violated no regulations," Data said. "I also understand the significance of this accomplishment. For that reason, I intend to notify Starfleet Research and Development about Lal, and to keep them apprised as we progress."

"I can only hope that will satisfy Starfleet," Picard said. He pushed back from his desk and stood up, intending to ease his apprehensions with a cup of tea. "You have certainly taken on quite a responsibility, Data." Picard started toward the alcove that contained his replicator.

"Indeed," Data agreed. "In preparation, I have scanned all available literature on parenting." The last word stopped Picard, and he turned back toward Data. "There seems to be no consensus on this issue. Human approaches range from punitive to laissez-faire, while other species, such as the Tellarites—"

"Data, I am not talking about parenting," Picard interrupted. "I'm talking about the tremendous consequences of creating a new life."

Again, Data regarded the captain quizzically. "I do not understand," he said. "Does that not describe what it means to become a parent?"

Picard waited a beat, inhaling deeply and exhaling slowly in an effort to quell his mounting exasperation. After a moment, he returned to the chair behind his desk. "Data, you are striving to achieve what only one person—your creator—has ever been able to achieve: to make another functioning, sentient android—to make another being like you."

"I am aware of that, sir," Data said. "That is why I must do this. Reproduction is a necessary component of humanoid life; without it, a species cannot sustain itself. Since the loss of Lore, I am the last of my kind." Created by Dr. Soong prior to Data, Lore had been located and reactivated more than two years ago, but when he tried to sacrifice the *Enterprise* crew to a powerful alien entity, he'd been transported out into open space. "If I were to be damaged or destroyed," Data went on, "my lineage would end, but if I succeed with the creation of Lal, then it will continue."

Picard nodded. "You do make a compelling argument, Mister Data."

"Thank you, sir."

Unsure what else he might need to know, and wanting more time to reflect on the unexpected state of affairs, Picard dismissed his second officer. Data rose and headed toward the door of the ready room. Before he reached it, the captain called after him. "Keep me informed of your communications with Starfleet Research."

"Aye, sir."

Data exited, and Picard watched him go. The captain felt that he better understood Data's motivations in creating the new android, but his grasp of what drove Data did little to alleviate his concerns about what might follow. Picard recalled a conversation he'd had with Guinan during the time of the hearing on Data's legal status—a conversation in which his old friend had highlighted Data's value to Starfleet. A second android, not a member of the service and with no life experience, could actually prove even more valuable, should the recentness and the circumstances of its manufacture allow Starfleet to seize control of it.

Picard got up and walked over to the alcove. He peered down at the replicator, but then decided against a cup of tea. Instead, he returned to the bridge and resumed his duty shift.

Picard sat on the sofa in his quarters on deck eight, a glass of 2364 Chevalier de Bayard on the low table before him, an old-fashioned hardbound book propped open on his knee. He'd owned the antique volume since his days in secondary school in Moulismes. Picard had enjoyed the collection of French plays often over the years, though not in some time. He'd read halfway through Sartre's existentialist opus, *Huis Clos*, when a short sequence of electronic tones signaled a visitor calling on him.

"Come," he said. When the door opened, it did not surprise him to see Commander Data standing in the corridor with his new charge. In the days since he had created the android, Data had informed Starfleet Research of his efforts, then had followed up by transmitting regular status updates to the division's facility on Galor IV. The personnel there had twice requested additional information from Picard, but he anticipated that as time passed, they would seek more than just an observer's role; they would want to manage Lal's development. He remembered all too well Commander Maddox's intense interest in learning how to produce more Soong-type androids. Consequently, the captain had chosen to keep himself educated on the new android's progress, offering his own, minimal counsel in the hope that his labors could forestall any efforts by Starfleet to take direct control of the situation. He had therefore asked Data to report to him periodically.

"Would this be a good time to see you, Captain?" Data asked.

"Yes, come in," Picard said, setting aside his book. He watched as the two entered, the occasionally stiff, not-quite-human movements of the new android echoic of its—of *her*—creator. Data had allowed Lal to elect her own gender and appearance from among several thousand composites he had programmed in the holodeck. She had opted for the form of a human female, aged twenty-five or so years, with short black hair and dark eyes. Her pale skin approximated flesh tones far more realistically than did Data's. She wore a lavender vest and matching ankle-length skirt, over a long-sleeved purple blouse. "Please sit," the captain said, indicating the two oversized chairs facing the sofa. The pair took the seats, Lal watching Data as she did so, then moving with a deliberateness that seemed awkward, as though she had only just learned how to sit down—an accurate description, Picard realized.

"Good evening, Captain," Data said. Looking at the book Picard had placed beside his half-filled wineglass, he said, "We did not intend to interrupt your reading."

"Not at all," Picard said. Shifting his attention to the new android, he asked, "How are you, Lal?"

"I am functioning within normal parameters," she replied stiffly.

"Lal," Data said gently, "you are fine."

Lal peered at Data for a moment and seemed to process the information, then turned back toward Picard. "I am fine," she said.

Picard felt the side of his mouth curl up in amusement. As difficult as he found it to credit the view of Lal being Data's child, he could certainly see something resembling a father-daughter dynamic in their relationship. She seemed receptive to his efforts to teach her, with an eagerness that belied her emotionless existence.

"I am endeavoring to assist Lal in improving her conversational skills," Data explained.

"A worthwhile venture, but not a simple one," Picard said. "Good conversation requires not just skill, but art."

Art," Lal said. "The production, quality, or expression of beauty or significance according to aesthetic principles."

"That is correct," Data said.

"But people speak to each other with great frequency, merely for the purpose of imparting information," Lal said, confusion tingeing her voice. "How can that require art?"

"There are different forms of conversation," Picard said. "I did not mean to say that *all* such forms require art. But depending on the setting and the interests of the participants, personal dialogue can engage and even stimulate the mind. It can possess movement, like dance; it can flow, like writing; it can arouse visualization, like painting or drawing."

"I . . . do not understand," Lal said. "People converse . . . to create works of art?"

"Not precisely, but I have observed examples of that which the captain is describing," Data said. "In fact, Lal, are you intrigued by the premise of conversation as art?"

"Yes, I am."

"Then perhaps Captain Picard has just demonstrated an example of it," Data said.

Lal looked to one side, neither toward Picard nor toward Data, as though gazing into the middle distance. "Yes," she finally said, turning back to the captain. "Tell me more."

"How about we simply talk?" Picard said. "As many a philosopher has noted, the best education lies in the doing."

"Indeed," Data said. "In his *Ethika Nikomacheia*, Aristotle wrote, 'For the things we have to learn before we can do them, we learn by doing them.'"

"And because he wrote this, it is so?" Lal asked.

"Not necessarily," Picard said. "One can certainly seek wisdom in the words of others, but be wary. As the English writer Somerset Maugham observed, a 'gift for quotation' is but 'a serviceable substitute for wit.'"

Data and Lal glanced at each other, as though searching for guidance. "That would seem paradoxical," Data said. "You decry quotation by repeating another's words."

"And that," Picard said, "can be described as dry humor."

"I . . . do not understand humor," Lal said. "I do not understand humor of any kind, dry or wet."

"I do not believe that there is such a thing as wet humor," Data told Lal. "But do not concern yourself that you do not understand humor. I do not understand it either. In this especially, we can make our journey together." The two androids sat quietly for a moment, perhaps contemplating the concept of human comedy.

"So, Lal," Picard said into the silence, "how do you find the *Enterprise?*"

"I do not need to find it," Lal replied. "It is right here. We are aboard it."

"Lal, I believe you are interpreting the word *find* differently than Captain Picard intends it," Data said. "When he—"

"*Bridge to Captain Picard,*" came the voice of Commander Riker.

"Go ahead, Number One."

"*Captain, we've received a distress signal from New Providence,*" Riker said.

"That's one of the Federation's outermost colonies, is it not?" Picard asked.

"*Yes, sir. It's on Jouret Four,*" Riker said. "*The message provided little detail before it cut out, but indications are that they might be under attack.*"

"Attack?" Picard asked, glancing over at Data. "By whom?"

"*Unknown,*" Riker said. "*But we're the nearest starship.*"

"Best possible speed to the Jouret system," Picard said, standing up from the sofa. "Inform Starfleet Command. I'm on my way. Picard out."

Data rose from his chair as well, and Lal followed his lead. "Captain," Data said, "though much closer, Jouret Four lies in the general direction of our encounter with the Borg."

"I know, Data," said Picard, anxiety welling within him. The *Enterprise* crew had first encountered the Borg fifteen months earlier, but more than seven thousand light-years from Federation space. Starfleet had begun preparations to protect against a possible invasion, but had anticipated a lead time of at least three years to allow for the design and production of new armaments and defenses.

"Captain, if the Borg have already reached the edge of Federation territory," Data said, "then their vessels must possess a source of power considerably more advanced than our own."

"Yes, I know, Data," Picard repeated. He also knew that, if the eve of combat with the Borg did loom, the enemy would find Starfleet ill-prepared for battle.

The alert reached him through the shared consciousness of the Borg, overtaking his concentration on Data and the construction of Lal. He opened his eyes to see the overhead lights flickering, and he knew—because others knew—that the vessel, headed for the heart of the Federation, had fallen out of warp, its power distribution network damaged. An instant later, a rash of prioritized thoughts flowed to him, and through him, identifying the nodes that had failed: a cluster of three that had come under attack.

Phaser fire, he thought, reflexively recalling that the *Enterprise* crew had retuned the frequencies of both the ship-mounted weapons and their handheld units. He immediately tried to direct his thoughts elsewhere—back to Lal, back to La Barre, back to anywhere but aboard his vessel. He did not want to give up the technical specifications of the adjusted phasers, did not want to aid the Collective in adapting to the modified weaponry.

Too late, he realized, as he glimpsed through the eyes of several drones personal forcefields snapping into place, absorbing varicolored phaser beams. Tendrils of smoke drifted to his nose, while the whine of energy weapons and the flare of sparks resounded in his ears. Only when he had to step across the body of a fallen drone did he become aware that he no longer lay supine atop a Borg operating table.

Up ahead, several drones turned into a corridor from which emanated the high-pitched hum of phasers. He heard a voice— "They're adapting to the new frequencies"—and knew it belonged to Lieutenant Commander Elizabeth Shelby of Starfleet Tactical. He thought to call out to her, but could not manage to do so. He felt himself moving his own body, his brain sending impulses to his muscles, but he no longer controlled his own volition. He came abreast of the corridor and halted.

"Jean-Luc," beckoned another female voice.

Crusher, Beverly, he thought, spontaneously supplying information to the Borg hive mind. *Commander, chief medical officer,* U.S.S. Enterprise. *Human.*

He turned to face her, and something in him reveled at the sight of her long red hair. *I'm here, Beverly,* he thought, understanding that he could say nothing, could do nothing. *I'm here. It's me, Locutus.*

Locutus?

"Captain!" called Worf. *Lieutenant, chief tactical officer,* U.S.S. Enterprise. *Klingon.*

Yes, I'm the captain . . . Captain Jean- . . . Captain Jean-L— . . . Jean-Luc—

Locutus!

Worf rushed down the corridor toward him, obviously bent on retrieving him and returning him to *Enterprise.*

Yes, yes, take me back! he screamed with his mouth closed, his face immobile. His personal forcefield flared green when Worf struck it. The security chief fell backward, striking the deck hard.

"*Enterprise,* get us out of here now," Shelby barked into her communicator.

He watched Worf climb back to his feet, then disappear with the others—Shelby, Crusher, and Data—amid the dulcet purr and white sparkle of a Federation transporter beam.

Reroute, the Borg said as one. Decentralized systems permitted the redirection of power throughout the vessel, facilitating the bypass of nonworking equipment. He closed his eyes and watched as those Borg sufficiently specialized to execute such a task moved throughout the ship, throwing switches and realigning the currents of power through conduits. It would require only minutes before they restored warp capability.

Repair. In his mind, he saw other Borg retrieving materials and approaching the locations where power-distribution nodes had been destroyed. Drones utilized their individual, specialized tools to begin replacing the demolished machinery.

Recycle and complete termination. Eight Borg had perished during the attack by the *Enterprise* away team. Other drones approached the corpses and recovered various technological components from them, triggering the dissolution of those fallen.

Communicate. He opened his eyes, understanding that the imperative had been targeted to the lone Borg who satisfied the criteria necessary for the delivery of the final message to the *Enterprise* crew: Locutus . . . Picard himself. Above, the lighting continued to flicker, but less frequently as drones redistributed power throughout the ship. A group of Borg neared, and he understood that they would accompany him to the nearest communications terminal.

He fell in behind the eight drones and marched with them through the ship. At last, they turned down a corridor, at the end of which hung a viewscreen. The Borg stepped aside to allow him an unimpeded line of sight. The screen flickered to life, revealing Commander Riker and Lieutenant Commander Shelby standing together at the center of the *Enterprise* bridge.

"I am Locutus of Borg," he said, even as he exclaimed, *I am Picard*, inside his head. "Resistance is futile," he continued, hearing an unnerving robotic quality in his own voice. "Your life, as it has been, is over. From this time forward, you will service us." He saw the horrified expressions on the faces of the people who had become his family: Beverly and Wesley, Deanna and Worf, even Data appeared gripped by the unfolding events.

Riker stared, stone-faced, from across the gulf that separated the Borg and Federation starships, and Picard knew what his former first officer would do—what the new captain of *Enterprise* must do. In that moment, the Borg also knew, but too late. They had sought the information from Picard, had searched for whatever new weaponry the Starfleet crew might have improvised, but he had managed to hide it from them until now.

"Mister Worf," Riker said, *"fire."*

A thousand Borg minds functioned as a single entity, studying the information Picard recalled from his meeting with his first officer. *Geordi and Data want to install higher-capacity power transfers to the deflector dish so that they can generate a concentrated energy burst at a specific frequency,* Riker had informed him. *The Borg systems showed susceptibility to the phasers when they fluctuated into a high, narrow band.* A thousand drones focused on conceiving an adaptation, a means of thwarting the efforts of Picard's crew.

"Deflector power approaching maximum limits," La Forge said at a rear station on the *Enterprise* bridge. *"Energy discharge in six seconds."*

Six seconds, Picard thought, whatever part of him that had become Locutus of Borg agonizing at the too-short time frame.

"Firing, sir."

The part of him that remained a Starfleet captain rejoiced at the words. He heard the growing hum permeating the *Enterprise* bridge, then felt the jolt as the high-intensity deflector discharge slammed into the Borg vessel. As systems overloaded, the collective consciousness of a thousand drones raced to find a solution. A titanic blast ripped through a section of the Borg ship to Picard's left, exposing its interior to space. He saw scores of Borg blown out into the void even as emergency forcefields crackled into existence to protect the rest of the vessel.

For just an instant, Picard saw out in space the forward starboard quadrant of *Enterprise*'s primary hull. Then another explosion tore through the Borg ship, and then another. The hive mind crumbled as the infrastructure supporting their communications collapsed. Unexpectedly freed from the embrace of the Collective, Picard regained full control of his mind and body.

In the last moment of his life, knowing that the *Enterprise* crew—*his* crew—had vanquished the Borg, Picard smiled.

2

William Riker gazed through the small circular window at the blue and white surface of the world below. He realized that he couldn't recall the proper name of the planet. He'd known it at some point, but for years, he'd simply referred to it by its Starfleet designation of Starbase 234.

"Must be losing my mind," he said, his voice seeming strangely loud and out of place in the small, empty compartment. He reached his hands up to the escape hatch and leaned against it, bringing his face close to the port. His breath fogged the lower part of the window. He peered left and right, not looking for anything in particular, but spying off to starboard an *Akira*-class starship. Riker couldn't read the name or registry number on its hull, but he knew the identity of the vessel. *U.S.S. James T. Kirk* had drawn a temporary patrol assignment for this sector during *Enterprise*'s refit.

Riker reached over, wiped away the condensation of his breath on the port, and looked downward. From his vantage far out on one of the upper arms of Callendra Station, he couldn't see *Enterprise* in its berth of more than five weeks. After the destruction of the Borg cube, La Forge and his engineering teams had needed the better part of a day to patch up the main deflector and other ship's systems. The lower three decks of the saucer and the forward half of the secondary hull had remained uninhabitable because of exposure to the high levels of radiation emitted by the improvised energy weapon. When finally capable, *Enterprise* had limped to the Callendra facility, a repair dock in orbit of Starbase 234. Nearly complete, the refit had consumed thirty-nine days of round-the-clock work.

Initially, Riker had thrown himself into that work. Once Starfleet Command had debriefed him, they had quickly made permanent his field promotion to captain. They'd let stand their offer for him to command *U.S.S. Melbourne*, but they'd also pulled out the center seat for him on *Enterprise*. He'd accepted the latter because—

"Because what else could I do?" Riker asked himself. While he'd long aspired to one day command his own vessel, he'd also passed up several such opportunities—he'd intended to decline the *Melbourne* captaincy when it had first arisen—in order to remain aboard the exemplar of the fleet. When Riker's two ambitions had coincided, there really hadn't been anything for him to debate.

Except that as completion of *Enterprise*'s repairs drew closer, his new position hadn't proven particularly satisfying—nor did he feel much anticipation for the ship's imminent return to active duty. During the past couple of weeks, he'd begun delegating more and more supervision of the refit to Worf, Shelby, and Data. At the same time, he'd spent more and more time off the ship, either down at the starbase or up on Callendra Station. Evidently concerned by his behavior, Deanna had sought him out a few times, trying to speak with him about it. He'd managed to say little, and of late, she'd taken to allowing him some space.

Behind Riker, the fastening mechanism of the inner hatch unlocked with a clang. He turned to see the door pull open, a row of environmental suits hanging just beyond it. He expected a member of the station's maintenance crew to appear, but instead, Admiral Hanson stepped into the airlock.

"Going somewhere, Captain?" Hanson asked in his low, gravelly voice. The stocky admiral had a craggy face and a high forehead, his head crowned by a semicircle of silvering hair.

Riker forced a smile onto his face. "Just thinking of a little orbital skydiving," he joked.

Hanson regarded him with what felt like a penetrating stare. "With or without a chute?" he finally asked.

Riker furrowed his brow, immediately uncomfortable. "Now how am I supposed to take that, Admiral?"

"Take it the way I intended it," Hanson said. "As the opening of a conversation that you and I need to have."

"About what?" Riker asked, though the answer seemed plain.

"Captain," Hanson said, the single word a clear reproach. "Do you really want to dissemble?"

Riker couldn't bring himself to reply.

"I have to tell you," Hanson went on, "that I'm far less concerned about the lack of respect that demonstrates for me than I am about the lack of self-respect it demonstrates for you."

"Self-respect," Riker said, a note of uncertainty creeping into his voice.

"Yes." Hanson waited, apparently providing him the chance to address the situation.

"And you want to have this discussion here?" Riker asked, aware even as he did so that he simply sought to avoid talking about this for as long as he could.

"This is where you are, Captain," Hanson said, raising his arms to take in the relatively cramped confines of the airlock. "And not to be a martinet about regulations, but you're out of uniform." The admiral raised his hand to indicate his own combadge, a piece of equipment Riker had intentionally left behind in his quarters aboard *Enterprise*.

"I didn't want to be found," he explained.

"Obviously," Hanson said. "Not exactly the sort of conduct Starfleet Command expects from its starship captains."

Riker smiled humorlessly. "And yet you did find me, Admiral."

"Because I know every square centimeter of this base," Hanson said, "and I know where personnel go when they want to be by themselves, when they want a place to think."

"Oh, I didn't come here to think," Riker said, wishing at once that he hadn't.

"You didn't come here for orbital skydiving either," Hanson said. "So why did you feel the need to get away by yourself, and to take yourself off the comm grid?"

"I just . . ." Riker shrugged, not really knowing what to tell the admiral. "I guess I needed a little quiet." He turned and peered again through the port.

"But I understand that you've already had a considerable amount of quiet over the past few weeks," Hanson said. "Alone in your quarters, having minimal contact with your crew."

Riker whirled back around to face the admiral, understanding the implication of his observation. "Somebody spoke to you," he said, more statement than question. He thought that Hanson would deny it, or at least refuse to give up his source, but he did neither.

"Counselor Troi came to me," he said.

Riker felt his mouth drop open, shocked to learn that of all people, Deanna—his *Imzadi*—had shown such disloyalty.

"Don't look so crestfallen," Hanson said. "Your counselor didn't betray you. She acted professionally, fulfilling her duties out of a concern for her commanding officer. And she didn't come to *me* first; she went to *you*, on more than one occasion, and you refused to speak with her."

Riker felt himself deflate, like atmosphere rushing from the airlock. He couldn't honestly challenge the admiral's statements, and he knew that if he continued to say nothing, Hanson wouldn't allow him to leave Starbase 234 with *Enterprise*. Deciding to tell the admiral the truth—deciding to face it himself—Riker looked Hanson in the eye and said, "I killed my captain." Unable to hold the admiral's gaze, he looked away before adding, "I killed my friend."

Silence descended once more in the compartment. Except that sounds reached Riker: his own breathing, the impossibly loud beating of his heart—and in his head, the command he'd issued that would change his life, and end Captain Picard's. *Mister Worf . . . fire.*

Time seemed to elongate. Riker didn't know how he could leave without saying more, and yet he didn't know how to say more than he already had. He found himself hoping that the admiral would just leave, even if that meant Riker would be deemed unfit to continue as captain of *Enterprise*.

Instead, Hanson stepped forward and took hold of Riker's upper arms. Much shorter than Riker, he had to reach up to do so. And still, Hanson said nothing, until at last Riker met his gaze. "Will," the admiral said, for the first time calling him by his given name, "you destroyed a powerful, relentless enemy intent on enslaving the whole of the Federation. You didn't kill Captain Picard. You killed whatever the Borg made of him. *They* ended Captain Picard's life, not *you*."

"I want to believe you," Riker said. "I mean, I understand the truth in what you're saying. It's just that . . . it doesn't *feel* that way."

"No, of course not," Hanson agreed. "Which is why you need to talk about it, to deal with it. It's the most obvious example of why we include counselors among our starship crews." The admiral gave Riker's upper arms an encouraging squeeze, then stepped back away from him. "So you'll see Counselor Troi or one of her staff?" he asked.

Riker understood that his answer—his *real* answer, not merely how he replied to the admiral—would dictate whether he would continue and succeed as *Enterprise* captain. He wrestled with his emotions, with his guilt and his ambition, searching within himself for the wherewithal to proceed as the admiral had bade. Finally, he found what he needed for his response: "Yes, Admiral."

"Good," Hanson said, his demeanor turning in an instant. "Now then, about your choice of first officer . . ."

Riker appreciated that the admiral required no additional assurances, no prolonged dialogue about the matter, nothing more than his word that he would deal with the emotional fallout of the battle with the Borg. He valued Hanson's straightforward manner, as well as the trust he clearly had in Riker.

"My first officer," Riker said, clumsily following the admiral's abrupt conversational transition. "I know in what high regard you hold Commander Shelby. I do too. I'm sure she's told you that we've butted heads a bit during her time on the *Enterprise,* but I seriously considered her for the position. It's just that—"

"Captain," Hanson said, holding up a hand to stop Riker in midsentence. "Starfleet Command has reviewed your recommendation and we're in complete agreement. Mister Worf's promotion to Lieutenant Commander and his reassignment from the *Enterprise*'s chief of security to its exec will be effective once you notify him."

"Thank you, Admiral," Riker said, genuinely pleased. "I'll also inform Lieutenant Commander Shelby. I know she'll be disappointed, but I'd like to offer her the position of security chief. I'm sure she'll still be a valuable asset to the ship."

"No, she won't," Hanson said.

"Sir?"

"I'm afraid you're going to have to find another security chief," Hanson said. "Starfleet Command isn't convinced that the Borg threat has passed. You defeated one ship, but the Borg completely eradicated the New Providence colony, and they were likely responsible for the dozens of Federation and Romulan outposts that disappeared two years ago. That being the case, we may not have seen the last of them."

"And so you want her to return to her position as the head of Borg tactical analysis," Riker concluded.

"Yes," Hanson confirmed. "That might not jibe with Commander Shelby's own career plans, but we need her there right now."

"Who's going to tell her?" Riker asked.

The admiral laughed once, a harsh, guttural sound. "You're off the hook, Captain," he said. "I'm meeting with Shelby as soon as we're done here—which I think we are."

Hanson started to turn toward the inner hatchway, but Riker

stopped him by saying, "Admiral." When Hanson looked over, Riker said, "Thank you."

The admiral seemed to take his measure, then said, "Jean-Luc thought very highly of you, Captain Riker. So do I." Then he continued through the hatch.

Riker stood in the airlock, listening to the admiral's footfalls recede into the distance. For the first time in weeks, he felt positive about the future. He made his way through the inner hatch, on his way back to his first command.

Deanna Troi sat at a table in Ten Forward, her hands resting on either side of a cup of what had once been hot chocolate. It had doubtless cooled, since she hadn't dared drink from it for the past ten minutes, as she'd been alternately laughing and groaning her way through Specialist Pacelli's comedy routine. The evening's unexpectedly entertaining performances underscored how good it felt to be under way aboard *Enterprise* again.

Pacelli stood in front of the large central window of the ship's main lounge, in a pool of light in the otherwise-darkened room, the starfield beyond him composing a dramatic backdrop. "So my dilithium crystals have destabilized," he said, "forcing me to set my shuttle down on Nedboi Two."

A few titters drifted up from the crowd, though Troi didn't know why; she'd never heard of Nedboi II, and had no idea whether it truly existed or had been invented for the joke. As she glanced around, she saw that Ten Forward had filled to capacity, with many of those present standing amid the room's tables. She sat with Beverly, Geordi, and Data.

"Now, I don't know if any of you have ever been to Nedboi Two," Pacelli continued, "but it's populated by the Cadecians, a humanoid race of cannibals." More people laughed, obviously amused by the joke's extreme setup. "I end up landing in the middle of the jungle. My replicator's out and I've got no emergency provisions, meaning I have to head out and forage for food. So I'm making my way through this dense foliage, trying to locate some nuts or some fruits, when all of a sudden I hear voices. I peek through the leaves and I see two Cadecians mixing something in this huge black cauldron." Pacelli put his fists one atop the other and mimed an exaggerated stirring motion.

"And one of the cannibals says to the other, 'You know something? I really hate my mother-in-law.'

"'So,' the other cannibal says, 'just eat the vegetables.'"

Troi chuckled, but she heard roughly equal amounts of laughter and groans around her. Pacelli waved and thanked his crewmates for indulging him. As he stepped down from the area that had become a makeshift stage for the evening, the lights came up and he received a nice round of applause.

Leaning in over the table, Troi said, "Who knew Alfonse was so funny?"

"I still don't know he's funny," Geordi grumbled.

"Oh, come on," Beverly said. "A lot of his jokes were good."

"What about you, Data?" Troi asked. "What did you think of Alfonse's routine?"

"As you know, Counselor, I am still far from adept at understanding humor," Data said. "But I did note that Specialist Pacelli's monologue did elicit a good deal of laughter throughout his performance."

Beverly reached across and patted Geordi's forearm. "Sounds like you're outnumbered," she teased.

"Well," Geordi said with a comic shrug, "I guess humor must be in the *eye* of the beholder." His eyebrows went up above the VISOR appliance he wore across his eyes, which allowed him to "see," even though he'd been blind since birth. He clearly waited for a response from his friends.

Troi gave him one by groaning.

"Hold on," Geordi said. "*That* was funny."

Troi shook her head and rolled her eyes, then looked back to the stage when she saw Ten Forward's new host step up to it. "A fine job by Data-Flow Specialist Alfonse Pacelli," he said. Another polite round of applause followed. "Our final act of the night will be up next, in just a couple of minutes." On his way back to the bar, he walked past Troi, who flagged him down.

"Mister Okona," she said, "I just wanted to tell you what an excellent idea this was."

Thadiun Okona smiled broadly at her, the usual glint in his eye. "Everybody does seem to be having a fine time," he agreed.

After the loss of Captain Picard aboard the Borg vessel, Guinan had decided not to return to the ship once it had undergone repairs. She'd originally come aboard two years prior, specifically to oversee the operation of Ten Forward. She'd been personally invited to take the position by Captain Picard, who'd been a very close friend.

When the time had come for Captain Riker to fill the job, he'd recalled the crew's encounter with the charismatic Okona a couple of years earlier. A bit of a rogue, with an abundance of charm and a quick wit, he'd cut the figure of a dashing swashbuckler, though in reality he'd done nothing more exciting than captain his own small interplanetary cargo carrier. While Guinan—arch, mysterious, and wise—would be difficult to replace, Will believed that Okona might develop into a worthy successor. So far, in his first few days aboard, he'd gotten off to a fine start. Certainly his notion of presenting a talent show, where members of the crew could share their artistic abilities, had proven popular.

"Is your hot chocolate unsatisfactory?" Okona asked, pointing toward her untouched cup.

"No, just not hot anymore," Troi said. "I was laughing too much to drink it."

"Let me warm that up for you, then," Okona said, grabbing up the cup. "Would anybody else like anything?" he asked the others at the table. When they all declined, Okona offered another smile and headed for the bar.

"So, Data," Troi said, "it's a shame that Lal didn't come out with you tonight. I think this would have been a really good experience for her." Since the battle with the Borg vessel, Troi and her counseling staff had spent a great deal of time helping numerous members of the crew cope with their grief. As a result, she hadn't had much occasion to see Lal. Nor apparently had Data, whose responsibilities during the repairs to *Enterprise* had kept him exceedingly busy. He'd only recently found the opportunity to complete his final neural transfers to the android he considered his child.

"I agree that Lal may have benefited from attending this evening's activities," Data said, "but she is not absent."

"She's not?" Troi asked, surprised. "Where is she?"

"When last I saw her," Data said, "Lal was standing near the far end of the bar, in the port aft corner of the room."

"What?" Beverly said. "Data, why didn't you have her join us?" Troi stood and craned her neck, but couldn't see through the crowd around her.

"Lal did not wish to be distracted while she prepared," Data said.

"While she prepared?" Geordi said. "For what?"

As though in reply, the lights in Ten Forward dimmed. Data pointed to the stage. Thadium Okona deposited a steaming cup of hot chocolate before Troi, then crossed to the front of the room and stepped back into the light. The audience greeted him with appreciative clapping. "Thank you so much for coming, everybody," he said. "I'd like to introduce our final performer of the evening. Please welcome one of the newest additions to *Enterprise,* the daughter of Second Officer Data . . . Lal."

Troi watched for her as Okona descended from the stage, but only caught sight of her once she'd started up the steps. She wore a long blue dress that looked nice on her, though it didn't quite hang properly. Troi wondered what she would do. Okona's rules for the event permitted performers the use of only their natural abilities, without the aid of instruments or props of any kind.

Lal moved to the center of the lighted area and turned to face the audience, who greeted her with warm applause. Before the clapping even stopped, she opened her mouth and began to sing.

> *"The skies are green and glowing*
> *Where my heart is,*
> *Where my heart is,*
> *Where the scented lunar flower is blooming,*
> *Somewhere beyond the stars,*
> *Beyond Antares."*

She sang quietly, but perfectly on key. She stood completely still, her arms at her sides. Her face wore an expressionless mask.

> *"I'll be back, though it takes forever;*
> *Forever is just a day.*
> *Forever is just another journey,*
> *Tomorrow a stop along the way."*

Lal displayed no signs of enjoying herself, though Data surely would point out that, since his daughter did not possess the capacity for emotion, she couldn't possibly experience enjoyment. While her stationary stance and impassive face lent Lal an awkward air, Troi noticed that she had improved her simulations of human responses, such as breathing and blinking.

> *"And let the years go fading*
> *Where my heart is,*
> *Where my heart is,*
> *Where my love eternally is waiting,*
> *Somewhere beyond the stars,*
> *Beyond Antares."*

When Lal finished singing, she closed her mouth and immediately left the stage. Troi, caught off guard by the hasty departure, didn't respond to the performance right away, nor did anybody else in Ten Forward. But as Lal moved through the crowd toward the door, several people began applauding. Troi quickly joined them, as did others.

Data left the table and followed after Lal. In the wake Data left through the crowd, Troi saw Okona dart out from behind the bar and intercept Lal before she left the room. When Data reached them, he started speaking to Lal.

"Do you think he's proud?" Beverly asked.

"I'm sure Data would find another word for it," Geordi said, "but yeah."

Troi saw Okona point back toward the stage. Lal looked to Data, then allowed Okona to lead her back up to where she'd performed. Once there, Okona sidled away, leaving her alone in the spotlight. The audience's show of appreciation rapidly grew until it had become a rousing ovation. Lal appeared confused for a moment, but then she did something Troi would never have predicted: she smiled. It seemed clumsy and out of place on the android's face, an obvious attempt to mimic human behavior. Still, Troi thought it one of sweetest smiles she'd ever seen, and she matched it with one of her own.

"I haven't been sleeping well," Riker confessed. It troubled him to be seeing a counselor only days after beginning his first mission as the permanent captain of *Enterprise,* but he knew better than to let pride stand in the way of his mental health—especially given the weight of his new responsibilities. He also knew that, because of their history together and their current friendship, it wouldn't be appropriate for him to consult Deanna.

"And is something in particular preventing you from getting your rest?" asked Lieutenant Lueke.

"Oh, I don't know," Riker said with more than a little annoyance. The two men sat in the assistant counselor's office, in comfortable chairs, a small, circular table between them. Riker leaned forward, feeling adversarial. "Maybe it's because I lost at poker the other night." Although Matthew Lueke had only joined Troi's staff during *Enterprise*'s refit at Callendra Station, he had been fully briefed on the loss of Captain Picard, and on what that loss meant to the crew he'd left behind.

With an even bearing, the young counselor peered out from beneath his mop of thick, dark hair. "Sarcasm often masks anger, and as you may know, anger is one of the stages identified in the Kübler-Ross cycle of grief," he said. "Of course I know that you've suffered a terrible loss with the death of your captain."

"Not just my captain," Riker said. "My friend."

"Yes," Lueke said quietly, in a way that touched Riker, as though the counselor genuinely understood the depth of his emotion. "When I asked if something in particular was keeping you from sleeping, I wanted to know specifically how your restlessness manifests. Do you lie awake in bed, replaying the tragic events in your mind? Do you fall asleep, but then wake up after experiencing nightmares? Do you—"

"Worf to Captain Riker."

Lueke stopped speaking, folded his hands together in his lap, and looked down.

"Yes," Riker said, "go ahead, Number One."

"Captain, you have an incoming transmission from Galor Four," Worf said. *"Admiral Anthony Haftel. It is coded as urgent."*

Before Riker could respond, Lueke stood and started toward the door. "I'll give you your privacy, sir," he said softly, and exited to the corridor.

Riker nodded his thanks, then crossed the room to a companel, which he activated with a touch. The Federation emblem appeared on the screen, a brace of stylized laurels surrounding a circular starfield. "Pipe it down here, Mister Worf."

"Aye, sir," Worf said.

The companel chirped, and the admiral appeared on the monitor. He had a long, rugged face, with a cleft chin and a high hairline. His gray eyes matched his hair. *"Captain Riker, I hope I'm not disturbing you."*

"Not at all, Admiral." Riker had never before spoken with Haftel, but he knew that Galor IV housed an annex of the Daystrom Technological Institute, which served as a major installation for Starfleet Research and Development. "What can I do for you?"

"As I'm sure you're aware, your Commander Data has been forwarding progress reports on the android that he created," Haftel said.

"Lal," Riker said. "Yes, sir."

"Commander Data recently informed Starfleet Research that he completed the neural transfers from his positronic brain to that of the new android," Haftel said. *"That being the case, we have concluded here on Galor Four that our facilities and personnel would be best equipped to oversee the development of the new android."*

"I see," Riker said, not at all pleased with the prospect of losing one of his officers—and one of his friends. "Have you informed Mister Data of your decision?"

"I am informing his commanding officer," Haftel said with a belligerent quality Riker believed unique to Starfleet admirals and small children.

Riker nodded. "Data's transfer is compulsory, then?" he asked.

"You misunderstand me, Captain," Haftel said. *"We are interested in bringing only the new android to Galor Four. If Commander Data were to accompany it here, his presence would undoubtedly hinder its progress."*

"Forgive me, Admiral, but I'm not sure I concur with that assessment," Riker said. "I've observed Data working with Lal, and he seems to be making tremendous strides with her."

"Captain, you are hardly an expert in cybernetics."

"No, but surely nobody has a better understanding of Soongtype androids than Commander Data," Riker argued. "The total population of which includes Data and Lal."

Haftel looked away from the monitor, then inhaled and exhaled heavily, as though barely maintaining his patience. When he turned back, he asked, *Are you refusing to accede to this request, Captain?"*

Until that moment, Riker hadn't even considered the possibility that the admiral's proposal could be rejected. But Lal was not a member of Starfleet, and so he realized that she couldn't be compelled to relocate to one of their installations. Riker supposed that any such attempt could be deemed kidnapping.

"Admiral, let me take your concerns and your proposition to Commander Data," he said. "I know that he wants what's best for Lal, so it's possible that he'll agree with your assessment."

"Very well," Haftel said begrudgingly. *"Just keep in mind that Starfleet maintains a strict protocol on research and development. No matter Commander Data's assessment, he may be in violation of those protocols."*

And there's a shot across the bow, Riker thought. He offered a smile he hoped would disguise the rising antipathy he felt. "I'll inform Data of that as well," he said.

"See that you do, Captain," the admiral said. *"Haftel out."* A quick tone signaled the end of the communication, and the Federation seal reappeared on the screen.

Riker stood alone in Counselor Lueke's office for a moment, thinking about his conversation with the admiral. There could be no mistake that it had concluded with a threat—if not to the captain, certainly to Data and Lal. He knew that he couldn't simply ignore what had just transpired, if for no other reason than he would assuredly hear from the admiral again. And though Riker had only just spoken to him for the first time, he'd come away from their interaction knowing two definite things: he neither liked nor trusted Anthony Haftel.

3

L al picked up the paintbrush, not for the first time. She examined the blank canvas on the easel before her, then gazed down at the palette she held in her other hand. She had arranged the few paints in order of the spectrum, with black—the absence of color—at one end and white—the combination of all colors—at the other. The selection of a hue, though, seemed a virtual impossibility for her.

Standing in the living area of the quarters she shared with her father, Lal alternately studied the expanse of white canvas and the variety of paints. After ten minutes, she set both the palette and the brush down on the low table in front of the sofa, then sat down and attempted to work through her dilemma.

Visual comprehension had been among the most difficult abilities for her to master, but she had improved markedly in that area, both with continued practice and with each successive neural transfer her father had made. All the pathways of her positronic brain had been laid down identically to his. Despite some variation at the quantum level, she should be capable of storing and processing the same information as her father. It therefore made sense that, since he had completed a number of paintings, she should be able to do so as well.

Except that Lal had so far been unable even to start—at least not beyond making the appropriate preparations. When the idea had first occurred to her, she had quickly assembled all of the components necessary for the task. Her father sought to understand and emulate human behavior, and he guided her in her own pursuit of those goals. Art, as a staple of human expression and a bellwether of societal progress, provided a ready path to follow.

Then why can I not take the first step? she asked herself. After all, she had already participated in an artistic pursuit when she sang in Ten Forward. When Mr. Okona had invited her to perform, she had initially demurred, but her father had proposed that she reconsider; he had made the case that joining the crew in their recreational activities could aid in her socialization. She had agreed, but at a loss for what to do, she had decided on singing "Beyond Antares" only when Mr. Okona had suggested it.

I need a suggestion, Lal realized. In striving to engage in artistic endeavors, she lacked well-defined procedures. When she solved an equation, she could proceed from one step to another following the logical dictates of mathematics, but to create a painting, no definitive step ensued after collecting and setting up the needed materials. When her father arrived home after his shift on the bridge, she would ask him to tell her what she should paint.

Lal stood up and began to clear away her canvas, palette, and brush, but as she did, she caught sight of a painting hanging on the wall. It showed a pair of dark brown orbs, each connected by small spokes to an outer rim, an artistic representation by her father of Zylo eggs. Lal wondered if anybody had suggested the subject of the painting to him, or if he had chosen it on his own. She hypothesized that, to truly engage in humanlike behavior, he would have executed the work completely on his own.

Why then can I not do that? Lal asked herself. She needed only to pick a subject, and then she could set it down on canvas to the best of her ability. That choice rested at the heart of her struggles, but she saw that it need not; she would simply paint the current object of her attention: her father's canvas of Zylo eggs.

Lal moved the easel so that it stood in front of her father's painting. Then she retrieved her palette and brush. She inspected the color of the Zylo eggs in her father's work, then mixed red and black on her color tray. Not entirely satisfied, she cut the blend with a minute amount of yellow. Collecting the result on her brush, she at last reached forward and swiped an arc of brown across the canvas.

It gratified Lal to have finally begun an artistic expression she had conceived on her own, and she wanted to continue. She carried the arc around until she approximated a circle, and she realized that there would be complexities for her to resolve as her work progressed. She strived to represent, in two dimensions, a two-dimensional representation of three-dimensional objects. She stepped past her easel for a moment and scrutinized her father's painting, searching for clues to the techniques he had employed.

A brief series of electronic tones sounded in the room, and Lal recognized the door chime. She accessed her social-skills subroutines, then said, "Please enter."

The door opened, and Captain Riker and Counselor Troi stepped inside. "Hello, Lal," the counselor said.

"Hello, Counselor Troi," Lal replied. "Hello, Captain Riker." The captain nodded.

"You're painting?" the counselor said, moving over to glance at her canvas.

"I have just begun," Lal said.

"I think it's wonderful that you're exploring your creative side," the counselor told her. "You know, it took your father a lot longer in his life before he did anything like this."

"I have the benefit of my father's guidance," Lal said. She thought for a moment, consulting the information she maintained on manners. Then she placed her palette and brush on the table and invited her guests to sit down.

"Thank you, but I'm afraid we can't stay," the captain said. Where Troi had smiled and spoken warmly to her, Riker appeared preoccupied, perhaps even concerned. "We've come to ask you a few questions."

"I will do my best to answer them," Lal said.

"Did Commander Data tell you what he would be doing when he went on duty today?" the captain asked.

"Only that he would be assuming his regular duties as operations officer for alpha shift," Lal said, "and that he would return to our quarters immediately afterward."

"Did he do or say anything out of the ordinary this morning?" the captain asked. "Have you noticed him acting . . . differently . . . in any way? Today or any other time recently?"

Lal considered the question, looking off to the side as she recalled and analyzed her interactions with her father that morning, and then for the past week. "No," she ultimately answered, peering back up at Riker. "When plotted on a Wilkes-Takiyah Normalized Behavioral Model, my father's conduct falls within one-point-two-five standard deviations of the mean."

The captain looked inquiringly at Counselor Troi, who said, "Well within his expected range."

Lal thought about the nature of the questions that had been put to her, and she realized that something unanticipated must have happened with respect to her father. "What is the reason that you are asking me these things?" Lal wanted to know.

"Lal, I'm sorry," the captain said, "but Data is acting very strangely. He's unaccountably taken control of the *Enterprise*. He's locked himself alone on the bridge, changed our course and speed, and he won't respond when we try to speak with him."

"I do not understand," Lal said. "Why would he do this?"

"We don't know," the counselor said softly. "We came here hoping that you might have noticed something recently—something your father did or something he said—that would help explain it."

Lal again reviewed her interactions with her father over the course of the past week. "I have noticed nothing unusual," she said. "Is my father in danger? Is the crew?"

"Not at the moment," the captain said. "But until we know

where he's taking the ship and what he intends to do, we can't be sure that won't change." He paced forward to stand directly in front of Lal. "Would you try contacting your father for us? Would you ask him to stop what he's doing and return control of the ship to the crew?"

"Yes," Lal said at once. "I will try."

"Computer," the captain said, "open a channel to Commander Data on the bridge."

"Channel open," the computer reported.

When the captain nodded at Lal, she said, "Father, this is Lal. Can you hear me?" She waited for a reply, but none came. The captain indicated that she should continue. "Father, I have been informed that you have commandeered this vessel. I ask that you relinquish control back to the *Enterprise* crew." Again, she received no response.

The captain waited a moment, then closed the channel and told her, "Thank you, Lal." To Troi, he said, "I'm going back to engineering. Maybe La Forge has made some progress."

"I'll stay with Lal just in case Data decides to contact her," the counselor said.

The captain strode out, and Troi crossed the room to sit on the sofa. "I hope you don't mind me staying," the counselor said, but her actions demonstrated that, regardless of Lal's wishes, Troi would remain.

"What's going to happen?" Lal asked.

"I don't know," the counselor told her. "But I've known your father for a few years, and even if something has happened to his physical body or to his programming, I have to believe that he can be repaired and that everything will be all right."

Lal contemplated this for a moment as she moved to sit beside Troi on the sofa. "No," she said, "you don't *have* to believe that."

"Well, no," the counselor admitted, "but I *want* to—wait. What did you just say, Lal?"

"I said, 'No, you don't *have* to believe that.'"

"You said *don't*," the counselor told her. "You used a contraction."

"Yes," Lal said, confused. "Is that not correct?"

"It is," Troi said, "but it's something your father's not capable of doing."

"Then I will desist."

The counselor smiled. "I don't think you need to do that," she said. "I'm sure your father won't mind. In fact, he'll be proud when he learns that you have mastered a skill that he hasn't."

"My father cannot feel pride," Lal noted.

"Well, yesterday, you couldn't use contractions," Troi said.

Lal doubted that her father would spontaneously develop the ability to feel pride, but she could not explain how her abilities had suddenly exceeded his. Without warning, her circumstances had changed, and obviously so had his. She wondered if their lives would ever be normal again.

Data felt himself jerk forward, then saw that the operations console had vanished. No, the ops console hadn't vanished, he realized; rather, he found himself no longer on the *Enterprise* bridge—or anywhere else aboard *Enterprise,* as best he could tell. Instead, he sat on a chair in a cluttered, unfamiliar place. From directly to his left, somebody peered at him.

Data regarded the man, whose wispy white hair contrasted with both the blotchy pink skin of his face and the dark brown garments he wore. Wizened by age, he hunched over in apparent infirmity. Data rose to his feet, glanced quickly at his surroundings, then addressed the old man. "I fail to recall how I arrived here."

"I sent for you, in a manner of speaking," said the old man. He chuckled, then added, "You got here quickly, so you must not have been very far away."

"Who are you, sir?" Data inquired.

Again, the old man chuckled, then turned his back and moved

away. Data utilized the opportunity to tap his combadge. "Data to *Enterprise,*" he said. He received no response. "*Enterprise,* do you read me?"

The old man returned, reached up, and took Data's face in his hand. The gesture seemed more familiar than threatening. "I always loved that face," the old man said. He patted Data's cheek and moved away again. "Please, sit down."

Perplexed by the situation, Data searched his memory. "We were headed for a diplomatic summit. I was seated at my station on the bridge and—"

"I'm sure your starship will return for you soon," the old man said. "Now please, sit down."

"I must find a means of contacting the *Enterprise,*" Data said.

The old man crossed back to Data again and gazed up at him. "Tell me," he said, "do I look at all familiar to you?"

Data studied his features. "Yes, you do bear a resemblance to Doctor Noonian Soong, the cyberneticist who constructed me."

Chuckling, the old man turned and crossed the room, which looked to Data like equal parts laboratory, library, and storeroom. Sophisticated equipment stood scattered about the space, mixed in among pieces of old furniture and shelves and stacks of numerous books. In one area, a large, fossilized skull overlooked a diorama teeming with miniature models of dinosaurs. The old man weaved through the disarray and ascended a ladder against the far wall, where he retrieved a large volume from a high shelf. "Noonian Soong indeed," he said triumphantly.

"Am I to understand that you purport to be Doctor Soong?" Data asked.

"I don't 'purport' to be Soong," the old man said. "I *am* Soong."

"I am afraid that Doctor Soong died soon after constructing me," Data said. "He was killed in an attack on the Omicron Theta colony by the Crystalline Entity."

"Gödel's incompleteness theorems notwithstanding, you can't prove that because it isn't true," the old man said. "Your father is alive, Data." He carried the book over to a table and dropped it with a thud.

"But the entire colony was destroyed," Data protested. "There were no survivors."

The old man thumbed through the tome, clearly looking for something. "I never felt comfortable living anywhere without having a pre-arranged escape route. Of course, I never thought I'd have to run for my life from a giant snowflake, but you do what you have to do."

Something about the old man's description of the Crystalline Entity persuaded Data. Somehow he saw in his face, heard in his voice, the creator he had never known. "It really is you," he said.

"Yes, it really is me," Soong said. He stopped paging through the book and beckoned Data toward him with a wave. "Come over here."

Data walked over and looked down at the book. He saw handwritten notes, equations, sketches. A drawing in one corner resembled Data's own neural transfer port. "These are your technical specifications for my construction?"

"Well, it's not an instruction manual," Soong said, "but, yes, I recorded a lot of my ideas here. I have—" He waved vaguely in the direction of the shelf from which he had pulled the book. "—I don't know how many volumes. A lot of what I wrote isn't even scientific . . . just the musings of a father-to-be and a father-at-last." Once again, Soong ambled away.

"You said you sent for me," Data said, following behind him. "Why have you done this?"

"Why?" Soong said. "Why not? Perhaps I wanted to check on your progress." He turned to face Data. "Here, do this," he said, and moved his hand in a circle in front of his midsection, as though rubbing his stomach.

Data did as the doctor asked.

"Okay, now keep doing that," Soong told him, "but with your other hand, pat the top of your head."

Data did so.

"Good," Soong exclaimed, laughing heartily. He moved over to an ornate, high-backed chair and dropped into it. "That's wonderful, Data. Tom Handy bet me you'd never master that."

"Tom Handy, sir?" Data asked, dropping his hands back to his side.

"One of the colonists on Omicron Theta," Soong said. "What about whistling? Can you whistle?"

"Not well."

"Go ahead, let me hear you," Soong urged.

Data pursed his lips and attempted to whistle a simple tune. It sounded fuzzy, as though partly a hum.

"All right, all right, that's enough," Soong said.

Data stopped. "Are these simple exercises how you propose to check on my progress, sir?" he asked.

"No, Data, no," Soong said. "I'm aware of your progress, more or less."

"Then my question remains: why did you send for me?"

"Always asking questions," Soong said. "I like that."

"I have many others," Data said. "But there is one in particular that I have always had, but to which I believed I would never receive an answer."

"Why did I create you?" Soong said.

"Yes."

Soong sighed deeply, as though facing something long anticipated. He motioned to a chair beside his own, and Data sat down. "Why does a painter paint?" he said. "Why does a climber climb? A dancer dance? A writer write? Do you know what Michelangelo used to say? That the sculptures he made were already there, hidden within the marble, even before he began. All he needed to do was remove the pieces that didn't belong. It wasn't quite the same with you, Data, but my need to reveal you to the universe was no different than Michelangelo's need."

Data listened intently, but he didn't know if Dr. Soong had

actually answered his question. Data knew that people who achieved objectives often felt driven to do so. Identifying the desire to accomplish a particular goal did not equate to explaining that desire. Before Data could articulate this, Dr. Soong continued.

"Now let me ask you something," he said. "Why are human beings so fascinated by old things?"

"Old things?"

"Yes. Old buildings, structures, artifacts. Ancient things, antique things. Clocks, lanterns, tables, anything at all."

The query seemed ill-phrased to Data, far too vague to admit of a single answer. "There are many possible explanations," he said.

"Look," Soong said, "if you brought a Noophian to Earth, he'd probably take a look around and want to tear down any of the old buildings he saw. He'd want something with state-of-the-art technology, something efficient. But for a human, that old building is something to hold on to, something to celebrate and cherish. So I ask you again, why?"

Data thought about this. "Perhaps, for humans, such things represent a tie to the past."

"But what's so important about the past?" Soong demanded. "In the past, people got sick easily, they wanted for food and water, they needed money. Why preserve any links to that?"

"I think it is because humans are mortal," Data said. "As a species and often as individuals, they seem to require a sense of continuity."

"Yes, but why?"

"I believe it helps them provide their lives purpose and meaning."

"That seems reasonable," Soong said, "but does that sense of continuity run only to the past?"

Data considered what carrying on into the future would entail for humans, both as individuals and as part of their culture. "I suppose it can be a factor in the human desire to procreate."

"So then, you believe that having children gives humans a sense of forward continuity," Soong said. "Maybe even a feeling of immortality?"

"It is a reasonable explanation to your query, sir," Data said.

Soong leaned forward in his chair. "And it is to yours as well, Data."

He again patted Data on the check, then stood from his chair and walked away, leaving Data to think about what he had said. Dr. Soong's explanation of fulfilling a procreative need in creating him did not clarify why he had not simply had natural children. Still, the description satisfied Data in a way he had not thought possible.

From beside a worktable, Soong asked, "Shall I show you why I brought you here?"

"Yes, please," Data said, rising from his chair.

"First let me ask you one more thing," Soong said. "I've been able to keep track of you periodically, since you've become something of a celebrity in the cybernetics community. And when I hear of you out in space, aboard a starship, I wonder why you elected to enter Starfleet. I gave you the ability to choose whatever you wanted to do, to be whatever you wanted to be. So why Starfleet?"

"Starfleet officers retrieved me from Omicron Theta and reactivated me," Data said.

"And so you chose to emulate your rescuers," Soong said. The doctor bent down over the table and picked up a pair of tweezers. "Very disappointing."

"What choice of vocation would have met with your approval?" Data wanted to know.

"I had hoped that you would pursue a career in science," Soong said as he reached for a small, circular container. "Perhaps even in cybernetics."

"You wished me to follow in your footsteps, as it were?"

"I don't see anything wrong with that," Soong said.

"Nor do I," said Data. "But your hopes for me might not have been misplaced."

Soong looked up, apparently startled. "Say again."

"Sir, I *have* followed in your footsteps," Data said. "Though I am in Starfleet, I have recently engaged in a major cybernetics project."

"Data," Soong said. He absently tossed the tweezers back onto the table, where they clattered across the metal surface. "What are you saying?" He took two steps forward. "What have you done?"

"I am saying that I have a daughter."

Captain Riker stood beside Counselor Troi outside the holding cell, watching as La Forge plucked a tool from his kit, which sat beside Data on the sleeping surface in the bare room. The engineer pressed a button on the Y-shaped instrument, then brought it up to the crown of the android's head. Riker heard an audible click, then saw La Forge reach up and open a flap beneath the hair on Data's skull.

Riker waited. After a moment's inspection, La Forge said, "I see what Doctor Soong described, Captain. It looks like the top of a mount. I've seen it in here before. It always looked and scanned like a support for the circuitry."

"Can you verify what it is before removing it?" Riker asked.

"I can try," La Forge said. He exchanged his tool for a tricorder, which he utilized to inspect the component in question. "I'm not reading anything concrete," he said, "but it appears to connect into the circuit, like a ground for microcurrents."

"Can you remove it safely?" Riker asked.

La Forge closed the tricorder and walked over to Riker and Troi. From the other side of the cell's forcefield, he said, "Yeah, I can remove it, but I'd like to attach another ground first, just to be safe. When we get the component clear, we can run some tests to verify its true function."

"Is there any danger to Data?" Troi asked.

"There shouldn't be, particularly if I add a secondary ground," La Forge said. "But there's always the possibility that if Soong's not telling us the truth, this could impact Data in some unexpected way."

"Would you recommend removing the component?" Riker asked.

"I think we have to, Captain," La Forge said. "After what happened, we can't have Data walking around with an unstoppable homing device in his head."

"Agreed," Riker said. After Data had seized control of *Enterprise*, he'd taken the ship to Terlina III. There, he'd transported down to report to Dr. Noonian Soong on the otherwise-uninhabited world. According to Soong, he'd activated a simple homing device in Data's brain, shutting out all the android's higher functions but those necessary to reach Terlina III without harming anybody. Once Data had arrived, the doctor had restored him to normal operation, though keeping in place a block on the memory of how the android had reached his creator.

Soong further claimed to have fashioned an "emotion chip" for his progeny. His need to bring Data immediately to him had arisen because of the doctor's impending death from Burkhardt's disease. Before installing the new chip, though, Soong had learned of Lal. Both fascinated and elated by the mere fact of her existence, he had restored Data's memory, and the two had transported back up to *Enterprise*. Once back aboard, Data had released the ship back to the crew's control.

"Mister Data," Riker said, "what is your opinion about the component Commander La Forge found?"

"I believe Doctor Soong is telling the truth about it," Data said, "and I think it should be removed."

"Counselor?" Riker asked.

"Doctor Soong remains in a distressed, restless state, making him difficult to read," Troi said. "His agitation stems partly from his reunion with Data and his desire to meet Lal, but also from his sudden exposure to people. He's apparently been living completely alone for quite a long time now."

"I'm sure he's also not too happy to have been arrested," La Forge said.

"I didn't have much choice in the matter," Riker said, uncomfortably aware that he sounded defensive. When Data had beamed back to *Enterprise* with Dr. Soong, the captain had listened to their stories before taking them both into custody. He had ordered Soong confined, under guard, to sickbay, where Dr. Crusher treated the symptoms of his medical condition, though she had yet to finish running the tests that would corroborate the diagnosis of the incurable Burkhardt's disease. "Data hijacked the *Enterprise,* and Doctor Soong essentially kidnapped Data."

"Well, despite the doctor's transgressions and his deep anxieties," Troi said, "I'm convinced he's telling us the truth."

"All right," Riker said. "Mister La Forge, remove the component as you see fit. Let me know when you determine whether or not it's the homing device Soong says it is."

"Aye, sir," La Forge said, and he headed back across the holding cell toward Data.

Riker and Troi left the detention area and entered a turbolift. The captain ordered it to take them to the bridge. They began the ride in silence, but then Troi asked, "How are you holding up?"

"Just great," Riker snarled, tensing up at the question. "I've been in command of the *Enterprise* for a couple of months, and I've managed to damage it enough to require a month and a half of repairs, then when it's finally spaceworthy again, my second officer is abducted and my ship hijacked. Oh, and it all started when I killed Captain Picard."

"Will—"

"I know, I know," he said, raising his hands in a placatory gesture. "I did what I had to do. It's just . . ." He shrugged. "I'm sorry, Deanna. It's just that some days are more difficult than others."

"I know," Troi said, her tone sympathetic. "Computer, hold." The turbolift glided to a stop. "Counselor Lucke tells me that you haven't been back to see him since your first session."

"No, I haven't," Riker said. "I haven't wanted to talk much."

"I understand that, but you need to," Troi said. "You saw somebody at the end of our stay on Starbase Two-Thirty-Four."

"And that was extremely difficult," Riker said.

"Of course it was," Troi said. "But that's why you need to keep seeing a counselor: to make it easier."

Riker shook his head slowly, unable to find any words to respond.

"Will, I care about you, and so I always want what's best for you," Troi told him. "But this is more than that." She stepped forward and took his hand, then waited until he looked her in the eyes before continuing. "I'm your counselor, Captain," she said, though the touch of her hand in his diluted the confrontational nature such a professional statement might have carried with it.

Riker nodded. "Okay, I'll make an appointment with Lieutenant Lueke."

"Good," Troi said.

Riker withdrew his hand from her grasp and ordered the turbolift to resume its journey to the bridge.

Worf passed between the two security officers standing sentry at the door and entered the guest quarters. He had initially been opposed to housing Dr. Soong, once he'd been released from sickbay, in anything other than a holding cell. It would not be long before they reached Starbase 133 and could remand the doctor to the appropriate authorities. But once La Forge had confirmed the nature of the homing device he'd removed from Data, and Worf had spoken with Data directly, the *Enterprise*'s first officer had relented. Though he still did not approve of the means by which Soong had drawn Data to Terlina III, he at least appreciated the motives behind the doctor's actions. Worf could not imagine his android friend with feelings, but it seemed as though Data leaned toward having the emotion chip installed.

Inside, Worf looked around for Soong. He saw him off to the left, standing with his stooped back to the door. "Doctor Soong," Worf said.

"What?" the doctor barked, not turning from where he stood facing a bulkhead. "What do you want?"

Worf approached Soong cautiously, concerned that he might be trying to hide something, possibly a weapon. "Captain Riker has asked me to—" Worf stopped speaking when he got close enough to the doctor to see a handful of isolinear optical chips and a panel of some sort sitting by his feet. "What are you doing?"

"What?" Soong said again, at last turning to face Worf. When he did, the first officer saw that the doctor had partially disassembled the replicator. He must have seen Worf's eyes narrow in anger, because he jerked a thumb back over his shoulder and said, "This thing's unbelievably inefficient, and really not all that good at what it does. I was just making some improvements."

"This ship does not require 'improvement,'" Worf said. He wondered for a moment where Soong had gotten tools, since his replicator had been programmed to offer only food and drink, but then he saw the knife and fork in the doctor's hands.

"I don't know," Soong said, dropping the utensils onto the carpet and shuffling across the room to the sofa. "Seems to me that thing could also use a little personality." As he sat he down, he muttered, "And it's not the only thing."

Again, Worf felt his eyes narrow, but he controlled his irritation. "Doctor, it is unacceptable for you to dismantle, modify, update, or destroy anything in these quarters, or anything else on this vessel," he said. "You are already being detained for the crime of hijacking a Federation starship."

"That wasn't me, that was Data," Soong said, but in a way that suggested even he knew the folly of such a statement.

Worf chose to ignore the comment. "Given your reason for

wanting to see Data, as well as your contributions to society, it is possible that the charges against you may be reduced or even dropped," Worf told him. "But that will not happen if you do not follow the rules aboard this ship."

"Well, fine," the doctor said. "But I could really use a decent cup of *raktajino*."

Worf responded with a single, hearty laugh. "You do not need to tell me that," he said, desirous himself of good Klingon coffee.

Soong studied Worf for a few seconds, then snickered. "No, I don't suppose I do," he said. "So what is it you want?"

"I have been sent by Captain Riker to inform you that Commander La Forge has confirmed the details of the homing device he removed from Data, and that Doctor Crusher has confirmed the existence and particulars of your disease."

"In other words, everything I told you turned out to be true," Soong said. "So the captain had you come down here to apologize."

Once more, Worf laughed. "For not assuming the veracity of assertions made by a man who forced one of our own crew to commandeer our ship?" Worf asked rhetorically. He started back over to the door. "No. I came here to tell you that, despite your methods, the captain believes what you told him and understands your intentions. He has therefore decided to permit you visitors."

"Visitors," Soong said, almost spitting the word. "I don't want any visitors."

Worf stepped forward, and the door to the corridor opened. Data entered, followed by Lal.

"Hello, sir," Data said.

Worf watched Soong rise slowly to his feet, the doctor's mouth agape. "Is this . . . is this Lal?" he finally managed to ask.

"Doctor Noonian Soong, may I present my daughter, Lal," Data said. "Lal, this is . . . this is your grandfather."

★ ★ ★

Soong sat across from Lal in his well-appointed prison aboard *Enterprise,* and he could not take his eyes off her. That Data had even conceived the idea of creating her amazed him. Soong had programmed Data with neither a specific interest in cybernetics, nor an imperative to procreate; neither personality trait had even occurred to the doctor.

As time had passed, though, and as Soong had followed Data's career and life as best he could, he'd yearned for a closer connection with his creation. The doctor could have emerged from his solitary life on Terlina III and sought out Data, but to what end? To fulfill his potential, Data needed to live on his own, to learn and grow outside the shadow of the person who'd brought him into existence.

Or that's what I told myself, Soong thought. As he reveled in the presence of Lal—in a very real sense, his granddaughter—he found it necessary to admit to himself that he had always been far from adept socially, finding it extremely difficult to interact successfully with almost anybody he met. He hadn't chosen an isolated life as much as it had been the default setting for him. Even when love had finally, unexpectedly entered his world, he'd ultimately failed to climb out of his own insecurities and self-involvement to make it last.

Soong watched Data and Lal, listened to them relate the story of her first artistic undertaking, singing at a gathering of some of the ship's crew. Until that moment, despite having accomplished what no other scientist ever had, the doctor had believed that the results of his genius had mimicked the truth of his own life, namely that his creations had been outsiders—strangers in a strange land, as the old phrase went. Because Data had achieved the closest thing to a normal life, though, Soong had stayed away, knowing that he could never have offered him anything more—at least not until the doctor had completed work on the emotion chip.

"Tell me, Lal," the doctor said, "what is it you want to do?"

Lal tilted her head in apparent confusion, a mannerism she shared with her own creator. "Can you be more specific?" she asked. "I want to do many things."

"What career do you aspire to?" Soong clarified.

"Lal was activated less than three months ago," said Data. "It is unrealistic to expect her to select a vocation with so little experience."

"But you laid down her neural pathways by duplicating your own," Soong said. "She possesses the same vast body of knowledge as you, and she has the same ability to process that knowledge. Why shouldn't she be able to choose what she wants to do?"

"I do choose," Lal said. "I want to fulfill my function."

"Your function?" Soong said. "And what is that?"

"My function is to contribute in a positive way to the world in which I live," Lal said.

Soong felt himself straighten on the sofa, as though Lal's answer had pushed him backward. "Did you teach her that?" he asked Data.

"Father has taught me many things," Lal said. "We both have access to the sum of recorded human knowledge, but I lack the experience to understand as much as he does. He is wise, and I look to him for guidance."

"Seems like you have a fan, Data," Soong said.

"I have a daughter," Data said. "We are close."

The doctor could have interpreted the comment as a slight, pointing out his own deficiencies as a parent, but he knew better. "You're close, but without emotion," Soong noted. "That's impressive. Just wait until you experience the real thing."

"I look forward to doing so," Data said.

A rush of excitement coursed through Soong. "You've decided to install the chip, then."

"Yes."

Soong smiled widely. "I couldn't be happier, Data. Maybe this'll make up for . . ." He waved the thought away, unable to

find the right words. Instead, he peered over at Lal again. He
wondered if he had enough heartbeats left to fabricate an emotion chip for her as well. He watched her body simulate the
rhythms of breathing, watched her eyelids flash down and up,
and thought her a thing of beauty, a piece of art made flesh and
blood—or their cybernetic equivalents.

"You have her blinking in a Fourier series?" he asked Data.

"Actually, we have been experimenting with different patterns," Data said, glancing over at Lal.

"We're presently employing a bilateral Laplace transform," she
said.

Data stared at Lal, and at first, Soong didn't understand why.

"Lal," Data said, "you utilized a verbal contraction."

"Yes," Lal said. "Counselor Troi told me you wouldn't mind."

"You have done this before?" Data asked.

"Yes," Lal told him. "I did it for the first time while you were
away."

"Did you do it consciously?" Soong asked, awestruck that
Data had not only created a functioning android, but that he had
crafted one that clearly improved on his own design, even if he
hadn't intended to do so.

"After I used a contraction for the first time, I asked myself if
I had done so consciously," Lal said. "It is a difficult question. I
think and respond to internal and external factors, and I select
the ideas I wish to articulate. Words arise in my mind . . . it is a
difficult question. But I did not specifically decide to say *We're*
instead of *We are*." She looked at Data. "Do you disapprove,
Father?"

"I do not," Data said. "I want your abilities to exceed my own,
but I do not understand how this has occurred." He fell silent, as
did Lal, obviously both contemplating the turn of events.

"Data," Soong said while gazing directly at Lal, "this is quite a
remarkable girl you've got here."

★ ★ ★

Riker stared at the monitor on his desk, where the stern image of Admiral Haftel stared back. *"Captain, I understand that you had an incident with Commander Data,"* said the admiral.

"We did," Riker said, sure that he knew where Haftel would take this conversation. "He was essentially abducted by his creator," the captain said, doing his best to derail any implication that Data might be unfit, either for duty or in overseeing Lal's development. "But we resolved the situation, with no harm to the crew or to the ship."

"You say 'abducted,' but there was more to it than that, wasn't there?" Haftel asked. *"Commander Data lost his ability to function consciously and took control of the* Enterprise, *did he not?"*

"Doctor Soong activated a homing device that replaced Data's priorities with an impulse to get to Terlina Three," Riker explained. "None of us, including Data, knew the implant existed. As I said, it did no damage to Data, and it has since been removed."

"And what's to say that there isn't some other unknown component inside Data?" Haftel asked.

"Doctor Soong assures us that is not the case."

"Forgive me, Captain, but Doctor Soong has hidden from society for decades, allowing the people of the Federation to believe that he was dead," Haftel said. *"And now he remotely took control of a Starfleet officer and made him do his bidding. The doctor can therefore hardly be considered a reliable source of information about Data or anything else."*

"I understand your point, Admiral," Riker said. "But the *Enterprise* has resumed normal operation, as has Commander Data. We're now on our way to Starbase One-Thirty-Three so that we can turn Doctor Soong over to the proper authorities for the crimes of subjugating a Starfleet officer and hijacking a Starfleet vessel."

"That's all well and good, Captain," Haftel said, *"but my concern is for the new android."*

That didn't take long, Riker thought. The admiral had made it quite clear during their last conversation just where his interests lay. Whatever Haftel's concerns about Data and Soong, he really wanted only one thing: his division's supervision of Lal. "Let me assure you that Lal is doing very well here, Admiral."

"Your assurances aside, I have taken my concerns to Starfleet Command," Haftel said. *"Once you reach Starbase One-Three-Three, you are to remain there until I arrive. I will then review the new android's development for myself."*

"Sir, that really isn't necessary," Riker said. "Commander Data and I have fully complied with all requests for information from Starfleet Research, and we will continue to do so."

"I'm afraid that's simply not sufficient at this point, Captain," Haftel said. *"I should also inform you that if I am not satisfied with what I find, Starfleet Command has authorized me to transfer the new android to the Galor Four facility."*

"Transfer?" Riker said. "Admiral, may I remind you that Lal is not in Starfleet. She can't simply be displaced against her will."

"Let me remind you, Captain Riker, that the new android is a technological achievement carried out by an officer while in the service of Starfleet," Haftel said. *"It is therefore property of Starfleet."*

Riker flew back in his chair as though he had been punched. He took a beat, working to prevent himself from committing insubordination. Finally, he leaned forward and looked earnestly at the image of Haftel on his monitor. "Admiral, almost two years ago, Starfleet's own JAG office ruled that sentient androids are free life-forms."

"No, they didn't," Haftel said. *"Captain Louvois specifically ruled that Data was free to choose whether or not to allow Commander Maddox to disassemble him in the name of research. In this instance, nobody's requesting anything of Data, and nobody's requesting the disassembly of the new android."*

"She's not just a 'new android,'" Riker snapped, bringing the flat of his hand down loudly on his desktop. "Data views Lal as his daughter, and she views him as her father."

"Father and daughter?" Haftel said. *"Really, Captain? You're going to make the argument that one android constructing another makes them parent and child?"*

"Yes, I would make that argument," Riker said. "I *will* make that argument, if necessary, and other arguments as well."

"Well, you're certainly entitled to your opinion, Captain, and to do what you feel you have to do," Haftel said, seemingly unimpressed by Riker's stand. *"But you will make the new android available for my inspection at Starbase One-Three-Three, and you will also continue to hold Doctor Soong until I have a chance to speak with him. Haftel out."*

The admiral's visage vanished from the screen, replaced by the Federation emblem and the words END TRANSMISSION. Riker slumped back in his chair, feeling defeated. He remembered how fiercely Captain Picard had fought for Data's rights. Riker foresaw a time coming soon when he would have to make a similar stand, not just for Data, but for Lal as well. He only hoped that he could find the strength and endurance to fight the good fight.

4

Data sat at the operations console on the *Enterprise* bridge and could not stop laughing. At first, he managed to confine his spurts of amusement to mere snickers, but before long, he could not prevent himself from erupting in full-throated guffaws. It felt—*felt*—good.

"Data," Counselor Troi said from behind him, from where he knew she sat in her chair beside the captain. "What's so funny?"

Even without looking at her, Data could tell from the pronunciation of her words that she had spoken with a smile on her face. He had from time to time during his existence witnessed the so-called infectiousness of laughter, but never before had he participated in it. That bit of glee in the counselor's voice drove him to laugh even harder.

"Commander?" Captain Riker said.

Despite the seriousness of Riker's tone, Data still could not contain himself. He reached up and touched a control to secure the ops station, then spun in his seat to face the captain and the counselor. Lieutenant Commander Worf also sat in his regular location beside Riker, and he regarded Data with a stern, disapproving countenance. "'So just eat the vegetables,'" Data said by way of explanation, quoting Specialist Pacelli's final punch line from his performance in Ten Forward.

The captain and first officer looked at each other with no sign of understanding, evidently nonplussed by Data's remark. Counselor Troi, though, sputtered as she tried and failed to keep her own merriment in check. Riker glanced at her briefly before standing and heading toward his ready room.

"Walk with me, Commander," he said as he passed ops.

Data rose and followed the captain. As they exited the bridge to the captain's ready room and the door closed behind them, Data fought to establish a straight face and then to maintain it. It lasted only until the captain turned to regard him.

"Mister Data," Riker said, wholly unamused. "Data, you need to get a hold of yourself." He spoke firmly, but not angrily.

Even as Data continued to laugh, he apprehended the sincere concern of his captain. The good humor Data felt faded by degrees, a hollow sense of foolishness left in its place. "I'm sorry," he said. "I did not expect that emotions would be so difficult to master."

"I don't know if you have to master them," Riker said, "but you certainly have to find a way to deal with them in a mature manner." He made his way around his desk and sat down, and with a gesture, invited Data to sit opposite him, which he did.

"I am trying, sir," Data said.

"I believe you, but it's been three days," Riker said, "and frankly, your behavior seems to be getting more out of hand."

"I seem to have developed a sense of humor just today," Data explained. "I am finally understanding why things I have heard in the past were considered funny by those around me. Those jokes are, essentially, brand-new to me, and I am experiencing their comedic effect for the first time." Geordi had installed Data's emotion chip under the watchful eye of Dr. Soong.

"By tomorrow, we'll be at Starbase One-Thirty-Three," Riker said. "Soon after that, Admiral Haftel will be reviewing Lal's progress. We already know that his stated preference is to have her moved, without you, to Galor Four, so that Starfleet Research can take over her development. If you provide him even the slightest indication that you're not fit to continue guiding and teaching Lal, I'm convinced that he *will* take her away from you."

Any residual good feelings within Data receded completely, driven back by anxiety, disappointment, and fear. "I am not in favor of Lal being taken from me," Data said. "Not only is she my daughter, but because we are the only two of our kind, there are numerous lessons that I exclusively can teach her. My lifetime of experiences, including the mistakes that I have made and all that I have learned, make me singularly qualified to raise her."

"I agree with you," Riker said, "which makes it all the more important that you convey those sentiments to the admiral, and that you demonstrate your fitness, both as a parent and as a teacher."

"I will do my best," Data said seriously. "Is there anything else, sir?"

Riker nodded his head slowly, as though deciding whether or not to say more than he already had. When Riker sat back in his chair, Data thought that the captain would dismiss him. Instead, Riker said, "I know how long and how intensely you've striven to comprehend what it means to be human. And I also know how much you've wanted to be as human as you can be."

"Pinocchio," Data said, recalling how Riker had characterized him when they had first met each other.

"Yes," Riker agreed. "But perhaps now is not the right time for you to be dealing with this. I think you should consider removing the emotion chip temporarily, until you've satisfied Admiral Haftel with your guardianship of Lal."

"But, Captain," Data said, "I chose to equip myself with emotions at this time specifically because of the situation with the admiral."

"I don't understand," said Riker. "Since Commander La Forge installed the chip, you frequently seem overwhelmed by what you're feeling, and sometimes even unstable. How will that help you with Admiral Haftel?"

"I did not expect that it would be quite so difficult for me,"

Data said. "Regardless, my decision to experience emotions was motivated by the admiral's questioning my abilities as a parent."

"I don't know that he's really done that," Riker said.

"But he has, sir," Data said, "by suggesting that other individuals would be better qualified than I to oversee Lal's development. Since there are no sentient androids at the Daystrom Institute annex on Galor Four—or anywhere else in the Federation—there can be no better android guides for Lal than me. Therefore, the primary distinction between the researchers on Galor Four and me is their ability to feel emotion. By having my emotion chip installed, I have removed that distinction."

"I see," said the captain, who appeared to ruminate on Data's point. "I still think you should consider removing it for the short term. Emotions won't help if they make you seem erratic. Should Admiral Haftel cite a lack of feelings as a reason to take Lal from you, then you can always have the chip reinstalled."

"I will think about it," Data said.

"Good," Riker said. "That'll be all, then."

"Thank you, sir," Data said. He got to his feet and started for the door, but after taking a step, he began laughing again.

"Data?" Riker said. "There's nothing funny about this situation."

Data turned back toward the captain. "I know, I agree, sir," he said, though he continued to laugh. "I cannot help myself." A jolt of energy surged through his body, causing him to wince. "I think something is wrong." His mouth opened again in raucous laughter, totally disassociated from anything he thought or felt.

Riker rushed out from behind his desk as another shock coursed through Data. Several of his axial servos seized up. He heard himself cry out, as though in pain, and then another fit of laughter racked him. Captain Riker arrived at his side and tried physically to steady him.

All of Data's senses failed him. He saw a field of white as a rush of static rose in his ears. He could no longer feel the captain's hands on his arms. His proprioceptive apparatus shut down, and for an instant, he lost the ability to recognize his corporeal self.

When his system reset, Data saw an overhead. He sat upright to find himself on the deck in the captain's ready room. He heard the chirp of a combadge.

"Riker to La Forge, emergency. Commander Data is experiencing major system problems."

"Understood," Geordi responded. *"Is he conscious?"*

"He appears to be," Riker said. "He collapsed, but now he's sitting up on the deck."

Everything seemed to take place at a remove from Data. He knew that, whatever had happened, he'd recovered only in a rudimentary fashion. "I believe the emotion chip has overloaded my positronic relay," he concluded.

The captain repeated this to the chief engineer, then said, "Geordi, you'd better bring Doctor Soong."

The ensign—a tall Andorian whose wavy white hair beautifully framed his blue-skinned face—ushered Riker into the inner office. According to Admiral Nguyen, commander of Starbase 133, the use of the suite had been granted to Admiral Haftel for the duration of his stay there. That Haftel had ordered Riker to bring Lal to the base, rather than the admiral seeing her aboard *Enterprise,* had not been lost on the captain. To Riker, it seemed more than mere posturing; it felt like an endgame.

Leaving Lal in the anteroom, the captain entered the inner office to see Haftel seated behind an outsized, arc-shaped desk, the main focal point of the well-appointed but impersonal room. A large rectangular window adorned the rear of the space, overlooking the interior of the starbase's space dock, where several starships sat attached by various umbilicals to maintenance ports. Riker adopted a friendly, professional demeanor and paced forward with an outstretched hand. "Admiral, a pleasure to meet you in person," he said, even as he thought, *Thank goodness he's not an empath.*

"Captain," Haftel acknowledged evenly. He stood and offered Riker a weak handshake. "I understand you've had another problem with Commander Data."

Riker dropped the admiral's hand, but fought to remain calm. Where Haftel had stated his intention to review Lal's development, the result of that review seemed foreordained. "I wouldn't characterize it as a problem, Admiral," Riker said.

"No?" Haftel asked, his voice rife with disbelief. He sat down behind the desk, and Riker took the middle of the five chairs facing it. "Your own log states that Commander Data decided to install in his positronic brain an emotion chip designed and built by a man you're detaining for his part in a kidnapping and a hijacking."

Riker understood that the admiral sought to cast uncertainty on Data's stability and judgment. "Whatever Doctor Soong's recent indiscretions," the captain said, "he created Data and remains the foremost expert on him."

"And yet this emotion chip overloaded Commander Data's positronic matrix," Haftel persisted.

"Only momentarily," Riker said. "Doctor Soong fabricated the chip so that it would ultimately integrate seamlessly into Data's neural net. He simply thought it more likely to happen later rather than sooner."

"The chip has fused to Commander Data's neural net, has it not?" the admiral asked. "Which means that he is now stuck with his emotions."

Riker leaned forward, feeling a smile bloom on his face. "Aren't we all?" he said, believing that his simple rhetorical question defanged Haftel's argument. But the admiral did not even hesitate before responding.

"Yes, but emotions aren't new to the rest of us," he said.

Riker felt disheartened, but he pressed on, explaining to Haftel that Data had elected to experience emotions so that he could become an even better parent for Lal.

"Don't misconstrue what I'm saying," the admiral said. "I'm not impugning Commander Data's motives, or even his abilities. But the work that he's doing with the new android, he's doing in effective isolation."

"Does that matter," Riker asked, "if he's the best guide for Lal?"

"That's what I'm trying to find out, Captain," Haftel said, making no attempt to disguise his growing impatience. "I asked you to bring the new android with you."

Riker stood up and glared down at the admiral. "Her name is Lal," he said quietly. "You keep referring to her as 'the new android,' but she's a sentient being, and her name is Lal."

Haftel returned Riker's angry stare with what the captain could only describe as the strength of his rank. The admiral rose slowly to his feet, touched his hands to the desktop, and leaned in toward Riker. "Are you going to bring the new android here," he demanded, "or do I need to send a security detail to what is *currently* your ship?"

The intensity of the threats and the insistence on control staggered Riker, though he worked not to show it. *What choice do I have?* he asked himself, and knew that he had none. "Lal is waiting in the outer office," he told Haftel. "I'll ask her to come inside."

As he walked back to the door, he imagined himself telling Lal to run and hide. Such an action would amount to sheer folly, neither protecting Lal nor keeping Riker in a position from which he could attempt to help her and her father. While unclear just what assistance he could actually provide them, he knew that he would have to do an end-run around Anthony Haftel, climbing the chain of command.

In the outer office, Riker saw Lal sitting on a sofa, dressed in a brown-print skirt and a pink blouse that he knew Deanna had helped her pick out. Lal focused her attention on a personal access display device. He couldn't see what she read on the padd, but he'd observed her voracious appetite for self-improvement. Reluctantly, he invited her inside.

Riker allowed Lal to enter before him, then followed her to the desk. Still standing, the admiral peered at him, and for an uncomfortable few seconds, the captain thought that Haftel would order him to leave. When he didn't, Riker introduced Lal to the admiral.

"Please," Haftel said with a smile, "have a seat." Lal did so, and the admiral returned to his own chair. Riker opted to remain on his feet. "Well, Lal," Haftel continued, "I've been looking forward to meeting you." When he said her name, he studiously avoided eye contact with Riker.

"Thank you," Lal said, accepting the implicit compliment with manners that Riker had watched improve considerably. "May I ask if there is a particular reason you wanted to meet me?"

"You're quite important to us at Starfleet Research and Development," Haftel said. "We have an impressive cybernetics facility on Galor Four, one of the finest such complexes in the Federation. I would like very much to show it to you."

Lal listened to the admiral, then looked over at Captain Riker. "Has my father visited this facility?" she asked.

"Actually, I believe he has," Riker said. "Perhaps you can ask him what he thinks of it." Haftel glowered at him, but Riker didn't care.

"I'm sure Commander Data would confirm how important the Daystrom annex is to the field of cybernetics," the admiral said. "In fact, we would like to relocate you to Galor Four so that you can take advantage of its services and staff."

Again, Lal looked to Riker. "I do not understand," she said. "Am I no longer welcome aboard the *Enterprise*?"

Riker opened his mouth to answer, but Haftel spoke first. "No, not at all," he said. "But we would like to bring you to

Galor Four in order to expand your horizons. After all, there's only so much you can learn on a starship."

"That is true," Lal said. "Therefore, the logical conclusion would be that, once I have learned all that I can aboard the starship, I will relocate to Galor Four."

Riker wanted to cheer. No matter the admiral's plans, the captain could not imagine Starfleet allowing Lal to be forcibly moved against her will.

"That is not the logical conclusion," Haftel said.

"I believe that it is," Lal said.

The admiral regarded her for a moment, then said, "You're contradicting me, Lal. That is considered a breach of good manners, a failure in the selective verbalization of your thoughts. It is also an example of how we can help you learn and grow on Galor Four."

"My father is already helping me learn and grow," Lal said. She glanced up at Riker, and something seemed to occur to her. "Does my father wish us to relocate from the *Enterprise*?"

"Lal," the admiral said, "Commander Data serves on a starship, where he lacks the resources necessary to aid you fully in your development. All of those resources, and more, are available on Galor Four."

"You did not answer my question," Lal observed.

"I did answer your question," Haftel said, "but perhaps not in the way you desired."

"I'll answer your question, Lal," Riker said, the words spilling from him in a rush.

"Captain, you—" Haftel tried to interject, but Riker spoke over him.

"Your father wants to stay on the *Enterprise*," he told Lal, "and he wants you to stay with him."

Lal looked at Riker with something surprisingly resembling relief. She stood and faced the admiral. "Then I choose to stay with my father aboard the *Enterprise*."

Haftel sighed, in what Riker thought must finally be an acceptance of his defeat. Instead, he said, "I'm afraid that's not an option."

"What?" Riker said, stunned. "How can that not be an option? Lal is a free—"

"Captain Riker, you're dismissed," Haftel ordered. He started out from behind his desk, and Lal backed away from him.

"No!" she cried, the expression on her face unmistakably that of fear. "No!" She began jabbing at her midsection, as though something there pained her.

"Lal," Riker said softly, trying to calm her. "It's all—"

As she continued to step backward, her foot caught the leg of a chair and she fell. Both Riker and Haftel moved to help her, but she quickly clambered back to her feet. "No," she said again, and then she turned and headed for the door.

"Lal," Haftel said, but she ignored him. "Lal, stop."

The door opened, and she left.

The admiral activated his combadge with a touch. "Haftel to security," he said.

"Admiral," Riker said.

"Security here."

"Admiral," Riker said again. "There's no need for security."

Haftel's eyes narrowed. Riker thought to say more, but knew that, despite their differences, the admiral understood.

"Belay that, security," he said. "Haftel out."

The channel closed, and then the admiral hurried for the door. Riker followed him out.

Data peered at Lal and wondered where he had gone wrong—or in some sense, what had gone right. She stood in the experiment chamber of the *Enterprise* science laboratory in which she had initially been activated. Captain Riker and Admiral Haftel looked on.

"She learned that she would be leaving you and the *Enterprise* and moving to the Daystrom Institute annex on Galor Four," Riker said. "She looked and acted terrified."

Since Data had himself experienced fear—he had first worried that his daughter would be taken from him, and now he worried that she would not survive the day—it pained him to know what she had felt. At the same time, that she had so quickly outgrown her programming, that she had achieved in a matter of weeks what he had not in years, thoroughly delighted him. He only hoped that she would outlast the occurrence.

"She did regain her composure, and then made her way back here without saying another word," Haftel said. "Her motor skills appeared to deteriorate along the way; it became more and more difficult for her to walk."

"Lal is programmed to return to the lab in the event of a malfunction," Data said.

"And that's what you think this is?" Haftel asked. "A malfunction?"

"I do not know with certainty that what has transpired should be categorized in that way," Data said. "Clearly, though, Lal has perceived it as such, otherwise she would not have come here."

"Data, I know it sounds crazy," Riker said, "but she *was* scared. I could see it on her face and hear it in her voice." As the captain spoke, Admiral Haftel nodded soberly.

"I believe you, Captain," Data said. "It appears to be a symptom of cascade failure. The solution would be to reinitialize the base matrix without wiping out the higher functions."

"I agree," said the admiral, his expertise in cybernetics at last a boon rather than a threat. "But is that even possible?"

"I do not know," Data said. "But there is somebody on board who may."

Troi sat in a comfortable chair in her office and waited for her newest patient to speak. When he gave no sign of doing so, she realized that her guidance would be required, even simply to get started. "So tell me what you're feeling," she prompted.

"I am feeling many things, Counselor," Data said. He sat in the chair across from her, his posture as always ramrod straight. "So many different emotions, in fact, that I am finding it difficult to concentrate."

"Considering what you've been through in the last two days, I'd say that's understandable," Troi told him. Forty-eight hours ago, Lal had unexpectedly experienced emotions for the first time, which had in turn brought her to the brink of a complete system failure—cybernetic death. "You must be exhausted," Troi said, before realizing her folly: androids didn't tire.

To her surprise, though, Data agreed with her. "Though I typically do not require physical rest," he said, "I believe that the depth and variety of my emotions have somehow contributed to a sense of fatigue."

"Such a reaction to emotional turmoil is not unusual," Troi said. "Why don't you talk about what you're feeling?"

"At this moment, I am more than anything else elated that Lal has survived the procedure to correct her cascade failure," Data said.

Will had told Deanna that only the extensive efforts of Data, Admiral Haftel, and Dr. Soong, over the course of two days, had managed to save Lal. Data had worked without surcease, with Haftel and Soong taking short breaks to rest whenever they could no longer stay on their feet. Perhaps most remarkably, the trio had been able not only to prevent Lal's permanent shutdown, but to preserve her newfound emotional awareness.

"I am also grateful that Doctor Soong was here to assist Admiral Haftel and me," Data continued. "I do not believe that, without his help, we would have been able to repair Lal."

Troi waited a moment to see if he would say more. When he didn't, she asked, "And are there flip sides to those emotions?"

"'Flip sides?'"

"Yes," Troi said. "You feel elation at Lal's survival, but surely that calls to mind the possibility of her demise. You are thankful for Doctor Soong's aid, but if his presence was necessary to save Lal, how vulnerable does that make her?"

"Such thoughts did occur to me, primarily after the successful completion of the procedure," Data said. "I find myself worrying about her even now."

"I want to assure you that's not an unusual reaction," Troi said. "When people are forced to confront the mortality of their loved ones, and by extension their own mortality, it can focus the mind and the emotions in various ways."

"Those fears are consuming a significant amount of my processing power," Data said. "I seem unable to let them go."

His face, for so long an impassive façade, revealed the depth of his dread. Troi still had not grown accustomed to seeing emotion reflected in his aspect, much less sensing it in his presence. Although she could feel a confusing mix of the affects of which he'd spoken, it emanated from him at a low level, confirming his weariness.

"Those feelings should fade with time," Troi said. "As you and Lal live your lives—" She wondered briefly about the propriety of the words *live* and *life* when used with respect to androids. "—your concerns will lose their immediacy. When not faced with death in the near term, people have a healthy tendency toward denial."

Data's brow furrowed, and he looked away from Troi, not at anything in particular, but as though in deep thought. "Data?" she asked. "Is everything all right?"

Glancing back up, he said, "I am just recalling something Admiral Haftel said after we had stabilized Lal. He mentioned that, more than the internal threat to Lal, he worried about an external threat to the two of us."

Troi felt her own eyebrows knit in confusion. "I'm not sure I follow," she said. "What kind of 'external threat' did he mean?"

"The admiral suggested that if the *Enterprise* were to engage in battle, it would put Lal and me at risk," Data explained. "If we were both destroyed, it would mean the effective extinction of Soong-type androids."

"That's true," Troi said, "but I suppose Doctor Soong could always create another."

"That is unlikely," Data said. "Doctor Soong has a terminal illness which will result in his death well before he could complete such a project. And it is unclear just how willing and how able the doctor is to pass on the knowledge he has amassed through his work."

"Then I guess we'll just have to prevail upon Captain Riker to keep the quadrant at peace," Troi said. She'd intended the sentiment as a joke, but as she articulated the thought, it evoked the memory of Captain Picard's violent death aboard the Borg ship. She tamped the horrible recollection back down, but as she did so, she thought of something else. "Data, why did Admiral Haftel make that argument to you? I mean, why do you think he felt the need to say that to you just after you'd saved Lal?"

Data slowly moved his head from side to side. "I do not know," he said. "I would infer that it was simply the verbalization of another reason that the Admiral believed that Lal would be better served by being relocated to the Starfleet Research facility on Galor Four."

A terrible feeling of dread suddenly overcame Troi, and she fought not to let it show on her face. "Where is Lal now?" she asked.

"She remains in the laboratory for now, so that her condition can be monitored continuously."

"I see," Troi said. "She's still activated, then?"

"Yes," Data said. "She is fully sentient, so it would be inappropriate to deactivate her."

Still working to stay composed, she tapped her combadge. "Troi to Lal." She waited, and when she received no response, she tried again. No reply came. Unable to completely contain her anxiety, Troi stood from her chair. "Computer," she said, "locate Lal."

"Lal is not aboard the Enterprise," came the distinctive female tones of the ship's computer.

Data rose to his feet. "Computer, open a channel to Lal aboard Starbase One-Thirty-Three."

Seconds passed, and Troi hoped that the silence would be

broken by the voice of Data's daughter. Instead, the computer spoke again. *"Lal is not aboard Starbase One-Three-Three."*

Troi peered over at Data to gauge his reaction, but already he raced for the door.

Data stood beside Riker in front of the desk in the captain's ready room. Counselor Troi sat off to the side, on the sofa. They all faced the desktop monitor, which displayed the image of Admiral Haftel. They had located him aboard *U.S.S. Teton,* being ferried to the Daystrom Institute annex on Galor IV.

"This will not stand, Admiral," Riker said, the obvious anger in his tone not something Data had often heard directed at a superior officer.

"I understand the difference of opinion we have on this matter," Haftel said, with the arrogance and self-satisfaction of somebody who knows that they have successfully achieved their goals despite the resistance of others. *"Let me assure you again that we are only looking out for the best interests of Lal."*

"Whether or not I choose to believe you is irrelevant," Riker said, his outrage not abating. "What matters is that you have taken Lal from this ship against her will and against the will of her father. This goes beyond the mere violation of orders; you have carried out an act of abduction."

"On the contrary, I have neither disobeyed Starfleet orders nor committed a Federation crime," Haftel said. The admiral looked down and worked the controls of the companel at which he sat. When he glanced back up, he said, *"I've just transmitted two data packets to the* Enterprise. *The first contains Starfleet Command's orders for me to move Lal to the Galor Four facility, both for her sake and for reasons of Federation security. The second packet includes a ruling I received from Starfleet's judge advocate general's office, this sector. In that ruling, you will see that the JAG concurred with the contention that, as the product of the efforts of Starfleet personnel and matériel, the new android meets the criteria to be considered the property of Starfleet."*

"That cannot be," Data said. "Lal is a living, sentient being, and as such, she cannot be deemed property, either morally or legally." The very thought disgusted him.

"Again, I have official orders and a JAG decree stating otherwise," Haftel said.

"I'll go to Starfleet Command with this," Riker threatened.

"I am Starfleet Command," Haftel blustered, his irritation plain. Then, seeming to moderate his temper, he added, *"I understand that this is difficult for you, Commander Data, but I'm confident that if you examine the situation objectively, you'll see that this is what's best for Lal and for the Federation. I can promise you that Lal will come to no harm in our custody. Ensuring her safety is, after all, why we brought Doctor Soong along with us."*

Riker peered over at Data, a look of confusion dressing his features. Data understood the feeling. He shook his head to indicate to the captain that he had not known of Dr. Soong's participation in Lal's relocation. Considering the outstanding charges against the doctor, Data wondered how much of that participation had been voluntary.

"Admiral," Riker said, "I don't doubt that you and the scientists on Galor Four will see to many of Lal's needs. But that's not the point. You intend to hold her against her will, which is more important than ever now that she has emotions."

"Lal's will is irrelevant," Haftel said, and the similarity to the attitudes and statements of the Borg reverberated for Data. *"And this conversation is irrelevant. I have my orders, and now I'm giving you both yours: drop this now. Haftel out."* The monitor winked off to standby mode, the Federation emblem appearing on it.

Data did not know what to do. He had received orders he had no desire to follow, but it seemed unclear what else he could do. He looked at Captain Riker, whose face had grown flush with his ire.

Activating his combadge, the captain said, "Riker to bridge."

"Worf here, sir," came the immediate reply.

"Commander, make preparations to depart space dock," Riker ordered. "Set course for Galor Four."

"Aye, sir."

"Captain," Troi asked, "what are you going to do?" Data wanted to know the same thing.

"I don't know," Riker said, "but we can't do nothing while a resident of this ship is kidnapped."

Troi stood up and briefly touched her hand to Data's forearm. "Forgive me, Data," she said before addressing the captain, "but Lal's already been taken. All of the arguments in opposition have failed to prevent that. So what do you propose to do? Win her freedom by force?"

"Perhaps," Riker said. "If that's what's needed."

"Really?" Troi said. "You're prepared to fire on the *Teton,* or on the Daystrom Institute? You're willing to unleash phasers and photon torpedoes against Starfleet personnel?"

"I'd like to do more than that to Anthony Haftel," he said, though Data could see that Riker understood Troi's perspective. The captain patted his combadge once more. "Riker to bridge."

"Worf here."

"Mister Worf, cancel preparations for departure, and contact Fleet Admiral Shanthi. I need to speak with her on an urgent matter."

"Aye, captain."

Riker said, "We'll take care of this, Data. We'll get Starfleet to do the right thing." He appeared earnest.

"No, sir," Data said. "We will not."

"Data, I'll talk to Admiral Shanthi, make her understand," Riker said.

"I appreciate what you wish to do," Data said, "but I believe that if Admiral Shanthi did not endorse what Admiral Haftel has done, then it would not have happened."

"You may be right," Troi said.

"Data, we have to fight this," Riker insisted.

"I agree," Data said. "But what has transpired has repercussions and redresses far beyond Starfleet." He reached up, plucked his combadge from his uniform, and set it down atop the captain's desk.

"Data, what are you doing?" Troi asked.

"Starfleet has permitted an act that has not only defied both my wishes and Lal's, but has transgressed morality and, I believe, legality," Data said. "The wisest course, then, would seem to be to pursue a legal remedy. I am therefore resigning my commission in Starfleet."

5

Cluttered with scores of padds, stacks of hardcover volumes, and bound copies of legal extracts, the studio apartment had grown smaller with each passing day. At the moment, the air inside smelled stale and felt uncomfortably close. As Data sat in a hard-backed chair and scoured the information he had amassed, a sense of claustrophobia began to creep over him. When the tones of a nearby carillon pealed out across the neighborhood, ultimately striking the afternoon hour of three, he could no longer stay seated.

Data hied across the room and pulled open the French doors. Unseasonable heat greeted him as he stepped out onto the Juliet balcony. Despite the stifling temperature, it felt good to be outside, if only just for a respite. With the joys and hopes and delights of an emotional existence had come sorrow and despair and pain, and Data had yet to discover how to deal with such disadvantages.

Except that I have learned to cope with negative emotions, Data thought. *I simply do not like them.*

It had been nearly four months since his resignation from Starfleet and his departure from *Enterprise*. He had been right to leave, as Captain Riker's occasional messages demonstrated. The captain's efforts to sway Starfleet Command continued even to the current day, but had met only with resistance.

Seeking to correct the wrongs perpetrated against him and Lal, Data had traveled to Sector 001. As both home to Starfleet

Headquarters and the seat of the Federation government, Earth seemed the best place to conduct a legal action against Starfleet. He had taken up residence just outside Paris, in Hauts-de-Seine, and in short order, he had retained an attorney.

Data peered over the neighborhood, out toward the skyscrapers of La Défense, and beyond it, past the River La Seine to the City of Light. The great metropolis and its environs afforded him an exceptional location in which to conduct the research he needed. The area boasted some of the most significant historical and legal libraries, not just on Earth, but in all the Federation.

Because of the paucity of truly sentient androids within the UFP, laws respecting their rights and privileges essentially did not exist. The two JAG decisions—the one two years earlier regarding Data, and the more recent one regarding Lal—fell strictly under the purview of Starfleet, and even had they not, they would have provided no help. Accordingly, Data's attorney—a human named Gregory Desjardins, originally from the Alpha Centauri system—wanted to ground their argument in case law that best approximated their cause.

Since Data did not sleep, he could contribute continuously to the legal effort, and thanks to the speed and storage of his positronic brain, he could provide rapid analyses of a large number of cases. He'd started with the most obvious of records, examining those findings brought under principles established by the most significant and revered legal charters, such as the Fundamental Declarations of the Martian Colonies, the Statutes of Alpha III, and the Vulcan Bill of Rights. In the course of his research, he'd found a number of rulings that his attorney believed would be beneficial to their cause of action.

Data gazed down the front of the building, past the ornate wrought iron of the balcony and the first four floors of the apartment complex, to the tree-lined street below. As he'd done so often during his time in Hauts-de-Seine, he watched people walking along the pedestrian thoroughfare, some making haste, others moving at a more leisurely rate. Data saw people of many species—humans, Vulcans, Orions, Andorians, and others— some strolling by themselves, some in couples or larger groups. The pairs with a single adult and a single child always drew his sharpest attention.

Down the street, one such duo emerged from a building across the way. Both appeared human, the man perhaps in his thirties or forties, and the young girl, ten or so. Data imagined them father and daughter, though the reality of their situation mattered less to him than the emotions the impression stirred in him. He watched them all the way to the end of the street, walk- ing hand in hand, until at last they disappeared around the far corner.

Data turned and walked back inside. He ignored the mounds of collected information spread throughout the apartment, head- ing instead for the small companel on the wall to his left. There, he sat down and activated the recorder with a touch to the ap- propriate control.

"My dear Lal," he said, "I am sending you another message, although I have little new to say to you." He did not mention how many messages he had sent to her since she had been taken from *Enterprise,* because despite the Federation's clear legal prohibitions against blocking, intercepting, copying, or altering personal transmissions, he had no expectation of privacy. If Lal had received all forty-seven of his previous messages, then she would know how many he had sent; if she had not, then he nei- ther wished to distress her, nor to provide those who held her a reason for not passing his message through to her.

"I wish to tell you again how sorry I am that I did not do enough to prevent our separation," Data said. "I am hopeful that the people around you are providing you a comfortable, stable environment in which to live. The stated intention for removing you to Galor Four was to help you develop, to guide you in a way that I could not. For your sake, I want this to be true." He felt a knot in his midsection, a feeling of emptiness that he had come to recognize well. No matter the aims of Admiral Haftel and his staff, Data remained certain that his daughter could have no better and no more suitable guardian and teacher than himself.

Data forged ahead. "Please do not lament our parting. At this time, our external circumstances are not entirely in our control, but we both retain the ability to choose what happens within us. Continue to strive for the things important to you, for the personal growth that you began almost immediately after I activated you." He felt pressure behind his face, in the channels that controlled the flow of lubricants to his eyes. In programming Data's emotion chip, Dr. Soong had not neglected to endow him with the ability—and in fitting situations, the compulsion—to weep. Data fought that compulsion, wanting to avoid upsetting his daughter.

"I am very proud of you," he said. "I miss you, Lal, and I love you." He ended the recording, then transmitted the message without reviewing it to the Daystrom annex on Galor IV. As always, he could only hope that it would make it through; he had received no verification that any of his previous messages had done so, much less any replies from Lal. Nor had Admiral Haftel responded to any of the various entreaties that Data had sent to him.

A rapping sound startled Data, causing him to flinch, another physical reaction engendered by his emotion chip. He realized that somebody had knocked on his apartment door, and he could think of only one person who it would be. He crossed the room and opened the door. His attorney stood there with his usual slight hitch in one shoulder, his hair the same color as Data's but shot through with flecks of gray, his swarthy complexion a vivid contrast to Data's normal pallor.

"I have news," Desjardins said, "and I wanted to deliver it in person." He held up a padd, though in such a way that Data could not see its screen.

"Please come in."

The attorney walked into the apartment past Data, who closed the door behind him. Desjardins continued to hold the padd aloft, as though in triumph. "Data," he said, "we have a court date."

This time, the flutter in Data's abdomen measured not discontent or frustration, but excitement.

"One degree to overlap," said Lieutenant Laresk, *Enterprise*'s alpha-shift operations officer. Even after the months that had passed since Data's resignation from Starfleet, Riker had not yet gotten used to seeing the Arkenite crewing the ops station. She had performed well so far, receiving high marks from all who worked with her, including the captain himself, but—

But Data was my friend, Riker thought. In the back of his mind, the hazy awareness of how he had failed Data returned to him, as it often did. As a captain, and as a man in an ongoing battle against more than just that one demon, Riker pushed his failures away. He didn't have the time, and his crew didn't deserve his self-indulgence. And if he even entertained such thoughts while on duty, Deanna would be certain to bring it to his attention.

Turning in his chair to Troi, he remarked dryly, "Nothing like a mapping mission to satisfy the appetite for exploration."

"We are very close to the Cardassian border, Captain," said Worf, seated on the other side of Riker. "My only concern is for *their* appetite for conflict."

"I don't know, Worf," the captain said. "The treaty between the Federation and the Cardassian Union has held for an entire year. I don't think they're hungry anymore."

Before Worf could reply, Laresk announced, "Stand by to record." She paused, then said, "Mark."

"Recording," acknowledged Astrometrics Specialist Fortin from his aft station.

"Captain," said Ensign zh'Kal from the tactical station, surprise registering in her voice. "I'm picking up a vessel closing on our position at high warp."

"Cardassian?" Worf asked, reaching at once for the console beside his chair and working its controls.

"Getting a fix now," said zh'Kal. "It's definitely coming from their side of the border."

"Is it a patrol vessel?" Riker asked. "Cardassian Central Command knows we're out here, but they can still be skittish about vessels near their territory."

"Not a patrol vessel," Worf said, consulting his readouts. "It's a *Galor*-class warship."

"Shall I raise the shields?" zh'Kal asked.

Riker's gut told him to protect his ship and crew, but he'd also learned from Captain Picard that even acting to defend oneself could be considered provocative action. He reminded himself that hostilities with the Cardassian Union had ended more than a year ago, and that a treaty had been formalized soon after—a treaty that, as far as he knew, remained unbroken and in force. "Negative, Ensign," he told zh'Kal. "We're at peace with Cardassia. Hail them."

Riker heard the telltale chirrups that signaled an attempt to open communications. "No response, sir," zh'Kal said.

"Keep try—"

"Captain, they're powering their weapons," zh'Kal said.

Riker knew that the armaments of a *Galor*-class vessel did not measure up to those of the *Galaxy*-class *Enterprise,* but he would not simply allow the Cardassians to damage his ship. He looked to his first officer and nodded.

"Shields," Worf ordered, and a moment later, zh'Kal confirmed operation of the ship's defenses.

"They've dropped out of warp," said Laresk, "and are now within visual range."

Riker stood and moved to the center of the bridge. "Let's see them, Lieutenant. Maximum magnification."

The image on the main viewer shifted and the Cardassian vessel appeared. Though basically linear in shape, the *Galor*-class ships had always put Riker in mind of a snake. The forward structure spread like the hood of a cobra, while its narrow aft section split like the forked tail of a Filian python.

As Riker watched, a fiery pink beam flashed from the Cardassian ship and pounded into *Enterprise*. The captain rode out the fleeting disruption of the inertial dampers, then saw a second beam streak toward his ship. "What the hell is he doing?" he wondered aloud.

"Damage report," Worf ordered.

"Shields at ninety-three percent," zh'Kal said. "No damage to the ship, structural integrity intact. No casualties." The tactical officer paused, then added, "They're firing again."

Riker waited for the jolt, then moved back to his command chair. "Ready main phasers," he said. "Target their weapons. Let's show them we don't appreciate taking 'friendly fire.'"

"Phasers ready," zh'Kal said.

"Continuous fire," Riker said. "I want their weapons disabled."

"Yes, sir," zh'Kal said, even as the captain heard the electronic tweets that indicated phaser activation. Riker saw his ship's weaponry leap forth, at first slamming into the warship's forcefields, and then slicing through them. The captain waited until his tactical officer reported that the Cardassian ship's aft shields had collapsed. "Firing on their spiral-wave generator," she said, and then, "Generator down."

"Let's see if they're willing to talk to us now," Riker mused. "Hail them, Ensign."

"Hailing," zh'Kal said. "Channel is now open."

"Imagine that," Riker said under his breath, just loud enough to allow his first officer and counselor to hear. Worf offered him a knowing grin. "Cardassian vessel, this is Captain William Riker of the Federation *Starship Enterprise*. Please identify yourself and your intentions."

On the main screen, the image of a Cardassian bridge replaced the view of the ship in space. *"I am Gul Macet of the warship* Trager,*"* said the commander of the enemy vessel, the scales along his neck and lining his face reminiscent of reptilian features. *"And I believe I've made my intentions clear."*

"That you have," Riker said. "What's also clear is that your ship poses no real threat to mine." He waited, allowing Macet the chance to take in that harsh reality. "Your actions, though, do pose a threat to the peace treaty between the Federation and Cardassia."

"That threat does not come from us," Macet protested. *"It comes from the Federation starship that destroyed our unarmed space station in the Cuellar system yesterday."*

Again, Riker looked to Worf, but the first officer appeared as thunderstruck by the claim as Riker felt. "Are you sure you have your facts right, Gul?" he asked his Cardassian counterpart.

"I saw the distress signal myself," said Macet.

"Can you confirm that?" Riker asked Worf, who worked for several seconds at his console.

"Negative," he said.

"So what's it to be, Captain?" Macet demanded. *"Are we at war?"*

Riker shook his head, but he could only think, *I wish I knew.*

Captain Riker followed the first officer of *U.S.S. Phoenix,* Commander Sokar, out of the turbolift. It had been a while since Riker had been aboard a *Nebula*-class starship, and its smaller, boxier command deck struck him as almost primitive when compared with *Enterprise*'s expansive, circular bridge. *Still*, the captain told himself, *this ship destroyed a science station and a supply ship.*

The latter action had come as Riker's crew had pursued *Phoenix* into Cardassian territory. After *Enterprise*'s confrontation with *Trager*, Starfleet Command had confirmed *Phoenix*'s unprovoked destruction of the Cardassian space station in the Cuellar system. The ship's captain, Benjamin Maxwell, refused to respond to repeated messages from Starfleet as he continued an apparent and unexplained rampage through Cardassian space. Central Command had agreed to allow *Enterprise* free passage to locate and stop *Phoenix,* with Gul Macet and two of his aides coming aboard to monitor the search. When *Enterprise* had finally intercepted the rogue vessel, Maxwell had agreed to meet with its captain.

As Riker trailed Sokar across the lower tier of the bridge, several of *Phoenix*'s command crew glanced up at him, each of them looking immediately away as he met their gaze. On his trip up from the transporter room, Riker had tried to gauge Sokar's state of mind, but the Vulcan had displayed nothing but the stoicism so common among his people. On the bridge, though, the anxiety of the crew seemed palpable.

Sokar ushered Riker into *Phoenix*'s ready room, where Captain Maxwell sat at his desk, intent on reading the contents of the computer interface there. "Captain Benjamin Maxwell," the first officer said, "this is Captain William Riker of the *U.S.S. Enterprise*." Maxwell looked up but did not stand. The two captains greeted each other by title, but neither extended their hand to the other.

Sokar stepped aside, but did not leave the ready room. As he had when he'd initially come aboard, Riker noted the handheld phaser holstered at Sokar's side, and he realized now that the first officer meant to stand guard over his captain. "I'd prefer to speak with you privately," Riker told Maxwell. Then, spreading his arms wide, palms up, he added, "I'm unarmed."

"Thank you, Sokar," Maxwell said. "I'll be fine."

"Yes, sir," Sokar said, and he departed the ready room.

Maxwell gestured toward one of the chairs in front of his desk, and Riker sat down. "I'm glad they sent you after me," Maxwell said. "I'm glad they sent somebody who knows what it's like out here."

"Captain?" Riker said, unsure what to make of his counterpart's comments.

"I read your reports on your battle with the Borg," Maxwell explained. "That was impressive work."

Riker nodded slightly, uncomfortable with Maxwell's characterization of his efforts against the Borg. "It was *necessary* work," he said.

Maxwell took his meaning right away. "And this work in Cardassian space, my work, isn't necessary? Is that what you're telling me?"

"I really haven't told you anything," Riker said. "But why don't *you* tell me about your work out here. The *Phoenix* isn't even supposed to be in Cardassian space."

"Somebody has to be here," Maxwell said. "The Cardassians are re-arming."

Riker felt his eyes squint involuntarily as he tried to assess his colleague. "*Re*-arming?" Riker asked. "The Cardassians already have a healthy military."

"I mean along their borders with the Federation," Maxwell said. He rose and came partway around the desk, half-sitting on its edge as he brought his face close to Riker's and lowered his voice. "That so-called science station we destroyed was nothing more than a military supply depot—a military depot on the threshold of three Federation sectors."

"If what you say is true, such an act would be a contravention of the treaty."

"Oh, it's true, Captain," Maxwell said. He pushed himself up off the desk and paced over to the narrow window in the corner. Through it, Riker could see the imposing sight of his own ship. "Think about it. Of what possible value could a science station be in the Cuellar system? A main-sequence star, luminosity one, spectral class G, right in the middle of the Hertzsprung-Russell diagram. Seven absolutely ordinary planets in an absolutely ordinary region of space."

"I see your point," Riker said. "Have you got proof?"

Maxwell tapped one knuckle on the window. "The proof was on that science station."

"Which you conveniently destroyed," said Riker, not bothering to mask his suspicion.

"You think *this* is convenient?" Maxwell said. "Being dressed down by a fellow Starfleet captain? A captain with less seniority and a far-less-impressive service record?"

Riker offered a sarcastic smile, undaunted by Maxwell's taunts. "No, I'm sure it's not convenient," Riker agreed. "But without proof of your claims—"

"There's proof all over this sector," Maxwell snapped. "All we need to do is find one of their alleged science transports. Then you can see for yourself."

Riker considered the suggestion. Captain Maxwell did indeed have a long and distinguished service record, lending credence to his assertions. At the same time, his record—and his life—had been marred by tragedy when he'd lost his wife and children in the Setlik III massacre—a massacre conducted by the Cardassians during their war with the Federation. Riker could not even imagine how much such a loss must color Maxwell's worldview.

Riker stood up and addressed Maxwell. "My orders don't include chasing down Cardassian vessels in Cardassian space," he said. "I'm sorry, but they do include removing you from command and bringing you back home."

Maxwell looked down, his shoulders slumping, a defeated man. Riker took no pleasure in the sight. Maxwell trod across the room to the door, but before exiting, he turned back. "You're a fool, Riker," he said quietly.

"Maybe so, Captain," he said. "But I'd rather be the fool who keeps a fragile peace than the one who triggers an unnecessary war."

Something like a laugh escaped Maxwell's lips, hissing his evident disgust. Then he walked onto the *Phoenix* bridge. Riker followed.

As Maxwell headed for the turbolift, Sokar rose from where he sat in the command chair, perched at the front of the raised aft section of the bridge. "Commander," Riker said, "I am confining Captain Maxwell to his quarters. In the interim, you are in command of the *Phoenix*. You are to follow *Enterprise* and vacate

Cardassian space along the shortest possible route, and from there, set course for Starbase Two-Eleven."

"Aye, sir," Sokar said.

Riker crossed the bridge and entered the turbolift behind Captain Maxwell. The two men descended in silence.

"Captain, the *Phoenix* is breaking formation," reported Lieutenant Laresk from the ops station.

Riker jumped up from the command chair at once, and Gul Macet quickly joined him in the center of the *Enterprise* bridge. On the main viewscreen, Riker watched the *Nebula*-class starship peel away to starboard. He could only deduce that Maxwell had retaken command of his vessel. "Pursuit course, Mister Wallace," he told the officer at the conn. "Ensign zh'Kal, hail the *Phoenix*."

"Yes, sir," zh'Kal said, and then, "No response."

"Where is he going?" Macet asked, his voice low and deep.

"That's a good question," Riker said. "Lieutenant, project the course of the *Phoenix*. Where could they be headed?"

Laresk operated her console. "The nearest planetary system to their route is —" she began, but then cut herself short. "Wait. Captain, there's a Cardassian supply ship directly along the path of the *Phoenix*."

"That's where they're headed," Macet said. "They're going to destroy that ship and crew just as they destroyed the science station and the other supply ship."

Though he hated to agree, Riker could think of no other reasonable interpretation of events. "Do you know what this particular supply ship might be?" Riker asked, recalling Captain Maxwell's accusations.

"In this area, I presume it's taking scientific equipment to the research station in the Kelrabi system."

"I see," Riker said, though just as Maxwell had questioned the need for a science station in the Cuellar system, he wondered why one would be needed in the Kelrabi system. Regardless, though, he could not permit more Cardassian lives to be taken by Starfleet personnel. "Mister Wallace, increase speed to overtake."

"Accelerating to warp six," Wallace said.

"Sir, the *Phoenix* has increased velocity to warp nine," Laresk said. "We won't be able to overtake them before they reach the Cardassian ship."

"Match their speed," Riker said. He turned toward the tactical officer. "Ensign zh'Kal, arm phasers and photon torpedoes, then warn the *Phoenix* off. Tell them we will not hesitate to fire on them if they attack that Cardassian vessel."

"Yes, sir," zh'Kal replied, her hands already moving rapidly across her console.

Riker returned to the commander, and Macet seated himself back at his side. Minutes ticked away, the atmosphere as tense as that of the *Phoenix* bridge. Macet leaned in close to him.

"Will you really fire on a Starfleet vessel?" he asked quietly.

"We'll do what we need to do to prevent a war," Riker said. *I've already killed one Starfleet captain,* he thought morosely, *so why not another? And maybe take some of his crew along this time, too.* He did not tell Macet that the very last thing he wanted to do was discharge *Enterprise*'s weapons against Starfleet personnel.

"Captain," Laresk said, "the *Phoenix* has dropped out of warp and has reached the Cardassian vessel."

"Slow to impulse," Worf said. "Prepare to fire on the captain's order." Riker felt the thrum of the warp engines decline as the ship dropped out of warp.

"Sir, the ships are within visual range," said zh'Kal.

"Show them to me," Riker said.

On the main viewscreen, a terrifying tableau appeared. *Phoenix* floated in space behind the smaller Cardassian vessel, as though about to pounce upon it. "Has the *Phoenix* armed its weapons?" Riker asked.

"No, sir," said Laresk.

Of Macet, Riker asked, "What sort of armaments and defenses does the supply ship have?"

"Virtually none," said Macet.

"Lieutenant Laresk, status of the Cardassian shields?" Worf said.

Riker watched as Laresk punched in several commands, then repeated the process. "Sir, I'm unable to read either the defensive or weapons systems aboard the supply ship because they're operating a high-powered subspace field."

"A high-powered subspace field?" Riker echoed, turning to face Gul Macet. "Why would a ship transporting scientific equipment run with such a field?"

"I'm sure I don't know," Macet said smoothly. "After all, I'm not a scientist."

"Captain, we're being hailed by the *Phoenix*," said zh'Kal.

Riker stood and moved to the center of bridge again, looking back over his shoulder and nodding to the tactical officer as he did so. Captain Maxwell appeared on the main viewer. "You said your orders didn't include chasing Cardassian ships, Riker," he said without preamble. "Well, this one you don't have to chase."

"Captain Maxwell, you were removed from command and confined to your quarters," Riker said. "You've violated direct orders."

"If that's what it takes to prevent the Cardassians from ambushing the Federation, so be it," Maxwell said. "Board the ship. You'll find the proof you need."

Riker regarded the renegade officer, then peered over at Macet, who looked on quietly. Admiral Haden's orders had been clear: uphold the treaty between the Federation and the Cardassian Union. *But if the Cardassians have breached the treaty . . .*

He gazed back at the viewscreen. "I'm not going to board the supply ship," he told Maxwell. "I have assurances from Gul Macet that it is not carrying military gear, but rather scientific equipment for their research station in the Kelrabi system." He glanced again at Macet, who remained quiet.

"You're going to take the word of a Cardassian?" Maxwell said. "I don't think so. If you won't board that ship, I'll destroy it."

Riker had expected as much. He rounded on Macet. "We both

know he's not bluffing," he told the gul. "He's already destroyed one supply ship, *and* a space station."

As though in support of Riker, Laresk said, "The *Phoenix* just raised their shields and they're arming their phaser banks."

Macet leaped to his feet. "You can't allow him to do this."

"And just how can I stop him?" Riker asked. "I can fire on the *Phoenix,* but it'll be too late to save your supply ship." He paused, giving Macet a moment to process the information. Then he said, "So before I arrest Captain Maxwell and bring him back to the Federation in irons, why don't you order that ship to deactivate its subspace field? That way we can put the lie to Captain Maxwell's accusations."

Macet appeared to seethe, an unseen rage percolating just beneath his outward quietude. "That would be an infringement of Cardassian sovereignty."

"Or might it reveal an infringement of our treaty?" Riker asked. He turned partially back toward the main viewer so that he could address both Maxwell and Macet. "I don't know the answer to that question." And he didn't. What the *Phoenix* captain counted as suspicious behavior by the Cardassians might easily be the result of what Maxwell had suffered at their hands, and an attempt—conscious or not—to reap vengeance for the deaths of his wife and children. Or the Cardassians might actually be preparing to launch a new, surprise offensive against the Federation.

"Ensign zh'Kal, target the supply ship's power systems," Riker said. "I want the minimum phaser spread required to bring down their grid. I want the ship and crew left otherwise intact."

"I protest this action," Macet said.

"As you should," Riker replied. "If I'm wrong, if Captain Maxwell is wrong, I'll place the two of us in your custody to take back to Central Command."

"Captain," Macet said imploringly, "you are jeopardizing the peace."

"Maybe," Riker allowed. "Let's find out." He looked over at zh'Kal. "Fire."

"Firing at seventy percent," zh'Kal said. "A volley of four."

The bridge fell silent, but for the small sounds that signaled the unleashing of *Enterprise*'s main phasers. On the viewscreen, Maxwell looked off to one side. Riker studied Macet, but the gul had grown stone-faced.

"Direct hit," said Lieutenant Laresk. "And another. I'm reading fluctuations in the subspace field." She examined her readouts. "Two more hits. The supply ship's power systems have failed, its subspace field is down."

"Ensign zh'Kal?" Riker said.

"Scanning," she said. "I'm reading four cargo holds, two larger, two smaller. Sensors show . . . spiral-wave emitters, plasma cannons, photon torpedoes, shield generators . . . the ship is packed with military equipment."

Riker looked at Macet, who could only stare back at him. Turning to the main viewer, he said, "Captain Maxwell, I need you to transfer command to your first officer, and to transport yourself over to the *Enterprise,* where you'll be confined to quarters until we reach Starbase Two-Eleven."

"You're not going to let them go," Maxwell said, incredulous.

"No," Riker said. "Mister Worf, I want you to oversee the transport of the supply-ship crew onto the *Enterprise.*"

"You're going to destroy the ship?" Macet asked.

"I'm sure you'd like me to do that," Riker said. "Destroy the ship and all the evidence with it. No. We'll be towing it back to the Federation." He tapped his combadge. "Security team to the bridge." When Macet gave him a questioning look, Riker said, "You'll be joining your two aides and the crew of the supply ship in the brig."

"You're abducting us," Macet said defiantly.

"Not at all," Riker said. "Consider yourselves prisoners of war."

6

Data walked across the *Cour du Mai,* approaching the wide, stone stairs that led up to the entrance of the *Palais de Justice.* His boot heels clocked along the three-sided courtyard, the ground dusted with the season's first snow. The overcast morning sky lent the day a gray countenance, promising no reprieve from the winter chill that had overcome Paris in the past few weeks. Though he could readily control his body temperature in such conditions, Data had taken to wearing a long wool coat because he simply liked the feel of it, the weight of it, in the cold conditions.

As he started up the stairs, he gazed upward at the four Doric columns that formed the colonnade framing the building's main entryways. Atop the pediment stood four statues, one above each column, symbolizing Justice, Fortitude, Plenty, and Prudence. Data knew that the regal edifice had endured for centuries as a center for the administration of the law, and that the site on *Île de la Cité* had served as a location for government going back millennia.

Data climbed the steps and entered the venerable structure. In one hand, he carried a single padd, on which he had stored his notes for the coming trial. He did this not for his own perusal, since he had also recorded all of the information in his internal memory systems, but for the purpose of communicating any of that information quickly and efficiently to his attorney, though he doubted that would become necessary. Over the past nine months, Data had watched Desjardins at work, had listened as he'd explained legal principles and practices, had observed as he'd combined facts and precedents to formulate a strategy for their case.

After consulting a diagram of the building's interior, Data made his way to the proper courtroom. It did not surprise him to find his counsel already there, though their action would not begin for another hour. Data advanced past the empty gallery to the table at which he would sit with his attorney. Once there, he saw Desjardins consulting a built-in interface, checking off an automated list of the items they required for their case, all of which had been securely transported to the court the day before.

"Good morning, Mister Data," Desjardins greeted him, a slight lilt audible in his voice, a remnant of his upbringing in the Alpha Centauri system.

Data removed his overcoat, revealing the dark suit he had worn for the proceedings. "Good morning, Mister Desjardins." Though the two had common goals—in the general, affirming equal rights for sentient artificial life-forms, and in the specific, gaining Lal's freedom—their relationship had remained both professional and formal. For his part, Data appreciated that reserve; he did not want a friend, he wanted an advocate.

"I trust you feel prepared and confident," said Desjardins.

"I do," Data said. "I am in fact anxious for the proceedings to begin." It had been half a year since Desjardins had secured time on the court's docket, three-quarters of a year since Data had departed *Enterprise* and begun this journey. In that span, he had established no contact at all with Lal, other than the numerous messages he had sent to her; he had received not a single word from her. Only Starfleet's responses to court-ordered requests for information had even confirmed his daughter's continued existence.

"We've got a strong case, Mister Data," Desjardins told him. "An important case, a quest for real justice."

"I believe that is true," Data said. "I am—" He stopped talking as two uniformed Starfleet officers entered the courtroom. Each wore the maroon of command and the rank insignia of a captain. The pair—a Bolian man and a Denobulan woman—made their way to their table. As the woman activated the interface there, the man walked over to Data and Desjardins.

"Allow me to introduce myself," he said. "I am Captain Nekar Rovilg, assistant counsel representing Starfleet in this matter."

"Gregory Desjardins, representing Mister Data." He spoke without inflection, neither welcoming nor cold. He did not offer his hand for a handshake, nor did he present an opening for any other ritual salutation. Data found his behavior practiced and reassuring.

"I wonder if I might speak with Mister Data," Rovilg said.

Desjardins looked at the captain and seemed to assess him for a moment. "There is a small conference room just across the corridor," he said. "We can meet with you there."

"Yes," Rovilg said, "except that I was hoping that I could speak with Mister Data privately." Data noted that Rovilg had followed Desjardins's lead, employing a formal term of address when referring to Data.

"Under the circumstances, that would be highly inappropriate," Desjardins said without hesitation.

"Of course," Rovilg said. "Starfleet has a proposal, and I simply wished to present it without interruption."

"I represent Mister Data's legal interests," Desjardins said. "Whatever your proposal to him, it should be made in the presence of that representation."

Rovilg appeared to consider this, then relented. "Very well," he said. "May I speak with the two of you, then?"

Desjardins looked to Data, who nodded his assent. The two men followed Captain Rovilg from the courtroom to a much smaller space set aside for confidential meetings. The room held a rectangular conference table that seated eight. Data and

Desjardins sat down at one long side of the table, while Rovilg remained standing across from them.

"Simply put, Mister Data," Rovilg began, "Starfleet's proposal is to provide you with what you most want: to be reunited with Lal."

"I would be in favor of that," Data said. He felt a flicker of excitement, though he did not imagine, after months of preparation for the impending trial, that Starfleet would suddenly accede to his requests.

"Is Starfleet then prepared to release Ms. Lal to Mister Data?" Desjardins asked. "Is Starfleet willing to forswear any claims of property ownership in Ms. Lal? Is Starfleet willing to recognize the reality of her existence as a sentient being, replete with the rights afforded all citizens of the Federation?"

Captain Rovilg hesitated, clearly displeased with Desjardins's questions, doubtless the sort of interruptions he had hoped to avoid. "There are matters of Federation security at issue," he said, "and so Starfleet's proposal would necessarily be unable to meet all of those conditions."

Desjardins glanced over at Data before replying. "We have seen reference made to 'Federation security' time and again in Starfleet's filings with this court," he told Rovilg. "We have asked for more detail—or *any* detail—about it on numerous occasions, but it's connection with Ms. Lal has yet to be adequately explained."

"Nor am I at liberty to do so now," Rovilg said.

"Forgive me, Captain Rovilg," Desjardins said, "but it strikes me that Starfleet is unwilling to discuss 'Federation security' with respect to this case because it is *unable* to do so. The contention that Ms. Lal should be taken from her father and held as property as a matter of Federation security fails on the face of it. Mister Data and Ms. Lal are two of a kind, and the lack of security issues with respect to his freedom and to his divorcement from Starfleet demonstrate that such would be the case with his daughter."

"As I said, I am not at liberty to discuss matters of Federation security," Rovilg told them.

"Then it seems we have nothing more to discuss," Desjardins said. He pushed back from the table and stood up.

Rovilg held up the flat of his hand. "Please wait," he said. "I would like Mister Data to at least hear the details of Starfleet's proposal."

Data peered up at Desjardins. "I would like to hear what Captain Rovilg has to say."

"Of course," Desjardins said, and he sat back down beside Data.

"Thank you," Rovilg said. "Starfleet is willing to bring Mister Data to Ms. Lal."

"So that Mister Data can be detained with Ms. Lal?" Desjardins asked.

"As you know, the office of Starfleet's judge advocate general ruled several years ago on Mister Data's status," Rovilg said. "And as you already pointed out, Mister Data has parted from Starfleet, and since no one in Starfleet created him, it leaves the organization with no claim on him whatsoever."

"Until somebody cites Federation security," Desjardins said. "And then Mister Data finds himself as much a prisoner of Starfleet as his daughter."

"That is not what Starfleet intends," Rovilg said.

"What precisely does Starfleet intend?" Data wanted to know.

Rovilg peered at Data and seemed happy to address him directly. "Starfleet Research genuinely believed that separating Mister Data and Ms. Lal would provide a better opportunity for her development. Her time on Galor Four has borne this out. But Starfleet Research—perhaps too late—does recognize the moral implications of that forced separation, and it now wishes to reverse this injustice."

"I get nervous when Starfleet starts talking about morality," Desjardins said. "This is the organization whose members have consistently violated its own Prime Directive, who annihilated a colony of innocent civilians on Renevant Six, who prolonged the bloody civil war on Neural, who—"

"Please, Mister Desjardins," Rovilg said. "No group of people is perfect, and every group is only as strong as its weakest members. I'm sure that neither you nor I would appreciate being branded individually by the actions of the worst of those in our own legal community. Now, if I may continue?" When Desjardins said nothing, Rovilg went on. "Starfleet will provide transportation to Mister Data so that he can join his daughter. Accommodations will be provided, and he is free to remain with her for as long as he chooses."

"That's it?" Desjardins said. "Not even a timetable for Ms. Lal's release from captivity."

"I am informed that Starfleet Research does foresee such a time in Ms. Lal's development," Rovilg offered vaguely, "but I have no more information than that."

"Is there anything more?" Desjardins asked.

"No," Rovilg said.

"Then I would ask for time to confer with my client," Desjardins said. Rovilg bowed his head in acknowledgment, then exited the conference room. Once he had left, Desjardins turned to Data. "What do you think, Mister Data?"

"I am inclined to accept Starfleet's offer," he said.

"Starfleet's proposal offers far less than we are seeking in our legal case," Desjardins observed. "It fails to address equal rights for sentient artificial life-forms."

"While this is true," Data said, "the proposal effectively meets the conditions I would have accepted while serving in Starfleet. Had I been permitted to transfer from the *Enterprise* to the Daystrom annex on Galor Four in order to accompany Lal to Starfleet Research, I would have done so."

Desjardins looked away, evidently in thought. When he turned back to Data, he said, "I will be disappointed not to bring this case.

I believe it speaks to important issues, not only for you and Ms. Lal, but for all of Federation society. No civilization can rise to its heights as long as there are those within it who are subjugated in some way, who are not treated as equals. But I also know that these proceedings will consume weeks, perhaps even months, of your life, and that a final determination will be unlikely for years, pending appeals. If you accept Starfleet's proposal, that is time that you would be spending with your daughter."

"Those are my thoughts as well," Data said, anticipation suddenly blossoming within him.

Desjardins rose, and Data followed suit. The attorney offered his hand, and Data took it. "If you ever wish to pursue this matter, I will be here," Desjardins said. "Regardless, it has been an honor standing by your side."

Data thanked his attorney, then left to find Captain Rovilg.

Riker sat at the desk in his ready room and combed through the reports of Cardassian activity along the nearby border. He made some notes on a padd as he attempted to estimate their troop and ship strength. He also searched for tactical patterns, striving for any possible advantage should the current tensions erupt into a shooting war.

Six months had passed since Captain Maxwell's actions had led to the unmasking of Cardassian treachery. In constructing a number of military bases along their borders with the Federation, they had violated the standing peace treaty between the two powers. Exacerbating their offenses, they had concealed their misdeeds, lying about the nature of the bases. The capture of the military supply vessel by *Enterprise*'s crew had led to a standoff in the Kelrabi system. Central Command's new base there remained incomplete and uncrewed, but the Cardassians had moved a large number of ships into that sector, right on the edge of Federation space.

It's only a matter of time, Riker thought darkly. Although he had continued for the last year to meet regularly with Assistant Counselor Lueke, the captain's outlook seemed to have grown more pessimistic. He couldn't blame the young counselor for that, since at some point, Riker had stopped being honest during their sessions. It had simply become too difficult, too altogether wearying, to continue to revisit the events surrounding the death of Captain Picard. Whatever it had cost Riker then, and whatever it still cost him, he kept it to himself.

I keep everything to myself, he thought. In the last year, and particularly in the last six months, he and Deanna had drifted away from each other. At least in part, his reticence had taken its toll, despite—or perhaps because of—her empathic abilities. She still sensed that things troubled him, but their personal distance had allowed him to discover how to veil the specifics of that trouble. As long as Riker continued to see Lueke, Troi could require no more of him in her role as ship's counselor.

Riker realized that his attention had roamed from the task at hand, and he focused again on the Cardassian activity reports. As he did, Worf's voice reached him.

"Bridge to Captain Riker."

Riker tapped his combadge. "Riker here. Go ahead, Number One."

"Captain, we're receiving a distress call from Dre Mirale," Worf said. *"The colony reports that it has detected unauthorized activity in their system, and they fear an attack."*

"I'm on my way," Riker said. He keyed off his interface and padd, then headed for the bridge. There, Worf relinquished the command chair, settling himself into his regular position to the captain's right. Counselor Troi sat on Riker's other side. "What have we got?" the captain asked.

"Dre Mirale is a Federation colony at the very edge of our patrol zone," Worf said. "It has a population of two million, with only limited defenses. The head of their security forces reports reading at least three and perhaps as many as five ships within their system in the last two days. The readings are sporadic and not completely clear, as though intentionally jammed."

"What is the colony's proximity to Cardassian space?" Riker asked.

"Half a light-year," Worf said.

"Too close," Riker said.

"Yes, sir," Worf agreed.

"What about Starbase Two-Eleven and the Kalorna system?" Riker said, inquiring about two of the major settlements within the region of space *Enterprise* had been assigned to protect, the two closest to the Cardassian border.

"They report only normal activity," Worf said. "Some movement outside Federation space, but otherwise no encroachments."

"Very well," Riker said. "Ensign Wallace, set course for Dre Mirale, warp nine."

"Aye, sir," answered the conn officer.

The captain watched Wallace work his console. In response, Riker felt *Enterprise* spring to life beneath him, the pulse of the warp drive translating rhythmically through the deck. As he had numerous times before, he wondered if this would mark the beginning of renewed hostilities with the Cardassian Union. Though rumors of high-level talks between the two governments persisted, the buildup of ships on both sides of the border made for a political environment of uncertain stability.

"What's your assessment, Worf?" he said.

Worf shook his head slowly. "I do not trust the Cardassians."

Riker laughed, though Worf's manner seemed decidedly serious. "You have a talent for understatement," he said. "I don't know if anybody in the entire Federation trusts them."

"Indeed," Worf said. He pointed to the interface beside his chair. "Dre Mirale is a small colony in a planetary system with only one significant resource."

"Its location," Riker surmised.

"Exactly," Worf confirmed.

"So you think the Cardassians are scouting the system?" Riker asked. "Perhaps in preparation for seizing it?"

"It's quite possible."

"Let's hope not," the captain said. "The last thing the Federation needs is another war with the Cardassians." Riker believed what he said, but as the words left his mouth, another feeling rose within him, surprising him not only in its content, but in its intensity: he was eager for a fight.

As the shuttle descended toward a large, circular landing pad, Data peered through the forward ports from his position at the rear of the main cabin. When he had last visited Galor IV, the pad had not existed. In the distance, he saw the buildings of the Daystrom Institute annex, past a range of low mountains.

The shuttle set down heavily on the pad, the dome that covered the landing area already rotating back into its closed position. Data stood up, preparing to disembark. Other than the dome swiveling back into place, he saw no movement outside the forward ports.

The Starfleet officer who had piloted the shuttle, Ensign Gee/13/Blue, sat at the forward console, in a chair clearly modified to fit his segmented, insectile body. Beside him, Lieutenant Trask, a security officer, turned toward Data. "You'll need to wait for your escort before you can exit the shuttle."

"I understand," Data said, though the amount and rigor of the security procedures at Galor IV surprised him. He had also encountered heightened measures during the past two weeks of his journey from Earth. He had come to realize that the increased friction with the Cardassian Union and the resultant fears of a looming war had contributed to the tightening of security throughout the Federation. As best he could tell, many more Starfleet vessels had been assigned sentinel duties, with their crews more strictly controlling the movement of people and ships within the UFP. Data and his belongings—a small carryall and a larger trunk—had been scrutinized numerous times during his trip from Earth to Galor IV. The journey had taken longer than he had expected, requiring him to travel on four different shuttles and two different starships.

Five shuttles, he amended, since he had not been permitted to transport to the Daystrom Institute annex from *U.S.S. New York.* Data had not known why at first, but during the trip from the ship down to the planet surface, the annex's shuttle had passed through defensive shields, a measure that had not been in place when last he had visited the facility. Also, up in orbit, Data thought that he might have spied an automated weapons platform, which would mark another new feature of the complex. He could only conclude that the ongoing Borg threat, coupled with the possibility of the resumption of war with the Cardassian Union, had induced the decision for such defenses.

Motion beyond the ports of the shuttle drew Data's attention. He looked out to see a lift rise up in one corner of the landing pad. Within stood a man and a woman, one of whom Data recognized: Admiral Haftel.

The woman waved toward the shuttle, and Lieutenant Trask said, "They're ready for you now." She touched a control, and the rear hatch folded downward with a hum. "Your trunk will be handled by the facility's internal transporters."

"Thank you," Data said. An amalgam of exhilaration and nervous anxiety churned within him. He gathered up his carryall and headed aft.

Outside the shuttle, he saw lining the perimeter of the landing pad a row of five more shuttles, their assignment to the annex, as with the shuttle Data had taken, spelled out across their hulls. He rounded the craft and walked across the pad to the lift. His footsteps echoed loudly within the dome—yet another apparent security system that hadn't existed on his prior trip to Galor IV. As he neared the lift, Admiral Haftel stepped forward and reached out his hand. Data had not expected the social gesture, but he interpreted it as a good sign. He shook the admiral's hand.

"Commander Data," he said. "Welcome to the Galor Four annex of the Daystrom Institute."

"Thank you, Admiral," Data said. He thought to remind Haftel that he had left Starfleet almost ten months ago and should therefore no longer be addressed as *commander,* but as a matter of courtesy, he chose not to correct his host.

"This is our chief of security, Commander T'Kren," he said, indicating the tall Vulcan woman by his side. She bowed her head in greeting, her bearing formal and unemotional. "Right this way," Haftel said, standing aside so that Data could enter the lift.

As they descended, apparently to an underground portion of the facility, the admiral said, "I imagine you must be anxious to see Lal."

"I am," Data said. He wanted to ask if his daughter had received any of the messages he had sent, but if she had not, and if the admiral had kept those messages from her, then such a question might discomfit Haftel. Data did not wish to have an adversarial relationship with the admiral, or with any of the personnel on Galor IV. He wanted only to see Lal. "Is she well?"

"She is," Haftel told him. "All of her systems are working perfectly, including her emotions."

"I am very glad to hear that," Data said, and until that moment, he had not realized the extent of the fear he had carried around with him for so long. He had missed Lal, to be sure, but having not heard from her, or really even *of* her, since she had been taken from *Enterprise,* he had also worried constantly about her well-being.

The lift eased to a stop, and Haftel led Data out into a security area, with T'Kren following behind them. A pair of guards processed the trio, sending them into a second turbolift. "For security purposes, the lift from the landing pad doesn't connect directly to the complex's internal lifts," the admiral explained.

They descended again, until exiting into a long, bare corridor, with doors lining either side. "This is one of two residential levels in this part of the facility," the admiral said. "It may not look like much, but we've got a mess hall down here, a gymnasium, a natatorium, an arboretum, one large and two small holosuites . . . our people have plenty to keep them occupied when they're not working."

Many questions occurred to Data, as the nature of the complex seemed to have changed dramatically. The first impressions he drew from the emphasis on security and the obvious physical changes to the facility were of a pervasive bunker mentality. That did not match up with the open, academically oriented atmosphere normally associated with the Daystrom Institute, or with what Data recalled from the time he had spent there previously. Again, though, he opted to hold his curiosity in abeyance.

They had walked almost to the end of the corridor when Haftel turned into a short side hall. Data immediately noticed when he passed a pair of control panels side by side on the wall, with a column of forcefield emitters between them. Though it appeared suspicious, he still said nothing. Instead, the admiral stopped him and pointed everything out to him.

"We have additional security in place especially for Lal," he said. "And now for you." He placed his hand on the panel closer to the long corridor, and a forcefield hummed into operation, separating Data from Haftel and T'Kren.

Alarm gripped Data at once. In an instant, he realized that he had been lied to, that he had not been invited to reunite with his daughter, that Starfleet had maneuvered him to Galor IV in order to quash his legal action and prevent him from ever reviving it. It seemed Machiavellian and convoluted, extreme, even nonsensical, not to mention antithetical to what he knew of Starfleet. Why would—

Haftel touched his hand to the panel again, and the forcefield dropped. "We put this in place in the unlikely event that somebody broke in to the complex with the goal of abducting Lal," the admiral explained. "It can be activated and deactivated from outside—" He tapped the panel closest to him. "—and inside." He tapped the other panel. "I am authorized to use it, as are T'Kren, several other security personnel, a number of cyberneticists working with Lal, and Lal herself." He tapped a control at the bottom of the panel, then said, "Computer, recognize Haftel, Anthony, alpha two clearance." To Data, he said, "And if you'll place your hand here, I can grant you authorization as well."

Data reached up and flattened his left hand against the glossy black surface of the panel. "Recognize Data, former Starfleet, serial number—?" He looked at Data.

"Ess cee one zero one dash five one seven."

"Authorize full privileges for this forcefield," Haftel finished. A brief tonal sequence signaled success. "Give it a try."

Data stepped back and touched his hand to the inner panel. The forcefield jumped back to life. He touched the panel a second time and it disengaged. "Thank you, Admiral," he said.

Haftel peered over at T'Kren and said, "You can return to your other duties." Then, to Data, he said, "Shall we?"

Only two doors lined each wall, and they made their way to the first one on the right. Haftel stepped up to the door, causing it to open before him. "These will be your quarters during your stay," he said. "Perhaps you'd like to leave your belongings here."

"Thank you," Data said as he stepped past the admiral. He unslung his duffel from his shoulder and set it down inside the door. He glanced around only perfunctorily—he saw a small, standard living area, with an open doorway beyond that doubtless led to a bedroom—before moving back out into the hall.

Haftel then led Data to the last door on the right. The admiral reached for the door chime, but then dropped his hand back to his side. "Mister Data," he said, "I know that you consider Lal your child, and that having her taken from you must have been exceedingly difficult. I want you to know that I truly believe the greater good was served by bringing her here alone. I hope one day, you'll see that, too."

Data did not know what to say, though he did notice that Haftel's reason for relocating Lal to Galor IV by herself had evidently changed, from being for the good of her development to being for the greater good. Before Data could determine how best to respond, the admiral tapped the door chime. A moment later, the single-paneled door glided open.

Inside, across the room, stood Lal.

She wore a lavender vest and matching ankle-length skirt, over a long-sleeved purple blouse—the first outfit he had ever replicated for her. She looked exactly as he remembered her. She looked beautiful.

"Lal," Data said softly, as though speaking too loudly might cause her to vanish.

"Father," she said, her eyes filling with the ocular lubricants that her emotions transformed into tears. "You let them take me," she said, her voice full of anger and accusation. "How could you let them take me from you?"

Data felt as though he had been stabbed—as though he had stabbed himself, as though he had taken a knife and begun slicing out portions of his neural net. He had waited so long to see Lal again, he had worked so hard to earn her freedom and bring her back, and none if it mattered. She hated him.

But then she hurried across the room and through the doorway, her arms encircling his back. She hugged him tightly to her, and he wrapped his arms around her. His own tears slid down his face and dropped with a whisper into her hair.

They stood that way for a long time, holding each other tightly, father and daughter, loving each other as they never had before.

"Captain, we are approaching the Dre Mirale system," declared Lieutenant Laresk from the ops station.

It had been more than a day since *Enterprise* had received the distress call, but it seemed as though it had been even longer. The hours had dragged since they'd begun their journey, and Captain Riker had not slept well in the interim—*When do I these days?* he asked himself. He felt angry and tense, and he had to force himself not to grip the armrest of his command chair too tightly. He knew that Deanna must have read his agitation. The captain assumed that, because she hadn't spoken to him about it, she likely believed the possibility of a Cardassian incursion wholly responsible for his stressed emotional state.

"Let's stay on our toes," Riker said. "Go to yellow alert."

"Ordering yellow alert," Worf replied, operating the console beside his chair to make it happen.

"Slow to impulse." As Ensign Wallace complied at the conn, Riker could hear and feel *Enterprise*'s warp engines shift to a non-operational state, dropping the ship back into normal space-time. On the main viewscreen, the blur of light halted, the stars becoming visible as fixed points once more. "Readings, Ensign zh'Kal."

"Scanning," confirmed zh'Kal as the tactical station chirped beneath her practiced touch.

Riker waited, and he knew that the rest of the bridge crew did too. What they found in the Dre Mirale system could define all their lives for months or even years to come. It could mean more than that, more even than the safety of the two million inhabitants of the colony. The *Enterprise* crew needed to confirm the presence or absence of Cardassian vessels within the system, and if absent, then whether or not they had scouted the region. If the Cardassians intended Dre Mirale to be where they established a foothold in Federation territory, they had to be stopped before that could happen.

"Captain, I'm not reading any Cardassian ships in the vicinity," zh'Kal said. "But I am picking up some indications of starship traffic in the area."

"Can you isolate it?" Worf asked. "Identify it?"

"Possibly, but sensors are picking up only scant traces of possible starship activity," zh'Kal said. "Those traces may be naturally occurring, perhaps caused by the detritus of a comet."

"Naturally occurring?" Riker asked doubtfully.

"If there are such traces in the system *not* caused by starships," Worf said, "then wouldn't the colonists have detected them before now?"

"Indeterminate," zh'Kal said. "If it was a comet with an unusual core, the traces might not have occurred until now."

"What do you recommend, Ensign?" Riker asked.

"A detailed scan of the system," zh'Kal said. "If we look closely enough, we should be able to make a precise determination whether or not the Cardassians have been here."

"How long would that take?" Riker asked.

"That depends on what we find, sir," zh'Kal said. "If we find nothing and we have to scan the entire system, it could take six to seven days."

The captain looked to his first officer for his opinion, and Worf nodded once. "Do it," Riker told zh'Kal. But in his mind, he thought, *Make it so.*

He tried not to bolt to his feet as he rose from the command chair. "I'll be in my ready room," he said as evenly as he could. "Mister Worf, you're in command."

Riker couldn't leave the bridge quickly enough.

Data sat in the mess hall across from his daughter, a plate of raw vegetables before him, and a plate of spaghetti before Lal. Around them, most of the two dozen or so tables stood empty, though a handful of people had come by for a late lunch. For the most part, though, the half-dozen replicators that served the facility remained idle.

When Lal had suggested to Data that they share a meal in the mess hall, he had immediately agreed, although he had also been puzzled. Lal explained that, while she obviously did not require nourishment, she wished to demonstrate for Data the improvement of her social skills. It delighted him not only that he would see that aspect of her development, but also that she *wanted* him to see.

Four days has passed since the *New York* had delivered Data to the Daystrom annex, and he had never been happier. The time he had spent missing Lal and working toward their eventual reunion seemed more like a dream than a recollection of reality. The two of them had spoken for many hours since his arrival, with each of them asking many questions about each other. She had never received his messages, for which Admiral Haftel had offered an apology, though he maintained his belief that initially removing Lal from Data's influence had been the wisest course.

"Do you often visit the mess hall?" Data asked. He speared a piece of cauliflower and ate it.

"Not very often," Lal said. "For the first few weeks after I was brought here, the cyberneticists accompanied me to the mess hall every day. They wanted to use the experience of dining as a means of improving my capacity to simulate human responses."

"At that, you are doing quite well," Data told her. "In many ways, you seem quite human." He had noticed, among other things, that Lal had gained a facility for spoken communication. Where before she had often struggled to articulate her thoughts, she now spoke with easy confidence. Also, with her ability to feel emotions, she no longer needed to *simulate* certain human responses.

"Thank you, Father."

As Data ate a broccoli floret, he watched Lal deftly spin a fork through her spaghetti. When she had finished, she lifted the tightly wound pasta to her mouth, a feat that impressed him. He had seen people eat spaghetti many times through the years, and rarely had he witnessed any of them lifting a forkful of their meal that did not have at least a few strands of pasta hanging from it.

"Have you kept up with your singing?" he asked. He knew that Lal had continued to paint because of the canvases she had shown him in her quarters, but he wondered if she had found any other creative outlets.

"No, I haven't," Lal told him, her use of a contraction still a marvel to Data. "But the cyberneticists have encouraged me to engage in creative activities, and that's something I felt the need to do myself. In addition to my painting, I recently began to write and record music."

"That is wonderful," Data said. "What types of music do you write?"

After another mouthful of spaghetti, Lal said, "Electronic music."

"I see," Data said. "Although I know a great deal about the genre, I have experienced virtually none of it."

"I would enjoy playing some of my work for you," Lal said, a shy smile blooming on her face.

"I would like that very much," Data said, returning her smile. "Do you practice any other forms of art? Writing? Dancing?"

"No," Lal said. "I do write, but not creatively. I've been keeping a journal of my life on Galor Four. You may read it, if you like."

"Perhaps," Data said noncommittally. "I would not want to intrude on your privacy." While he might be interested to learn his daughter's thoughts and feelings about her time away from him, he also thought that it might sadden him to do so.

"Since I have invited you to read it," Lal said, "it would not be an intrusion."

"No, I suppose not," Data said. "Do you think—" He stopped as he saw a woman in a red Starfleet uniform enter the mess hall. He watched her as she walked to the string of replicators.

"Father?" Lal asked, following his gaze. "Is everything all right?"

"That is Commander Shelby," he said.

"Commander Shelby?" Lal asked. She looked away for a

moment, as though considering the name. "Yes," she finally said. "She was aboard the *Enterprise* for a short time while I was there."

"Yes," Data said. "But I am curious why she is here."

"I do not know."

"Have you seen her at the annex before?" Data asked.

"Yes," Lal said. "I believe she has been here for many months, but I have never spoken with her."

"I see." Data did not understand why, but something about the commander's presence at the annex troubled him. "Lal, would you excuse me for one moment?"

"Yes, Father."

Data rose and strode over to the replicator bank. He arrived there just as Shelby lifted several dishes of food onto a tray. "Commander," he said.

Shelby turned and recognized him at once. "Commander Data," she said, then regarded his civilian clothing. "Or is it *Mister* Data?"

"I resigned my commission nearly a year ago," he said.

"Are you here at Galor Four now?"

"Yes, I am," he said. "I have come to be with Lal."

Shelby nodded, then offered an awkward smile. "That's wonderful." Looking down at the meal on the tray she carried, she said, "Well, this is hot, so . . ." She smiled again, then went around him toward a table.

"Commander," Data said, and she stopped and peered back at him.

"Yes?"

"Why are you here?" Data asked.

Shelby shrugged. "Just some research," she said.

"Are you still with Borg tactical analysis?"

Again, Shelby shrugged. "I'm afraid that's classified information, Mister Data," she said. "And since you're no longer a member of Starfleet . . ." She let her voice trail into silence.

"I understand," Data said. "It is nice to see you."

"And you," Shelby said, then continued on her way. Data watched her pace to the far side of the mess hall. She sat at a table by herself, keeping her back to Data.

"Is something wrong, Father?" Lal asked, walking up beside him.

"No," Data said. "I was just saying hello to Commander Shelby. Let us return to our lunch." He and Lal went back to their table, where they resumed their meal and their conversation. When finally they finished and started back to their quarters, Data glanced back across the mess hall. To his surprise, Commander Shelby had gone, though he had not seen her leave.

On the fifth day of their scans, the *Enterprise* crew found the evidence they sought.

Riker listened as Worf and zh'Kal stood in front of the desk in his ready room, delivering their report. "The ionization trail indicates the possibility of a starship," zh'Kal said, pointing to a padd she held, "but the faint traces of a warp field in a cloud of micrometeorites remove all doubt."

"We have contacted the Dre Mirale colony and confirmed that none of their vessels traveled through the area in question within the last month," Worf added.

"It wouldn't have mattered if they had," zh'Kal said. "None of their vessels produce warp fields sizable enough to cause traces to remain in matter this size. And the ionization trail left a signature."

"A signature?" Riker asked. "Something definitive?"

"Yes, sir," zh'Kal said. She raised her padd so that she could see its display, and she read a list of three elements and the manner in which they had become charged, one negatively, two positively. "Federation starships don't leave an ionization trail like that."

"And neither do those of the Romulans, the Gorn, or the Klingon Empire," Worf added.

"In fact, only one type of starship leaves this kind of an ionization trail," zh'Kal said.

"You're sure about this, Veridantha?" Riker asked.

"I am, sir," said zh'Kal.

"Worf?"

"Affirmative," said the first officer. "There is no doubt: the Cardassians have been here recently."

Riker stood up and came around his desk. "Good work, zh'Kal," he said directly to the alpha-shift tactical officer. "Dismissed."

"Thank you, sir," zh'Kal said before returning to the bridge.

After she had gone, the captain turned to Worf. "So they've been here," Riker said. "The question is: are they coming back? Is this where they intend to break through?"

"Yes," Worf said. "It required five days of concentrated effort to find what we did. In another day, there won't be any traces left at all."

"It could be a clever ruse," Riker said.

Worf nodded, though not in a way that suggested he agreed. "It *could* be," he said. "But I don't think so."

"I don't think so either," Riker said. "Get me Starfleet Command, priority channel, scrambled." He paused, then added, "Code factor one."

"Invasion status," Worf said.

"Yes."

"Aye, Captain," Worf said, then he too turned and exited to the bridge.

Left alone in his ready room, Riker waited for the signal to be put through to Starfleet. While he did, the captain paced over to the window and peered out at the depths of empty space surrounding *Enterprise*. In just a matter of days or weeks, he knew, half of Starfleet would fill those skies with phaser fire and photon torpedoes, defending everything they held dear.

★ ★ ★

Data waited for Lal in the living area of her quarters. Although Admiral Haftel had assigned him those next door, when not with Lal, Data preferred to spend as much time as he could around the artifacts of the existence she had led for nearly the past year. It pleased him that she had continued her painting, of which many examples hung on her walls. As he sat on the sofa, he gazed admiringly at an impressionist landscape that she said she'd recently completed. He reveled in studying the different styles in which she had engaged, particularly with respect to those pieces that evoked the most emotion in him.

Data got up from the sofa and walked over to Lal's bedroom. Inside, he looked at the two paintings he most valued. One of the photorealistic portraits, painstakingly achieved, depicted Dr. Soong; the other, Data. It had saddened Data to learn that his creator had died from his illness within weeks of coming to Galor IV with Lal. As Data had surmised, Starfleet had seen to the dismissal of the kidnapping and hijacking charges the doctor had faced, in return for his cooperation in aiding Starfleet Research with Lal's development. Lal referred to him as her grandfather, and she said that he had been very kind to her.

Lal's schedule at the Daystrom annex left her a great deal of free time. Admiral Haftel and his staff required four to six hours of her time daily, most of which she spent in various laboratories around the facility. According to Lal, they had geared a lot of their efforts toward developing her human abilities, from basic behavior to coping with and understanding her own emotions. The scientists also ran copious numbers of tests, analyzing every aspect of her android mind and body.

During Lal's time away from her quarters over the past days, Data had taken the opportunity to tour the Galor IV complex. He had not seen Commander Shelby again, but as he had noted when he had first arrived, the annex had greatly expanded since his last visit. Although the scientists still utilized the structures on the surface of the planet, all of the newer laboratories and support facilities had been built underground. Data had been able to determine no reason for the subterranean construction other than a desire for increased security.

Data returned to Lal's living area and sat back down on the sofa. Something troubled him, though he could not explain just what. Data had yet to master many aspects of his emotional life, but he had at least come to a fundamental understanding of how to deal with most of what he felt. That did not include intuition. Since the installation of his emotion chip, Data had on several occasions felt something that he could not define, much less cultivate. He had that sense now, about both Commander Shelby and the massive security measures in place on Galor IV.

But why? he asked himself. Not why had Starfleet sent Commander Shelby to Galor IV, not why had they enacted such major defenses for a cybernetics lab, but why did it trouble Data? What else did he know or feel that made the idea of increased security at the Daystrom annex unsettle him? He did not know.

As he pondered this, the door to the corridor slid open and Lal entered. "Hello, Father," she said.

"Good afternoon, Lal," Data replied. He walked over to her from the sofa and hugged her. He could not entirely believe the satisfaction that such an action gave him. To hold his child, to know that she was safe from harm, to feel the joys that had come and that would come from watching her learn and grow . . . he had never known anything more fulfilling.

When they parted, Lal moved to sit on the sofa, and Data followed her over. "Did you have an enjoyable afternoon, Father?" she asked.

"I did," he said. "I admired your paintings again." Lal smiled, a full, wide, toothy smile that contained no hint of awkwardness. Data felt immensely proud of her. "And how was your time in the lab today?" he asked.

"It was fine," Lal said.

"Whenever I ask about your day in the lab, you tell me that it was fine," Data said. "What did you actually *do* today?"

"I do not know," Lal said nonchalantly. "I was deactivated for most of the time."

"What?" Data said. He thought that perhaps he had not heard her correctly.

"I was deactivated for most of my time in the lab today," she said again.

Data stood up quickly and strode across the room, not because he wanted to do anything, but to cover the sudden distress he felt. Coupled with how he'd been troubled just moments ago thinking about the security of the complex, he almost could not control his emotional state. He wanted to run, he wanted to find Haftel and make the admiral tell him for what reason he had allowed his child to be deactivated, perhaps had even ordered it.

"Father, did I say something wrong?" Lal asked.

Data did not wish to worry his daughter. Carefully, he collected himself and turned to face Lal with equanimity. "No," he told her. "I am . . . I am . . ." He did not want to tell her what bothered him, for she would surely ask questions, which could lead to her feeling troubled herself. "I am overcome with my pride in you," he finally said—not what he had been thinking, but also not a lie. "In such a short time, you have become a re-markable, talented—" *What? Android? Girl? Woman?* "You have become a remarkable, talented human being."

"Father," she said, with emotion that Data had somehow given her, that she had somehow developed, and that Dr. Soong had managed to protect and preserve in her.

She truly is remarkable, Data thought. That anybody would ever deactivate her for any amount of time seemed an unconscionable act. But the next day, when Lal left for the lab, Data would find out why they had done so.

★ ★ ★

Riker sat at the desk in his ready room, his first officer standing at his side. Via a subspace transmission boosted by a string of starships and relay stations across the Federation, Fleet Admiral Shanthi spoke to them. *"We're getting reports of activity in Cardassian space near Starbase Two-One-One and the Kalorna system,"* she said.

Riker peered up at Worf, who responded with an almost imperceptible shake of his head. To Shanthi, Riker said, "What kind of activity, Admiral? Is it something significant, something well-defined?"

"At the moment, it's neither," Shanthi said. *"The sensor contacts are sporadic, but given the situation, we're concerned about it."*

"I understand," Riker said. If Starfleet committed most of its resources to Dre Mirale and the surrounding space, that would leave the region that included Starbase 211 and the Kalorna System largely unprotected. "We can split our forces across both Dre Mirale and Kalorna," Riker said, "but if we do, that would leave both regions susceptible to defeat if the Cardassians launch a full assault."

"It doesn't sound like we have enough good options here," the admiral said.

Again, Riker looked at Worf. This time, the *Enterprise* first officer spoke up. "Admiral, we have thoroughly examined the evidence of Cardassian incursions into the Dre Mirale system, and we are convinced that it is accurate."

"That may be, Commander," Shanthi said, *"but does such an incursion definitively tell us that the Cardassians will invade in that region? It could be a ploy."*

"It could be," Riker allowed, "but we are of the opinion that the sporadic sensor contacts around the Kalorna system are meant to coax us away from protecting Dre Mirale."

On the desktop interface, Shanthi looked away, then inhaled and exhaled deeply. *"Very well, then,"* she said. *"We'll rendezvous with you at Dre Mirale as we planned."*

"We'll see you there, Admiral," Riker said.

"I hope you're right about this, Captain," Shanthi said. Her image vanished from the screen, replaced by the Federation emblem.

Riker turned in his chair to face Worf. "Let's continue our drills," he told his first officer. "When the Cardassians get here, I want to be ready."

After Lal left for the laboratory, Data found the padd on which she kept her journal. She had invited him to read it, but he had not looked at it until then. On page after page, he saw the one word he had hoped he would not: *deactivated*. Lal's experience in the lab the day before had not been an aberration; over time, she had been shut down again and again. He thought a great deal about that, and he could conceive of only one reason that Haftel would allow it.

Data returned to his own quarters with only a vague plan, but as he searched his memory, he settled on the tactics he had employed to commandeer *Enterprise* and take it to Terlina III. He activated the companel in the living area. "Computer," he said, perfectly imitating the admiral's voice, "recognize Haftel, Anthony, alpha two clearance." He had heard the admiral employ that level of security authorization.

"Priority clearance recognition, alpha two," responded the computer.

"Isolate all commands from this location and disable all records and notifications of computer activity sourced here," Data said, still utilizing Haftel's voice. He wanted no one in the complex to learn of his unauthorized actions.

"All localized commands isolated, all records and notifications disabled."

"Computer, display complete internal map of Daystrom annex on Galor Four, including all secure and classified areas." A three-dimensional map appeared on the companel monitor. Data read down the legend beside it, swiping his fingers across the screen to turn the image. He found three classified areas that remained unidentified on the map. One formed the lowest level of the complex, filling it entirely.

"Computer, display complete map of the lowest level of the Daystrom annex on Galor Four."

"Unable to comply," said the computer. *"No such map exists."*

Data considered attempting to make his way down to the lower level, but even if he could use the admiral's security clearance to gain access, somebody would undoubtedly see him. Then he remembered how his trunk of personal belongings had been delivered to his quarters from the shuttle: via a transporter system internal to the facility.

"Computer, is there a transporter pad on the lower level of the Daystrom annex on Galor Four?"

"Affirmative. There are four high-capacity transporters and two lower-capacity transporters."

"Is that level equipped with internal sensors?" Data asked.

"Affirmative."

"Access internal sensors on that level, disabling all records and notifications of that access," Data said. "How many individual life-forms are currently present?"

"Accessing," the computer said. Several beats passed before it said, *"There are currently eleven personnel on the lower level."*

"Computer, analyze," Data said. "Is there a location on the lower level to which I can transport without being detected by the personnel present, where I can remain undetected for ten seconds?"

"Analyzing." Again, several seconds passed before the computer completed its response. *"Affirmative."*

Data did not hesitate. "Computer, initiate site-to-site transport, disabling all records and notifications of that transport, and block internal sensors on the lower level from detecting my presence. Beam me to the location just described, and ten seconds later, transport me back to this location."

At once, the white glimmer of a transporter beam enveloped

Data. His quarters dissolved from his view, and an indeterminate amount of time later, a different place appeared before his eyes. He heard movement, but at a distance. He had materialized beside several metal crates, and he cautiously peeked out from behind them.

Cavernous, with high ceilings and bare walls, the area looked like an industrial site. Machinery of a configuration Data did not recognize filled the space. But he did recognize the products of the machinery: body parts. He saw android arms and legs, a torso—

And then he dematerialized again, reappearing in his quarters. He went directly to the companel. "Computer, state the purpose of the production of androids on the lower level of the Daystrom annex on Galor Four."

"Unable to comply. That information has not been provided."

But Data knew anyway. The drastically increased security. The talk of Lal being taken to Galor IV as being necessary for Federation security. The transfer of Commander Shelby to the annex. First there had come the threat of the Borg—which Starfleet Command still considered serious—and then there had come the threat of a new war with the Cardassians. Suddenly, Data's intuition made sense.

"Computer, access transit logs for the Daystrom annex on Galor Four," he said. "How many different Starfleet vessels have arrived here within the last month?"

"Within the last month, thirty-seven different Starfleet vessels have arrived at Galor Four."

More than one a day, Data thought, horrified. The assignment of the new androids had already begun. Starfleet was girding for war, and populating their starships with disposable troops.

Captain Riker walked up to the bridge's upper level and glanced over Ensign zh'Kal's shoulder. Starfleet symbols dotted the sensor map. The armada had arrived.

Now where are the Cardassians? he thought.

★ ★ ★

Standing in his quarters, Data looked at Lal, at the clothes she wore that he had replicated for her. He had explained the situation to her, and told her what he wanted her to do. He had also let her know what *he* intended to do—although, for both her own protection and plausible deniability, as well as to prevent her from growing fearful for his safety, he had not told her precisely how he would accomplish his goal.

Data checked the companel, still under his control utilizing Admiral Haftel's security clearance. He studied the sensor readings of the android-production facility and of the landing pad. With a Starfleet vessel newly in orbit, he expected that a group of new androids would shortly be transported from the lower level of the Daystrom annex to the pad, where they then would be taken aboard a shuttle into orbit. That period, Data thought, would provide him the only opportunity he would have to save Lal from her unwitting participation in Haftel's appalling scheme.

As Data studied the companel readouts, he saw the confluence of events for which he had been waiting. He quickly activated the transporter, then turned to watch Lal disappear in a coruscation of white light. They had already said their farewells.

Once the hum of the transporter faded, Data turned back to the companel. He reinitialized the screen, which had also been displaying an image of *U.S.S. Galatea,* a new class of Federation starship originally designed as a defense against the Borg. Data had learned a great deal in recent days, all of it culled from various classified reports. He had spent many hours searching through the computer for whatever information he could find on the work being done on Galor IV. He had employed Admiral Haftel's security clearance, as well as that of Commander Shelby. Before taking action, he had needed to be sure that he was right.

He was.

Lal had been deactivated time and again so that she would

not know to what purpose she had been put. Her neural net had been employed as a template for other androids, much as Data had utilized his own neural net in laying down Lal's. Those other androids had then been programmed essentially as war machines, any hint of their humanity removed, given the lone purpose of going into combat, without choice, without the possibility of dissenting.

Whatever the process Haftel's cyberneticists had used to download Lal's neural net to the other androids, they had been unable to use that same process with those androids as a source. They needed Lal. Without her, they could not produce a functioning positronic brain.

On the companel, Data called up a readout of Galor IV's orbital sensor grid. According to one of the annex's schedules he had found, the starship in orbit would depart at 2310, slightly more than an hour away. If it didn't, if the vessel remained at Galor IV until the next morning, then Data's plans would be dashed. When Lal did not appear at the lab on time, they would come looking for her. When they did not find her in her quarters or in Data's, they would look elsewhere. They would also suspect Data of abetting her escape attempt.

At 2310, the starship had not broken orbit about Galor IV. Data waited. The ship had not departed by 2315, nor by 2330. But at 2337, it finally departed.

Data then issued orders to the computer, once again with Admiral Haftel's voice, and various materials from around the Daystrom annex materialized in a haze of white light in his quarters. He did not think it would take much longer for the alarm to go up, despite his precautions. Fortunately, he would not need much more time.

When he had completed his preparations, he returned to the companel. "Computer, record command sequence Data-one."

"Recording command sequence."

"Begin command sequence. Transport all individuals on the

lower three levels of the Daystrom annex to the mess hall. Transport me and my cargo from this location to the center of the lower level. Ten seconds later, transport me to the landing pad. End sequence."

"Command sequence recorded."

Data turned and walked over to the device he had assembled in the middle of his quarters and laid his hands atop it. "Computer," he said, "initiate command sequence Data-one."

"Initiating command sequence."

A moment passed, and then the glistening white motes of a transporter beam swirled about him. He materialized in the center of the android production factory. He reached down to the bomb he had built and activated its fifteen-second timer. Then another transporter beam swept him away.

A massive chemical explosion tore through the entire lower level of the Daystrom annex on Galor IV, destroying everything in its path.

7

The android, constructed as a female and clad in the uniform of a Starfleet ensign, walked purposefully down a corridor aboard *U.S.S. Galatea*. When she arrived at the quarters to which she had been assigned, she entered and made her way to the companel inside. There, she recorded a message detailing what had been taking place on Galor IV. She then asked that the information be disseminated to the media, beginning with the Federation News Service. Finally, she asked to be extracted from *Galatea* as soon as possible.

Then Lal pressed the transmit control, sending her message to Gregory Desjardins, Paris.

The Tears of Eridanus

Steve Mollmann & Michael Schuster

Your heroes are warriors . . . your myths and legends tell of battles won—it is *natural* you turn to *violence*! Yet, I cannot *condemn* this! For it shows a great *spirit*—a spirit which properly channeled can take you beyond the stars!

—The Old-Timer
Green Lantern volume 2, issue 79 (September 1970)
"Ulysses Star Is Still Alive!" by Denny O'Neil

KUMARI: ONE

On every starship, in every service, in every quadrant, there was one command that no flight officer ever liked to hear. "Hold her steady."

Was there any flight officer whose natural inclination was *not* to hold the ship steady? Hikaru Sulu had heard the order from any number of commanding officers over the years, and yet here he was uttering it himself. At the helm, Vanda M'Giia's antennae twitched in what Hikaru recognized as annoyance.

But M'Giia just offered an "Aye, sir" without a trace of insolence, and she hunched over her console just a tiny bit more, plainly doing her best to keep the *Excelsior*-class starship steady within the energies of the Ashen Scar.

Hikaru looked up at Phelana Yudrin. Standing next to his chair, his executive officer was even more imposing than usual. Like M'Giia, she had the characteristic Andorian antennae, though hers were unflappably still as they protruded from her platinum hair. "How much time do we have?" he asked.

"Twelve minutes," replied Yudrin without glancing at a chronometer.

Twelve minutes. Twelve minutes to cross the Ashen Scar and make it back into friendly space before the nearest Klingon patrol was scheduled to reach this region.

Suddenly the deck seemed to heave and drop out from beneath Hikaru. He grasped the arms of his chair.

"I thought you were keeping her steady, Lieutenant." Though her voice was sharp, Yudrin seemed to have been physically unaffected by the jolt.

"I *am* keeping her steady!" M'Giia's antennae stood up aggressively.

Hikaru noticed Yudrin's antennae standing in response, and quietly murmured, "Not now, Subcommander." The Ashen Scar was difficult enough to navigate on low power without the distraction of one of Yudrin's infamous reprimands.

Hikaru took a look around the command deck. The blue emergency lights gave everything a hard look and made even the few non-Andorian bridge personnel look like they had blue skin. The bridge was tense: no one had expected the mission to be this difficult. Normally their covert border crossings were very well planned and coordinated. He spun his chair to take a look behind him. "Status of the Klingon patrol?"

"Still out of range of our sensor drones," replied Lieutenant th'Eneg. Coming as he did from the highest mountains of Andor, his voice was a sibilant whisper in standard atmosphere.

"Is it possible the drones are being interfered with by the Scar?" asked Yudrin.

"Unlikely," replied th'Eneg. It was possible that the intelligence officer was piqued at the notion that his equipment didn't work, but he only answered factually. "My team determined their placement precisely, just to avoid such an occurrence."

"Yet according to the Klingon patrol schedules they should be arriving in twelve minutes," said Hikaru. "If they're that close, the drones should be picking them up."

"Eleven minutes now, Commander." Yudrin's tone was all business, but Hikaru could see the slight trace of a smile.

Standing up, Hikaru crossed the command deck to examine the large map on the bulkhead next to th'Eneg's console. It was currently displaying a three-dimensional chart of the Ashen Scar and its surrounding environs. A swirling rift to another dimension created by subspace weaponry deployed during the early

Klingon expansion, the Ashen Scar straddled the border between the Klingon Empire and the Interstellar Union. The amount of gravitational and photonic energy it generated blinded sensors and was responsible for the destruction of a dozen starships over the years. *Kumari* was going to be the first vessel to pass it successfully at such a close range—if they survived.

It certainly hadn't been Hikaru's plan to take this route. *Kumari*'s short hop into Klingon space to access the logs of an automated communications satellite had taken longer than projected, thanks to an unexpectedly high quantity of comsat data. Hikaru had decided to take the extra time to download it all. But in that extra time, a Klingon battlecruiser had filled the gap in the patrol patterns they'd used to cross the border.

Now their only chance of not getting caught was to go past the Scar, but even its sensor-jamming capabilities weren't absolute. If this sector's patrol got close enough, they'd see *Kumari* just fine, and that would be it for his ship and his crew—and possibly much more depending what was in that data.

The map showed the position of *Kumari* and its sensor drones, as well as the expected Klingon patrol routes of the area, which would bring the Klingons within sensor range in—he checked the chronometer—ten minutes. But the sensor drones *Kumari* had deployed all along the border in this region should have picked up a patrol by now—if it was on its way. Though he was grateful for the potential extra time, Hikaru was more worried about the idea of a trio of Klingon battlecruisers he couldn't even see.

"Is it possible some of the sensor drones have been destroyed? We deployed those things months ago."

Hikaru turned from the map to see who had spoken, though he'd known just fine from the man's deep—*immensely* deep—voice. Thirrilan ch'Satheddet was *Kumari*'s chief tactical officer, and despite the fact that one of his antennae had been replaced with a mechanical implant, the other's flatness still indicated that the man was on edge.

"Impossible," hissed th'Eneg. "They have been inactive up until now; the Klingons have no way of knowing they were even there."

Kumari rumbled again; Hikaru turned to face the map and saw a tendril of the Scar briefly light up and then return to normal. He turned to look at th'Eneg, who shook his head. Still no Klingon patrol.

"Commander," said Big Lan, waving a hand to get his attention. The Andorian man was also large—*immensely* large—with fingers twice the diameter of Hikaru's own. Just seeing them reminded Hikaru of his promise to never shake the man's hand again.

"What is it, lieutenant?"

"They've got to be out there somewhere," he said. "I advise a full torpedo spread forward, then we gun it out of the Scar and across the border. They have to know we're here by now."

Th'Eneg laughed, a rasping laugh that always gave Hikaru the shivers. "You would suggest that," he said. "No appreciation for subtlety. If my drones say there are no Klingons, then there are no Klingons. But calling attention to ourselves by firing weapons and going to full power will bring them here soon enough. I recommend holding position until we can gather more information."

Hikaru just nodded, looking over at Yudrin, who was still standing beside the command chair. "Subcommander?"

"I don't like it," she said. "But we have a plan: passing the Scar on low power. I advise we stick with it."

Th'Eneg hissed in annoyance, and Big Lan slammed one hand into another. They rarely agreed, but they certainly did on their dislike of *that* idea.

The ship rumbled yet again, even worse than before. Hikaru grabbed on to the console below the sector map to keep his footing, watching the Ashen Scar light up even brighter.

They *were* coming, he realized. He needed a new plan, and fast. But the only thing he knew was that he didn't know enough about the situation.

Well, that wasn't all. He knew he could rely on his people. "Lan, I want a full torpedo spread prepared."

"Aye, sir," said the tactical officer, his blue face lighting up in anticipation. "Arming photon torpedoes."

Th'Eneg cut in. "Commander—"

Hikaru held up his hand, bending his fingers slightly in imitation of the Andorian antenna movement of command. "Not now, Lieutenant. I want you to activate your sensor drones' thrusters. Bring them this way."

The intelligence analyst complied without comment. Hikaru touched the map in four spots just ahead of *Kumari*'s position; the map put a marker at each point as he did so. "I want one to each of those locations." He turned to face tactical once more. "Lan, when those drones are in range, I want you to fire a torpedo at each one."

Ignoring the perplexed glances of his crew—it was rare that Hikaru could so completely take a group of Andorians by surprise—he returned to the command chair. "How long until the drones are in range?"

"About two minutes," replied Big Lan.

"One minute, forty-seven seconds," added Yudrin, but quiet enough so that only Hikaru could hear.

"Lieutenant M'Giia, when those torpedoes hit, I want you to take us forward at warp one."

"Commander!" Yudrin had been keeping quiet about the plan so far, but she'd obviously had enough. "Even if the Klingon patrol is way behind schedule, they'll see *that*."

"No, they won't."

Hikaru glanced around the command deck. The crew looked even more tense than they had before. "I don't have time to explain what we're about to do, but I trust all of you to do your duties as laid out. We're going to get across the border just fine, and we're going to get that intelligence back to Interstellar Headquarters. We've got a job to do."

Everyone just looked at him for a moment, then Yudrin answered, "Yes, sir." The crew turned back to their consoles, readying themselves for action. Hikaru hit the comm button for engineering on his armrest. "Th'Rellvonda."

"Here, Commander."

"We're about to fire a spread of torpedoes. As soon as they're away, I want enough power for warp—but not a moment before."

It would be hard to ramp up the warp reactor that quickly, but th'Rellvonda said nothing of it. *"You'll have it, commander."*

Hikaru switched the comm off, glancing to see the map. The sensor drones were almost here. He looked at the viewscreen, and there they were: four dull gray dots barely visible against the silver energies of the Scar.

"Torpedoes away," reported Lan.

Hikaru watched as four blue bolts streaked outward.

A whirring of instrumentation announced the restoration of full power. He blinked as the dim emergency lights were replaced by full illumination.

The torpedoes hit their targets, each one flaring bright red.

"Engaging warp drive." M'Giia slid a lever forward on her console.

The screen flared silver. The ship creaked and moaned for a second, and Hikaru was thrown backward in his chair, gripping even harder than before. "Oh, my." The silver light on the screen grew brighter as *Kumari*'s engines struggled against the power of the Ashen Scar.

Hikaru could hear the strain in the engines as they grew louder; he felt everything *twist* as the ship sprang violently into warp space. They weren't going to make it—he could hear Yudrin praying quietly beside him—he wondered what Demora was up to—

And seconds later, everything was fine. The silver light on the screen faded away, to be replaced by normal space, the stars streaking by slowly as *Kumari* moved forward at warp one.

"Position, M'Giia," barked Yudrin. Of course she'd recovered first.

The flight officer looked down at her instruments. "IU space," she replied. "We're in the clear."

"Resume normal patrol," ordered Hikaru. "By the time those Klingons get out of the Scar, I want us looking perfectly normal."

"What Klingons?" demanded th'Eneg. "My drones never detected any."

"The Klingons who were coming at us from behind," said Hikaru, trying to keep the smugness from creeping into his voice. "The Klingons who were deeper within the Scar than we were, out of range of our drones. The Klingons who will shortly find the wreckage of four sensor drones, and decide that they must be the irregularity they had detected."

"But how did you know?" asked th'Eneg. There was nothing more guaranteed to aggravate him than someone else knowing something he did not.

"Because of the tremors." Hikaru stood up and began heading aft. "For M'Giia to not be able to handle them meant that they had to be greater than expected. And for that to be true meant that something had to be impinging on the Scar's subspace field."

Understanding dawned on Yudrin's face. "Like a patrol of Klingon battlecruisers."

"Exactly."

It wasn't long before Big Lan reported three Klingon battlecruisers climbing their way out of the Ashen Scar, dragging the remains of the sensor drones in their tractor beams. There was no indication that they'd detected *Kumari*: the explosion of the drones had evidently covered up their escape, exactly as Hikaru had planned. Satisfied, Hikaru told th'Eneg to get to work analyzing the data from the satellite, turned command over to Yudrin, and prepared to head to his quarters.

"How did you know about the Scar, Commander?" asked M'Giia as the bridge door slid open with a loud clunk.

Hikaru grinned. "It pays to be a scientist as well as a starship captain."

Hikaru stared at the situation reports and sighed.

He'd known that something big had to be going on, given the

size of the dataload on the satellite, but he hadn't expected *this*. He closed the analysis from Lieutenant th'Eneg and flipped open the updated conjectural map of the Klingon Empire that had been attached to the report.

The data on the satellite had revealed that Klingon forces had taken Gamma Hydra, meaning the Empire had now reached what most experts considered their point of maximum coreward expansion. Beyond that point lay the Typhon Expanse, a vast area of space rumored to contain dangerous abnormalities in the fabric of reality itself. Some considered it spacers' superstition, but the Klingons knew the rumors too and were unlikely to push further coreward. This meant that the ever-hungry Klingon war machine would soon be turning its eyes in a new direction, and few disagreed on what *that* might be.

Hikaru closed the report, approved its forwarding to Interstellar HQ, and shut off his desktop unit. He leaned back in his chair for a moment, contemplating his quarters.

By the standard of the Interstellar Guard, they were positively spacious—the new *Excelsior* class were the largest ships ever fielded by the Guard—but at twenty square meters, he wasn't exactly overwhelmed by space. The architecture of the cabin was as Spartan as ever for an IG vessel, but at least the *Excelsior* class had seen the color of choice shift from unrelenting gunmetal gray to some soft off-whites. Hikaru had done his best to spruce the place up with some personal effects, mostly a few exotic plants and some prints of astral phenomena, but it was still cramped and unfriendly.

Which he supposed was the point—the Guard wanted its personnel out and about on the ship, doing their duties, not languishing around in their quarters. Even the ship's commander. Especially on a day like today.

Hikaru finished off the cup of *srjula* on his desk, grimacing as he did so. As helpful as it was for keeping him awake and alert, the Andorians had never managed to brew what Hikaru considered a decent cup of tea. He checked his uniform in the mirror to make sure everything was right and headed out into the corridor, stewing all the while.

They'd spent two years out here on the Klingon border, alternating between long periods of boredom and short flares of intensity like this morning. Why did his ship have to be the one patrolling the border, snooping for whatever information they could find? Well, he knew the answer to that: they were good at their jobs. But sometimes he wished that they really were on the mission to chart gaseous anomalies that was their official excuse to linger on the border.

He reached the end of the central corridor spanning the long neck of the ship, coming to the massive door that led to the bridge. A touch of the keypad next to it, and the door opened. As usual, the command deck was a hive of activity, officers crossing back and forth between its many stations, coordinating all the functions that it took to operate a starship with a crew of over seven hundred. But that did not allow Hikaru to escape the notice of Phclana Yudrin, who immediately stood up from the command chair and saluted sharply.

He returned the salute in a somewhat sloppier fashion. "Good afternoon, Subcommander."

"Commander Sulu," the Andorian woman acknowledged. Yudrin wore her hair in a no-nonsense cut only a few inches long, from which a pair of antennae protruded. "We are back in position as ordered, three parsecs out of Mu Arae, within one light-year of the border." She handed him a data slate displaying *Kumari*'s current position and operational status.

"Any sign the Klingons realized we were there?" he asked, giving the slate a quick once over and returning it.

"No, sir," she answered, slipping the slate back under her arm. "The *Jartokk* and the other ships have resumed their normal patrols."

"Have you seen Lieutenant th'Eneg's report?" he asked as he settled down into his chair.

"Of course not, sir. It has not yet been cleared for general release." Her black eyes were absolutely passive, but her slightly twitching antennae betrayed a different story.

"Right."

"Do you doubt my devotion to regulations, sir?" Yudrin stood as straight as possible, hands clasped behind her back.

Even after she'd spent almost three years as his executive officer, Hikaru was still unable to tell when she was trying to be funny. The Andorians were a subtle people—sometimes too subtle for him. "What I don't doubt is your devotion to the Interstellar Guard, which is why I suspect you already know what I'm about to tell you anyway. The Klingons have taken Gamma Hydra."

She nodded, just once. "Unfortunate."

"It's more than that," he said, quietly, trying not to be overheard. "The Klingon Empire now stretches from the Typhon Expanse to the Delta Triangle. They're cut off in both directions, and they've got to expand somewhere. Their entire economy depends on an active military. You know it, I know it, the whole Interstellar Union knows it."

"Space is vast," said Yudrin, "and full of many directions that are not coreward or rimward."

"And all of them," said Hikaru, "are filled with obstacles to the Klingon Empire."

Indeed, they were hemmed in on all sides—the Interstellar Union, of course, occupied a substantial portion of the border, but there were also the Gorn Hegemony, the Holy Order of the Kinshaya, the Metron Consortium, the Guidon Space Pontificate, the Taurhai Unity, the Ksahtryan Regime. Each of them pressing in on the Klingons from a different direction, each of them with a reputation for dealing ruthlessly with those who disturbed them.

But the Klingons had to expand *somewhere*. And if Hikaru were Chancellor Korrd, he knew which way *he'd* go.

Yudrin didn't respond to his statement, but instead informed him that she had to head down to engineering to take care of something. She was an efficient executive officer—it wasn't so much that she dealt with the problems before they reached Hikaru, it was that everyone dealt with their own problems because they didn't want *her* dealing with them. Hikaru headed over to the map display, bringing up the border shared by the IU and the Klingons.

What th'Eneg had found out had been so much worse than they'd expected. The Interstellar Union had never been at war in its one-hundred-twenty-year history. For most of that time, the Interstellar Guard had been subsisting on the fearsome reputation of its predecessor, the Andorian Imperial Guard. But the might of the IU's Guard had never been tested, and even Hikaru had to admit—though only to himself—that he had doubts about how well the IG would do against an enemy as fierce as the Klingons.

Over a century of absolute peace was about to come to an end.

He shouldn't be thinking about it now—the conflict would be a problem for Field Marshal Thelian and the rest of the General Staff. But if it *did* come to war, *Kumari* would be right there on the front lines, and the eighty planets of the Interstellar Union would all be targets for invasion, including mainstays like Risa, Yridia, Earth, and Andor itself.

But he needed to think about it, to put his mind at ease. He was zooming in on different sections of the border, trying to see where the IU defenses were better or worse, when he suddenly became aware of a presence looming behind him. He turned around to see Big Lan.

"Excuse me, Commander." Lan filled in for Yudrin when she wasn't on the bridge.

Hikaru switched off the map. "Yes, Lieutenant?" He automatically looked at Lan's antennae to get a read on his emotions, but that mechanical one always threw him off.

"There's a signal for you from IHQ," Lan said, beginning to move back to his console.

"Who's it from?"

Lan paused for a moment in mid-stride, apparently lost in

thought. Finally, he shrugged. "I don't know, sir. It's a private signal."

They must have read th'Eneg's report, Hikaru realized. "Have communications pipe it into the briefing room," he said. "I'll be there in a moment."

The briefing room was always one of Hikaru's favorite places on any IG starship, and the *Kumari*'s was no exception.

It was one of the few places that IG ship designers actually cut loose a bit and put some space in, allowing for some accessorizing and personalization. His predecessor as commander of *Kumari*, Thelin th'Valrass, had created a display of the seven previous vessels to bear the name *Kumari* along one wall, and Hikaru had left it intact in his memory. The two hadn't gotten along well as captain and executive officer—"cultural differences" would have been a polite way of putting it—but they'd mended their relationship while Thelin lay dying, the victim of an attack by a Klingon terrorist. Thelin had a keen strategic mind; Hikaru would have gladly remained exec to have his insight on a day like today.

Hikaru sat down at the head of the briefing room table and flipped on the three-sided viewer in the table's center. The emblem of the Interstellar Union—a faux constellation of the IU's four founding planets—briefly appeared before being replaced by a face covered in bushy gray hair, but mostly notable for the large upturned snout in its center. A very familiar snout, belonging to a very familiar Tellarite.

"Gav!" exclaimed Hikaru. Perhaps some delight slipped through, but he managed to keep his voice as gruff as Gav would expect. "I see age hasn't done you any favors. Every time I see you, you look uglier. And as for your uni—"

Brigadier General Gav cut him off. *"Unfortunately, we have no time for civil conversation, Sulu. I'm afraid I have bad news."*

"I know." Gav, who'd served as executive officer during Hikaru's time on the old *Charter*-class *Enterprise I,* now occupied a position in the IG Security Bureau. It was nominally concerned with internal IU matters, making him a strange choice for handling this Klingon situation.

"You do?" asked Gav. *"Then you've already heard?"*

"Heard?" Hikaru wasn't sure what Gav was getting at. "We sent in the report!"

Gav blinked his sunken black eyes in confusion for a moment. *"I believe we're talking at cross purposes. Perhaps there is time for civil conversation, after all, Sulu: you're an idiot. I'm not talking about some insignificant scrap of intelligence you've picked up with your spy-rays or whatever. Your daughter's in trouble."*

Hikaru had thought that nothing could make his day worse, but he could feel his stomach sink right out of him at that. "Demora?"

"Do you have another?" snarled Gav. Hikaru took in a sharp breath at that—he and Susan had been trying their best to have a second child when—

Gav obviously recognized Hikaru's reaction for what it was, because his next words had a somewhat apologetic tone, though he didn't actually apologize. *"A report crossed my desk today—you know where she'd been posted, right?"*

"A hidden observation outpost on a prewarp planet," Hikaru said. "Commanding its security detail."

"The planet has no native name—or at least none that its evolutionarily challenged natives can agree upon—so it's officially known by its IU astronomical designation, UGC 36A-2B. It's not entirely clear what's happened, but we do know that the outpost is no longer in the hands of our personnel."

"Are there any leads on what might have happened?" He was trying to keep his voice steady—especially in front of Gav, who he'd never seen react with an emotion other than disdain. If the team had been killed—

"It's not clear, but we do know that the natives have access to the equipment—the Science Directorate received a set of what would seem to be demands. They're working on translating them. Slowly, of course."

"Have they been taken hostage?" If the natives were making demands, then surely they had some sort of bargaining chip. Hopefully it was the lives of the outpost crew. Though if they'd made it to the communications equipment, they must have over-whelmed the security staff—

No, he couldn't allow himself to think that.

"You know everything that I know." Gav laughed. Tellarites placed a high value on insult and riposte, but Hikaru was grow-ing impatient. *"Well, not everything I know, of course, but in this one case, it might be true."* His face became grim once more. *"It goes without saying that you didn't hear this from me."*

Hikaru nodded, trying not to react visibly to Gav's jabs. "Of course I didn't. Has a rescue ship been assigned yet?"

"Not yet. The Pompous Ass Himself is dealing with this one, and Phinda knows he can't make a decision that quickly." The Pompous Ass Himself was General Shras, one of the members of Field Marshal Thelian's General Staff. Gav and Shras had a somewhat ancient antagonism, and Gav had never forgiven himself for let-ting Shras get so far ahead of him in the ranks of the IG.

An outline of a plan was already forming in Hikaru's mind. "Thank you, Brigadier." He began extending his hand toward the disconnect button. "Now if you'll excuse me, I have some calls to make."

"Thank goodness, I thought you'd never shut—"

Hikaru didn't wait to hear the rest of Gav's retort. He quickly looked up the planet on the monitor to refresh his memory. It was a desert world, colloquially known as "Eridani," after its Earth astronomical designation of 40 Eridani A II. Preliminary observations had indicated that the native intelligent species was extremely warlike and brutally savage—hence the reason it had gone relatively uncharted despite its proximity to the core planets of the IU; it was a mere thirteen light-years from Andor.

He opened a channel to the bridge. *"M'Giia here."*

"Lieutenant, at maximum warp how long will it take us to reach 40 Eridani A?"

"I've never heard of that planet, Commander. It can't be important."

Normally, Hikaru was amused by his flight officer's flippancy. "Lieutenant, answer my question. *How long* will it take us?" Not today.

A pause. *"At warp eleven . . . about two days."* She sounded uncertain.

Two days. Two days where Demora might be dying in an alien desert.

No time to waste, then. "Set a course and engage at maximum warp."

"Aye, Commander."

The comm unit gave a tone that indicated someone else had joined the conversation. *"Commander, this is Subcommander Yudrin."*

She must have solved that problem in engineering. "Go ahead, Subcommander."

"Sir, have we received new orders?"

Hikaru's voice was filled with confidence as he answered. "We will."

They had to. And he was going to make sure they would.

It took some doing for Hikaru to find someone who could help him, but he finally had his man—or woman—in Major General Lamia. She'd served with Hikaru as *Enterprise*'s chief of security, and had gone on to serve as the first commander of *Kumari*. It had been at her insistence that Hikaru had been transferred back to space duty, as *Kumari*'s flight officer.

"You said at the time, ma'am, that you owed me one."

"I thought I had paid you back, Hikaru. You spent a mere two years as flight officer and then you were promoted to exec." When Lamia had been promoted to general, Thelin had been promoted to take her place, and Hikaru had taken *his* place as executive officer. Neither of them had been particularly happy about it at the time. *"And now look at you! Commander of the flagship of the Guard!"* Her green eyes, unusual for an Andorian, made her look like she was staring.

His assignment to *Kumari* had been a point of contention.

He'd have been happy to remain on Andor—or any planet, as long as Demora was there—but during his nine years of teaching at the Interstellar Institute he'd also become involved in the project to develop transwarp drive, the so-called "Great Experiment," and given *Kumari* was a testbed for that technology, he'd been deemed indispensable to the ship upon its launch. "I didn't ask for the captaincy. I need you to talk to General Shras for me."

She lost her smile. *"What is it you want?"*

"I need you to recommend *Kumari* for an assignment. And you can't ask me why." If she learned what Hikaru's stake was in this, she'd reject him in a heartbeat. "I know I'm asking a lot, especially as Commander Thelin used to always tell me that the Andorians had few sympathies."

"That's true enough." Andorians tended to believe that if you couldn't make it on your own, you just didn't make it. They were ostensibly a warrior race, after all. Some delighted in circulating persistent rumors that they left infants with disabilities in the ice-fields of Andor to perish in the harsh elements.

"But this is about one of those sympathies you *do* have. You have to trust me."

Hikaru liked to think that he'd picked up a few things during his time in the Interstellar Guard, how to deal with Andorians being one of them. Maybe he was right, because before the conversation was over, Lamia had agreed to recommend *Kumari* for the Eridani mission to General Shras.

As she signed off, Hikaru could hear the words of Thelin echoing in his mind: "A warrior race has few sympathies, but one that we do have . . . is for family."

Thank you, Thelin.

He didn't know how to answer Demora's question. "But why, Dad? Why?"

When he and Susan had gotten married, they'd made an agreement. One of them would go back into space; the other would take a ground assignment on Earth to be with Demora. After all, there was no room for children on an IG battlecruiser. But after five years, they'd trade off. Neither of them could give up the stars for longer than that.

They flipped a coin to see who went first.

So Hikaru had gone back out into space aboard a refit Enterprise, and Susan had taken a position at the San Francisco Interstellar Observatory.

That was simple enough. But how could he explain that the stars had just called too much—that Susan had been unable to resist a six-week survey of Marris III? She'd left Demora in the care of Hikaru's parents and shipped out on Kanlee.

Four weeks later, Hikaru had gotten word that she was dead. Sakuro's disease. Perfectly treatable—unless you were over two weeks from the nearest starbase.

Commander Kirk had given him leave, of course. "Take as much as you need."

Now here he stood with his daughter. The first time they'd seen each other since it had happened. And he had no idea what to say.

Except: "I don't know. But I'm here now."

MINSHARA: ONE

Demora woke slowly, with sand between her teeth. Merely thinking took effort, almost as if her mind didn't want to wake up. It kept important things just out of reach, making it difficult for her to do what she was trained to do: determining her situation and assessing her chances of survival. The truth was, she had no idea where she was. Worse, she didn't remember what exactly had happened to her; everything was a blur.

She was lying on the ground, and as her eyes focused, she discovered that she must be in a cave of some sort, sounds echoing from wall to wall. It was night-dark, but that didn't mean anything. Most likely, whoever had brought her here didn't want to waste energy on illumination.

With great effort she pulled her arms toward her, gathering enough strength to push her upper body from the ground and lift her head to take stock of her surroundings. As suspected, she was inside a dwelling, but it didn't look like a natural cave to her, more like a room hewn into the rock. At the edge of darkness there was a door with a tiny window set into it, through which she could see a distant flickering flame.

She wanted to spit, to rid herself of the sand grains, but her mouth was dry. Judging from her dry lips and the growing headache, she had been without water for at least ten hours, if not longer. That meant that it had to be almost noon, because the

IU outpost had been overrun late in the night; she recalled that much, at least.

Demora propped herself up on her hands and pulled her legs closer so that she was able to sit. Her left shoulder hurt, as if somebody had punched her there repeatedly. That, together with the dehydration-induced headache, aching ribs, and a sore right ankle, meant she was less battle-ready than she would have liked, but at the moment she didn't have to be. What was important now was finding out where she was and if there were other members of the team being kept here.

Now that she was able to use her hands, she inspected herself. Her uniform was dirty, but intact. Her pockets had been opened, however, and there was no trace of her handscanner or of her blaster. Even her *flabbjellah* was gone. Not that she'd expected them to be there, but she couldn't afford not to check.

Despite her loss of equipment, she couldn't sit around expecting to be rescued by a transporter beam. The observation outpost had been constructed on the fringes of an electromagnetic dampening field, where the area that locals called the Forge met a mountain range. It had seemed like the perfect place to build a hidden observation post, because a lot of the natives came by the area to meet and, in some memorable cases, fight to the death. Never had Demora thought that the team she was assigned to protect would be the target of such a fight.

Memories stirred, although only in fragments, leaving her the dreadful task of piecing them together. She couldn't make much of them yet, the sequence of events eluding her. Still, the picture became clearer the longer she thought about it.

It was not pretty.

Demora gasped with shock as she remembered the sickening crunch of Vrani's neck breaking. Mere minutes before, the two of them had shared a joke. Then the attack came. They were easily overpowered, too easily. Demora still couldn't believe what had happened. In the ensuing battle, a native resented being the target of *fivri* moves—how proud Vrani had been about making second belt!—and decided to kill her for it. The yellow-haired security trooper had no chance.

What had happened to the others? Where were they? Had they been killed? If so, why was *she* still alive? If not, what did the Eridanians hope to gain from the kidnapping?

As she tried to stand up, she realized painfully that her injuries were worse than she'd thought. Her ankle was in no condition to support her full weight, forcing her to hobble to the doorway, each step causing fireworks of pain to shoot up her right leg.

Reaching the door, she leaned against it, closed her eyes, and listened. It was very hard to discern, but she heard something . . . it was muffled, but it seemed to her like people talking in a low voice. Her captors? Or members of the observation team?

Demora opened her eyes again. She needed all her senses now, if she wanted to have any chance at all at getting out of here. *Observe closely,* she told herself. *Every little thing can be significant. If it tells you where you are, good. If it lets you escape, even better.*

The light coming through the little window in the door wasn't enough to help her see the room she was in. Putting her palms to the flat rock, she felt her way around the room. By necessity, she favored her left leg and steadied herself by keeping contact with the wall.

Roughly five meters by seven meters in size, the room did not contain any furniture. The only notable discovery she made was a spot in a far corner where water had made it through the rock and trickled down onto the sand-covered floor where it seemed to seep away into whatever lay beneath.

She thought about similar places she knew about. On Earth, many cultures had preferred hollowing out hills and mountains to building houses, and on Andor, several peoples, most notably the Zhevran tribes, built whole cities in the ice caves. More often than not, the reason for digging into the rock was the inhospitable climate, just like here on Eri.

From the corner of her eye she saw something move, and

when she turned, she noticed the flickering flame was much closer. It dipped out of sight for a moment, and then reappeared as the cell's door swung open. The flame barely illuminated its bearer, a male native in dark garments made colorless by the poor light. His long brown hair entirely covered his peculiar diabolical ears that had so spooked Demora when she'd first seen them. It had been a childish reaction, and she had felt shamed by it.

The native approached her, candle in hand, and stared at her. He didn't say a word.

"What do you want from me?" she asked him, determined not to let him see any weakness.

It didn't matter that he didn't respond, because she wouldn't have understood him if he had. The translator set inside her skull wouldn't work, if what she knew about the dampening fields around here was true, and she had unfortunately declined the offer by Doctor Grayson to be taught the local *lingua franca*.

Poor woman. The mission's senior scientist had always been so kind to everybody, and she had thought the warring natives belonged to a culture that the Union could learn so much from.

Shit, she was doing it already! Thinking of Doctor Grayson as if she was dead, even though there was no evidence of that. She knew that the linguist hadn't been killed on the spot, unlike several of her security detail. There was still a chance.

"I'd like to go home, if you don't mind. Don't get me wrong, I am grateful for your hospitality, but I think you guys are overdoing the Spartan bit." Her mouth was moving faster than her brain, just like always. Usually, that got her into trouble, but thankfully the natives wouldn't understand her English—or Andorii, for that matter.

"*Kroykah,*" the man said. It sounded like an order, but she didn't feel compelled to follow it.

"Yeah, whatever. Fancy place you got here, and with running water, even," she said, pointing at the far wall.

"*Nam'uh ralash-fam!*" He shouted, displaying his yellowed teeth. It was easy to see that he was angry, as the team's observation had shown that the locals' emotional displays were similar to those of humans. *"Fa-wak shroi ri nemut zhitlar."*

Candle Guy took another step toward her and grabbed her shoulder. Demora had been trained to keep her cool in situations such as this, but under the circumstances, it just wasn't happening. She wanted to protest, but deep inside her, an unknown force kept her jaws clenched together, and all her willpower wasn't enough to open them.

Her mind started to cloud up again, like it had been before, when she woke up. She glared at him, trying to fight against the intrusion. It was obvious to her that Candle Guy must be one of those strong espers about whom the observation team had found out disappointingly little during their months here.

The native removed his hand again, and immediately she regained control over every aspect of herself. He gestured at her in a way she interpreted as a warning. *"Ikap'uh t'du ru'lut."*

The meaning was clear. *Keep your trap shut, or else.*

Well, Demora Sulu could take a hint. She also knew that ranting at Candle Guy might make her feel better, if only for a moment, but it wouldn't help her escape.

She'd noticed something, though: he'd grabbed her shoulder to shut her up, so he likely needed physical contact to establish a telepathic connection. This was important information, and she filed it in her mental Major Clues drawer.

The Union as a whole had had blessedly few experiences with powerful mind control, aside from the reclusive Ullian State, until Science Director Usbek-Wran had pushed for an exploration of a previously ignored trinary star system in the Eridani constellation.

The past five months had yielded a few interesting results—for the scientists, anyway. It hadn't taught Demora anything about defeating a telepathic attack, however, something she was now sorely regretting.

She'd had a plum position for a recent Institute graduate, in charge of a team of eight noncommissioned security troopers, and quickly earned the respect of her subordinates, from Vrani to Gohoy, by doing her job well and still remaining a decent person. She might be a bit too young for the taste of some old warriors, but even they had to respect someone who'd gone through the Institute's intense Security College.

Would they still respect her now, if they knew she was at the mercy of bloodthirsty natives? She didn't want to think about it.

The man motioned at her to move, and she did so, not having another option. Taking the lead, she walked past the doorway through which he had come, and then forward, knowing that he'd let her know what route to take.

Walking along bare walls, Demora had little to do but think. It was tempting to believe that she was in no immediate danger— after all, the natives could have killed them all in the attack, instead of leaving her alive. But under the circumstances, nothing was certain.

And to think that everything had gone so well! The past few months had simply flown by, while the team collected data about the various Eridanian tribes and factions. There'd been blessedly little to do for the security detail, but that had not hindered Demora from doing her job, and doing it well. She'd drilled her team repeatedly and never when they expected it. She'd worked out various scenarios involving an attack by the natives—their common flaw now obviously being a complete underestimation of Eridanian abilities.

Hindsight could be such a curse sometimes. What if she'd done this or that differently? Let's say she had paid closer attention to the surveillance cameras—would she have noticed the camouflaged tribesmen creeping patiently closer and closer at a snail's pace? Their first warning had been the explosion—already too late. In a rush, dozens of armed men had poured into the hidden building that Demora, Doctor Grayson, Doctor Dax, and the others had called their home. They'd been no match for local ingenuity and inhuman strength.

Perhaps she had neglected her duty. But before a tribunal could judge her, the important question of how the natives had even known about the outpost would have to be answered.

It was her training that was keeping her going now. She knew there must be a way out for her. She only had to find it. The few facts she had collected so far didn't help her much, but she was able to come up with something that resembled a plan.

Candle Guy could influence minds, but apparently not easily if he needed physical contact. For Demora, this made what she intended much easier. She resolved to use whatever chance presented itself. The most important thing was to keep from touching the man. Surprise was her only available tool, and she was damned if she lost it to him.

After a few minutes' walk, going up a flight of stairs, they passed through a hallway, at whose end they turned a left corner. Their destination was a wooden door. It turned out to be locked, but Candle Guy had a strange-looking key that opened it.

Inside, fires burned within standing braziers, filling the sizeable chamber with a warm orange light that belied the stark austerity Demora had witnessed previously. There were a table, four chairs, and a number of metal chests in the far corner.

Most importantly, however, the room was already occupied—and by a familiar face.

"Doctor Grayson!" she cried as she entered.

The old woman sitting on the leftmost chair turned and squinted at the newcomers. When she recognized Demora, her face lit up briefly, but then she spotted the man holding the candle, and her features returned to the stony façade they had displayed before.

The man pushed Demora into the chair next to Grayson. He then placed the candle on a small stool near the wall and glared at the two women.

Grayson spoke, seemingly unimpressed by his presence. "Ensign Sulu, I thought you had been killed with the others."

"I was just about to say the same thing about you," Demora said, not daring to take her eyes off the man completely. "Have they been treating you well?"

"As well as can be expected. They didn't exactly smother me with kisses."

"Same here. Found out yet what they want?"

"No, but I—"

"Vrukah!" shouted Candle Guy.

"Nam'uh hayal. Lof t'etek ri aisha vatlar," replied Grayson. Demora was once again impressed by the linguist's fluency in the Eridanian language. "I told him to calm down, we're not here to make trouble."

"Thanks, Doc, but speak for yourself. My plan is to make as much trouble as possible."

"Ensign, you know how swift and deadly they are. They'll stop you before you can even execute your first move."

"Not this guy. He needs to touch me to read my thoughts, and I won't let him."

The linguist just shook her head. Doctor Amanda Grayson was the mission's seniormost scientist, and Demora had always regarded her with an almost daughter-like affection. A former professor of xenolinguistics at the Makropyrios, Grayson had worked for the Union's Science Directorate for many years, studying the new cultures discovered by the Guard's explorers. Her career had been ending when she came to Eri; from day one, she'd told everybody who had been close enough to hear that this was to be her final bow. "I'd like to go out with a bang," she'd said to Demora once, showing how important she considered the Eridanians to be, both culturally and scientifically. She hadn't expected it to be quite so literal.

Candle Guy spoke and Grayson immediately added a translation of their exchange for Demora's sake: "What are you? Who sent you here? You do not want me to have to ask you a third time."

Tough questions, especially when talking to members of a primitive culture. Standard IG policy in similar situations (although Demora couldn't recall any xenostudy projects that had gone *this* badly) was to admit nothing. Total compliance with that guideline was almost never possible, but it usually went well enough for the higher-ups at IHQ to be satisfied.

"We are scientists from a distant world who have heard good things about your people. It was decided to observe you before we initiated contact."

A good answer, if a bit too informative.

"Why have you aligned yourselves with the Nashih?"

"As I told you before, we are not aligned with anybody. We have not met or talked with Clan Nashih."

"Don't try to fool me by feigning ignorance. Why do you work with our enemy?"

"We don't. We came here in peace, with good intentions and the will to cooperate with *all* of you."

That drew what Demora interpreted as a derisive laugh. Perhaps there were some things that were universal, whether you had pointy ears or not. "You're insane if you really believe that! Minshara is as fractured a world as can be, and nobody cooperates with anyone unless forced to do so! You can't be so stupid as to believe what you say, so think again and tell me the truth."

"You don't want the truth; you want what you'd like to hear, and I won't give you that. No matter how often you ask, I'll give you the same answer: we're here to prepare for official first contact between our community of worlds and the people of your planet."

At that, the man grew considerably angrier. He took a step toward Grayson, bringing himself within reach of her. He put his hand forcefully down on the older woman's shoulder, and immediately the two of them took on a somewhat distant expression, Grayson more so than he. However, the entire episode didn't last long, and he pulled back his hand and scowled at her.

Demora didn't know what had just transpired, but obviously things had not gone according to his plan. She shot Grayson a questioning look.

"He tried forcing me to reveal my 'real' objective, but I gave him some of his own medicine." At Demora's lack of comprehension, she elaborated: "I've been trained by an expert to protect myself against telepathic intrusion. One of the survivors of the Gorn attack on Beta Zeta V was very helpful in that regard."

The old woman looked frail, but appearances were often deceiving, and rarely more so than in Grayson's case. Demora could only wish that she turned out to be so wise and agile when she reached—

"Bath'paik!" the man yelled, his features distorted by rage. In one swift move, he drew a green-bladed knife.

"Watch out!" she cried, but it was too late. Boiling with anger, he lunged at Grayson. Almost instantly, dark blood gushed from a deep, angled cut across her throat and down her chest. The linguist tried to speak, but no sound other than a sick bubbling came forth. In a matter of seconds, she collapsed on the chair, her life-force rapidly leaving her.

Witnessing Grayson's murder caused something to snap inside Demora. Without thinking, she shot up and hurled herself at the native with a loud battle cry.

It was summer in Laikan, which meant that the temperature was just above freezing. He reminded himself that this was the warm part of Andor.

They'd been on the planet almost a year now. He'd taken a position at the Interstellar Institute because it was the only ground posting available. He lectured in astrophysics, his first love. And to his surprise, he actually liked teaching. Well, when his students weren't whining about how hard their exams were.

She'd taken to the change of location fairly well, but there was one thing that troubled her. "We never get to go outside," she would say. "I never get to see the stars."

But it was summer now, and he'd promised her that they would go out when it was warm. From his memories of four years here as a student at the Institute, he knew it typically didn't get much warmer.

So when night fell, they bundled up and went outside. Fortunately the gas giant Andor orbited was a mere crescent tonight—nothing to outshine the stars.

He spent some time pointing out the Andorian constellations he knew: the Eagle, the Hybor, the Bull. He caught sight of a barely visible star, pointing it out to her. "That's Sol, where Earth is. That's home."

She shook her head, then looked at him. "No. Home is here now. Earth is gone."

KUMARI: TWO

*C*ommander Sulu, I've elected to pull Kumari *temporarily from border patrol.*"

Hikaru had to give General Shras credit. From the way he said it, you'd think it was *his* idea.

"May I ask why, sir? The situation with the Klingons—"

"*—will not be resolved by probing their communications. Atlirith will be taking over your position once they conclude their relief mission on Nimbus. You are to set course for UGC 36A-2B immediately.*" Shras was an older Andorian; most of his hair had fallen out, giving him a fringe that he had grown out to create an unconvincing comb-over.

"I'm unfamiliar with that world, sir."

"*It's a prewarp planet in Sector 005. Because of the impending threat from the Klingons, it's recently acquired a certain level of . . . significance.*"

Oh, really? Now this was something Hikaru hadn't discovered in his research thus far. Though, now that he thought of it— the time of the establishment of the outpost on Eridani almost exactly corresponded to when the Klingon Empire's rimward expansion had been halted by the Metron Consortium after the Battle of Cestus. "How so?"

"*For one thing, the planet falls between Andor and the projected path of the Klingon invasion, making it a pivotal part of the defense of the capital. If we can secure a military base there, it could prove instrumental in the coming conflict.*"

It was very telling, Hikaru thought, that Shras seemed to be consistently referring to war with the Klingons as a done deal. If the situation had been different, he would have been highly alarmed—not even the General Staff at IHQ thought there was a way out. But in the present situation, the fate of the Interstellar Union was just a minor worry. "Is there another consideration, sir?"

"With the volatility of the current diplomatic situation, information is on a strict need-to-know basis, Commander." Hikaru was all too aware of his rank with *that* comment. *"We'll determine exactly what's required once you evaluate the situation on the planet."*

Hikaru was about to ask if there had been any further word from the outpost when he remembered he ostensibly didn't know *anything* about Eridani beyond what Shras had just told him. *Stupid*, he thought. He couldn't afford to let Shras know the general had been manipulated into sending *Kumari* on this mission—Hikaru would be off the job, and probably the ship, in a heartbeat. So instead: "What *is* the situation on this planet, sir?"

Shras gave him the rundown of what was known. Unfortunately, there wasn't any more information than Brigadier Gav had already provided him. *"Commander, you are to do whatever it takes to get those outpost personnel back alive—assuming they still* are *alive—but absolutely do not antagonize the native population any more than you have to. A good relationship is essential to IHQ plans for the defense of Andor—"* His chest puffed up at this point. *"—and, indeed the entire Interstellar Union."*

Hikaru could certainly see why Gav had given the man his nickname. Pompous Ass, indeed. "On this backwater planet?"

Shras rolled his eyes. *"Commander, I believe Earth was an insignificant planet itself before the Andorians transformed it into an interstellar power. And then it went on to be a co-founder of the IU. Don't underestimate the power of a 'backwater.'"*

That was hardly how Earth had entered the interstellar stage, but Hikaru knew better than to get into *that* now. He decided to change approach. "Any word on the situation with the Klingons?"

Shras's antennae stuck straight up in a sign of aggravation

and posturing. *"Officially, commander, there is no 'situation' with the Klingons. The Klingon Empire has never antagonized the Interstellar Union and never will. The Prefect is currently seeking assurances to that effect from Ambassador Azetbur."*

"And are they forthcoming?"

Shras sighed, but very quickly regained his stiff-backed bearing. *"Not yet. But rest assured, Commander, that the situation is well in hand at IHQ. Nothing for you to worry about."* He smiled. Hikaru couldn't remember a time where Shras's smile hadn't come across as patronizing, and this one was no exception.

"But, sir—is the Interstellar Guard ready to face an all-out invasion? We haven't been at wa—"

"The Guard was a tiny fraction of its present size when it handled the Xindi; it can handle the Klingons just fine. Commander Sulu, you have your orders; these discussions are beyond your purview. Proceed to UGC 36A-2B at all due speed and report in immediately. Interstellar Headquarters out." Shras's image vanished from the screen to be replaced by the IU emblem.

The emblem was made up of four dots representing the four founding planets of the Interstellar Union—the one representing Andor was slightly larger, and lines connected it to the dots representing each of the three cofounders: Earth, Tellar Prime, and Coridan. It was no abstract depiction; this was how the four planets were arrayed when viewed from above the galactic plane, and Hikaru's eye wandered to the line running between Andor and Coridan. Roughly on that line was the location of 40 Eridani A II.

The planet where Demora could be dying at that very moment.

No, he mustn't allow himself to think about it.

The problem was, between Demora and the Klingon invasion, he didn't have anything positive *to* think about.

"The natives have a wide variety of designations for UGC 36A-2B, including Minshara, T'Khasi, Vulcanis, and Ti-Valka'ain." Hikaru was impressed that th'Eneg pronounced that last one without even stumbling. But then, given the man's own first name, perhaps it was child's play. "For the sake of convenience and neutrality, it is typically referenced as 'Eridani' by its contact team, because this Terran designation is the longest-established alternative." As usual, th'Eneg spoke everything in a hoarse whisper that Hikaru found vaguely unsettling.

The whole senior staff was assembled in the briefing room now, examining the images that th'Eneg was projecting onto the viewer in the table's center.

"Can't they just agree on calling it something simple—like, 'the world'?" This comment came from *Kumari*'s chief engineer, Corpek th'Rellvonda. Rarely to be found outside of engineering, he had made the trip up to the briefing room for the senior staff's mission description.

"I think you will find that the Eridanians agree on relatively few things," replied th'Eneg. "Their planet has been in a constant state of war for over ten thousand years."

"Ten *thousand*? Infinite Uzaveh." That was M'Giia—Hikaru could feel Yudrin at his right side flinching at her irreverent use of the name of the Andorian deity. "How have they even survived that long?"

"That is one of the things the contact team was attempting to ascertain," said th'Eneg.

On one of the IG's more exploration-oriented starships, such as *Enterprise,* it would have been the purview of the chief science officer to conduct such a briefing. But *Kumari* was, like most of the IG, *not* exploration-oriented, and so there was no science officer on the senior staff. Instead the duty fell to the intelligence officer. Before *Kumari,* Hikaru had never served on a starship with an intelligence officer, but he'd rapidly come to appreciate th'Eneg's keen analytical mind. Rare was the situation that th'Eneg could not find an advantage in.

But Hikaru, who'd started his career in the sciences, had to admit that at times like this, he missed having a science officer. Th'Eneg knew as much about anthropology as he did about baking Nausicaan pastries.

"What do we know about the Eridanians?" That soft-spoken voice came from Chirurgeon Jabilo M'Benga, *Kumari*'s chief medical officer.

Th'Eneg tapped some buttons on the control panel in front of his seat, displaying an image of a man in profile—or at least Hikaru assumed he was a man—with dark black hair in a bowl cut and upswept eyebrows. But by far his most distinctive feature was his left ear, which came to a sharp point at its end. He looked like nothing so much as an elf of old Earth legend.

"A fairly typical andorianoid species," said th'Eneg, "with similar deviations to the norm as humans. Only two sexes. An unusual copper-based blood."

"Copper-based." M'Benga frowned. "Like the Orions. I'm afraid I don't have much experience with it."

"Well," said Hikaru, interrupting the briefing for the first time, "it's not the Eridanians you'll be treating, is it? Casualties among the survey team are what *we're* worried about."

M'Benga nodded. "Fair enough." But he still looked anxious.

"What kind of weaponry do these guys have?" Big Lan had *his* concerns, of course.

Th'Eneg gave a hiss of frustration. "Unfortunately, that sort of data is fragmentary. Certainly, the natives have a wide variety of hand weapons." He quickly flicked through some images of things vaguely similar to swords and axes and bludgeons. "Sporadic use of projectile weapons has been observed—especially large artillery. Certain parts of the planet show evidence of a limited nuclear exchange at some point within the past two millennia, indicating that at one point they possessed atomic capability. It is uncertain if this is still the case."

Big Lan was opening his mouth to ask another question when a chime resounded throughout the room. Subcommander Yudrin answered the companel set into the table. "Yudrin here. Go ahead."

"This is Ensign s'Bysh. The Science Directorate has sent us a translation of the Eridanian demands."

Yudrin glanced at Hikaru, who nodded. "Pipe it down here," she ordered.

"Yes, ma'am."

A hissing sound emanated from the tri-monitor, then some indistinct mutterings, as if whoever was speaking was standing too far from the pickup. Hikaru could vaguely make out a second, deeper voice, and then the first one became much clearer, now obviously that of a woman. *"Foreigners, we are aware of your presence on our lands. Your spies have been found. Many of them have already been dealt with. We know not what kind of creatures you may be, but you bleed as we do, and you die as we do."*

Hikaru tried to restrain his joy—they weren't all dead! The outpost had had a staff of two dozen; Demora might be among those still alive!

"We know someone is listening to this. We demand you show yourselves, or those who still survive will be joining their friends in Sha Ka Ree. Come quickly, or more blood shall run upon the sand, more tears shall be shed by your brothers. This is—" The hissing sound suddenly increased in volume, overwhelming whatever else the woman might have said.

Grim looks were exchanged between the various officers around the table. M'Giia looked highly distressed. Yudrin's face was as impassive as always.

Big Lan was the first to speak. "It sounds like we have a hostage situation here." His natural antenna was now as erect as his artificial one—a typical Andorian sign of hostility. "We should be able to handle these primitives, easy."

"No doubt that is what the outpost personnel thought," snapped th'Eneg. "Obviously we must not underestimate these Eridanians—they are capable of operating a subspace communicator, for example."

Big Lan waved his hand dismissively. "Their opponents were a bunch of professors and clerks. We'll see how these pointy-eared freaks handle the security team of the flagship of the IG Fleet."

Th'Eneg rolled his eyes, but stayed silent.

Hikaru stood up. "Unless there's anything else, you are all dismissed. ETA to 40 Eridani A II is—" He looked at M'Giia expectantly.

"Nineteen hours," she supplied.

"Nineteen hours," he echoed. "By that time, I want a security team ready to go and prepared for all contingencies. I'll be leading the landing party, which will of course also have medical and intelligence support."

Normally, Hikaru liked to linger after a staff briefing to deal with any questions that might come up, but in this case he was the first out the door.

Demora might still be alive!

It was a slim chance, but it was all he had.

One of the few spaces on *Kumari* that took up multiple decks was the security force's training ground. It was actually three decks high, filled with obstacle courses and exercise equipment—whatever Big Lan thought was necessary for the training of his troopers.

The third level was ringed by a walkway, allowing someone to observe the entire room and what was going on in it. Which was exactly what Hikaru was doing as Lan took his troopers through a formations drill—he would call out a formation number and then time how long it took them to assume it, immediately calling out another one, and so on.

"A model of efficiency, are they not?"

He glanced to his right to see that—as the voice had indicated—th'Eneg had joined him at the railing. Of course, he had not heard the Andorian man approach. No one ever did, unless he wanted them to. It still unnerved Hikaru somewhat, but he had learned to not let it show, not if he wanted to maintain his crew's respect.

"Yes," he replied. He was indeed impressed by the speed at which Lan's troopers could move; he always had been.

"Well, some of them, at any rate." Th'Eneg sounded amused. No doubt he had identified problems in the formations that were beyond Hikaru's ability to recognize.

Not wanting to get involved in yet another Security/Intelligence dispute, Hikaru changed the subject. "That was a good briefing, Lieutenant."

Th'Eneg's antennae shrugged. "Compiling a report on the activities of a group of prewarp primitives is child's play compared to what I normally do," he said. "I was glad of the change of pace. A bit of light work, for once."

"Then you won't be disappointed to leave the Klingon border?" asked Hikaru.

"Not strictly speaking. I am only disappointed that *Atlirith* was selected to take our position. I hope Interstellar Headquarters had not grown too accustomed to high-quality analyses and reports."

Hikaru snorted. "Modest as ever, Lieutenant."

"If their intelligence officer was the best in the Fleet, would not *Atlirith* have been posted to the border to begin with?"

Hikaru had to admit that the man had a point. It wasn't just any ship you sent on a years-long mission to spy on the Klingons. Hikaru liked to think, though, that it was also a reflection on the capabilities of *Kumari*'s commander as well.

A series of footsteps coming from the left caused Hikaru to look up. It was M'Benga. "Chirurgeon," said Hikaru as the dark-skinned human settled in next to him. "What brings you down here?" He had known better than to ask th'Eneg such a direct question, but the chief medical officer would actually answer if asked.

"I just like to watch," replied M'Benga, gesturing at the still-shifting group of security troopers. "It's quite beautiful, in its own way."

Hikaru frowned. "Do you think so? They're military formations and maneuvers; they're unfortunately necessary, not beautiful."

"Oh, definitely unfortunate," said M'Benga. "Hopefully even

Lan wouldn't disagree with that. But my own skills are no less an unfortunate necessity—a world where a ship's surgeon never had to repair a blaster wound, never had to administer treatment for Haslev-Rahn disease, would be a much preferable one to this. Yet that doesn't make medical skill any less admirable."

"I hadn't ever thought of it like that," said Hikaru. But it made sense. The Interstellar Guard never lacked form to go along with its function. Everything it did not only worked well, but looked good. The *flabbjellah*—simultaneously a deadly weapon and a beautiful musical instrument—was perhaps the pinnacle of this idea. Perhaps security forces could still be beautiful.

Hikaru had found it hard to adjust to that mode of thinking. He was still more a scientist than anything else in many ways, and the antipathy between scientists and the military was much older and ran much deeper than the one between Intelligence and Security. He'd joined the Interstellar Guard to see the wonders of space, not to combat alien threats.

It bothered him that for *Kumari,* the most advanced ship in the Fleet, a mission to chart gaseous anomalies was nothing more than a cover story. Back during his days on *Enterprise,* that would have been the *real* mission. Even if there was something beautiful in the way that Lan's troopers moved from formation to formation with forthright efficiency, he could not help thinking that there was more beauty in the irregular pulses of a quasar, in the emissions of a dark matter nebula, in a sudden conglomeration of *n*-dimensional spectral rays.

Today, though, he would take the military force of Big Lan and his security troopers, beautiful or not. Demora needed it. *He* needed it.

Hikaru turned to his right to ask th'Eneg his opinion on the beauty of combat formations, only to find that the intelligence officer was gone. He'd departed just as suddenly as he'd come, and just as mysteriously.

He did, however, see Subcommander Phelana Yudrin coming

straight for him. Which meant it was time to get out of here. "I'll see you later, Jabilo." M'Benga nodded in acknowledgment, still captivated by the drills unfolding below.

Hikaru made his escape. Perhaps not as stealthily as th'Eneg had, but no less effectively.

It took over a day, but Yudrin finally caught up with him.

Ever since the briefing, Hikaru had scrupulously avoided situations where he'd be alone with her. Unfortunately, she knew him too well.

Before he went to bed each night, Hikaru would go out to the end of one of *Kumari*'s two "wings." These branched off from the narrow body of the ship's main hull, holding weapons and sensor pods best kept away from the main body of the *Excelsior*-class ship. At the very tip of each wing, however, was an observation pod that allowed a viewer to gaze at both the sweep of space and *Kumari* herself.

Hikaru liked to spend a few moments counting his blessings and pushing his burdens to the side for the moment. Sometimes, only half in jest, he would thank the Great Bird of the Galaxy for the former and ask It for strength in dealing with the latter.

He had a lot of strength to ask for today. *Kumari* was about ten hours away from Eridani. So far there hadn't been any further signals from the outpost. He was hoping that no news was good news.

Being out here among the stars made him think of simpler times—when he'd been an astrophysicist on the old *Enterprise* under Commander Kirk. Certainly, the ship had had its share of close calls, but rarely had Hikaru had to worry about them. Unfortunately, the advancement opportunities for a science officer in the Interstellar Guard were limited, and after the mission had ended, he'd undergone retraining as a flight officer. From that point on, he'd carried a lot more responsibility.

But for a few moments, sitting here amidst the stars, all that melted away. The Klingon invasion, dealing with General Shras, everything.

Everything except for Demora. There was no way he could put her out of his mind.

His thoughts were interrupted by the hatch to the observation pod swinging open. Phelana Yudrin stood in the hatchway, hands clasped behind her back. Despite the fact that at sixty, she was a good five Earth years older than Hikaru, the black IG uniform looked much better on her than it ever had on him; he was beginning to show a bit of a paunch. She gave him a curt nod. "Commander."

He nodded back. "Subcommander." He looked out at the stars, which were slowly drifting by as *Kumari* flew through IU space at maximum warp. Slowly from a cosmic standpoint, of course—in reality they were going by at thousands of times the speed of light. "Nice night, isn't it?"

Yudrin stepped into the pod, the hatch automatically swinging shut behind her. She seated herself on the bench across from Hikaru. "Everyone in space says that line like it's original," she said. "It's not."

"It's not original, or it's not a nice night?"

A half-smile briefly flitted across her face. "Both. It's a rotten line, and it's a rotten night."

"I take your point," said Hikaru. "We seem to have exchanged one misery for another."

She nodded. "At least a hostage scenario is something we can deal with—unlike an invasion. Well, most of us can deal with it."

"What's that supposed to mean?" Hikaru did his best to make the question sound genuine. He might have been trapped, but he didn't intend to give up yet.

"It didn't take a genius to figure out you had a personal stake in this," said Yudrin. "Setting course for 36A *before* we received our orders? Secure communications with Brigadier Gav and General Lamia?"

"So?" he asked. "I daresay many things go on that are outside of your purview as a lowly executive officer."

"I briefly contemplated that," she said, "but number seven on the list of duties of an executive officer is 'be an inquisitive bastard,' so I had th'Eneg give me the outpost's personnel roster."

"Ah" was all Hikaru would say.

"And then I spent the next day trying to get you alone."

"I'm impressed," said Hikaru. "I didn't think anyone knew I spent time out here."

"Oh, I knew, Commander. I've always known."

"Where is 'knowing the whereabouts of your commander' on your list of duties?"

"Number two." She closed her eyes and recited from memory. "Ensign Demora Sulu. Graduated from the Interstellar Institute five months ago. First assignment: commander of the security detail of the anthropological outpost on 36A-2B."

"Someone on the outpost staff has the *same name* as me? What a coincidence."

Yudrin opened her eyes. "You never were very good at sarcasm, sir." She closed them again. "Father: Hikaru Sulu, commander, *I.U.E.S. Kumari II,* AAN-2000. Mother: Susan Sulu, lieutenant. Last post: San Francisco Interstellar Observatory. Sixteen years deceased."

Hikaru smiled, but it was a smile bereft of genuine feeling. "Yes, you got me. What are you going to do?"

"Does General Shras know?"

"Do you think he'd have sent *Kumari* on this mission if he did?"

"Not very likely," she said. "I suppose you worked your charm on Major General Lamia?"

"Something like that. Do I need to work it on you?"

She shook her head. "You're not my type, Commander. Too tiny."

"Speaking of which, how are things working out with Chirurgeon V'Larr?"

"Let's not get sidetracked into my personal life."

Hikaru amazed himself by actually letting off a small chuckle. "That bad, huh? The Phelana Yudrin I know normally can't hold herself back from describing her current romantic relationship . . . in every detail." In fact, he'd found out about her interest in the Caitian doctor before she'd even told V'Larr himself.

"Let's just say that dating a cat is every bit as aggravating as you'd imagine." She sighed and rubbed her forehead. "But re-gardless—we're letting the point escape us. You are involved in this mission on a personal level. And *that* is going to affect your command judgment."

"But you understand why I had to go."

She nodded. "I cannot have offspring. But if one of my sib-lings was in such danger, you can rest assured that I would be doing everything I could to protect them." She paused for a mo-ment, giving Hikaru quite a scrutinizing stare. "However, I am not the commanding officer of a starship. If I were to endanger the mission or the crew, my commanding officer could overrule me. You have no such safety net."

"Then can I trust my executive officer to give me one?" Inside, he was thinking as hard as he could, *hoping* as hard as he could. He didn't think he believed in the Great Bird of the Galaxy, not really, but he was praying to It and all the other deities he could think of. If Yudrin objected, it would be child's play to get *Kumari* called off the mission and another ship sent in its place. They weren't exactly the only ship in the quadrant.

But he didn't trust anyone else to bring his daughter home.

"If you swear that when I tell you that you've made a mistake, you let me take control of the situation."

Anything to get his daughter back. "That's a lot of authority."

"Commander, you abrogated your right to that authority the moment you manipulated a member of the General Staff." Her tone was sharp, but her black eyes didn't seem so unfriendly.

"Agreed, then." He breathed a sigh of relief. That was another obstacle overcome.

Yudrin switched benches to sit next to him, placing a hand on his shoulder. "Don't worry, Commander. *Kumari* is the best ship in the Fleet. We'll get your daughter back."

He looked at her and offered his best smile, which wasn't much at the moment. "I knew you'd come round. A warrior race may have—"

Abruptly, Yudrin withdrew her hand and stood up. "Commander, if you *ever* trot out Commander Thelin's old saw, so help me, I will go call General Shras *right now*."

"I thought that was a traditional Andorian saying."

Yudrin nodded—somewhat frantically, Hikaru thought. "Oh, it is. It is. And so is 'A good cook doesn't mix his *xixu* with his *hari*,' but you don't hear me saying that every fifteen minutes either. It's just as original, and just as annoying."

"I'll keep that in mind," he said.

"You'd do well to," she said. She stepped up to the hatch, which opened automatically. "Enjoy the night, Commander."

And with that, Hikaru Sulu was once again alone with the moving stars.

I'm coming for you, Demora. Don't worry.

Hikaru was on a rare leave from Enterprise. Rather than sit at home the whole time, they'd elected to go on a family trip, camping in Rocky Mountain National Park.

Hikaru had invited his great-grandfather Tetsuo along, since the old man was always complaining about never seeing his family. It was nonsense, of course; he just liked to complain. This meant they couldn't do anything too intense, but bringing Demora along pretty much guaranteed that already.

They took the aircar as far in as it was allowed, and then hiked the rest of the way, stopping frequently for Tetsuo. After a little while, Demora declared that she was tired of walking and she absolutely was not going to walk any further no matter what. It turned out to be quite true, so Susan carried Demora the rest of the way.

Hikaru tried to show Demora how to set up a tent, but she didn't seem all that interested. Which was probably for the best, as it had been a long time, and Hikaru wasn't very good at it. She seemed more interested in playing with her great-great-grandfather—or, more accurately, playing in front of him while he watched and laughed.

Susan, who had been setting up their food supplies, came over to see how he was getting on. "I'm glad you're back," she said, giving him a hug.

He watched his daughter and his great-grandfather ramble in the grass, Bear Lake shimmering in the background.

MINSHARA: TWO

It all happened in a matter of seconds. The man, his knife raised, tried to slash at her, but she used a *fivri* move that her muscles had memorized long ago. Running on automatic, she kicked and boxed, and she barely even noticed the burning sensation on her left forearm where the blade had cut straight through her uniform undershirt to touch her skin.

The murder of Doctor Grayson had transported Demora to another level altogether, and the native didn't stand a chance.

Stopping was the hard part, and it took her a while before she ceased pummeling the man's body with well-placed punches. She reined in her emotions as much as possible, letting Guard training take over; she knelt to check his pulse. There was one, leaving her with the decision about what to do now. According to regulations, she ought to incapacitate—not kill—if possible.

The longer she thought, the more her sense of duty prevailed, and eventually she decided to let the man live—but not without giving him a reason to regret attacking the outpost.

It was a nonstandard way of incapacitating an enemy, she had to admit, but it did the job. Gripping his ankles, she felt around for anything that resembled an Achilles tendon, and when she found something, she took the jade knife and cut into the heel. The tendons separated with a loud snap. When he woke up, he wouldn't be able to walk.

That done, she allowed herself some time to think. So far, she had only seen one native. Where were the other attackers? More important, were there other surviving members of the outpost staff? If so, where were they?

So many questions, and she had no answers to any of them. She did know, however, that she needed to get out of here, and fast—but this place looked like a maze of corridors and chambers, and without a map she would likely never see daylight again.

Calm down. She realized that she was still suffering from shock, and the double adrenaline rush, from witnessing a murder and then attacking the murderer, didn't exactly help. *Think about what you've been taught. You'll find the way out of this.*

If there was an ideal time for believing in herself, this was it, but she didn't, not really. It threatened to overwhelm her: the dreadful experiences of the past day, the exhaustion, the hunger and thirst, the pain, and her slight claustrophobia.

In any case she couldn't afford to just stand around.

She stuffed the knife into her belt. It must've been a ceremonial weapon, Demora judged, because nobody they'd observed on Eridani used stone knives for actual combat. If so, then there was more to Grayson's death than she'd first thought. Candle Guy had wanted to make a statement, even if he'd been the only one who had been able to understand it.

How can I be alive when Grayson is dead? It was my duty to die for her, wasn't it? The guilt she felt was a predictable reaction given the circumstances, but she couldn't do anything about it. Being trained to deal with these situations didn't stop her from having questions without answers.

She needed to focus on something else, so she began to undo the fastenings of the dark brown desert cloak Candle Guy was wearing. It seemed to her that she'd be less conspicuous if she wore native clothing, at least from a distance.

The cloak was woven, a coarse fabric that gave her the shivers just touching it. She'd always been somewhat sensitive to such natural materials, and contact with them gave her gooseflesh. The IU had long since abandoned the use of nonsynthetics; even her usual leather-like uniform had never been part of an animal.

The fastenings were curious; two hairy pieces of fabric consisting of tiny loops and hooks lay against each other, but they came apart easily with a ripping sound when she pulled. She yanked the cloak out from under the unconscious man and put it around herself. That left one important thing to do: search for more weapons. Fighters as effective as these natives couldn't be armed exclusively with ceremonial blades.

She patted the body down from head to toe, and halfway down she found something: a projectile weapon, from the look of it. Similar in appearance to a standard CE62 flechette, it seemed deadly enough. Demora spent a precious minute examining it closely before she was satisfied that she'd be able to fire it. It certainly helped that there were pretty few alternatives to standard small arms design throughout the galaxy.

Satisfied that she'd gotten everything she could—and wasted enough time—she scooped up the candle from its stool, said a silent farewell to Doctor Grayson, and set out in a jog along the hallway they'd come just minutes before. It irked her to leave Grayson's body lying there, but she didn't have the time to do anything else.

She turned left at the end of the hallway, opposite the way she and Candle Guy had come from. It was a long tunnel that had numerous doorways, usually closed, set into its walls. At the end of the tunnel, she was faced with a decision to go right or left. She took a look at the candle, to see if it flickered even if she wasn't walking. When she held it to the left, it promptly did.

Aware that she might be walking into a trap, she picked the left hallway. It was narrower than the others she'd seen, and its end presented her with a problem: there was a metal door, and it was closed. There was no button or handle.

Long moments of frantic search yielded nothing. Angrily, she kicked the door, realizing immediately that had been unwise: now her foot hurt, *and* the impact made a loud, resonating clang.

She had decided to turn around when she heard the sound of metal scraping on metal. The door was opening, sliding back into one side of the hallway.

Not thinking twice, Demora hurried along. She was faced with four more of those doors, but she became better at forcing them open with a well-placed kick every time, convinced now that this was the intended way of opening them, for whatever reason.

Eventually, she found herself in a large, cavernous room, filled with military paraphernalia, such as things that looked like mortars and other forms of artillery, as well as a number of tall bipedal mechanical walkers. A few llama-like creatures were tethered in a corner.

At the far end of the cavern, she spotted another door. Walking toward it, she gripped the handle of the flechette gun beneath her cloak and let her index finger rest close to the trigger.

"Darakah!" someone shouted and Demora flinched involuntarily. So, she'd been discovered, had she? Looking around to see where the call had come from, she saw another native standing at the aft end of a walker, holding tools of some kind. He was waving at her, but his gestures didn't seem all that hostile. Torn between options—walking on and approaching him—she remained on the spot, perhaps a moment too long, before she turned and walked briskly toward the man. Once she was close enough, she drew the gun out from under the cloak, pointed it at the mechanic and said, even though she knew he wouldn't understand, "Quiet. Do as I say, and you won't be harmed. Now get over there." She motioned with the gun, a language universally understood.

The mechanic stared at her blankly, but after a few moments he did what she wanted. Demora directed him toward the booth-like structure near the door—presumably a tool shed of some kind—her gun pressed into his back. He didn't try anything, even though she'd half-expected more mind-tricks. Perhaps not every native had the ability?

Or maybe he was just waiting. After all, she had a gun in her hand, and he couldn't know that she hadn't had even an hour's training with it.

They were almost at the shed when she got her answer. Without warning, he stopped and turned toward her.

"Hey!" she said. "Get moving, Mister."

Instead of complying, he lunged at her, reaching for the hand holding the flechette, but she pulled it back, just out of his reach. A quick step backward caused her to stumble, and she fell down hard.

The mechanic didn't waste any time. In a blur he was over her, making as if to grab her and hold her down. She pointed the flechette at him. He continued as if she wasn't holding anything at all, coming even closer than before.

Without warning, the flechette gun discharged. Demora hadn't known that she was pressing the trigger. It wasn't a loud sound, but it echoed around the vehicle hangar. The force of the impact threw the native backward, freeing her.

A bit shaky, she got up and carefully walked over to inspect the wound she had caused him. The dart from the gun had torn a small hole in his abdomen, from which green blood was flowing at a high rate. Aware that though such a wound would be fatal to a human or Andorian, it very well might be nothing to an Eridanian, she stood just outside his reach and waited.

It would have been common sense to shoot him again and get it over with, but her training and her own sense of right and wrong stopped her. She held the gun pointed at the man's chest, watching it rise and fall with each pained breath. His eyes were closed, but he was still alive.

And he was still a threat.

Any moment now hordes of angry telepaths might be flooding

into the hangar in search of the alien who'd attacked one of their number. However, if she left him, the mechanic might be able to sound an alarm.

She couldn't afford to be squeamish. She needed to move, and every second she spent deliberating brought her potential pursuers closer. Sighing, she took aim and shot the mechanic in his left knee. It left him alive, but unable to move anywhere—the best option.

Trying in vain to ignore his cries of agony, she made for the large doors that presumably opened directly onto the rocky desert outside. But how did these open? She doubted it was by kicking.

To the left of the vehicle doors, she spotted a black metal box mounted on the wall. It was closed, but flipped open easily. Inside, she found just what she'd expected: a set of levers arranged in a vertical column that could only have been designed for one use. Without wasting time second-guessing herself she tried them all, one after the other.

The third one did the trick. Hidden gears began to turn, the sounds they made the only indication of their existence. After a while the heavy door, consisting of rust-colored segments, rose slowly, and Demora slipped under as soon as it was high enough.

As she'd hoped, it led outside, and she had never been so glad to stand in such an arid, dusty place. From what she could tell, this was the mountain range the natives called L-langon. The observation post had been set into the L-langon foothills, where the mountains gave way to the deadly and desolate Forge, but she was likely a long way from there.

Right now the only important thing was to get as much distance between her and this facility as possible.

Ignoring her sore ankle as best she could, she broke into a run. This proved difficult with the cloak, but she didn't want to part with it just yet, given it was her only protection from the intense Eridanian sun.

When she'd turned around a cluster of large boulders, she

contemplated her direction. The easiest way was to continue along the foot of the mountain that housed the compound, but as she looked up the slope, it seemed to her that the craggy terrain was an ideal hiding place.

Yet where was she running to? Even if she could find the outpost, she couldn't take on the natives who now occupied it. All she could do was hope that the unannounced end to the scientists' stream of reports rang some alarm bells back home and somebody—preferably an experienced commander with a ship full of elite troopers—got sent to investigate. Until then, she had to hold out and survive.

That last bit would be difficult, however, if she didn't manage to find food and water. The slopes of the mountains were not entirely bare; some hardy shrubs and succulents could be seen here and there, indicating that there must be some underground water. In her mind, Demora already saw herself digging holes with the stone knife as her only tool.

She climbed quickly, intent on making the most of her head start. It was hard going, with no actual path to ease her ascent. Stumbling more than once, each time cursing her ill-suited boots, within half an hour she reached an altitude that enabled her to turn around and take in the panorama. Under different circumstances, she might have actually enjoyed it. The sight of large craters dotted her view, evidence of the violent wars that had been fought here for millennia between ever-shifting factions of an aggressive people that made Andorians and Klingons look like boy scouts.

In the distance, hidden behind a shimmering veil of hot air, she thought she'd made out something resembling an aqueduct. The distant stone pillars weren't all intact; many of them had collapsed, leaving huge gaps in the remarkable structure. It was impressive, but she couldn't affort to waste time on sightseeing; she had to keep moving—put as much distance between her and the natives as possible.

Within an hour she realized she'd been overtaxing herself.

She was sweating profusely, and breathing became more difficult with each step, thanks to Eri's low-oxygen atmosphere.

Enough, she realized. *You're going to kill yourself if you don't stop right now.* Time to take a break and sit down for a while. She wanted a spot in the shade and out of the line of sight of possible pursuers. Some intense searching under the glaring afternoon sun located a group of large boulders that were placed just far enough apart for Demora to pass among them. They were also tall enough to shield her from daylight, so she hurried over and took shelter, keeping a close eye on the way she'd come, assuming her pursuers would follow the same path.

A strange noise distracted her. It was a sound unlike anything she'd heard before . . . except for those school trips to the zoo in Laikan. She listened intently, hoping she'd imagined it.

When she heard it again, it became clear this was the real deal. Tornellen Dax, the animal expert among the team, had once told her about the native predators, and the biology lesson had contained far too many warnings for her taste. There was almost no large animal on Eri that wasn't a danger to both natives and offworlders.

Demora was about to reach inside her cloak to grab her knife when she saw that she was already holding it. Filled with worry about her obvious lack of concentration, she quickly took the flechette in her other hand and pressed her back against the rust-red boulder behind her. It was hard to determine the noise's origin from in here, but she didn't want to leave her secure position.

It was an almost regular sound that had a wheezing quality to it. Distance was just as hard to judge as direction, but if she had to guess, she'd say it was too goddamn close.

Not having another choice, she opted for a distraction. She put the knife back inside her cloak, and with her free hand, she grabbed a smallish rock near her feet and threw it in a large arc down the side of the mountain. Its impact was immediately followed by movement to Demora's right, as a large creature decided to investigate.

Carefully, Demora peered around the boulder, and what she saw did not fill her with confidence. The animal she had momentarily lured away from her position was at least as large as the tigers in Laikan Zoo. It had a glossy fur that changed between hues of yellow and green, depending on how the sunlight hit it. The animal was sniffing the air, turning its head as it did so. The longer Demora stared at it, the more it became obvious that the thrown stone hadn't served its purpose. If anything, it had given the animal a whiff of her scent. It was only a matter of seconds before it would be on her trail.

Better to be on the offensive, then.

Giving up any pretense of safety, she got on her feet and walked around the boulder's cracked curve as silently as she could. She raised the flechette and aimed it at the still sniffing creature, knowing full well that she wouldn't be a good shot with the unfamiliar weapon. The animal was farther away than the mechanic had been, and it was moving.

Piece of cake.

Before she fired, she took the knife back out, just in case she missed.

The animal was still probing the air, but it had turned a little, and was now about to look in her direction. Pointing the gun at its head, Demora waited until it stopped moving. All it took was a tiny contraction of her index finger, and immediately a dart left the barrel of her gun.

It did not get the creature, but it did get something else: its attention. She could have done without that.

Advancing on silent paws, the yellow-green Eridanian tiger came to investigate what had just passed over its head. Then it stopped, moving not a muscle, and Demora knew that it had spotted her. She retreated back between the boulders, trying to find a passage that was just narrow enough for her to pass through, but not the animal.

She found none. Gathering the last remnants of strength, she started a desperate run up the mountainside, knowing full well that the tiger would follow her.

After only a few meters, she threw herself down, turning around as she did so—just in time to see the animal charge at her. Raising the flechette with both hands, she kept firing until no more darts came forth. Not wanting to witness what would happen next, she closed her eyes.

When no attack followed, she dared open them again, but she saw the animal was still on its feet. It had stopped, however, and was moving on unsteady paws that she now saw were armed with long, dark claws. Bright green blood was coming from a number of small puncture wounds, indicators that she had actually hit her target.

It staggered toward her, baring its teeth, sharp-edged and shark-like, and then its legs buckled and it collapsed—on top of her.

Its weight was considerable, and she felt it in every bone in her body. It was still alive—she felt its ribcage expand with every breath—but only barely so. She pushed against the body with all her strength, to lift it up and roll it to one side. Eventually she succeeded, but not without incurring pain and more injuries; as it slid off, the tiger's front paw grazed her right shoulder, slicing through the cloak and her undershirt as if they weren't even there, breaking her skin.

She hoped she didn't get an infection out of this, not after she'd beat the odds yet again. It would be somewhat anticlimactic to die of blood poisoning after having survived armed natives and a ferocious predator.

She remained on her back a few moments longer, taking deep breaths. It was a relief that she didn't feel any pain—at least, no *new* pain.

When she got back on her feet, she was still a bit wobbly, but confident she'd get back into form in short order. She threw away the now-useless flechette gun and resumed her flight up the slope, but not before giving the animal one last look. Despite what had happened, she could only marvel at its otherworldly beauty, the green skin underneath the similarly colored fur, and the graceful body, lithe and muscular, bred for the hunt.

She left the dying Eridanian tiger behind, her attention now focused ahead, hoping that these animals did not live in packs. If she was lucky, she might just have a chance at surviving this.

Of course, that still meant she'd have to continue to evade capture by the fanatics that had attacked the outpost.

She'd been hiking upward for another hour when thirst slowly but surely became her primary concern. Her lips were parched, and her head had already begun to throb painfully. Not only did she not have any water, but she also had no clue as to where she might find any.

To make matters worse, a strange sensation was spreading from her right shoulder, into her arm and down the side. The tiger's claws had to be responsible. Dread filled her when she followed that line of thought. Not enough time had passed for an infection, which left only one conclusion: poison.

There was no telling how quickly or strongly it would affect her. Was it lethal? Did it only paralyze? What were its effects on non-Eridanian species?

She was still pondering those questions when her legs gave in, and she crumpled in a heap, unable even to brace herself for the fall. Thankfully, she had lost consciousness before her head hit the dusty ground.

She came to him the night before the project was due, of course.

"How long have you had to work on this?" he asked, doing his best paternally stern voice.

"Two weeks," she said.

"So why are you coming to me now?"

She shrugged. "My group didn't decide what it wanted to do until today."

"Ah, so it's a group project," he said. "What did they decide to do?"

"They decided that I would make it."

He took her down to the small workshop in their basement. He was usually busy with his work at the Interstellar Institute and the Great Experiment, but he still managed to get down here from time to time. "Well, here's everything I have. Get to work." He made like he was leaving.

"Dad!" The exclamation was already so loud at her mere twelve years. How much worse would it be as a teenager?

"What is it, dear?" He sounded as oblivious as possible.

"Aren't you going to help me?"

"You said that your group decided that you would do it. Hop to it."

"Well, I decided that you would help me." How much worse would her sarcasm be?

He smiled at last. "I'll help you get started. It can't be too hard to make."

He was downstairs until well past midnight.

KUMARI: THREE

"Coming up on the 40 Eridani system."

Hikaru switched off his data slate. The first inklings of *Kumari*'s discovery had slipped their way into the newsfeeds. There wasn't much worry yet, but it was plainly about to begin. He just hoped that *Atlirith* and the rest of the IG could handle the problem for now. It made him feel awful to abandon the border, but he didn't have a choice. "Thank you, Lieutenant M'Giia."

Hikaru watched the main viewer as the yellow dot in the center rapidly expanded into a small disk; it suddenly stopped growing as *Kumari* decelerated from warp with a gentle shudder. 40 Eridani A was a little smaller and cooler than Earth's sun, but well within the typical range for a life-bearing star system.

"Plotting orbit for 40 Eridani A-II," reported M'Giia. As *Kumari* turned, the sun slipped out of view to be replaced by a dusky red planet, which quickly grew to fill most of the viewer. "Orbit achieved."

Yudrin had been standing behind M'Giia, keeping an eye on the helm station's star plot. Now she moved to the back of the bridge, where Ensign s'Bysh was manning the sensor controls. "Begin full intensive scans of the planet," Yudrin ordered the Orion woman. "Locate the observation post."

S'Bysh nodded, her fingers moving quickly across the control boards. Hikaru just waited quietly, knowing that Yudrin would have it well in hand.

It was killing him. He wanted to charge down to the transporter room *now*, Big Lan ch'Satheddet and a team of his best troopers behind him, and get his daughter back. But blindly charging into a situation wouldn't help save Demora. He had to remember that.

"I have the outpost," reported s'Bysh.

"On screen," ordered Yudrin.

The view of Eridani on the main viewer was replaced by a false-color topographical map, as imaged by *Kumari*'s various sensor packages. A blinking blue blip at the foothills of a mountain range (labeled "L-langon Mountains") indicated the location of the observation post, evidently where the mountains gave way to a massive plain.

"Low-level energy signal from the outpost," said s'Bysh. A waveform appeared on the main viewer indicating the makeup of the energy.

"That's the profile of a standard PXN fusion reactor," said Corpek th'Rellvonda. Yudrin had demanded his presence on the command deck for this moment, and the chief engineer had reluctantly complied. "Seems to be functioning normally."

That makes sense, thought Hikaru. While on their way here, they'd picked up another transmission from the outpost—the same Eridanian woman's voice giving much the same demands—and for the subspace transmitter to still be functioning, the outpost had to be in somewhat good working order, especially its power systems.

"Good," said Big Lan, who was poring over the data coming into his station as well. "Last thing we need is a bunch of primitives setting off a nuclear explosion."

"It looks like they've already done that," said Yudrin, leaning over s'Bysh to press some buttons on her panel. A diagram of a new energy signal appeared. "There are over twenty former impact sites spread over that entire plain. Evidence of a long nuclear winter in the distant past, with remaining low-level electromagnetic radiation across the region. Any people beaming down will have to be inoculated."

S'Bysh muttered something under her breath that Hikaru couldn't quite make out, but from her vehemence he suspected it was one of the more potent Orion swear words. "The radiation is interfering with our sensor capabilities within the region."

Yudrin turned to face Hikaru. "Indeed, all electronic and duo-tronic devices will have limited operating capacity while on the surface."

"The outpost had countermeasures, though, right?" asked Big Lan, obviously uneasy at the thought that his blaster might not function.

"According to Lieutenant th'Eneg's data, the external surface of the outpost should function as a Faraday cage to neutralize the effects of the radiation," said Yudrin.

"Of course," grumbled Big Lan, "it'll have been damaged in the attack."

Hikaru had waited long enough. "Any lifesigns?"

Yudrin shot him a meaningful glance, but he did his best to ignore it.

"Still working on that, sir," said s'Bysh. "The interference is pretty intense."

Hikaru waited and hoped.

Before long, they had identified several lifesigns *around* the outpost, but none within it. Unfortunately, they were unable to determine whether the lifesigns belonged to the outpost crew or to the Eridanian natives. Sporadic lifesigns dotted the foothills of the the L-langons, but they were all either Eridanian or indeterminate.

Kumari's transporters possessed sufficient power to punch through the interference, but for extra safety, th'Rellvonda suggested locking on to the outpost's own transporter units, which would give the signal a boost on the receiving end.

Having learned everything that it was possible to learn from orbit, Hikaru ordered Big Lan to prepare a landing party while he reported in to IHQ from *Kumari*'s briefing room.

To his surprise, his call was taken by General Shras. Why a situation like this repeatedly required the attention of a member of the General Staff escaped him, but it was making him wary. There had to be more going on here than a simple hostage situation—even Eridani's location in the Klingon invasion corridor didn't account for this.

"What's the situation?" Shras demanded without any preamble. His blue skin was paler than usual—Hikaru suspected that, like himself, the general hadn't been getting much sleep recently.

Hikaru sketched out what *Kumari* had been able to discover since settling into orbit. "I'm preparing to lead a team down to the outpost to ascertain the situation down there."

Shras nodded. *"If you make any contact with the natives, find out what they want and report in to me immediately."*

"Surely, General, we know what they want?" asked Hikaru. "They want their world rid of the invading offworlders." Offworlders that they were willing to kill to get rid of. How could the Science Directorate have been so foolish as to send a team into a situation like *that*?

"That very well may be the case, Commander. But in light of the Klingon situation, there may be other issues at stake." Shras said that with a sneer, as though Hikaru should somehow be aware of the facts that Shras was obviously holding back.

He decided to risk poking the dragon. "'Klingon situation,' sir? I thought you said there was nothing to worry about."

"There won't be if you do your job right!" Shras snapped. *"Examine the situation on the surface and report back in. Interstellar Headquarters out."*

Hikaru frowned at the IU emblem that had replaced the general's image on the tri-monitor. Obviously Shras was under a lot of stress from this Klingon situation—and just as obviously what was happening on Eridani somehow played into that.

But what could connect the two situations, Hikaru had no idea. And he didn't like being in the dark, especially where Demora was concerned.

But he couldn't exactly afford to sit around in orbit trying to solve the puzzle while Great-Bird-knew-what was happening to her on the surface. It was time to head down.

The transporter beam released Hikaru into darkness.

Barely a moment had passed before the room he'd beamed into was suddenly illuminated by a number of blobs of light—Lan ch'Satheddet and his security troopers had switched on the lamps mounted on their blasters. Of course, *they* didn't need them quite so much as Hikaru did, given that as Andorians, their vision extended into the infrared. But Hikaru appreciated it.

Belatedly, Hikaru fished his own handlamp off his equipment belt and flicked it on. The transporter room was located deep within the outpost, with no sources of natural illumination. He waved the light around, trying to avoid shining it into the eyes of Big Lan's three troopers as they fanned out around the perimeter of the room.

He stepped down off the transporter dais, crossing the room to take a look at the giant console that was its only other feature. Lieutenant th'Eneg was already there, looking over its inoperative controls. "The controls have been shut down," said the intelligence officer, his whisper of a voice more ominous than normal in the deserted room.

"Emergency cut-out?" asked Hikaru.

"Probably," said th'Eneg, pointing at an indicator light, which was steadily blinking on and off in blue—the only sign of activity on the panel. "Passive receive mode is still operative."

"Lucky for us." Hikaru glanced up—Jabilo M'Benga was standing next to the console, holding his handscanner.

"What is it, Chirurgeon?" M'Benga was the only other non-Andorian on *Kumari*'s senior staff, having done his internship in an Andorian ward. Hikaru had frequently found himself going to the man for advice in the early days of his command, struggling to come to terms with the different cultural norms. Not even a lifetime's service in the IG could prepare you for everything.

"Levels of electromagnetic radiation are somewhat high— looks like the outpost's outer hull was breached. Without the boost on the receiving end, there was a faint chance some of us could have ended up slightly scrambled."

Hikaru winced. When he had been flight controller on the *Enterprise I,* there'd been a particularly nasty transporter accident during the encounter with V'ger that had claimed the lives of a couple crewmembers, including the ship's chirurgeon, a man named McCoy. He couldn't think of many worse ways to go. "Obviously it's not too bad, though," said Hikaru, gesturing toward M'Benga's handscanner, which was chirping away—the only sound in the silent room other than the footsteps of Lan's troopers.

M'Benga nodded. "Most of our equipment should be fine. You might want to ask Lieutenant ch'Satheddet to check on the blasters, though."

Th'Eneg was flipping switches on the transporter console, and it was slowly humming back to life. "We know whatever happened to them, they had enough time for someone to activate emergency cut-out protocols." He pointed at a screen that was displaying the transporter's activity log; Hikaru took a look and saw that the unit had been shut off for the past three days.

Heavy footsteps caused Hikaru to look up and see Big Lan approaching their little group. "That's right," the security chief said. "The door's been flash-sealed shut."

"Emergency cut-out?" asked M'Benga, looking expectantly at the other three men.

Hikaru nodded at th'Eneg, who obliged. "All IU anthropological outposts have an emergency system designed to seal off sensitive technology in case of a breach," he said, "to prevent it from falling in the hands of a primitive culture. So, here we find that the door to the transporter room is sealed and the controls shut themselves off."

"But you just turned them back on," objected M'Benga. "Hardly secure."

"Had I attempted to access the console without first entering the appropriate alphanumeric code, the circuits would have fused themselves into an irreparable mess." The intelligence officer's voice showed his displeasure at having to explain what he saw as a basic concept, but if M'Benga picked up on it, he didn't show.

"We're going to shoot through the door, sir," said Big Lan. "It'll give us a chance to see how the blasters function down here, too."

Hikaru nodded his assent, and the security chief summoned his troopers with a quick hand gesture. Some hushed orders passed between them, and the three troopers took positions in front of the door, blue beams from their blasters causing the duritanium door to slowly take on an orange glow.

"If the outpost's subspace communications are still functioning," said Hikaru, "that means either the cut-out protocol was interrupted or the Eridanians managed to get the code from the base personnel."

"I have already considered both of those possibilities," said th'Eneg as he continued to inspect the console, not looking up at his commander. "I do not consider either of them particularly favorable." His focus shifted continuously between two of the console's screens.

Hikaru turned his attention back to M'Benga; obviously th'Eneg wanted to be left to his job. "Any lifesigns?"

M'Benga shook his head. "There's no one within this outpost except for us," he said. "Still picking up some life forms outside of it—probably Eridanian, but it's hard to tell." He slapped the side of his handscanner in frustration. "There may be some organic residue on the next level up."

"That is the outpost's control room," said th'Eneg without looking up.

"Bodies?" asked Hikaru, keeping a quaver from slipping into in his voice.

M'Benga nodded. "Probably."

Hikaru rejoined Big Lan, who was watching his troopers at work. There was now a sizeable hole in the middle of the door, which was rapidly becoming wider. "How's it going?" asked Hikaru.

"Slowly."

Hikaru had to look up quite a ways to make eye contact with the man. He'd always been somewhat sensitive about his height, especially among the typically statuesque Andorians. Someone as big as Lan just made it worse.

"Blasters still function, but their effectiveness is reduced, and it looks like the power packs are draining off faster than normal." He grinned and patted something on his equipment belt. "Fortunately, we'll be fine." All IG security personnel were trained in the use of the *flabbjellah*. Most carried something else besides; Lan's belt also bore an *ushaan-tor,* a nastily sharp instrument originally designed for cutting through the ubiquitous Andorian ice. His was enormous, so as to fit around his oversized fingers. "Do you have an alternative?"

Hikaru shook his head. The IG minimum weapons training requirement for officers was the blaster, and he'd never felt compelled to go beyond that. In his hands, a *flabbjellah* or even a good old-fashioned knife would be worse than useless. "I'll depend on you to protect me, Lieutenant."

Lan grinned again, his organic antenna coiled with excitement. Hikaru had always thought he got a little too excited about the wrong things. "As it should be, Commander."

The troopers turned off their blasters, and one of them—an Andorian man whose name Hikaru was embarrassed to realize he didn't recall—turned around to make his report. "Commander," he said with a curt dip of his antennae at Hikaru before shifting to address Lan. "Lieutenant, we're ready to head into the hallway."

Lan glanced at Hikaru, who nodded back. He was more than ready to get on the move. They had to find out where Demora had been taken. Unless, of course—

No, no. Demora would still be alive. She was smart, she was

cunning; Hikaru and Susan had raised her well. She *had* to be alive, and he would find her.

While Big Lan gave orders to his troopers, Hikaru went to rejoin th'Eneg and M'Benga at the transporter console. "We're about to move out, gentlemen," he said. "Anything to report, Jabilo?"

M'Benga shook his head. "I'm no more certain than I was five minutes ago. Best thing to do would be to take a look at what's upstairs and see for ourselves."

"Any movement from whoever's surrounding this place?" asked Hikaru.

"Nothing I can track. Readings are spotty."

"And you, Lieutenant?" Hikaru had toyed with using th'Eneg's first name for a moment, but decided that his tongue wasn't up for the challenge, especially not today.

Th'Eneg let out an exasperated hiss. "Before we materialized, the last use of this transporter unit was five days ago—three days before the attack. Whatever happened, it took them by surprise."

The disdain in his voice was obvious—th'Eneg might have a higher opinion of the Eridanian natives than Big Lan, but he was still not very impressed with IU personnel who weren't capable of defending themselves against them. "Anything else of interest?" asked Hikaru.

"I tried to connect to the rest of the outpost's computer system, but the network is under cut-out as well."

"Well, let's go, then," said Hikaru, trying to project a lightness with his voice that he did not feel. He suspected that he hadn't quite succeeded, but it probably didn't matter. M'Benga always maintained his own quiet optimism, and th'Eneg's emotional state never rose above "grim" in any case. They joined Big Lan at the door: one of his troopers was flashing his light through the hole; the other two had evidently gone through already.

A moment later, one of them returned and waved. Lan indicated that Hikaru and the other two non-security personnel should go through first.

The corridors of the outpost were even more ominous than the transporter room had been. At least that space had been small—their seven lamps might not have been capable of taking the whole room in at once, but Hikaru at least had the assurance that they'd examined every square centimeter of it. The corridor seemed to go off forever in either direction, and no matter how far down it Hikaru flashed his handlamp, there seemed to be more of it out there, filled with nothing but shadows and terror.

They soon fell into a formation, with two of the troopers in front, followed by th'Eneg, M'Benga, and Hikaru, and then Lan and the other trooper protecting their rear. Slowly they worked their way down the hallway, looking for an access ladder to the upper level. The others seemed capable of holding their lamps steady or at least moving them in nice, regular patterns; Hikaru's was jumping erratically every which way as he tried to take in the entire outpost at once. Other than the fact that all the lights were out and the systems offline, there was nothing to indicate that anything untoward had happened here. Everything was in order, just as it should be.

Somehow, Hikaru found that even more unnerving.

Suddenly, amidst all the standard IG gray of the corridor walls and floor, Hikaru's lamp caught something of a different color: a splotch of green on the floor. He held up his hand and the group came to a sudden halt. "What's that?" he asked. "A mold of some sort?"

M'Benga squatted down next to it, handscanner at the ready. "It's blood," he said after a few moments. "Dried, copper-based blood."

Big Lan grunted. "So at least they managed to hurt their attackers."

"We can now reasonably conclude it was the Eridanians," snapped th'Eneg. Hikaru shot him a glance. "It never pays to jump to conclusions," he said unapologetically. "I always consider the alternatives. Though it still may have been planted." He pursed his lips for a moment. "Or they may have been attacked by Orions."

That was unlikely. The IU might have been formed as a bulwark against the growing economic threat of the Orion Free Traders, but the Orions had been peacefully absorbed into the IU over fifty years ago now—as evidenced by lifetime IG officers such as s'Bysh. Hikaru didn't believe the rumors that the Syndicate had never been fully disbanded. "If it *is* Orion blood," said Hikaru, "it could have been a member of the outpost staff."

"There were none on staff," said th'Eneg, the "obviously" clear but unstated.

"It's a moot point," interrupted M'Benga before Hikaru could formulate a response. "This is *not* Orion blood, and its chemical makeup is consistent with the readings I have of local microorganisms." He stood up, snapping off his handscanner. "Definitely Eridanian."

Lan chuckled. "Another of th'Eneg's far-fetched conspiracy theories bites the dust."

"It still *could* be an elaborate ruse," pointed out th'Eneg. "Placing blood here would not be—"

"Gentlemen," said Hikaru, holding up his hands with his palms spread out. "Let's move on."

They continued down the corridor in silence. Finally they reached the access hatch for an emergency ladder. M'Benga did a quick scan to confirm that there were no lifesigns waiting for them in the control center above, and then Lan sent one of his troopers up.

The only sound in the corridor was the *clank clank clank* of the trooper scaling the ladder. Nervous, Hikaru glanced at M'Benga, who smiled wanly. Hikaru wondered if M'Benga knew about the Demora situation. He wouldn't put it above Yudrin to tell someone in the landing party, and the most likely candidate was the chirurgeon, who was compassionate enough to only make use of the information if the situation *really* required it. Th'Eneg would have figured it out himself, of course, but his only use for it would probably be to manipulate his commander.

The *clank*s stopped for a while, which only made Hikaru more nervous. But soon the trooper's voice echoed down the shaft: "All clear!"

Hikaru wanted to be the next up the ladder, but Lan pushed himself in front of him. He probably hadn't even noticed Hikaru trying to go up; normally Hikaru stood back and let his people do their jobs. But not today; he made sure he went up right after Lan.

The observation post was set into a rock outcropping in the L-langon foothills, and the control center had six large one-way windows set into its walls that looked out over the Forge. It was just after sunrise, local time, and the outpost faced east, which meant that the room was awash in a dim orange light.

Hikaru decided he preferred the darkness of the lower level.

The outpost's control center was a large, round room. In its center stood a table surrounded by a number of chairs; the computer consoles surrounded this in three concentric circles.

M'Benga came up right behind Hikaru, scanner back in hand. "This way," he said to Hikaru, who followed him. The access ladder had come up in the back corner of the room; M'Benga was leading him closer to the windows, weaving through the computer consoles.

The trooper caught his arm. "Commander," she said, "I'm not sure if you should—"

He shook her off. "I'll be the judge of that for myself, trooper," he said, continuing to follow M'Benga.

As they grew closer to the windows, Hikaru came to realize that what he'd initially taken for partitions dividing the windows were no such thing. They were far too blobby and irregularly shaped. The room actually had one large window.

Each of the five divisions was a corpse.

Metal poles had been driven into the floor, and the bodies violently shoved down on top of them, impaled straight through from between the legs.

Even worse, though, were their heads. None of their faces were visible, as they were almost entirely coated in blood. The blood had evidently streamed down from a cut made into their foreheads, completely bisecting their—

Hikaru's stomach nearly retched as he realized what the Andorian trooper's infrared eyesight had probably let her see from across the room. The top third of the skull of each body was missing.

And so were their brains.

"Damn," breathed M'Benga. "How *could* they? What sort of animals would do this?"

Hikaru looked from body to body, but the blood that covered their faces prevented him from discerning any of their identities. In the orange light, he couldn't even see what color their blood was.

He placed his hand on M'Benga's shoulder. "Steady, Jabilo. Just give me the facts."

M'Benga nodded. "Sorry, sir," he said, holding his handscanner up and waving it in the direction of the nearest corpse. "This one is Coridanite."

"That would be Guard Trooper Hollisjle Gohoy." Hikaru glanced over his shoulder to see that th'Eneg was standing right behind him. "He was the only Coridanite on the outpost's staff."

M'Benga continued to wave his handscanner around the room, identifying the species of the corpses while th'Eneg recited their names dryly.

"Tellarite."

"Guard Trooper Pol kj Onn."

"Triexian."

"Guard Trooper Yobob Ha Re."

"Nausicaan."

"Guard Trooper Myshellmaloni Mangol."

Hikaru held his breath. There was only one corpse left in the room. It certainly had long enough hair to be Demora, but it couldn't be, it couldn't be.

M'Benga waved his scanner up and down. He frowned and then hit some buttons on it.

"Well?" said Hikaru at last, unable to stand it any longer.

"Andorian," said M'Benga.

Hikaru exhaled a massive sigh of relief. He felt so terrible, being relieved that it was someone else impaled on that pole, someone else with a brain removed, someone else brutally murdered by the Eridanian natives. And not just someone else, but someone else's *child*.

But he was. These five security officers might be dead, but with every body they found, the higher the probability that Demora was among the survivors they were using as hostages.

"There were obviously multiple Andorian personnel on base," said th'Eneg. "Further identification is impossible without more data."

"Can't you tell just from the cut of her uniform?" asked Big Lan. *His* approach Hikaru had noticed; it was impossible not to. "You're usually better than that, Lieutenant."

Th'Eneg hissed. "I would have thought that we had higher priorities than your sarcastic comments, ch'Satheddet."

"I was unaware that showing off the ability to memorize personnel rosters was a high priority, th'Eneg." Lan's hand involuntarily jerked towards his *flabbjellah*.

Hikaru was about to intervene with a judiciously placed comment, but M'Benga beat him to it. "I've recorded all of their DNA, and transmitted it up to *Kumari*. Chirurgeon V'Larr should be able to run a check against the DNA profiles the Science Directorate sent us and come up with positive identifications."

"Thank you, Chirurgeon," said Hikaru. "Now—can we get these people *down* from there?"

He was glad that both th'Eneg and Lan looked suitably chagrined.

Lan and his troopers did most of the work in getting the corpses down from the poles. It was a bloody mess; the poles extended well into the corpses, in order to keep them somewhat upright. They were a nightmarish form of the scarecrows of ancient Earth.

Lan had asked th'Eneg for assistance, but the intelligence officer had claimed that he needed to examine the outpost's subspace communications system. Big Lan had guffawed, but a pointed glance from Hikaru had stopped him from making anything more of it.

Now Hikaru and M'Benga were standing over the corpses while Big Lan and the other security officers fanned out to investigate the rest of the control center and the other rooms on the same level. M'Benga's handscanner had indicated that there were other organic remains within the compound.

"What do you make of it, Jabilo?" asked Hikaru. There had not yet been any sign of the victims' brains—or the tops of their heads. "It reminds me of some tribal rituals I've seen on more primitive planets, like Capella Four. One of the tribes there would carve symbols into a defeated enemy's chest. But remove the brains?"

M'Benga slipped his handscanner back into its holster on his equipment belt. "Have you ever heard of the Aenar?"

Hikaru frowned. "An Andorian subspecies, aren't they?" he asked. "I remember hearing about them when I was at the Institute—but only from other aliens. The Andorians wouldn't ever talk about them." Despite their position as one of the founding members of the IU—and their homeworld as its capital—there were many things the Andorians often refused to discuss with members of other species, such as their complex four-sex reproductive system.

"That's right," said M'Benga. "They're all but extinct now, but I went on a medical relief mission to their settlement during my internship. They're telepathic, able to read and project thoughts."

"Really?" Hikaru had encountered a few species with such abilities during his time in the Imperial Guard, but no IU member species was supposed to have such capabilities. "I'm not sure I follow you, Chirurgeon."

"The Aenar venerated the brain. When they died, the aspect of the body they were most concerned about after death—the *only* aspect of the body they were concerned about, really—was the brain. It had to be preserved perfectly."

"Could the Eridanians be telepathic?" asked Hikaru.

M'Benga shrugged. "I don't know. The information the Science Directorate sent us didn't indicate it, but it *was* pretty scant."

Hikaru wondered if that was because the Directorate actually lacked the information, or because of General Shras's mysterious agenda. "So if they *are* telepathic, they might somehow consider removing the brain of an enemy an important act. Necessary to show that their enemies are truly no threat." He sighed and began pacing back and forth in front of the giant window, mostly because he was tired of looking at the ghastly corpses. "I wish *Kumari* had an anthropology expert aboard. I'm a bit out of my depth."

M'Benga grunted in acknowledgment or agreement. Once again, Hikaru found himself regretting that the trajectory of his career had taken him away from more science-focused vessels. *Enterprise* had had a bevy of experts in every conceivable scientific field. *Kumari* had some, of course, but they tended to be in "practical" fields such as astrophysics; there wasn't much in the way of the "soft" sciences. "What if—"

Hikaru's question was cut short by the sound of something whisking its way through the air right next to his head—he turned to see a metal arrow bouncing off the transparisteel window. "Down, M'Benga!" he cried as he dropped to the floor himself.

Hikaru pulled his blaster out of his belt, praying that the electromagnetic radiation hadn't depleted it too much. He crawled over to the nearest ring of consoles, poking his head over the top to get a view.

A group of about twelve men had entered the room. How had they gotten so close without anybody noticing? What had happened to Lan's troopers?

Ornate silver helmets covered the sides of the men's heads, including their ears, but from the sweep of their eyebrows he could see that they were Eridanians.

A couple were carrying bows. Most of them had large poles in their hands, one end with a sharp blade and the other with a blunt club.

Hikaru could only see one of the security troopers—and he was on the ground with an arrow in his back. Th'Eneg was scrambling to get away from an advancing Eridanian wielding the club/blade weapon, trying to grab the blaster on his belt.

Hikaru flicked the safety off on his blaster, pointed it at the Eridanian, and fired.

Nothing happened.

He looked at the blaster's power levels. It was nearly depleted. He shook it roughly and took aim once more. He pulled the trigger.

The blaster's response was sluggish, but an energy beam eventually lanced out, striking the Eridanian. It didn't render him unconscious or even knock him down, but it did send him stumbling, giving th'Eneg enough time to go for cover beneath the room's central table.

Hikaru glanced over at M'Benga, who had pulled his communicator out and was signaling *Kumari* for a beam-out. Hikaru couldn't quite make out the response, but Yudrin's voice did not sound reassuring.

He glanced back down at his blaster once more—and a knife blade heading for his throat.

From behind him, a voice rumbled in a language Hikaru needed no translator to understand.

"Kiv tehnau fa-wak stau nash-veh du."

One wrong move and he was dead.

"So no Andorians live in this cave?" she called back as she continued to crawl.

"Exactly," he said. "They abandoned it centuries ago—and built Laikan right outside it."

"Yes, I remember civics class, Dad."

"Watch where you're going!" He inched his way forward, her boots very nearly in his face. "Besides, you couldn't exactly live in this one, could you?"

The ice cave they were in right now was barely taller than he was thick. Actually, to be honest, he was probably slightly thicker than it—a ground teaching assignment had not kept him in the best of shape. It had narrowed suddenly and unexpectedly, and they'd been proceeding on their stomachs for the better part of fifteen minutes now.

"Let me take the lead!" he called. She grumbled, but obligingly let him pass her up. He turned his head to redirect the lamp on his helmet, to get a better view. Unfortunately he couldn't quite get a good angle. He detached the chin straps and took the helmet off, holding it in his hands to direct its light beams forward.

"Be careful," she admonished.

"It'll be fine," he replied. "I went spelunking in the caves of Exo Three; this is—"

"—nothing, I know."

He made a tentative move forward. His head promptly collided with the cave ceiling.

He taught her a few choice expletives that day, in English, Japanese, and Andorii.

MINSHARA: THREE

Pain nearly overwhelmed every other sensation. Demora's body felt like it was marred by a bunch of new bruises. The worst was her head, which was throbbing where she'd hit the mountainside.

She used all her willpower to open her eyes and found herself surrounded by stone walls. She'd been recaptured. They must've spotted her and taken her back; all her effort had been for nothing. Considering what she'd done to their people, though, she was at a loss to explain why she was still alive. They hadn't hesitated to murder before, so what did they want with her now?

And who were they? Another clan, perhaps these Nashih that Candle Guy had mentioned? If so, what did they want from her? Demora was afraid but, knowing fear wouldn't help her now, tried to concentrate on something else to take her mind off whatever terrible fate these others had in mind for her. She began to inspect her body, noticing that her hands were free. Pretty sloppy work, that—if she'd been responsible for a recaptured prisoner, she'd have made sure they were restrained first thing.

Her bruises and abrasions had already begun to scab over, but when she touched her shoulder (very gingerly), she felt something unexpected: a bandage. So, not only had they not killed her, they'd even dressed her wounds? Pretty forgiving lot . . . which didn't really mesh with her previous experience.

And there was more: she didn't seem to be in the same compound she'd been held in before. The walls were rougher, obviously unfabricated. This was a natural cave. A small fire burned a couple feet away from her. It was time to go spelunking.

She had barely gotten onto her feet—though with some difficulty—when a voice rang out.

"Hafa'uh! Nam'tor du kobat."

"Easy for you to say." Yeah, at least she'd still got it, that ability to stare into the face of danger and tweak the nose of terror. "Why don't you show yourself?" And all that with a charming smile.

Still, she stopped. Running away was not really the clever thing to do when you had no idea where to run to. It might have worked before, but her earlier feat of escapology was just a bit too improbable to be repeated.

An old Eridanian man emerged from the darkness, coming around a bend in the cave. He had sparse white hair reaching past his shoulders and was clothed in a loose-fitting shirt and equally loose trousers, made from a coarse, sand-colored fabric. His face was wrinkled, as were his hands, which held a metal bowl.

"Bolau tu shom."

"Is that so? Interesting."

"Nam'uh hizhuk. La masu," he said and handed her the bowl. It contained a clear liquid, hopefully water.

"Oh," said Demora simply, not expecting such generosity. She held the bowl to her lips, but did a quick examination with her nose first. It didn't smell like anything that would kill her, but it *did* smell, which water shouldn't. Still, she took a sip and found it drinkable despite its earthy taste. She emptied the bowl in one big gulp. "Thanks. That was very welcome."

He coughed very heavily, holding a hand over his mouth as he did so. *"K'shatrisu, ha'kel t'du wilat?"*

"Like I'd tell you. My lips are sealed."

Having decided that she was in no immediate danger from the

man, Demora sat down on the ground, not far from the fire. Her legs thanked her for taking the weight off them, even if her back now complained. To relieve it, she leaned back against the cool cave wall.

The old man sat down to face her. He stared at her, somewhat impolitely, but Demora ignored it. Neither of them said anything for a while, presumably since neither of them understood the other. Which was a pity, because she wanted to ask him some important questions—such as *What do you want from me?* And *Am I free to go?*

With nothing else to do, she studied the wizened man. He looked like a human would look if he reached a century—she knew the natives could reach twice that if they weren't killed in the clan feuds, and it seemed that this one had been lucky. Of course, living in a goddamned cave probably helped.

Realizing that *she* was staring at *him,* she began examining the cave in greater detail. The light was not great, but still surprisingly ample; some sunlight poured down on them through a crack above their heads. Hopefully that meant they weren't far from the entrance. Her eyes picked up traces of occupation everywhere: black marks on the ground, possibly charcoal; bits of wood; animal bones in a heap behind a rock whose top was so flat that it might serve as a table.

She handed the empty bowl back to him, motioning for a refill. He seemed to understand, because he took it and got up, disappearing back around the bend and into the darkness.

He returned after a short while with a full bowl. Again, Demora emptied it in one gulp. "Thanks," she said. "But I have to go now. I must find—"

The hermit moved suddenly. With one hand he grabbed her shoulder, and the other he pressed in her face, his fingers probing around her cheek. She tried to pull away, but he wouldn't let her and instead increased the pressure on her shoulder. His appearance belied his strength; he was able to easily overpower her. Demora could only rage inside her mind at the breach of the tentative trust she'd been feeling, and even that didn't last long. She resolved to fight him off, no matter what it took.

He whispered something. *"Nahp, hif-bi tu throks."* Eridanian gibberish.

And then, with no warning whatsoever, their minds merged.

There was no other word for it; it was painfully obvious that her thoughts were no longer only hers. She felt as though a milky-white glass wall had been erected between her consciousness and the rest of her. She could still form thoughts, but they were somehow more . . . ephemeral. It was difficult to even understand what was going on, much less put it into words. The man's presence was not something she could classify in any way; it simply *was*. Before, her thoughts had belonged to her. Now they did not.

Quiet, something—not quite a voice—said, or thought, or projected. It felt like a part of herself, but at the same time it was utterly alien. This was the mind of the Eridanian hermit, who had feigned helpfulness only in order to . . . she could not complete the thought, it upset her so much.

Quiet, woman. You are no longer in danger.

Was she really expected to believe that? After all she'd been through?

Thanks to the meld, I now know everything that has happened to you over the past two days. I also know how to speak your language. In return, I have given you the ability to speak mine.

Then release me!

I will, but I need to know more. You are from beyond Minshara. What brought you here?

You're asking? Can't you dig this info out yourself?

I could, but it would not be . . . polite.

Since when do you care about being polite? You know what I've gone through, so you know that I don't have any reason to trust you.

I had to find out why you lay in the sun outside my dwelling.

Couldn't you have done that while I was asleep?

Again, that would not be—

Polite. I get it.

You do? How remarkable.

Are you being funny?

I should think not. Will you give me the information I seek?

Why? I don't know you, and as I just said, I certainly don't trust you.

I know that.

And yet you expect me to give you what you want?

Yes.

Why?

Our minds intersect; we are now part of each other. My thoughts are entirely open to you. Examine me, judge me, decide on my sincerity.

How the hell am I supposed to do that?

Don't think about it, just do.

Thanks a lot, Zen Master.

You have a response to everything, don't you? Something to hide your doubts and fears, something that creates the illusion of aloofness, to protect yourself.

And now you're a psychiatrist. I hope you don't charge by the hour.

Enough! We can help each other. Don't make light of your situation; it does not suit you.

No! I've had enough of this! Let me go!

The entire telepathic experience was threatening to overwhelm her. With every thought she was less and less certain of her own identity. She needed to break out at once. But how?

You have nothing to fear. I want to help you.

By invading my mind? Is that what you call help? Get out of my head!

If that is your wish. I apologize for unsettling you.

He called what he'd done "unsettling"! That almost made it

even worse. Thoroughly disgusted, she barely noticed that he had retreated from her mind, as instantly as he'd entered it.

Demora once again had control over her body. She used that control to move away from him.

In this cave, though, that was difficult, thanks to the darkness at either end. Which direction was the way out? Did she even *want* to leave the cave? She didn't know what was outside, after all. She needed another encounter with those fanatics like a hole in the head.

Stumbling past him, she disappeared in the gloom, not having the slightest idea where she was going. She needed to move, to put as much distance between her and that . . . that criminal as possible. She continued even when the light from the cracks could no longer show her where to step, holding her hands out in front of her. When she finally made contact with the back side of the cave with her fingers, it was just barely in time to avoid a painfully close contact with her head.

Sitting down, she hugged herself, only in part to conserve warmth against the growing coolness. She felt disgust at what he'd done. She felt unclean. She'd never felt this way before.

It appalled her how easily he'd invaded her mind, with just a simple touch of his hand. Doctor Grayson had put up a fight against *her* assailant; why hadn't she? Demora was the one trained to be a fighter!

How could he do that? Just how lawless is this planet?

He was coughing again, an overwhelmingly loud cough that went on for at least a whole minute, but she ignored him. He didn't deserve her attention.

It was getting uncomfortably cool away from the fire. She longed for her stolen cloak, which had disappeared before her waking. Had he taken it off her when he'd carried her here?

What were this guy's motives, anyway? He had treated her wounds, had given her water, and then he'd invaded her mind without so much as a blink. Feelings were warring within her:

she didn't believe that he posed a real threat to her, but she couldn't be certain about anything these days, could she?

"Please, do not hide in there," he said, his distant voice echoing along the walls of the cave. "The *shatarr* do not like intruders. If they see you as a threat, they will attack you." His command of Andorii was impressive, his accent almost that of a native Laikana.

Telepathy was evidently a useful tool. But, like any tool, it was easily used for malevolent purposes. You could simply throw away your inhibitions and scruples, and enter another's mind unasked. Who knew what damage a trained telepath could cause? Deleting memories, scrambling thoughts, changing personalities, they all seemed possible to her.

She didn't reply to him, not ready to trust him. Her first goal was still to find a way to contact those sent to rescue her and the other survivors (if any remained), and then to leave this hot, dusty hellhole of a planet ASAP.

The crackling fire punctuated the silence that now existed between her and the native, sending glowing motes upward only to have them die out as quickly as they'd been created. As she grew colder, she closed her eyes, hugging her arms tightly around her knees.

A noise to her left startled her. It was almost inaudible, and only her complete stillness enabled her to hear it. It sounded like something moving on tiny legs across the ground.

Were these the *shatarr* he'd warned her about? She'd had enough attacks for one day. Despite herself, she asked, "What are *shatarr*?"

"Animals that sometimes live in caves like this one. If they feel threatened, they defend themselves. They are quite poisonous."

Good grief. Was *everything* deadly on this planet? Deciding she didn't need to risk another animal encounter, she made her way back to the fire, putting it between him and her as a sign that she didn't trust him.

He had another coughing fit, but said nothing, crossing his legs and folding his hands in his lap. Long minutes passed, uninterrupted by either of them. It was as if they had agreed to not disturb each other's ruminations.

Finally, he broke the silence. "My name is S'oval."

Big deal. Instead of replying, she studied him. He carried himself as if he were much younger than he looked. And for a man living in the wilderness he was surprisingly well fed. Whether he hunted his food or gathered it, he must be good at it.

There was one question she wanted answered. Fighting with herself over whether to ask him, she let her fingers trail over the uneven ground, feeling the sand and dry soil between them. It was an unconscious motion, and when she realized what was doing, she stopped.

"How did you get me here? And don't tell me you carried me."

If he was irked by her lack of politeness—something he seemed to care much about—he didn't let it show. Instead, he smiled. "I let Czei carry you."

So where was this Czei? And why didn't the cave appear to be occupied by more than one person?

As if he'd read her mind—*just about the worst simile you could've picked, girl!*—he continued, "Czei is my pet *sehlat*. I often use her to carry things for me."

That explanation would probably have helped if she'd known what a *sehlat* was. "It must be pretty lonely around here. Not much in the way of company."

"Company is not something I seek out," he said. "Well, unless somebody needs my help."

I could've done without your help. A trip in the desert can't be much worse than basic training at the Institute! "So that is what you call it. 'Help.' Interesting."

"I apologized for my behavior, didn't I? Among my people, such contact isn't frowned upon."

"I don't belong to your people."

"That much is obvious. But where are you from? What brings you here?"

"Too many questions."

"I think not. In fact, I've asked too few. There are a lot of things I want to know, and I would like your help."

"I wouldn't count on it."

"Need I apologize again to make you more kindly disposed toward me?"

"It won't help. I tend to dislike people who scramble my thoughts." She gave him a look of contempt.

"That was not my intent. How can I convince you of my sincerity?" His expression looked like one of sorrow, but she wasn't exactly an expert judge of Eridanian facial expressions.

"Best if you give it up entirely."

"What is it you want to know?"

She blinked. "What?"

"You obviously want to know something from me. Why won't you ask me? I have nothing to hide."

Did he really expect her to believe that? Fat chance. Demora shifted her position to keep her left leg from going to sleep.

S'oval took a piece of greenish meat from the stone table, stuck it on a metal pole, and held it close enough to the flames for it to sizzle. Its smell wafted over to her, setting off a memory of the barbecue in Grandpa Tetsuo's backyard, two weeks after her graduation from the Institute: her last actual meeting with her father.

Where would her father be right now? *Kumari* had been patrolling the Klingon border for two years now. She hoped he was all right, given the reports from the Klingon frontier that had reached her over the past months.

Her stomach grumbled, reminding her that she hadn't eaten in a very long time. S'oval looked up from the fire, surprised, and immediately offered her the pole. Much as she'd have liked to say no, she wasn't able to. Her hunger overwhelmed her antagonism, and she accepted the gift. Hopefully it wouldn't kill her. Sniffing gingerly at the steaming slice, she finally took an experimental bite that turned out to be far better than she was prepared to admit.

And yet, S'oval had probably seen the brief flash of delight on her face. He nodded almost imperceptibly and took another pole that he'd stuck between two rocks, fixed a piece of meat to it, and began roasting again.

"So, Soval," she began, chewing on the delicious charred meat, "how long have you been living here?" Hopefully he'd take her interrogation as small talk.

"Almost right. It is S'oval." This time he emphasized the glottal stop after the 'S' in his name. "I did use to be called 'Soval,' but that was before I changed my name to indicate my appreciation of a special branch of philosophy. It now means 'the one who bows' in your language."

"You're a philosopher?" she asked in between bites.

"A follower of philosophy of a certain kind."

"The kind that caused your fellow people to attack my friends and kill most of them?"

He merely shook his head. It was obvious that he wasn't easily provoked. Still, Demora would find out what he was up to one way or another.

"The precepts I observe—called *mnhei'sahe*—indicate I should only kill another person when threatened or wronged—and then only as a last resort."

"Well, that's good to know." She didn't buy a word of it. "That must be why your first idea for asking me where I came from was to invade my mind."

"Please try to understand me and my people. We differ from you in a great many ways. The ability to use our minds to directly influence the world around us has shaped us. Our history, our society, and thus our values, are remarkably different from yours."

Well, that's obvious. She snorted derisively. "I have eyes; I can see that. You people find nothing wrong with forcing yourselves upon others without explicit consent?"

"Indeed not. The very nature of our telepathic abilities make such considerations useless; to the most powerful there are no limitations whatsoever. Some, like me, cannot help but establish contact when we touch, and we make deliberate use of this ability only when it is absolutely necessary. It is not an act of an innate moral dimension, good or evil."

Demora said nothing and instead finished her tasty bit of local cuisine. She stared into the flames, letting their dance take her far away, back to those family trips to the Rocky Mountains, where they'd sat around a fire in the pine forests and Mom and Dad had told tales of distant worlds.

Thinking about it, Demora had to admit that what S'oval had said seemed plausible. She wasn't ready to forgive him, not by a long shot, but he *had* saved her life and given her food and drink. Personally, she'd have preferred it to remain a matter bereft of gray areas.

Perhaps he deserved to be given a chance to redeem himself. From his point of view, he hadn't even done anything wrong. There was still only so much diversity she could stomach, and even less when she herself was at the center of cultural misunderstanding.

S'oval continued, now munching on his own piece of meat, though he started cooking a third one. "If I'd known that my actions would cause you so much discomfort, I would have not gone through with them. It seemed the most effective way of establishing a common basis for communication. Language, after all, is the fabric that keeps civilization together."

That last comment had the feeling of a quote, presumably by a famous Eridanian author or poet. She idly wondered what works of art people would produce if they'd been at one another's throats for thousands of years, before she realized that this had been the case on Earth until first contact with the Andorians. And Earth's history was just as violent as that of Andor, Orion, and Xindus, to name only a few examples. Eri was no different from the rest of the galaxy.

Or maybe it was. How could it be explained that of these worlds, only Eri had not found an alternative to armed conflicts?

"If you guys can read each other's minds, why are you still fighting? From what we found out, there hasn't been a day of peace in the past twelve millennia!"

"It was once much, much worse. Would you believe that we once stood at the brink of destruction?"

Yes, as it happened, she did, but she didn't give him the pleasure of admitting it. "Do tell."

"One faction had developed immensely powerful bombs and decided to threaten its enemies with them. Its enemies developed the same. It all ended with the detonation of multiple atomic weapons across the planet, dropped from orbit by ships from opposing nations. They incinerated their enemies, and when they were done, little was left of Minshara. The death toll was in the billions, and virtually every major city had been reduced to slag and dust."

Demora said nothing. S'oval's account tallied with what the scientists had deduced. Evidence of the use of nuclear weapons was everywhere. Erosion had covered up some of it, but orbital examination of the surface, first by *Ravis* and then by *Ashoka,* the ship that had dropped them off here, had yielded a long list of suspected impact sites. Frankly, it was surprising that people could still live here.

"It took my people centuries, but eventually they increased their number enough to repopulate Minshara, in those areas least tainted by the Conflagration."

"Looks to me like you haven't learned a single thing since then." *Yes, perfect, girl! Annoy him even further! That's the way to freedom.*

To her surprise, he merely sighed and said, "I regret to admit that you're right. We still wage war on one another, we still sneak up on our enemies and kill them in their sleep, and we still refuse to use words when weapons will do."

"But why?"

"Demora, I suspect that no people, not even yours, has answered that question." He laughed, but it quickly turned into a cough.

She felt a brief moment of sympathy: despite herself, she was beginning to like the man. Well, not *like* per se, but she didn't think of him as evil personified any longer. It tore at Demora, that unbidden realization, and it made her angry, both at the man, for being so difficult to classify, and at herself.

"I lived in the city of T'lingShar in Tekeh Province until twelve years ago, when I came here to start anew. In all that time, I have had few visitors. I would like to thank you for breaking up my daily routine."

The words "You're welcome" were out of her mouth before she knew it. Snapping her mouth shut, she sat back and crossed her arms over her chest, an obvious sign—to humans, in any case—that she wanted some distance between them.

The white-haired hermit held up his hands, palms toward her, in a placating gesture. "It's clear that you still haven't forgiven me for my intrusion, and that pains me deeply. Is there a way I can undo what I have done?"

"Not likely." Her determination to keep her distance and be out of here at the first opportunity was beginning to waver slightly. The old man *did* look genuinely contrite. But even if what he said was true, he still had a lot to answer for.

"That is a pity. I had hoped you could see it from my perspective. All things considered, our people are not so different." He ignored her annoyed snort at this statement and continued. "You have one major advantage over me: you have encountered many other species of intelligent life-forms out there in the vast-

ness of space, and have learned a lot about them. Tell me, have
you always found them to be likeable, their philosophies easy to
understand?"

She tried not to give him the satisfaction of rising to the bait.
Cautiously, she composed her reply. "No. But most of them
don't attack me and my people, either."

"You're angry with me because some unknown clan killed
your friends? There is no kinship between myself and them."

"I'm angry because—" Demora stopped herself, not knowing
how to continue. For the past day, she'd been running on automatic. With all the murdering, running, hiding, and being poisoned, there had been little time to contemplate her emotional
state. Now, forced to confront her feelings, she had no answer
for S'oval. She needed to separate how she felt about the deaths
of Grayson and the others from her feelings about her own
desperate situation. "I'm angry. Let's leave it at that." As a peace
offering, she changed the topic of their conversation. "Tell me
more about yourself. Why did you come to live here?"

At that, S'oval's face lit up. Taking a gulp of water, he changed
his position on the floor slightly and then said, "I was no longer
interested in the direction my people were taking. Now, you may
say that it took me an awfully long time to discover that, considering my age—"

"How old *are* you?"

"Four hundred seventy-eight years," he said simply, but when
he saw Demora's astonished expression, he quickly amended his
remark. "Of course, this is calculated using the local calendar.
On your world, I would be . . . over two hundred sixty, give or
take a few years."

Though she gave no further indication of being surprised
by his age, she had to admit that she wouldn't have guessed it
by looking at him. To her eyes, he resembled at most a post-
centenarian human, like her great-great-grandfather. As a child,
she'd once said to her mother that Grandpa Tetsuo was made

entirely out of wrinkles. Her mother had found it funny, but not as much as Grandpa, who'd nearly fallen off his chair.

"But why? Why move out into the wilderness?"

"There's this lovely phrase in your father's language: 'to get religion.' Colloquial usage, evidently. You could say that I 'got philosophy.' A friend of a friend introduced me to the teachings of an almost forgotten thinker from our past, a soldier-poet who had lived during the Conflagration and still managed to publish his works and actually have people read them. There we were, bent on eradicating ourselves, and this man wrote poems about a version of our civilization that had no place for blind aggression and hatred."

"Sounds pretty utopian to me. I guess he didn't have many followers at the time."

"You could certainly say so. I was introduced to the poems of S'task—that was his name—and at first didn't know what to make of them. They seemed almost naïve in their optimism, but at the same them there was a lot about them that was pragmatic and, with a little determination, could be used as the basis for a new way of life."

Goodness, of all the people she could have stumbled upon in the desert, she had to meet an alien space hippie! Who was the naïve one here, old man?

He removed the pole from its position and gave it a thorough look. Then he offered the meat to Demora. "Here, have another."

Her stomach ordered her to accept the gift. "Thank you."

"Now, visitor from space, I would be glad if you could answer a few of my own questions. Surely that is only fair?"

Screw fairness. But he had a point: having received the bigger share of his sparse dinner, she couldn't well refuse his request for information. She nodded. "Yes. Fire away."

"Why are you here?"

A simple question that shouldn't be difficult to answer. IG

regulations about avoiding contact no longer applied to her situation, after all. "We wanted to study you. Some months ago, it was decided to put an observation post on your planet, staffed by scientists whose goal was to find out as much as possible about your people. If the information had satisfied our leaders, we would have initiated official contact between our peoples."

"I see. And who would have been Minshara's representative?"

"I don't know. *My* job was to protect the scientists. Fat lot of good that did them," she mumbled, more to herself than to S'oval.

"I'm asking because I couldn't single a person out. This planet is not unified; it has never been. Tribes, clans, organizations, and entire nations have been at war forever."

"Somebody said that 'Minshara is as fractured a world as can be,'" Demora said, quoting Doctor Grayson's killer. "Is that so?"

"Yes. It sounds as though matters have only gotten worse since I went into isolation. Your people picked a bad time to spy on us," he said, and only the increased wrinkling of his skin around his mouth and eyes led her to believe that he was attempting a joke. "Assuming you could have found one person to speak for us all, what would you have said to them?" S'oval stoked the fire, sending another flare of glowing motes into the air. One of them fell onto her left hand, and she winced at the unexpected sensation.

"That's outside my area of expertise. I'm a security officer, trained to save lives . . ." Her voice trailed off, and he immediately picked up on that.

"You feel you've let them down."

I don't need your pity. "Don't go there. Just . . . don't."

S'oval said nothing for a while, then he returned to his previous topic: "Even if you're not privy to the plans prepared by your superiors, surely you have some idea of what is going on?"

"I did, once," she admitted, "but I'm no longer certain. The Union needs to defend itself against the Klingons—they're a

warrior race bent on conquering the galaxy—" she added for his
benefit, "—and Minshara was ideally situated to slow the invasion. Your people's cooperation would have helped us." That last
statement sounded hollow, and it was; she was merely parroting
part of her original brief, the Science Directorate's orders that
had been authorized by Prefect M'Ress and General Shras. One
extra planet in the invasion corridor wouldn't slow a horde of
Klingons. No, if the statement was genuine, there must be something else Minshara could help them with.

When realization finally dawned, it was like a cold shiver running through her body, despite the fire still burning a mere meter
away. Somehow, M'Ress—or Shras, or both—must have found
out about the local telepaths and come up with a plan to use
them in battle. Demora herself had seen how effective telepaths
could be, and if those she'd met had been on the lower end of the
talent scale, then they could really be a formidable weapon in the
coming war. Just put one of the strongest in a ship on the border
and wait for the Klingons to arrive.

With enough mind soldiers, the Union stood a good chance
of surviving the coming storm. Presumably, one of the goals
Doctor Grayson and her staff had been ordered to achieve was to
establish a rapport with the natives, to ensure their cooperation.

"Bastards," she muttered, only aware that she'd spoken aloud
when she saw S'oval's raised eyebrow. "Not you. My people. I
think I know now why we're here."

"Oh? I take it you're not happy with that reason?"

"You can say that again. How would you react if you found
out that you've been used, and your friends died because of your
superiors' stupidity and incompetence?"

"I would become very angry, I suppose," S'oval said, barely in
time before he had to cough again heavily. It shook him thoroughly, harder than he'd been hit before. In those moments,
he was a frail, ancient man, unable to entirely control the con-
vulsions he went through. It was painful to watch, but before

Demora could bring herself to help him, everything was over, and the hermit had settled down again, visibly shaken but once more his own master.

"Are you all right?" she asked him.

Instead of a reply, he put the water bowl to his lips and drank deeply. Then, his throat cleared, he addressed her. "Don't worry about me. But," he said, pausing for one more cough, "let us talk about other things. Before we took this detour, we were discussing my reasons for coming here, weren't we? Now, S'task the philosopher lived here, in this region, for a time. In the time immediately after the Conflagration, he joined a group of te-Vikram—desert dwellers who eschewed technological changes and thus weren't affected by the weapons' side effects—and eventually devised the teachings he wrote down in a book that he called *The First Song*. There were others, but none as influential as this one. When I read it, I decided to follow in S'task's footsteps and explore the land between the Forge and the Womb, from the T'Kala Sea to the Kurat Mountains. Eventually I settled here, after a long journey."

"You traveled on your own?" Demora asked, more astonished than anything else, since he didn't strike her as still capable of such a feat.

"Not always," was the answer. "But she is gone now." His face betrayed little emotion, but Demora got the impression that the woman must've meant a lot to S'oval. But it wasn't something he was going to elucidate on.

"I'm sorry," she said, her anger at the man gone. The anger she now felt was directed at the Union in general, and at the Union's Prefect in particular. They shouldn't have put a cat in charge, after all.

"She left me a present, however. I was not prepared for it, but I accepted it nonetheless."

"Yeah? What was it?"

"S'task."

"Another book by him, you mean?"

"No. The man himself."

Now she was completely lost. "Didn't you say he'd lived thousands of years ago, at the time of the . . . 'Conflagration'?"

"Yes. His body died eventually, yet his mind lived on, carried by his followers."

This was something new. "What?"

"S'task's mind was deemed too important to be lost to time. Upon his death, it was transferred into the body of one of his followers."

The more she found out about this place, the stranger it became. "So, what you're saying is, he took over the guy's body?"

"Not at all. That is possible, but S'task was interested only in coexistence. The ritual gave him the opportunity to continue his work."

"Eternal life, that's what this is. Sounds to me like a guy who didn't want to die."

"On the contrary. S'task was looking forward to death, because it meant change, something new. The decision to move his *katra*—his spirit—was a late one, at the suggestion of the recipient himself. It was deemed an honor to carry S'task's *katra*, and I'm merely the last in a long line who have been chosen."

It was all too much, really. People volunteered for this? How crazy did you have to be to do that? "Chosen? How d'you mean?"

"All we can do is offer ourselves as carriers, but it is S'task himself who makes the final choice. It gives me new strength every day when I remember that I was deemed worthy."

He began to smile, but it was interrupted by another coughing fit. This one lasted even longer than the last. It was obviously painful for him; it was painful just to listen to. She moved around the fire to help him, but just as she made it to his position, he fell over and stopped moving.

"S'oval!" she exclaimed. "Are you all right?" She still might have been uncertain about the man, but if something happened to him, she didn't exactly have a lot of options.

He didn't answer, he just wheezed quietly. Breathing, that was a good sign. She rolled him over onto his back. He started coughing again, even harder. What could she do to stop this? She didn't exactly have a cough suppressant handy.

A few panicked moments later, S'oval was upright again, apparently fine.

"What happened?" she asked.

"I'm not well," he said. "I'm old, and I've lived a rough life."

"What happens to S'task?" she asked. "When . . . I mean, if, you die."

"If I die, he dies. Unless . . ." He looked at her expectantly.

"What!?" She backed away, narrowly avoiding the fire as she did so. "I'm not having some disembodied consciousness in *my* head, buddy!"

He smiled. "It is quite pleasant. S'task never ceases to amaze me, and our conversations are an infinite source of enlightenment for me."

To her, this whole thing reeked of a cult, and that wasn't such a good sign. Still, this old man had devoted his life to S'task. Perhaps . . . S'oval had saved her life, after all.

Damnit! How could she be even contemplating this? S'oval had already invaded her mind once before.

Yet, realistically, what options did she have? It was highly likely that he was the only one here not intent on killing her outright. Her goal was to get a message back to the IG, but it still might be worth finding out more. "So, if I wanted to ask S'task a few questions, would that be possible?"

"Certainly, if you melded with his carrier."

That caught her off-guard. Evidently, it wasn't as easy as having a quick chat. "Meld? Is that what you call it? Lord, it gets stranger by the minute." She considered her options and, since there weren't many, made her choice. "I'd like to talk to the man."

"Are you sure? You didn't seem to enjoy the previous meld."

"That's because you didn't ask me. I got no warning from you, in case you forgot. This time, it'll be different. I'll need your word that you won't try anything funny."

"Consider it given."

"Now, what do I have to do?" she asked as she got up and walked over to the man.

"Make yourself comfortable. Relax. It won't be an unpleasant experience, I promise you."

For some reason, she didn't quite believe him, but at least she was ready to give him the benefit of the doubt. Her reservations hadn't disappeared completely, though. Something could still go wrong, even if he didn't intend it.

Demora sat down to his right and crossed her legs. She looked him in the eyes. "I'm ready."

"Splendid. Let's begin, then." S'oval, looking much more ancient up close, reached out with his hand to touch her cheek. As before, his fingers moved in search of their destined spots, and then he spoke the same phrase as before, but in Andorii this time.

"In search of wisdom and truth we join our minds together. Our thoughts are merging . . . our thoughts are one."

After they'd been on Andor for a year, she finally got to take her first trip to the Institute, to see what her dad did all day.

It was a far cry from the little stone house they had in the Tumulus District of Laikan. The corridors were gleaming white, so bright it almost hurt her eyes, like the Issa Ice Cap. He took her to class with him, and she sat in the back while he lectured to a bunch of cadets about the Azure Nebula. She didn't understand most of it, but she liked the pictures.

He showed her off to his fellow instructors. She tried her best to be polite—he had drilled into her how necessary it was to maintain proper decorum in the Interstellar Guard.

But when a Tellarite had called her a "little runt," she replied with a comment on his porcine features. Her father had looked momentarily mortified, but the Tellarite had just laughed it off. "So young," he said, "and already conversant in civil conversation."

He took her up to Starbase 1 with him, to see the ship he worked on in his spare time.

She looked out the shuttle's viewport at the stars, at the other moons, at the gas giant, at Andor itself.

She'd always been prone to lashing out, and the world had never felt big enough for her. But out here, there was room to breathe, to relax. Out here, she was small. Out here, she could stay for the rest of her life.

KUMARI: FOUR

I surrender."

Hikaru opened his hands, dropping his blaster on the floor. He slowly moved his hands outward and upward—the universal sign for nonviolent cooperation.

"*Dvun'uh!*" the Eridanian behind Hikaru barked, making a swift jab for Hikaru's throat with his blade.

Apparently Hikaru's translator implant had not yet locked onto the language. Or maybe its function was being disrupted by the radiation, but he *really* hoped not. Praying the Eridanian hadn't told him to do something specific, Hikaru began rising to his feet. The blade was large and fan-shaped. And very sharp.

Again, the Eridanian shouted at him. "*Fa-wak tor du ra karthau!*"

"I said, I surrender." Hikaru tried to make his voice sound as calming as possible. "I'm Commander Hikaru Sulu of the *I.U.E.S. Kumari*. We mean you no harm. We simply wish to ascertain what happened to our people on your world."

The blade move a couple inches away from his throat and Hikaru suddenly found himself being roughly turned around by a hand on his shoulder.

Now face-to-face with his captor, he was finally getting his first good look at an Eridanian. The man wore a lightweight silver outfit that left his arms bare; it also had a skirt of sorts that went down to his knees, though it was divided in half in front. Beneath that he wore black leggings. The silver tunic had a low, square collar, allowing Hikaru to see that beneath it he wore a black shirt as well. A green sash was tied loosely around his waist.

Unlike the rest of the Eridanians in the outpost, this one did not have a helmet, allowing Hikaru to see his pointed ears. His hair was black, though he was balding a little and showing signs of gray. On the other hand, he was the first Eridanian Hikaru had seen with facial hair: a full beard and mustache. "Do you understand me?" asked Hikaru, hoping the translator was functioning.

The look of astonishment on the other man's face seemed to indicate that it was. "Yes, yes I do," he said. "But your words do not match your lips. How is this possible?"

"I'll explain later," said Hikaru. "First, call off your men." This Eridanian's lack of a helmet probably indicated that he was an officer.

"Call off yours," replied the Eridanian, moving the blade back toward Hikaru's throat. "Or learn to embrace your pain."

"Okay," said Hikaru. "Th'Eneg, ch'Satheddet, put down your weapons!" he shouted, his words echoing around the control center.

From behind him, he could hear th'Eneg's distinctive hiss of frustration, indicating his compliance.

"I mean it, ch'Satheddet!" He hoped Big Lan was within auditory range.

A desultory "Yes, Commander" from across the room indicated that he was, as did the musical tone of a *flabbjellah* falling to the floor.

"Now permit my chirurgeon to aid my fallen soldiers," said Hikaru. "Please."

The Eridanian nodded his assent. Hikaru could hear M'Benga scrambling to the aid of the security trooper who had been struck by an arrow.

The Eridanian leader barked some orders that the translator

could not decipher, and the Eridanian soldiers had soon rounded up Hikaru and the rest of the landing party around the table in the room's center—aside from M'Benga, who was still tending the fallen security trooper. Hikaru was pleased to see that though Big Lan, th'Eneg, and the other troopers had all taken injuries in the fight, none were particularly serious.

"Who are you?" demanded the Eridanian leader.

Realizing that his previous self-introduction must have been made before the translator kicked in, Hikaru repeated it. "My name is Hikaru Sulu. I'm the commander of the Interstellar Union *Starship Kumari*. These are my officers—First Lieutenant Thirrilan ch'Satheddet, chief of security, and First Lieutenant Yrrebneddor th'Eneg, chief of intelligence." From th'Eneg's wince, it looked as though Hikaru had mangled his first name, as usual. He gestured toward M'Benga, who was tending to the fallen trooper. "That man is Chirurgeon Jabilo Geoffrey M'Benga, chief medical officer."

"I am Sybok, son of Sarek, of the family S'chn T'gai, of the Clan Hgrtcha," replied the Eridanian leader. "These are my men. We are from ShiKahr. Where are you from?"

Hikaru had had enough. "Why did you kill these people? What happened to the rest of the personnel here?"

"You will answer my questions. How did you end up in here?" countered Sybok. "How did you get past our guards? Why do you invade our world?"

No, he wouldn't answer the questions. Instead, he had more of his own. "Where are the other personnel? What have you done with them?" Hikaru could feel his voice growing more and more desperate despite his best efforts to control it. "What do you want?"

"What do *you* want?" retorted Sybok.

A loud *clank* interrupted them, reverberating around the room and breaking the tense stand-off.

"Okay, everyone, *hands in the air!*"

Hikaru looked over to where the access hatch to the lower level had just swung open. Subcommander Phelana Yudrin was standing there, a blaster in one hand and an *ushaan-tor* in the other. Coming up the hatch behind her was one security trooper after another, all of them bearing not blasters, but what Hikaru recognized as old-fashioned "slugthrowers"—guns that fired projectiles.

Sybok laughed and drew his massive blade once more. "We know your strange weaponry does not work here." His archers began readying their bows.

"That's the third-biggest mistake you're going to make today," replied Yudrin. "Igrilan?"

One of the troopers took aim with his slugthrower and fired. The bullet hit the transparisteel window, cracking a large hole in it. Fracture lines radiated outward from it and pieces of transparisteel blasted in every direction.

"Do you care to make your second-biggest mistake?" asked Yudrin.

Sybok moved quicker than Hikaru would have thought possible—one second the Eridanian was standing next to him, looking at Yudrin and her troopers, the next he was once again behind Hikaru with his blade at his throat. "I have made no mistakes," he snarled. "But if *you* make another, your commander will lose his head."

"*Kroykah!*"

Hikaru looked over at the main door of the control center, to see a wizened old Eridanian woman come hobbling in. Despite her small stature and apparently frailty, her voice had reverberated throughout the entire control center.

Two of Yudrin's troopers moved to grab the old woman. But she held up what looked like a small stone, and the two troopers fell to their knees, their faces contorted in apparent agony as they clutched their antennae.

Hikaru opened his mouth to order his people to make a

counterattack, but stopped when he realized what the Eridanians gathered around himself were doing—all of them had fallen to their knees, facing the old woman, and they had placed their weaponry on the floor.

Not about to neglect this chance, Hikaru moved across the room to join Yudrin's group, motioning for the rest of his group to follow him. They did, M'Benga and Big Lan bearing the chirurgeon's patient, who was mostly patched up by now. Hikaru clasped a hand on Yudrin's shoulder. "Thanks, Subcommander."

"It was nothing," she replied. "Rescuing your commander is fifth on the list of the duties of the executive officer."

Hikaru allowed himself a small smile. "Right." He turned to face the old woman, who was still holding the stone out like it was a weapon. Given what had happened to the troopers moving toward her, it probably *was*. "I am Commander Hikaru Sulu," he said. "I have come to rescue my people here. Who are you?"

"I am T'Pau, matriarch of the Clan Hgrtcha," she replied. "And you will talk to me."

Hikaru recognized her voice—it was the one from the transmissions the outpost had been sending back to the Science Directorate. "Very well," he said. "I'm willing to do so now, if you'll answer my questions."

"No," she replied. "Not here. Neutral ground." And with that, she turned and headed out of the room. "Sybok!" she cried out. "Follow me."

Sybok and the other Eridanians picked their weapons up from the floor and began following her out of the room, their faces cast downward, avoiding eye contact with the *Kumari* landing party.

"What are you going to do?" asked Yudrin.

"Follow her," replied Hikaru. He needed to avoid antagonizing her until he knew the hostages were safe.

Silencing her objections, he gave orders for the corpses and wounded to be returned to *Kumari*. He would take M'Benga and three troopers bearing slugthrowers to the meeting with T'Pau; the rest would establish a base of sorts here in the outpost, since it was the only safe transport site in the vicinity, at least for the time being.

As he prepared to head out the door after the mysterious T'Pau, he stopped and turned. "Next time I call *Kumari*," he said, "I want to be patched in to General Shras. I'm starting to suspect I know what's going on here."

"Aye, Commander," Yudrin replied. "Oh, and sir?"

"Yes?"

"Remember—she might look like a harmless old lady, but this woman is a hostage-taker and a murderer."

"Oh, I know," said Hikaru, his mind filled by visions of Demora, mutilated like the members of her security team. He clamped down on them as best he could. This was not the time to allow his fears to get the upper hand. "I know."

Hikaru, M'Benga, and the three security troopers caught up to T'Pau, Sybok, and their soldiers right where the plain below the L-langon foothills began. The primary star, 40 Eridani A, was beginning to make its slow climb into the sky, and it was already quite hot. In his black pseudoleather uniform, Hikaru could only dread what he would feel like once it was high noon.

The 40 Eridani system was trinary, and the companion stars were close enough that he could make them out on the horizon opposite where the sun was coming up, even in the daylight. From this distance—about 450 AUs—they were nothing more than a bright blue and a bright red dot, however.

The Eridanian soldiers were setting up what seemed to be tents, one small and one large, undoubtedly to protect themselves from the rays of the climbing sun. T'Pau went into the small one. Sybok came up to Hikaru, looking somewhat meeker than he had earlier. "The matriarch wishes you to join her," he said. "The rest of your men may join me in my tent."

Hikaru nodded. Despite their actions before, the Eridanians seemed nonhostile now . . . but he should not let them lull him into a false sense of security. Fortunately, Big Lan trained his men too well for that. Telling M'Benga and the troopers to co-operate with Sybok, he joined T'Pau inside her tent.

This was the first good look he had gotten at the Eridanian woman. Her hair, like Sybok's, had obviously been pitch black at one point but was graying. She had a lot more hair than Sybok, though, and it was twisted into braids that were then looped or-nately around the top of her head. Of course, she had the typical Eridanian pointed ears, but a nasty scar through one of them in-dicated that at some point it had been very nearly severed in half. It was not her only scar—smaller ones dotted her face and hands. However frail she might be now, she had once been a powerful fighter. And he couldn't forget she probably still was, thanks to the stone she was still carrying it in her left hand.

"Commander Sulu?" she said.

"Yes," replied Hikaru. "And you are T'Pau."

"That is correct," she said, somewhat dryly. "Where have you come from?"

"What has happened to our people?" Hikaru countered.

"You will answer my questions first," she said, "and then per-haps I will answer yours. Each of us wants something from the other. It is in your best interests to cooperate."

Hikaru had seen Commander James Kirk give this explanation many times during his days on *Enterprise,* but he'd never had to give it himself. "Your world—I'm sorry, I don't know what you call it—"

"'Minshara,' sometimes."

"Minshara, then. Minshara is but one world among many, worlds that sit in your sky—"

"You talk to me as though I am a fool," T'Pau cut him off. "We are aware of other worlds—we had settlements on T'Khut, our sister planet, before they were destroyed in the Conflagration like so much else."

"My apologies," said Hikaru. He needed to stop underestimating these natives; despite their primitive appearance, they had been able to infiltrate and capture an IU facility. "We come from planets circling other stars. I myself come from a planet called Earth orbiting a star called Sol, sixteen light-years away. Earth is a member of an alliance of planets called the Interstellar Union—eighty worlds spanning a thousand light-years. Humans are but one of the many species who are members of this alliance."

"Such as the blue-skinned ones?" asked T'Pau. "The ones who look like insects?"

"Yes." Hikaru, who had grown up seeing Andorians everywhere, had never really considered how strange they must look to this species. Humans would seem like Eridanians with bobbed ears to these people; Andorians would be *really* strange. "They are called Andorians. They come from a planet thirteen light-years away from here, which serves as the capital of the Interstellar Union."

"What is this Union?" asked T'Pau, obviously intrigued.

He found himself giving a potted history of the IU, starting with the Andorian Empire and its domination of local space, as it squashed threats to itself such as the Tellarites and the Xindi, and manipulated smaller planets such as Earth and Nausicaa, and ending with the Andorians electing to enter into an economic alliance to stave off the competition from the Orion Free Traders, one that soon evolved into a military coalition and then a full-fledged unified political body. "The Interstellar Union has been at peace for over a hundred years now," he said. "War has been threatened on a few occasions, but never fought." Of course, there was no need to tell this woman *that* was about to change.

"War is something my planet has never been without," replied T'Pau. "Our recorded history goes back twelve thousand years, and during all that time, the Sons of Vulcanis have always fought one another. Some two thousand years ago, we fought a war so great it nearly consumed our entire planet in an immense Conflagration."

"Atomics," said Hikaru.

"Yes," she replied. "Most of our large-scale weaponry had always been that of the mind—which leaves the planet itself intact, if nothing else. We were unprepared for the scale of devastation we were able to release."

"Weapons of the mind?" he asked. "Like your stone?"

The old woman nodded, holding the stone out so that he could inspect it. He took it into his hands—though it had some runes etched into it, it looked just like ordinary rock. "Do you mind if I examine it thoroughly?" he asked. When T'Pau didn't object, he removed his handscanner from his belt and flipped it on. It might have looked like an ordinary stone, but the scanner showed its molecules to be aligned in patterns he'd never seen before. For this, the scanner offered one possible reason: telepathy was assumed by some scientists to be a form of quantum entanglement, and these patterns would be perfectly set to refocus or even magnify the effects. "You used this to incapacitate my troopers?" he asked, handing the heavy stone back to T'Pau.

"Yes," she replied. "It is the Stone of Gol. Not all of its powers are so direct, however."

"Of course!" Hikaru exclaimed. "You distracted our minds somehow—got into the outpost without us noticing!"

"We clouded your thoughts." T'Pau smirked. "A child's trick, but quite effective on your kind."

Presumably they'd pulled the same trick on Demora to attack the outpost the first time around. These Eridanians were formidable enemies. "But how did you know about the outpost in the first place?"

"For a species of touch-telepaths, a stray touch is a stray thought," she said. "When your people came among us in disguise, they could not help but reveal who they truly were. We quickly realized that you had the power to get us what we wanted."

"So what *is* it that you want?" Hikaru asked.

"We want peace," replied the matriarch.

He very much doubted that, especially since he'd seen the bodies left behind in the outpost. However, he had been given orders, and he would carry them out. "The Interstellar Union would be happy to send negotiators to your world," he said. "We have frequently intervened on other planets to end long, destructive conflicts—usually with agreements acceptable to all involved."

T'Pau spat. So crude a gesture from so regal a woman startled him. "We do not want this. We seek to dominate or destroy the other clans on our world. All of Minshara will be united under the Clan Hgrtcha. We know you have weapons we have never dreamed of. They might not work in the Forge because of the Conflagration's afterglow, but they will work on the rest of the planet. For the past two thousand years, the Sons of Vulcanis have fought each other mind-to-mind. Now we will fight a new way."

"But you just said that such fighting nearly destroyed your planet!" objected Hikaru.

"The Conflagration was devastating because *all* sides had the technology," said T'Pau. "If only Hgrtcha has the technology, this new war will be over quickly."

"Why should I cooperate with you?" he asked.

"You know why," she replied, a sinister grin spreading across her face. "If you do not, then those you sent to spy on us will all die."

"They want access to IG technology?"

"Any kind of weaponry we can provide. This T'Pau wants to rule the planet, and she will kill the whole outpost staff to do it."

"You can't give them that! They nearly wiped themselves out with nuclear technology—imagine what they'll do with an anti-matter warhead!"

"You don't have to tell me that. But we can't even *find* the outpost staff right now, much less *rescue* them."

Hikaru and M'Benga were standing a short distance away from the tents, the three troopers in a defensive circle around them to make sure none of the Eridanians eavesdropped on their conversation. "Then we need to cooperate with them just long enough to get a bead on the hostages," concluded M'Benga. "They don't know the extent of our transporter technology—for all they know, we can only beam in and out of the outpost."

"Exactly," said Hikaru, "and I intend to keep it that way. But first—I have a call to make." He pulled out his communicator and signaled *Kumari*.

"Yudrin here, Commander. How's it going down there?"

"This T'Pau is not an easy customer," he replied, sighing. "Any changes?"

"Ch'Satheddet and th'Eneg have established a defensive position in the observation post. Th'Rellvonda has some people working on repairing the exterior of the outpost so that it'll be shielded from the radiation again; he should be done in a couple hours, if he knows what's good for him."

"You going to get him if he doesn't?" he asked. Yudrin's dressing-downs could be brutal.

"I won't need to." Yudrin laughed. *"He's got Big Lan after him because his blasters don't always work and th'Eneg after him because his handscanners don't always work. The two of them in accord is more than enough to scare anyone into action."*

"I need you to pass on to th'Eneg and the others that the Eridanians' telepathic powers are touch-based. They need to avoid any and all physical contact with them from now on."

"They weren't touching us when they fooled us at the outpost."

"They can amplify their powers with devices called 'Stones,' but we can't do anything about that. Do you have that patch-through to General Shras for me?"

"He won't be happy about it, but we should. Give me just a moment." Hikaru had known he was leaving the job in the right hands. Shras might not appreciate a forceful Andorian subordinate very much, but he would probably find it just slightly more tolerable than a forceful human one. *"Got him, sir."*

"Commander Sulu, what is it you have to report?"

"General, is it the Eridanians' telepathic weaponry we're after?"

"By the Ice Caves of Poon, who told you that? Was it that fool Gav? I'll have him shot."

"No, General. It's simply logic—why else would the IU suddenly become interested in this planet right when the threat of Klingon invasion was becoming clear? Their telepathic powers are quite formidable. They certainly did a number on my men."

Shras grunted. *"If you say so. I suppose it doesn't matter. Seeing as you've now made contact with the natives, I would have given you your additional orders anyway."*

"Additional orders, sir?" Hikaru didn't like the sound of that.

"You are to do everything within your power to secure the cooperation of the Eridanians. The IG needs those telepathic weapons for itself, and if possible, the expertise in using them. We'd hoped to gain the knowledge simply through observation, but it looks like that won't be an option."

"It also looks like we don't have the time."

"Precisely. Prefect M'Ress has sent word to the field marshal that the government's been unable to extract any reassurances from Chancellor Korrd so far—so your mission is now of the utmost importance."

Hikaru reflected that things must be getting *really* tense at IHQ for Shras to admit to the problem. "They're requesting *our* weapons."

"If that's what it takes, then give them what they want. 36A-2B is insignificant in the current situation. We've got a thousand Aenar here, ready and waiting for whatever you manage to bring back."

"And the hostages?" Hikaru had seen IHQ's somewhat cavalier attitude toward non-IU members from time to time before, and though he might find it shameful, it didn't surprise him. The true litmus test of how bad the situation would be what Shras said about the captives. "Sir?"

To his credit, Shras hesitated slightly before giving his response. *"The lives of a small number of IU citizens are also insignificant when compared to the Klingon threat. As I said, your orders are to do everything within your power. Interstellar Headquarters out."*

M'Benga had been standing silently during the whole conversation, not betraying any reaction, but as soon as Hikaru switched his communicator off, he was seething. "What are they thinking? Do they not remember what happened on Neural Three? Or on Tezwa?" The IU had armed the residents of those planets—ostensibly neutral—with advanced weaponry to prevent the Klingons from taking them. The Klingons hadn't taken them, but there hadn't been much left for the planets' own inhabitants either.

Hikaru seethed at the notion that his daughter's life was insignificant, even if Shras hadn't known he was saying that. "Oh, I'm sure they do, Chirurgeon," he said to M'Benga. "But we're not trying to protect the Eridanians here—just ourselves."

"What are you going to do?" asked M'Benga.

Hikaru sighed. "I'm going to do whatever I have to to get those hostages back."

It wasn't at all what Shras would want to hear, but it was the truth: nothing else here mattered to Hikaru. Not even the fate of the Interstellar Union.

This should have scared him, considering that all their lives would likely be forfeit once the Klingons came, but if it would get his daughter back, right now he would have invited Korrd to tea.

"Before we begin talking about anything, I want to see that the rest of the personnel are safe."

T'Pau nodded her head. "Understandable. I will take you to them." She waved her hand at Sybok, who gave some orders to his soldiers. They began disassembling the tents. Hikaru was beginning to feel the sweat run down his face—he could only imagine how the Andorian troopers, born into a much colder climate than he, must feel. And 40 Eridani A was still climbing higher and higher into the sky.

Soon the tents were collapsed and stored, and Hikaru and his men were once again following the Eridanians across the Forge, along the base of the L-langon foothills. "This'll be nice later," said M'Benga. "When the sun starts going down, we'll be in the shade."

Hikaru looked up, shading his eyes from the sun with his hand. "That'll be quite a while, Jabilo."

A couple hours' hike brought them to the entrance of a cave. Fortunately, Big Lan had had the foresight to have everyone on the landing party equipped with water bottles before beaming down. Unfortunately, they weren't quite big enough, and Hikaru's throat was beginning to feel it by the time they reached the cave entrance. He was doing fine for oxygen, though, despite the thin atmosphere, as M'Benga had given him a shot of tri-ox before they got under way.

The Eridanians seemed to be doing well; Hikaru hadn't noticed any of them taking a drink the entire time. He supposed that was a benefit of spending one's entire life on a desert planet.

They halted their march, and T'Pau sent Sybok and a couple of his soldiers within. "You will find your people unharmed," she said.

Hikaru didn't say anything in response. "Unharmed"—except for the ones *whose brains they'd cut out.* M'Benga was fidgeting with his handscanner, downloading information from *Kumari.*

Finally, after about half an hour had passed, Sybok emerged from the mouth of the cave. "Here are all your people," he said. Shuffling out behind him was an assortment of people in either IG uniforms or drab civilian jumpsuits. He watched them file out of the cave mouth one by one: a couple of Andorians, an Ithenite, a Rigellian Chelon, some more Andorians, a Trill, a Tellarite. No humans.

No Demora.

He tried to keep his voice level. "Is this everyone?" he asked.

"It should be," said Sybok.

"It isn't," said M'Benga, sidling up to Hikaru. "According to our records, there are two unaccounted for. Doctor Amanda Grayson and . . . Ensign Demora Sulu. Sorry, sir."

Hikaru whirled around to where T'Pau was standing, as stolid as ever. "Where is she?" he demanded. "Where are they?"

"They are all here," she replied.

"They're *not*," he said. "There are two of them missing."

"Then they must have died in the attack on your outpost," she replied.

"We didn't see their bodies," countered M'Benga.

"Then perhaps we killed them already because we were tired of waiting for you," retorted T'Pau. "What does it matter? They are not here—these ones are, but they will not be if you keep this up."

Hikaru began to move closer to the cave mouth, in an attempt to talk to the hostages, but one of the Eridanian soldiers stepped in front of him, blocking his movement.

"I want to talk to them," he said, his voice seething with frustration. He was tired, and he was hot, and he was thirsty, and he wanted to know where Demora was. Had they sacrificed her as they had their victims in the outpost? Had she tried to escape and been murdered for her daring?

"You cannot," said T'Pau. "Sybok, take them back in. Commander Sulu has seen enough of them."

Sybok's soldiers indicated that the hostages should begin moving. The hostages—apparently confused as to why they'd been brought out here only to be taken back inside—began looking at each other. Finally, one of them—the Trill—broke away from the group. "Commander, what's going on?" One of the soldiers grabbed him by the shoulder, but he kept on talking. "My name is Tornellen Dax. I don't know what happened to Doctor Grayson or Ensign Sulu—we've all been in individual cells until a moment ago. Please . . . are you going to get us out of here? The others—"

Hikaru held up a hand. "It's all right, Doctor Dax." He'd heard of this Trill—a famous xenozoologist, somehow related to

Tobin Dax, himself a renowned engineer from the early days of the IU. "I'm Commander Hikaru Sulu, from the *Kumari*. We're doing everything in our power to—"

"But the others!" screamed Dax. "They cut out their brains! They made me *watch*! They *made me*—" All of a sudden he stopped talking, stopped moving entirely. Hikaru realized the Eridanian soldier guarding him had done something to his neck; the Trill man was now crumbling to the ground. The other hostages began growing increasingly agitated, and the Eridanian soldiers guarding them looked at each other nervously.

"That is enough!" shouted T'Pau. "Sybok, get them inside *now*!"

The Eridanian soldiers started to prod the hostages with their weapons, and reluctantly they began moving back inside the cave. The one who had rendered Dax unconscious picked up the Trill, slinging him over his shoulder. Soon, they were all gone, all back within the unknown depths of the cave network.

"Now," said T'Pau, "we shall talk."

And talk they did—for quite some time. T'Pau demanded hand weaponry—as well as the assurance that the IU would leave the planet and never return. Hikaru tried to broach the subject of telepathic weaponry, those "Stones" they had, but every time he did, T'Pau would radically increase her demands for arms, wanting atomics—and anything stronger if *Kumari* had it. No matter what General Shras had said, that was out of the question as far as Hikaru was concerned.

Or is it? he thought to himself. If the Interstellar Union could be spared the coming Klingon invasion, wouldn't it be worth it? An army of Aenar bearing weapons that could knock your enemies down with a mere thought—not even a fleet of D8 cruisers could stand against that. And who knew what else these people and their technology were capable of? Wouldn't one puny warlord armed with some photon torpedoes on one backwater planet be worth it? This was but *one* world . . .

Hang that. What he was really thinking was that if Demora could be saved, it *would* be worth it. What kind of people were these Eridanians? They'd supposedly had nuclear technology and spaceflight a millennium before Andorians, *two* millennia before humans. And what had they managed to do in all that time? Just nearly wipe themselves out. Here they still were, involved in their stupid squabbles; what would it matter if they were wiped out so that Demora might be saved?

But *could* Demora be saved? If these Eridanians knew where she was, they had given no sign of it. Or this Doctor Grayson, for that matter. All this was pointless if he couldn't find his daughter.

Abruptly Hikaru stood up from where they had been sitting cross-legged on the desert ground. "I see no point in continuing when two of our people are still entirely unaccounted for," he said. "We shall return to our outpost. If you wish to admit the truth, you know where to find us."

He left T'Pau sitting in the sand, the heat of 40 Eridani A beating down on her and everything else.

"Was that wise?" hissed th'Eneg once Hikaru, M'Benga, and the others had arrived back at the observation post. "You will not wish to antagonize this one."

"Considering what *she's* done," said Big Lan, "I hardly think that she has any room to be upset about someone walking away from the negotiating table. It's not as though *we've* brutally murdered five of her people and taken a dozen others hostage."

"Yes, keeping track of brutality points is an effective negotiating tactic," snapped th'Eneg. "These are obviously intelligent people, especially this matriarch, T'Pau. We should not underestimate them."

"If we're going to be giving these people atomic weaponry," said Hikaru, "then I want everything we can get in return—and *everyone*." Upon returning, he'd briefed the two men on Shras's new orders. Neither had voiced an opinion on them yet, but they'd both seemed quite intrigued when Hikaru had explained Shras's plan for the telepathic weaponry and the Aenar. "Now what have you men figured out so far?"

They were standing around the outpost's central table, and th'Eneg touched some controls on it to bring up a map of the area. His finger pointed at a large blue dot. "This is our current location, at the edge of the L-langon Mountains." He tapped some keys and another dot lit up, also at the edge of the mountains. "That is the entrance to the cave network where T'Pau showed you the hostages. The maps aren't very detailed; the electromagnetic interference is particularly strong in that area."

"There's no chance of beaming a rescue team in," said Big Lan. "We're looking at other options—that cave network permeates the whole area. There's got to be another way in. And if not—" He grinned. "—we'll make one."

Hikaru nodded. "Good. What about this 'ShiKahr' that Sybok mentioned?"

The map zoomed out to reveal the entire Forge. On the opposite side of it a red light blinked. "According to the data the outpost team had gathered," said th'Eneg, "ShiKahr is a prominent local city-state. It is primarily dominated by the Clan Hgrtcha, of which T'Pau is matriarch. Hgrtcha is a powerful clan; a number of cities within the area owe fealty or are otherwise allied to it. Of course, it is but one of many political powers jockeying for control over Eridani."

"This isn't their usual area, though," said Lan. "Almost everything they control is concentrated on the other side of the Forge. *This* side of the Forge is dominated by a clan known as the Nashih, who are technically at war with the Hgrtcha, though there's a cease-fire in effect right now."

"I'd wager that our friends from ShiKahr still aren't supposed to be here, then," said Hikaru.

"Exactly," said Lan. "Sybok's forces are probably small, to avoid attracting attention."

"That's good," said Hikaru. "That should let—"

He was interrupted by a chiming from Lan's communicator. The security chief pulled it out and answered the call. "Go ahead."

"Sir, this is Trooper Vaughn. We've got an Eridanian at the outpost entrance who wants to talk to Commander Sulu." There was almost no interference in the transmission; apparently th'Rellvonda's work on the outpost hull had been successful.

Lan looked at Hikaru, who nodded. "Copy that, Vaughn. We'll be down there in a minute. Make sure he's not carrying any weapons—conventional, telepathic, or otherwise."

"Aye, sir." The communicator squealed off.

"Sounds like T'Pau wants to talk," said Hikaru. "Let's go see what she wants."

A short while later, he was standing at the closed entrance to the outpost. Theoretically, its disguise as a large boulder meant that no one should be able to find it from the outside, but the repeated Eridanian access to it had certainly disproven that notion. Lan and M'Benga had elected to accompany him; th'Eneg had work to do in the command center.

Hikaru looked at the viewer displaying what was on the other side of the entrance. A lone Eridanian soldier stood there, a sack of some sort in his hand. A human security trooper that Hikaru presumed was Vaughn stood next to him, looking somewhat nervous. "Open her up," Hikaru ordered, and Big Lan complied, the large security door sliding open.

"Sir!" Vaughn saluted sharply as they stepped outside. "He checks out. Won't let me look at what's in the sack, but scans show nothing dangerous."

Of course, reflected Hikaru, there was the chance that the Eridanian had somehow telepathically distracted Vaughn, but he supposed that that was a risk they'd have to take in all their dealings with these people. "You have a message for me?" he asked the soldier.

Like the majority of his people, this man had black hair and a fair complexion. "You are Commander Hikaru Sulu of the *Kumari*?" he asked.

"I am indeed," replied Hikaru. "Might I know who I am addressing?"

"My name is unimportant," replied the soldier. "*This* is important." He drew the top of the sack open and put his hand in, pulling out—

A severed head.

The head looked almost human or Eridanian, until Hikaru noticed the pattern of dark spots along the hairline. It was the head of a Trill.

Tornellen Dax.

The soldier began to speak. "My matriarch T'Pau sends you the head of your comrade, together with this message: to get what you want, be prepared to give what we want. We know you do not wish to aid us. Unless you want the rest of your people to suffer the same fate as this one, you will negotiate in good faith. Forget about your daughter. You cannot save her. Remember the ones you *can* save."

There'd been a particularly violent storm that night. Normally the aircar landing pad was protected from these things by a low-level shield, but the storm had knocked out the power and the pad had iced over. He woke up, took in a cup of tea, then woke up Demora so that she could help him shovel off the ice and snow.

She wasn't too happy.

He agreed to let her shower and eat while he got started.

But after over an hour of back-breaking work—it had been a fierce storm—she was still nowhere to be seen. He made a snowball and threw it at her window. Fifteen more minutes and she still wasn't there. He went and thumped on the door. A surly "All right!" answered him. He went back to work. Finally, she emerged, shovel in hand, a scowl etched deeply into her features.

"I don't want to be doing this," she said.

"Well, that's evident," he snapped. "Do you think I want to be?"

"It's the weekend! I was going to—"

That was it. Was he supposed to do all this while she did her nails inside? "You know what, Demora? Life's cold."

He recognized the look she gave him. Her mother had given it to him a few times and it hurt. But she bent over and started to shovel.

MINSHARA: FOUR

The sensation was different this time. Before it had been relatively simple—there had been her, and there had been the Other. Now it was not so balanced.

Ah, company. How nice!

Well, thank you, she projected. She wasn't sure if she had to consciously think her messages or what, but it had worked well enough last time. She wasn't exactly trained for this. *You must be S'task. My name is Demora. I am—*

—a visitor on my world. I know. Indeed, I know all that S'oval does.

Great, that makes things so much easier.

You are not from T'Khasi. Why are you here?

For a philosopher, you're pretty demanding.

I was a soldier and a poet. Only those who do not truly know me call me a "philosopher."

Don't get snarky with me, pal. And I already told S'oval why I'm here, so shouldn't you know?

I seek a different knowledge. There is a hidden reason for your presence, and I sense that you know what it is.

There may be many reasons that I'm not privy to, simply because I do not need to know. I work better that way.

Interesting, was S'task's reply. **You know evasion is futile, yet you do so anyway. Shall we try again?**

Why should we? I'll tell you what I want to tell you.

She felt amused, but she certainly wasn't. Presumably she was picking up on this S'task's emotions. **I find your attitude refreshing.**

Oh? How so?

After two thousand years in the company of people who revere me, it is like a breeze of fresh air in an old house. He paused. **There is a barrier around you. Are you afraid of my trying to hurt you?**

Not afraid. Just cautious.

I understand.

The longer this conversation took, the more Demora felt she was getting the hang of it. This "meeting of minds" was an unusual experience, but it wasn't unpleasant. More than that she couldn't say. In fact, she'd be hard-pressed to describe it in any detail. Everything was through a layer of thick fog, close yet hard to pinpoint. It felt like diving in milk, with her perception altered and her movements slowed by the resistance of her surroundings.

She wondered how much of it was real, or if "real" was an entirely meaningless descriptor in such an environment. The only thing she felt she could really rely on were S'task's words. Maybe.

S'oval and I can help you. Without us, you will not survive the desert. My followers have weathered this environment for millennia, after all. And, of course, as T'Khasians we can help you through more encounters with our people.

Sounds great. Where's the catch?

"Catch"? How very amusing. I want an answer.

You don't give up easily, do you. Well, if it means so much to you—

Suddenly, she couldn't continue: her mind felt unsettled, and yet it wasn't her mind. The "substance" of the fog surrounding her was changing into something thick and hard, constricting her. Previously unseen walls were closing in on her. What was happening?

No, it can't be!

What is it? she barely managed to squeeze out.

S'oval . . . his life is leaving him. He is dying while still connected to you. You must hurry!

And do what? Tell me! Her claustrophobia was rearing up again, and this was worse than any cave. What should she do? What *could* she do?

You must end the meld. Take control of your body once again, and break physical contact with S'oval; the meld will end then.

How am I supposed to do that? I can't move a muscle!

Do not reject S'oval's strength, borrow it and add it to your own. Only with his help can you surive.

And what about him? Can't we help him?

No, as sad as this is. He is old—too old for his body to cling to life much longer. If you do not end the meld, your mind will die with his.

What? She couldn't quite believe what was happening but, having no other choice, she went along with it. If S'task was right about S'oval's condition, speed was essential.

She still felt disconnected from her body, blocked by the milky wall. She pushed against it, searching for a weak spot, but the more she pushed, the more constricting the fog became.

She began to panic, her mind flailing wildly.

S'task addressed her. It was as though he was talking to her from a great distance. **Do not resist. S'oval is still dominant; if you fight him, you will not have the strength to break contact. But he has lost control of the meld. He cannot help you.**

So I should just let him smother me, is that it? She wouldn't need to let him; it would just happen at this rate.

You need to pass through him. He wants nothing more

than for us to come to no harm. He knows there is no alternative to death for him, but the two of us may still escape.

With you inside my head.

It is the only option.

That doesn't make it better, y'know. She projected nothing more
for a while. At the edges of her perception, strange things were
happening, thoughts were bubbling through the wall, but when
she focused on them, they popped, and every pop felt like it took
a piece of her—and S'oval and S'task—with it.

A huge bubble formed, and when it popped, the whole wall
collapsed. She felt as though she was gasping for air, but she was
free. *What was that?*

He is close to death. The abyss will soon take him.

We'd better hurry up, then. Yet still Demora had not the faintest
idea what to do.

**Concentrate. You need to go through S'oval. Follow
your instinct.**

Easier said than done! And yet, she did as he instructed her. She
fell toward S'oval, a rapidly shrinking point of light/dark in the
milky fog. A ray extended out from him, and she felt herself grab
on as they both hurtled deeper and deeper. The chasm yawned
open ahead . . .

She could feel her body! She willed herself to bend and lift her
arms, then stretched them horizontally away from her. At first,
she thought it wasn't working, but then she could feel something
helping her—a push from S'oval. Elated, she put all her own
strength into it.

At the same time she felt herself hit the floor, the milky fog
disappeared, as did the chasm and the light/dark point. She was
herself again.

Well, aside from an ancient Minsharan philosopher who fan-
cied himself a poet.

Demora took a few breaths to give herself some time to recover from the meld, and not yet trusting herself to walk, she

crawled over to the prone form of S'oval and inspected him for lifesigns. He was still breathing, but barely. His eyes were open, and he was looking at her with a somber expression.

"Do not worry, Demora. I am about to join the High Masters, and I will have much to tell them. Leave me here. When I am dead, Czei will take care of my body. Now you must leave and help your friends. Take whatever you need." His voice was still strong, making it seem as though he would live another day. But if she believed him—and S'task—then he was dying. "I ask you to do me one favor, though."

"Of course." The words were out of her mouth before she knew it. Instantly she regretted it—the dangers involved were terrifying to contemplate. And yet . . . S'oval had helped her, despite their extremely unpleasant first encounter. What did it say about her that she didn't immediately refuse to help him?

The simple truth was, it was hard to refuse a dying man, even an Eridanian. "What do you want me to do?" She grabbed his hand and pressed it to reassure him. In an instant, she was connected with him again, and not just him. This was more like a three-way conversation within her head.

I thank you. My only concern now is for S'task. Carry him until you find somebody who's capable—and deserving—of caring for him permanently. Your mind is strong, but it is not built like ours.

Is there nothing I can do for you?

No. Look after yourself—that is more important. I've led a peaceful and long life, and that is more than enough. Now, go!

Leave him to his . . . *sehlat*? She couldn't do that, could she? He closed his eyes again, and Demora had the feeling that he would never open them again. Still, she held on to his hand.

You have been a good friend and a good student. S'task was projecting through her now. **I could not have asked for a better man to carry my *katra*.**

That's more than I could wish for. I'm glad that I was able to learn so much, *T'Kehr,* and to help you.

Your help has been crucial. I am proud to have known you; I will remember you as long as I exist.

I could not ask for more. Please, my *T'Kehr,* help Demora and keep her safe. Her friends may still be alive; if she can find them, perhaps further bloodshed can be avoided.

I will do as you ask, friend S'oval. Now prepare yourself to journey to the realm of the *sim're.*

S'task-*hel,* I will tell the High Masters to be patient while they await your arrival at their table. May you be successful in your endeavors! S'oval then addressed Demora: My new friend from space, I hope you find your friends alive and well.

May you rest in peace, thought Demora as she let go of S'oval's hand, breaking the connection. The man's chest rose once again and then no more.

He was dead.

After a few respectful moments, she got to her feet and began inspecting the cave for anything useful or nutritious, fighting with herself over what to do with the old man's body. His wishes were clear, but her upbringing required her to make sure the body was either interred two meters deep, or incinerated at such high temperatures that even the bones fell to dust. If only she still had her IG blaster! She could've taken care of S'oval's cremation without finding firewood.

What was she supposed to do? S'task must have sensed her dilemma, because he suddenly intruded on her thoughts. I realize that there must be different ways of taking care of the dead in your culture. Those who live in the wilderness know better than to deny their part in the cycle of life. Their *katra* lives on, so why should they care about what happens to their bodies? S'oval was consoled to know his body would serve his fellow creatures; you should be, too.

So I should just let his body lie there? Their acquaintance was only a few minutes old, and she was beginning to regret it. Philosophy had never interested her all that much, and she didn't suffer pretentious twits for long before telling them where to shove their "wisdom."

It is the *katra* that makes a person, and the *katra* endures.

I felt his being sucked into oblivion!

That is not so. The High Masters await him at their table, laden with food for a hungry mind.

Demora wasn't one for mythological mumbo-jumbo, but she kept her thoughts to herself as she worked. She found the cloak she'd taken off Candle Guy in a corner, folded into a perfect triangle, and put it back on, reattaching the curious loops and hooks that held it closed.

We call the material *vel-kroh,* S'task informed her. **You do not have something like it?**

I guess we humans just aren't as bright as you Minsharans. Now let's get out of here, though I still say it's wrong to leave him behind.

Only because you were raised to think so. There are different cultures that see things differently.

Oh, don't you dare patronize me! You may be a famous ancient poet, but so far, you've just been a nuisance. The sooner I get rid of you, the better.

She was beginning to get the hang of keeping her thoughts to herself. She was confident that she'd eventually be able to keep S'task packed in a corner of her mind.

Now, then, where was she supposed to go?

She hated to admit it, but S'task was a survival expert—had to be, after all this time in the desert. He had to know the lay of the land better than anyone.

Searching the rest of the cave yielded not much in the way of equipment and food, just a large canister that, once opened, smelled foul enough to kill a rhino. Around the bend at the far end of the cave, dangerously close to the *shatarr* refuge, she discovered S'oval's source of water, a small spring that seeped water through a crack in the wall. She washed the canister out thoroughly before filling it to the rim, screwing the lid back on, and stashing it in a leather bag.

One last look around, and Demora was satisfied that she'd packed what she needed—which was also all she could carry. There wasn't much point in taking so much that she collapsed from exhaustion after just a few hours.

S'oval still lay near the dying fire. Demora gave him a posture more fitting for a man of his state: his arms crossed over his chest, similar to the pose the ancient pharaohs on Earth were usually depicted in, and his legs straightened.

It was no use worrying about what she couldn't change, and so she headed for the cave mouth. When she reached it—after turning only a few corners and bends—she stopped far enough inside it to remain in the shade. Outside, it was high noon, judging from the shadows in the distance, since she couldn't see the sun from her vantage point. Certainly not the most ideal time for hiking, but time was of the essence.

Where do you want to go, Demora? S'task asked, having given her a moment of peace. Not long enough, in her opinion.

To my friends. I can't be more specific than that, since I don't know where they are.

I may be of help here. However, I require access to your memories from the other day.

Well, then, be my guest. She knew sarcasm wasn't worth much on this planet, but it did make her feel better.

Thank you. A short pause, then: **You know more than you realize. Your recollection of recent events is excellent; however, you have buried everything to avoid having to process it.**

What are you saying? she asked as she stepped over a number of large rocks that almost blocked her path along the side of the mountain. She was walking without any idea where she was headed. Her cloak was flapping in the weak breeze that did little more than send clouds of dust into the air around her, making every breath unpleasant.

I can help you remember. I can also make you understand.

Both for the price of one? You're too generous, buddy.

I do not think so. It is the least I can do for you.

Too damn right, she thought, hoping that he wouldn't catch it. *What you're saying is, you want to take my mind back to the attack? I'm not sure I want that. Wait . . . No, I'm sure I don't want that.*

It is the only way of getting any usable information about the attackers and the whereabouts of your friends.

It had all been so rushed; if S'task could cause her mind to go through everything again, but in slow motion, she'd be able to examine it all closely, and he might even be able to find some clues.

Okay, she projected. *Let's do it. Do you want me to sit down?*

Yes, preferably in the shade. There is a *qir'lal* bush over there, and I see it is even carrying fruit. It is not quite Irhheen yet, but they should already be ripe. You may want to eat some of them.

You're joking, right? With my luck, they're deadly to humans. Like everything else on this planet. I'll just sit down and drink some water.

As you wish.

She made herself comfortable in the shadow cast by the tall bush and took a big gulp of the no-longer-cool water from the canister.

I'm ready.

Of the three troopers she left behind, she spots only two. Gohoy and Creidranc cover the area outside with blaster beams, but Pol is nowhere to be found. However, when she moves closer, ducking to hide behind the upturned desk that serves as the troopers' cover, she discovers that the Tellarite has been hurt in the upper torso and is bleeding profusely. Demora kneels to help her, but Pol grunts and tells her with clenched jaws to give those bastards what they deserve.

Signaling the other troopers to take position, Demora picks a spot where she has a good view of the landscape outside. As she takes careful aim and shoots, she hopes that Doctor Grayson's worries about the Eridanians's mind-powers are unfounded. If Grayson's right, none of them has a chance.

The IG personnel keep firing, and before long, her blaster's energy is depleted. She reaches into her upper uniform pocket to take out another power pack but never finishes the move.

An unknown sensation overwhelms her, something she has never before encountered. It is as if a strange fog has crept up on her, dulling her senses and slowing her down. On the edge of awareness, she forms one final thought.

Damn.

And then she doesn't die, which comes as a surprise to her. Instead, she glimpses from the corner of her eye a person who wasn't there before. It is a native, and she points her blaster at him, pressing the trigger.

It doesn't fire.

The native, a tall, old man, dark-skinned and wearing much more ornate clothing than she has seen on any other Eridanians, smiles at her with no malice in his expression. "It is as I suspected," he says. "Demora, you are the victim of a psionic resonator. What you are now remembering is the effect of a very powerful artifact. Its existence and use by those that attacked you is a first clue as to their origin."

She has never seen him before, but from that tone of voice there is no doubting who he is. "S'task!"

"Of course," he says. He looks at her, and his worried expression reminds her of Grandfather Tetsuo. "Now let us find out what clan these attackers belong to. When we know that, we can deduce their location."

"Great! And then we can teach them a lesson!"

"I am afraid not, Demora," he says. "What we need to do is talk to them. I am confident that I can convince them of their folly. Mindless warring has never been a solution to any problem, and it pains me that my people have not learned a single lesson since my death."

"We can't talk to them if we can't find them," she points out.

"Indeed. We seem to have entered in the middle of the battle. I ask you now to refocus your memories and direct them toward the moments before you fell unconscious."

"What—how am I supposed to do that?"

"Concentrate. I will help you. Think about what happens next. You were involved in a close fight, so some of them must have been able to approach despite your impressive weaponry. How was that possible?"

Her mind is a blank. All she has are fragments of memory; she can't piece them together into a coherent narrative. "I don't know!"

"Between the trauma and the psionic resonator, it is understandable that you are confused," S'task says, managing to sound only half-patronizing. "Memory is fluid, and with enough effort, it can be directed. I am confident that you are able to achieve this; so far you have proven adept in matters of the mind. Now relax the bindings you tie around yourself. You need to be free of tension for this to succeed. Remind yourself that you are experiencing what has already happened. Nothing can hurt you now, do not forget that."

Demora tries, but she is too enmeshed in her own memories, holding the blaster as the Eridanians fire back with their projectile weapons. It is easy for S'task to talk about "relaxing the bindings" when he doesn't have to do it. It is impossible for her. "A little help here would go a long way, buddy."

"As you wish. I can but guide, however. You will still have to do your part."

Immediately, she senses a change in the world around her. It begins to distort, to move, to accelerate. Creidranc and Gohoy disappear. She herself has changed position, now standing next to a body that turns out to be Pol's. The Tellarite has been dragged over to the south wall, and her wound has been dressed. Of the medic, there is no trace.

There is a female native charging at her, weapon raised. It is a strange weapon, with a curved blade that fans out from the handle, designed more for hacking and slashing than stabbing. The woman shouts something at her that is barely audible because of all the other noise, but Demora has other things to worry about.

She falls back, step by step, until her shoulder blades connect with the cool titanium of the wall. The armed woman pursues her, and eventually she is close enough to push the blade under Demora's chin. The metal feels frighteningly cold, and it is obvious that any move will cause the woman to kill her on the spot.

Another native hurries toward them as still more flood the outpost, having finally overrun its defenses. He addresses the woman, and as the words leave his lips, Demora is amazed that she understands what he is saying. She couldn't the last time through!

"They are defeated. A few of them resisted capture, so we killed them. So far, we have captured eleven, but there may be more hidden elsewhere. We have been unable to access two rooms in the center of the building, but Decius and his team have promised to change that within the next hour."

"Good," is all the woman says. Neither she nor the man seems to spot S'task standing next to Demora, looking interestedly at both of them.

"Do you think she will be pleased?" the man asks. It is clear that he places great importance on "her" satisfaction, whoever that is. "True, we had expected that they would put up less of a fight, but victory is ours now. The dead will be mourned, of course," he adds after a stern look from the woman.

"Yes. Remember, Sybok, that our clan has always fought hard and suffered great losses, and yet we have always come back stronger than before. She will understand, even if she expected us to be more efficient." The woman smirks and points at Demora. "Take this alien to the others. T'Pau does not want us to kill any more of them."

At the name's mention, S'task's eyebrows shoot up in surprise, and almost immediately a smile tucks at his lips. Presumably this is a good sign.

Demora complies without resistance as the pressure of the blade against her throat decreases and the man grabs her arm to take her outside with him.

They have not yet passed the artificial threshold of the blasted hole in the wall when everything disappears around her, leaving her alone in the darkness.

When Demora opened her eyes again, she was momentarily surprised to see the arid mountainside, but she shook the confusion off. In the shade of the bush it was pleasantly cool, with an unexpected breeze that tucked at her sweaty hair.

You have been most helpful.

Oh, right. *He* was still here. *What do we do now?*

T'Pau is the feared matriarch of Clan Hgrtcha, which is located in ShiKahr, across the Forge. One of my previous carriers once located a hidden facility of theirs here in the L-langon Mountains. I suggest we go to it.

Ah. I hate to mention it, but I don't think they're going to be very friendly. I wasn't exactly nice to some of them when I managed to escape, and the general principle around here seems to be to counter violence with violence. I don't think they'll want to chat.

You forget that you have the benefit of my knowledge and experience. Together, we will be able to convince them to take us to T'Pau.

And then what?

We talk.

This is all easy for you to say; you're already dead.

In my present situation I have as much to lose as you do.

The man had a point there. Somehow she still had trouble wrapping her mind around everything. The IU had thrown them into a society where nobody thought twice about reading another person's deepest thoughts and—as if that wasn't enough!—minds could live on after a person's death and even be transferred to other people. This still sounded like a fairy tale, even though she'd witnessed it firsthand.

We need to hurry. Dusk is approaching, and we need to be clear of the basin before the *le-matya* come out to hunt.

All right. Let's get started. I just hope you're right about us making it out alive.

As do I.

"We fight. We battle. We destroy. The Interstellar Union is protected and the Interstellar Guard, and the Interstellar Guard is protected by the Security Forces. But this—" The dean of the Interstellar Institute's Security College held her flabbjellah over her head. "—this is not just an implement of war. We not only protect the Interstellar Union, we are the Union. And we protect the Union because it creates. It plays. It sings. And so do we."

The Coridanite woman held the instrument and began to play the IU anthem, "The Constellation of Unity and Multiplicity." And in unison with her, so did all of the newly commissioned security officers.

Hikaru had never been to the Security College's commissioning ceremony before, but he knew it was loosely based on Andorian traditions going back a millennium or more. Once the music had finished—and Hikaru had to admit that the new officers were fairly good—the dean dismissed them.

Demora found Hikaru easily, as he was one of only a few humans in the crowd. She looked like she had been born to wear the black IG uniform. "Congratulations," he said, giving her a quick hug. "But it's not too late, you know."

She frowned. "Too late for what?"

"You can still give up this foolish idea of becoming a security officer and be a scientist like your parents."

She rolled her eyes, but she was smiling. "Give it a rest, Dad."

KUMARI: FIVE

T hat's *it!*"

"What's 'it'?" Yudrin left a strategic pause. "Sir."

Hikaru, tired from the long day's exertions—not to mention eager to get out of his not-so-fantastically-smelling IG uniform—had beamed up to *Kumari* and taken the opportunity to shower. He'd then retreated to the starboard observation pod, only to find Subcommander Phelana Yudrin already there.

Once this crisis was over, he was going to have to find a new private retreat. For now, though, he was glad to have someone to talk to who wasn't Big Lan or th'Eneg—someone who was interested in something other than strategy or tactics.

"I'm tired of dealing with these Eridanians on their own terms," said Hikaru. "They break into our outpost, they butcher our people, they behead them—and I'm supposed to *negotiate* with them?"

"Those *are* General Shras's orders."

Hikaru sighed. "If this was *just* about the hostages, he'd have ordered me to go in there guns blazing, no problem. They might have their telepathic powers, but we still have a technological edge." Though whether or not the Eridanians were still ignorant of it was another matter. They'd obviously overheard his call to General Shras and his conversation with M'Benga, despite his belief that they'd been out of earshot; apparently these Eridanians had some phenomenal hearing. This meant they knew about the extent of the powers of the transporter—though they'd still be hard-pressed to do anything about it. Or so Hikaru hoped. "But we need their cooperation, not just our people back, and so Shras expects me to give advanced weaponry to a woman who thinks it's acceptable to send me a hostage's head in a sack!"

They'd locked the soldier—who'd given his name, Tal, but nothing else—in the outpost's cells, but there was precious little else they could do for Tornellen Dax. Hikaru had heard rumors that the minds of great Trill could last beyond their natural lifetimes, but the Trill were a secretive bunch, and he had no idea how it was done. If, indeed, it was even true; IU records had precious little to say on the subject.

"What choice do you have?" asked Yudrin. "We have our orders." Hikaru was never sure when she espoused a belief and when she was playing devil's advocate, and this time was no different.

"Our orders are to get the telepathic weaponry by whatever means are deemed appropriate," said Hikaru slowly, as he thought aloud. "But our negotiating position would be much stronger if the Eridanians' was much weaker . . . if they didn't have hostages to hold over our head."

"Are you proposing we liberate the hostages, *then* sit down with T'Pau again?" asked Yudrin.

Hikaru nodded. "Yes . . . yes, I think I am. I don't want to give these people antimatter weapons or even handblasters. They've almost destroyed their planet once before; I don't want them to go through with it now. And I *don't* want to add another head to our collection every time I do something T'Pau disagrees with."

Yudrin, who had been standing and staring out the window of the pod, sat down on the bench next to Hikaru, grabbed his shoulders and looked him squarely in the eyes. "Sir . . . this isn't about Demora, is it?"

Hikaru reflected inwardly for a moment. *Is it?* "No . . . I don't think so. It was at first," he admitted, "but not anymore. I don't know what's happened to her—and I'm starting to suspect the Eridanians don't, either. But when I saw the head of that young Trill scientist in the hands of that butcher, I realized that we were approaching this entirely the wrong way. It has never been the policy of the IG to negotiate with hostage-takers, and I don't know why we're starting now."

Yudrin nodded. "Good," she said. "As long as your priorities are right, then I'm behind you one hundred percent."

Hikaru smiled. "Glad to hear it, Subcommander." He stood up, ready to exit the pod. "Now let's get those hostages back."

He was glad he'd convinced her. He'd almost convinced himself.

With some prodding from Hikaru, th'Eneg and Big Lan had actually managed to come up with a plan that they considered mutually agreeable. Their scans still hadn't turned up another entrance to the L-langon cave network, and Lan had suggested using *Kumari*'s fighter squadron to do some aerial reconnaissance, but the idea had been dismissed as too overt, and th'Eneg had pointed out that any "backdoor" entrances to the cave network were likely to be guarded anyway.

So they'd decided to create their own. Their scans had turned up an area where a cave came pretty close to the surface, and not far from it was a good beam-down spot—a wide, open valley with sufficiently low levels of electromagnetic interference. In the middle of local night, *Kumari* beamed down some excavation equipment. The landing party was large: in addition to Lan and almost the ship's whole contingent of security troopers, there was Corpek th'Rellvonda and an engineering team to run the drills, Yrrebneddor th'Eneg and a couple of his intelligence analysts, and Jabilo M'Benga and his assistant, a Caitian named Tellameer V'Larr.

And, of course, Hikaru.

Subcommander Yudrin had asked for permission to come along—she was antsy, being kept away from the action planetside so much—but with two-thirds of the senior staff already on Eridani, Hikaru didn't think it was a good idea for his executive officer to be there, too. Besides, Hikaru wanted her up there to foist off any complaints from General Shras and also to keep an eye on the developing political situation with the Klingons—s'Bysh had picked up some disturbing rumors from the Gorn Hegemony and the Guidon Pontificate.

When the transporter beam released Hikaru, he actually shivered—evidently Eridani was much cooler at night. Or maybe it was because they were in the mountains. Either way, he was quite thankful for it. He could still see the two companion stars up in the sky, but at this distance, they provided neither heat nor light of any real substance. For once, the crew's black IG uniforms actually blended in with the Eridanian environment.

Hikaru quickly located th'Rellvonda. The *Kumari*'s chief engineer had very dark skin for an Andorian—a midnight blue rather than the typical sky blue—making him very easy to spot in a crowd. He was standing next to one of the laser drills, which was over twice his height, barking orders at the engineers who were crawling over it. Hikaru waited until he had finished yelling at a young enlisted Tellarite before he approached him. "How's it going?"

"It'd be going faster if you weren't all asking me questions!" snapped th'Rellvonda, not looking up from the data slate he was reading.

Hikaru *harrumph*ed. Th'Rellvonda looked up from the slate and went the palest Hikaru had ever seen him. "Sorry, sir," he said, snapping off a sharp salute. Hikaru was impressed—normally the engineer didn't bother. "These slackers have been letting me down today."

"What's the holdup?" asked Hikaru.

"We're trying to get the equipment secured for transport,"

replied th'Rellvonda, gesturing at where some tank treads had been attached to the side of the drill. "These things have antigrav units, but they're not trustworthy with the interference."

"Couldn't you have done this before we beamed down?"

"Probably, but there's more room and—" Th'Rellvonda turned his head to look at an engineer who had just dropped a mess of self-sealing stem bolts all over the ground. "—it *wasn't supposed to take long!*"

The engineer began frantically scooping up the bolts as best he could.

Hikaru gave the poor fellow a small smile. "I'm sure you're doing the best you can," he said. "Just make sure we're ready to go by daybreak." Lan had decided that it was too risky to spend much time moving through the unknown environment of the Eridanian mountains during the night—data from the outpost had indicated that the local predators were as ruthless and dangerous as their andorianoid cousins.

The engineer stood upright and saluted sharply, then fell back to his knees as he resumed picking up bolts.

Hikaru went to find th'Eneg. He eventually located the intelligence officer sitting in a lotus position on the rocky ground, surrounded by numerous data slates, apparently unperturbed by the squad of security troopers going through combat drills right behind him.

"How's it going, Lieutenant?" he asked.

The other man looked up. "I am worried, Commander." His voice was less raspy in the thin Eridanian atmosphere.

"Worried?" asked Hikaru. "What about?"

"The telepathic capabilities of this species are an almost entirely unknown quantity," replied th'Eneg. He held up one of the slates and handed it to Hikaru, who began flipping through what looked like analyses of an alien brain. "The outpost staff was only beginning to analyze them before the attack, and had learned next to nothing. There are suggestions that their mental capabilities are vast—they diverted our attention sufficiently to get all the way into the outpost control room before we noticed them. The T'Pau woman you talked to could cause our troopers to drop to their knees with a so-called 'Stone.' They blew a hole in the side of our outpost, and captured or killed all of its personnel. How do we fight that?"

"We can't," said Hikaru. "No one can. That's why we're here. They've got the ultimate weapon, and we somehow have to get it from them."

"I am worried," reiterated th'Eneg. "My analysts are scouting the surrounding area with handscanners—but what if we advance into hostile territory because what they think is an empty valley is teeming with natives? Or what if they're mentally induced to send an all-clear? Or what if they simply never return, their minds squashed like micrometeorites against a deflector shield?" He shook his head. "This is an enemy I do not wish to fight."

"Do you *ever* wish to fight?" asked Hikaru. "You've always told me that the key to winning a battle is preempting the need for it in the first place."

"That is true," acknowledged th'Eneg. "But when a battle must be fought—as this one must—then it is best to enter the fight with as much knowledge as possible about what the enemy can and will do."

"And here we have almost none," said Hikaru, staring up at the desert sky. So far from any fragment of civilization, there was no light pollution. Hikaru had not seen stars so plentiful planetside in a long, long time. Sol was below the horizon right now, but it didn't take long for him to locate the Andorian primary, Kuy'va, beneath whose light he'd spent so much of his life. How much simpler his duties had been when he'd merely had to teach classes at the Institute and participate in transwarp trials—how much easier it had been to keep Demora safe when the biggest threat they'd faced had been getting burnt by ice bores.

"We could be compromised right now," he said. "And there'd be nothing we could do about it."

"Exactly!" hissed th'Eneg. "I talked to Chirurgeon M'Benga about blocking out the thought waves, but we don't know enough about how telepathy works. If only we hadn't—"

Whatever action th'Eneg regretted, Hikaru would never know. A shrill whistling suddenly filled his ears. "Get down!" someone shouted, and Hikaru found himself being shoved roughly to the ground—just in time to experience the valley being rocked by an enormous explosion.

His ears were ringing like crazy, and he pulled himself up painfully to a sitting position. He'd been hit by scattered pieces of rock and scraped up a bit, but there didn't seem to be any serious cuts. The security trooper who'd knocked him to the ground hadn't been so lucky—blue blood seeped out of a gash on his forehead, which had come precipitously close to one of his antennae.

Of th'Eneg, there was no sign.

Hikaru knew he couldn't afford to think of either man now. He was in command, and he needed to affirm it. "Regroup!" he shouted. "Fall in behind the excavators!"

He looked around to get his bearings, but all the dust kicked up from the explosion made it impossible. He reached for his hand-scanner, only to find it wasn't in his equipment belt anymore.

Clipped shouts began to fill the air around him—Big Lan's security troopers calling out recognition and location signals. Hikaru grabbed the bleeding man before him and heaved him to his feet. "Move it, trooper!" He began heading toward where—at a desperate guess—he thought the excavators were.

Suddenly, out of the dust cloud came two more troopers, an Andorian woman and an Edoan man. "Commander!" shouted the Edoan. "Are you all right?"

"I'm fine," replied Hikaru. "But this man needs medical attention."

The Andorian took hold of the wounded trooper and laid him back on the ground. She removed a medical kit from her equipment belt. "She'll be able to stabilize him until we can get him to a chirurgeon," said the Edoan. "Right now we need to get you to safety."

Fortunately, the Edoan *did* have his handscanner, and he quickly got Hikaru behind the relative safety of the giant excavators. Lan was already there. "What's the situation?" asked Hikaru.

"Some sort of artillery shell," replied Lan. "Fortunately, it seems to be taking them a while to reload."

"Or maybe they're waiting for the dust to clear," said Hikaru. "It's not like we can mount an effective counterattack."

"That's where you're wrong, sir," said Big Lan with a grin. "Th'Rellvonda and I have had an idea." He gestured up at the excavator.

Hikaru followed his hand to see the dark blue engineer, barely visible in the thick cloud, scrambling over the top of the laser drill. "What's he doing?" he asked.

"Realigning the directional mirror," replied Lan. "To let this thing shoot sideways instead of down."

Hikaru shook his head. "You won't be able to aim it!"

"I'm hoping we won't have to," said Lan. "Blasting the side out of a mountain should be enough to startle these guys into submission."

"It won't be that easy," said Hikaru. "The Eridanians know what we're capable of—but they're *still* here! We need to fight them off, not just scare them off. What are your troopers' orders?"

"They're sweeping the area, making sure they find everyone. The chirurgeons are all right, but not all of the noncombat personnel are accounted for yet. Neither are all the troopers, actually."

Hikaru nodded, thinking fast. What should they do next? That rather depended on what the Eridanians did next. And he had no idea what that might be. Were they readying another artillery shot? Were they about to rush in on foot and butcher the landing party? Were they simply going to telepathically incapacitate everyone?

He had no way of knowing, and unfortunately, the Eridanians had a very easy way of finding out *his* plans as soon as he made them.

Yet he'd seen them surprised. They hadn't expected Yudrin's backup team in the outpost, nor Doctor Dax's outburst at the cave entrance. They weren't omniscient, despite th'Eneg's fears. It seemed that sudden moves or actions *could* take them by surprise.

He had the beginnings of a plan. But he couldn't think about it—he had to keep it off of his mind until just before he put it into action. But what could he think about until then? He needed something that would preoccupy his thoughts totally and utterly. He needed to think about—

Demora.

He thought of his daughter emerging from her mother's womb and taking her first look at the world, so small and helpless.

He thought of his daughter falling down the stairs as she tried to brave them for the first time and failed.

He thought of his daughter sleeping quietly as he bid her goodbye before assuming his place at *Enterprise*'s helm in a desperate attempt to stop an alien cloud from destroying Earth.

He thought of his daughter coming inside their new house in Laikan, all cut up and half-freezing from trying to brave an ice storm in nothing more than shorts and a tank top.

He thought of his daughter trapped in a cell in a cave beneath the L-langon Mountains, quietly starving.

He thought of his daughter lost in the Forge, wasting away in the heat.

He thought of his daughter dead, her head cut open and her brain extracted by Eridanians in a savage ritual.

He thought of his daughter.

He thought of Demora heading back out into that ice storm, this time clothed in an appropriate Andorian parka.

He thought of Demora taking her first steps across the kitchen floor, as he and Susan looked on and smiled.

He thought of Demora already looking the part of an IG officer in the sleek, gray trainee's uniform the day she left for the Interstellar Institute.

He thought of Demora trying her best not to cry at Susan's funeral, trying to be strong for him.

He thought of Demora taking top honors in the Institute *flabbjellah* tournament—in both combat *and* music.

He thought of Demora fighting back against the Eridanians, making her escape, fending for herself.

He thought of Demora.

Hikaru scrambled to the top of the rocky peak and came face-to-face with an Eridanian soldier.

He shot him in the chest.

Up behind Hikaru came the mass of *Kumari*'s security contingent—those that had survived the initial artillery shell, at any rate. Behind the massive excavators, they'd been safe from subsequent shelling, and Hikaru had waited for a particularly large impact.

At that moment, he'd finally let himself stop thinking of Demora and quickly gathered up as many able-bodied troopers as he could and charged straight up the mountainside. Because of all the dust kicked up into the air, they still couldn't see the Eridanian position—but th'Rellvonda had been able to calculate it from the angle of the shells' trajectory easily enough.

With all the dust, though, the Eridanians had no idea that the *Kumari* crew was coming for them until it was too late.

The trained troopers set upon the Eridanian soldiers. A few gunshots went off here and there—the Eridanians' slugthrowers—but those sounds were far outnumbered by the high-pitched shriek of IG blasters.

Hikaru himself contributed to those shrieks, doing his best to take down Eridanian after Eridanian. Their weapons were set to stun, of course, but in such a dangerous environment, falling unconscious could easily be fatal if you collapsed onto a pile of rock or tumbled down a treacherous slope. And of course the Eridanians were displaying no such reserve.

Hikaru's squad constituted the majority of the surviving fighting force, but not all of it. By the time most of the Eridanian contingent had moved to push back his force's approach, five of Big Lan's best troopers, led by the big man himself, had scrambled up the *other* side of the peak.

They quickly converged on the Eridanian artillery unit— which looked somewhat like what Hikaru remembered ancient humans had called a *mortar*—and made short work of it with their blasters. Good riddance. The weapon had certainly done enough damage. M'Benga and V'Larr had their hands full patching up wounded troopers and engineers down in the valley, but Hikaru knew several had been killed outright. Th'Eneg was still missing, as were all of his analysts.

A *whoosh* behind him made Hikaru duck and roll instinctively, coming up to face his attacker in a crouch, blaster at the ready.

It was Sybok, holding a long leather strip with two metal balls on each end—apparently Hikaru had narrowly avoiding having them whipped into his head. He recognized the weapon as an *ahn-woon* from the files th'Eneg had extracted from the outpost.

Hikaru's finger pulled on the trigger of the blaster—but nothing happened. A quick look at the indicator lights on the side confirmed his suspicions. Its power had already been depleted. He threw it at his approaching attacker, but the Eridanian man whipped the *ahn-woon* once more, striking the blaster in mid-air. Impressive aim.

He really wished he'd taken Lan's offer of a slugthrower, even if he'd never used one. The raging battle had moved some distance away; even if he yelled, the others were too preoccupied defending themselves to notice him.

With nothing else left to him, Hikaru resorted to issuing threats. "Release your hostages at once," he shouted, "or suffer the consequences!"

Sybok gave only a calm smile. "You amuse me, Commander Sulu. What consequences did you have in mind?"

"We want to trade with your species," he said, "but there's no reason we need trade with your *clan*. By your own matriarch's admission you are one of many. We can go to another tribe for the mental weapons we seek, give another tribe the antimatter weapons *you* seek."

"Or," said Sybok, "I can capture *your* team. That ought to bolster our negotiating position, don't you think? But you . . . I think you should die to show that we mean business."

Hikaru scrambled backward, away from the advancing fanatic, praying fervently that there wasn't a drop behind him. He reached for a rock with his right hand, but Sybok's *ahn-woon* whipped out and struck it just above the wrist. Overcome by the pain, Hikaru jerked the arm back and rubbed it with his left hand. Those little metal balls hurt like hell.

"The problem with you offworlders is that you are weakened by your pain," said Sybok. "Embrace your pain, as I do—it makes us who we are. Channeling your pain into strength and victory: that is the way of the Sons of Vulcanis."

"Is the way of the Sons of Vulcanis also to talk too much?" The sudden, whispering voice came from Sybok's left. Sybok and Hikaru both looked to see th'Eneg, crouched on a rock.

Hikaru recovered first and dove at Sybok's legs, knocking the Eridanian man to the ground. The *ahn-woon* went flying, but Hikaru ignored it, quickly pinning Sybok to the ground, sitting on his back to prevent him from moving. A few moments later, th'Eneg came to his side, the *ahn-woon* in his hands. Hikaru used it to bind Sybok's feet and hands together.

"We use our pain, just as you do," said Hikaru. "But we use

our pain to learn and grow from—if we hurt from something, we try not to do it again. Your people have been making the same mistakes for twelve thousand years, inflicting the same pain upon one another for all that time and learning the wrong lessons from it. You don't win by inflicting the greatest pain possible—you win by refusing to inflict pain at all." He stood up to admire his handiwork; Sybok wouldn't be going anywhere. "Which is why you won't die today."

Th'Eneg nodded in appreciation. "We Andorians are a hard people, but not a brutal one. Just like the humans, we learned our lessons."

Hikaru turned to face the Andorian. "Lieutenant! We thought you were dead!"

The intelligence officer smiled, a rare sight indeed. But his words contradicted his face: "I am distressed, commander."

Hikaru frowned. "By what?"

"I thought that I taught you better, yet I am gone mere minutes and you are already forgetting. If you don't see an asset destroyed yourself, always assume it is still in the fight. That is basic strategy."

Hikaru smiled. "You're right. Obviously I still need you around." He turned to get a better look at the raging battle—or rather, the formerly raging battle. It looked like the *Kumari* contingent had successfully incapacitated the Eridanian forces; Lan's men were rounding up a large number of prisoners. "It looks like we've won the battle without you, though."

Th'Eneg shook his head. "This battle is irrelevant," he said with a sigh, "if we are no closer to achieving our objectives."

With a sinking feeling, Hikaru realized how true that was. "And now, they know we're coming."

It took some time to clean up from the battle. Thankfully, only a few members of the *Kumari* party had been killed—two security troopers and one engineer—though many more had been injured, both by the shelling and the subsequent melee. Chirurgeon V'Larr had returned with them to the ship. And Lieutenant th'Eneg's missing analysts had yet to turn up. Ensign s'Bysh on *Kumari* had been unable to lock on to their transponders.

The captured Eridanians, including Sybok, had been rounded up and joined the soldier Tal in the observation post's cells, which were now somewhat crowded.

Fortunately, only one of the laser drills had suffered any substantial damage, and Lieutenant th'Rellvonda's engineers had been quickly able to repair the other two, as well as fit them with the necessary treads.

Hikaru was unable to see another way to go forward. Even if T'Pau's people now knew they were coming, they still needed to free those hostages if they wanted to get anywhere.

According to Yudrin's latest report, General Shras was getting impatient. *"Reading between the lines, Commander, it sounds like the situation with the Klingons is getting bad, fast."*

He frowned as he paced the outpost command center. "I can't believe they'd want to move against the Union this quickly," he said into his communicator. "I mean, we all knew they'd never stop their expansionist policies, but they only just took Gamma Hydra. I thought even Korrd would give it some time before pushing against one of the major powers."

"Which is probably why they're not waiting, and why the General Staff is in such a panic. I've been exchanging messages with your friend Gav—"

He realized with a start that she'd probably been doing this to keep tabs on *him*. As someone who'd served as Hikaru's superior officer for five years, Gav would be a good source of information on Hikaru's emotional states. No wonder Yudrin had been so insightful. But evidently they'd moved on to discussing other things.

"—and he says the word out of Intelligence is that the Klingons have acquired nonaggression treaties with the Gorn, the Guidons, and even the Kinshaya."

Hikaru was impressed. The Kinshaya and the Klingons had

been enemies for nearly a millennium now, and the Gorn never made treaties of any sort with anyone. "Allowing them to throw even *more* forces at us, without having to worry about their other borders." All three races shared significant expanses of border with the Klingon Empire, especially the supermassive Guidon Pontificate. "This *is* sounding bad."

"I'm surprised th'Eneg isn't having a fit. Well, he probably is and just not letting anyone else know about it. But Shras is definitely having one. He wants results."

"I don't even understand what he expects us to do here. Even if we get the telepathic weaponry from the Eridanians, it's not as though we'll be able to instantaneously deploy Aenar mind-troops. They'll have to train and practice first." Hikaru sat down in a chair with a resounding *plop*. He took a sip from the cup of *talla* he'd been holding in his left hand. No, cooling off had *not* improved it. Another Andorian tea to cross off the list.

"I get the feeling that Prefect M'Ress is putting a lot of pressure on Field Marshal Thelian to have a plan for the Klingon invasion," said Yudrin, *"and he in turn is putting pressure on the whole General Staff. If Shras has something, even something that won't work right off the bat, that'll probably still put him one up over all of his colleagues—and save him from being thrown out on the ice."*

"Fair enough," he said. So it wasn't just the Interstellar Union at risk—it was Shras's career. No wonder the man had seemed so urgent. "Well, I'll try to get some results." *I just can't promise they'll be the ones he wants,* he thought to himself quietly. No way was he giving people this barbaric *more* weapons. "Anything else to report?"

"Everything else is running smoothly," she said—too quickly and too patly. Obviously there was nothing wrong with the ship, as she'd have told him. It must be something else, possibly something involving Tellameer V'Larr, the chirurgeon who she'd chosen to spend her off-hours with. "Good," Hikaru said. "If that's all, I'll be signing off. It's nearly dawn, and I think Lan is anxious to head out."

"Just one thing, sir—are you sure you're making this decision for the right reasons? Is this about your daughter?"

"No," he said, "I don't think it is anymore. I told you it wasn't before—but I lied. When that soldier brought me Dax's head, it was Demora's head I saw in his hands. I was going to get T'Pau and all her people for that. But I thought about her a lot as we cowered behind that drill, waiting for the next shell to fall." He paused for a moment, recollecting.

"And?"

"And she might be my daughter . . . but she's a grown woman now. And she's always been capable of taking care of herself. She'll be all right. She doesn't need me right now. And as Tal said—those hostages do."

"Good to hear it, sir. But all that said—I hope you find her."

"So do I, Subcommander, so do I." Hikaru closed his eyes and released yet another prayer to the Great Bird. "With all my heart."

Dawn had broken across the Forge.

It was an awe-inspiring sight. The Forge was a broad, empty sweep filled with amazing rock formations, and the orange light cast by the rising sun alternated with strange and twisted shadows. Hikaru wished that he had the time to enjoy it—he could imagine sitting on one of the peaks of the L-langon Mountains and watching the sun come up. Or go down for that matter. But today was not the day for that.

The attack party had almost reached its destination. No one had come to stop them as they had progressed up and down the slopes of the mountain range. Despite the dangers of the night, they'd headed out a couple hours before daybreak, as there was no sense in letting T'Pau's people get too much time to recuperate. Some creatures—fearsome-looking ones identified in the outpost databanks as *le-matyas*—had attacked them, but fortunately the security troopers' blasters had made short work of them.

Hikaru was relieved they were almost there. He was getting tired of ingesting *talla* to keep himself awake. He could let his adrenaline take over once something was happening other than endless *walking*.

He'd allowed himself to slip to the back of the party, joining Jabilo M'Benga. He didn't have much to say to the chirurgeon at the moment, and the chirurgeon didn't have much to say to him—but he was glad of that. He'd been talked at by enough people the past few days, and to have someone walk next to him in companionable silence was refreshing. He'd always valued M'Benga's counsel—especially on the cultural quirks of his own crew—but unlike some ship's physicians Hikaru had known, the chirurgeon also knew when to keep quiet. He liked that.

Hikaru realized that they were about to be joined by a third, and much less quiet, person. Up ahead, Big Lan had stopped moving, allowing the party to move past him so that he could get to the back. Pretty soon Hikaru and Jabilo had caught up to him. "We're almost there, sir," the security chief said, brandishing his handscanner. "Once we go over the ridge just ahead, we'll reach the spot where we're going to drill."

"Good to hear, Lieutenant," replied Hikaru. "Are your men ready?"

Lan grinned. "They're as fit as *hyperblats*," he said. "That first battle was just a warm-up."

"I appreciate your enthusiasm, Mister ch'Satheddet," said Hikaru dryly, "but I can only imagine in horror what you consider a *real* battle."

Lan's remaining antenna stiffened into an upright position. "Begging pardon, sir. But we are ready, and we will win it." And with that, he stalked forward to the front of the group.

"He didn't like that," said M'Benga. "He wants *kanlee* on those who have wronged him, and an Andorian commander would have understood that."

"'For blood of mine, I shed blood of yours,'" Hikaru recited. He'd heard the phrase often enough in the IG. "Well, as I'm all too frequently reminded, I'm not an Andorian commander." He sighed. "Sometimes I wonder how interstellar history would have gone had Andorian ideals been less prominent in the early days of the Union. I have a hard time seeing someone like Bryce Shumar carpet-bombing the Xindi into submission like General Shran did."

"The Xindi attack on Andor happened before the formation of the IU," pointed out M'Benga. "And the reputation of the old Imperial Guard means that we've never been in a single war since the founding."

"True on both points," said Hikaru, "but—"

A shout from the front of the party, which had just crested the ridge Lan had pointed out, brought the whole group to a halt, excavators and all. Hikaru's communicator chimed. *"Please make your way up to the front, sir."* It was th'Eneg, but he did not even give Hikaru a chance to respond. Hikaru quickly jogged up to the front of the company, M'Benga close behind him.

Lan and th'Eneg were up there, flanked by several security troopers, who had their blasters at the ready. Before them was a somewhat flat area peppered by sinkholes—obviously the area close to the cave network.

Across the other side of the plain, having just come over a crest of their own, was an army of Eridanians, likely over a hundred in total. At their front was the wizened old matriarch, T'Pau.

It was clear they had not needed much time to regather their forces, even across the desert from their home base. One of the troopers said something in Andorii that Hikaru didn't entirely recognize—a particularly nasty epithet, in any case. He shot her a look, and the trooper looked suitably chagrined.

"We had no idea," said Lan. "Handscanners showed nothing."

"Interference either electromagnetic or mental," said th'Eneg with an exasperated shrug. "Who can tell?"

Hikaru sighed. Could they afford another clash? The Eridanians would probably be out for blood after the defeat of their brethren and capture of their commander earlier that night. There were far more Eridanians gathered now than they'd faced then, and the *Kumari* party had less force at its disposal, too.

He stepped forward. "I want to talk to T'Pau."

Lan and th'Eneg looked at him like he was crazy.

"I thought you said you were done with negotiating," said M'Benga.

"I did." He gestured out at the massed army. "But a willingness to talk is what sets us apart from them. That's why we're out in space and they're still squabbling over sand." Oh, *that* was respectful. "I'll give her one last chance."

He began walking out into the empty stretch between the two forces. Lan tried to follow him, but he held a hand up to indicate that he would walk out alone. He made quick, large strides— either the *talla* or his adrenaline had kicked in.

To his surprise, T'Pau broke away from her forces and was moving toward him. Alone, though Hikaru well knew what she could do with a thought.

But perhaps she knew what he intended—either through her telepathic powers or simply her acute Eridanian hearing. Perhaps she too did not want to see more of her people die today. Hadn't she said she wanted to bring peace to Eridani?

Behind him, his forces were silent, watching. Ahead of him, the Eridanians were silent as well, almost supernaturally so. Their black eyes bore into him from across the soon-to-be battlefield.

Hikaru weaved around a sinkhole in his path. He was within ten meters of T'Pau now. He opened his mouth to speak, but was interrupted by the sound of rocks clattering off to his right.

Both he and T'Pau looked over. A figure wearing a plain robe had just tripped over a pile of rocks as she descended from a hill at one side of the open area.

But despite the clothes and the long black hair, those were not the upswept eyebrows of an Eridanian on her face—and those were certainly not the distinctive Eridanian ears. A name rose unbidden to his lips.

"Demora!"

Her communicator continued to emit the connecting chime. She supposed it took a while to route a signal to an IG vessel on patrol. Though, for all she knew, he wasn't even there. Certainly his duties wouldn't let him sit in his quarters all day.

But she didn't close the connection. Finally the chime stopped and was replaced by a rustling—and a very distinctive yawn. "Hello?" He sounded confused.

Of course he was. "Hi, Dad."

"Demora? It's nearly four in the morning here on *Kumari*."

"It's not much better for me," she said. "I'm on Krios now, heading for home." He hadn't been too happy about her proposed sixteenth-birthday trip, but given that she'd legally been an adult in Andorian law for over a year now, there hadn't been much he could do about it. Not that he could have done much even if she wasn't an adult, what with him being in deep space, leaving her behind on Andor.

"What's the matter?" he asked, yawning.

"Nothing," she said. "I'm between flights and lonely and I wanted to talk to someone."

"I take it none of your friends would pick up," he said dryly.

She told him she'd made seventeen calls before finally trying him. But it wasn't true. She'd called him first.

MINSHARA: FIVE

After hardly sleeping all night—mostly for fear of being eaten—Demora was dead tired, but she kept on walking. She started before the sun came up and had made considerable progress, thanks to S'task's excellent local knowledge.

A breeze, stronger than the one yesterday, stirred up dust and sand around her, and she had to cover her nose and mouth with a cloth she'd found in the leather bag. Her water supply was almost gone, and there was no food left. If S'task's estimate was correct, she should shortly arrive at the hidden compound operated by Clan Hgrtcha. She suspected those fanatics wouldn't give her food and drink so much as hot lead at high velocities.

The air was thin, which didn't make climbing mountains any easier. Demora had to pause regularly to catch her breath, preferably in the shade, but it wasn't always possible.

According to S'task, there was even less shade at her destination. Considering its name, that was not very surprising. However, calling it the "Forge" was a bit too on-the-nose for her taste. Too poetic for so violent a people.

For most of the morning she hadn't been walking up the mountainside but down, often over almost impassable terrain. More than once, she'd stumbled, and her ankle hadn't exactly thanked her for it. It was a miracle that nothing was broken—nothing new, anyway.

Over the past hours, she'd repeatedly heard explosions in the distance, which she took to be evidence of an ongoing battle. One involving the Nashih and T'Pau's clan, perhaps? She could only hope—it would mean they'd be too preoccupied to keep looking for her.

The slope she was descending belonged one of a number of small hills on the edge of the Forge. She was going down the side of the hill opposite the plain to avoid the rising sun, already blistering even at this early hour.

What was that down there? There was a hill with a wide, flat top amidst the others; her hill intersected it on one side. Specks were moving about the flat area, difficult to make out but obviously not animals. Had she found the clan's camp already?

She squinted. The people on one side wore clothing that was different from any native's she'd seen so far. The black color made them appear like they belonged to the IG, but that was just wishful thinking.

And yet, she switched direction and increased her pace. Minutes later, she was close enough to make out people's faces. The uniformed ones were looking in the wrong direction, but her first guess had been right. It *was* the IG!

Without consciously planning to, she hurried down the remainder of the slope, sending rocks and pebbles flying in all directions. The sounds of their impacts caused the two opposing sides below to look up, and then she heard a familiar deep voice shout, "Demora!"

The shock of hearing her name nearly made her lose her balance, but she kept on going. Was it a heat-induced hallucination—or had her father really come all the way to save her?

"Dad!" she shouted, and practically ran the last few meters, making it to the bottom without accident only by sheer luck. Seemingly oblivious to the guns pointed at him, her father sprinted to meet her.

As they hugged each other tightly, she ignored her ribs' protests. Her father was here, that was all that counted. It was weird: even though she was a battle-trained graduate of the Interstellar Institute with a remarkable career despite her young age, the thought of her father having come to rescue her made her feel like she was five years old again, when he had woken her up at night, held her hand, and told her that Mom had died: helpless and sad, but at the same time glad that he was there for her. She could only guess at what he'd had to do to get himself reassigned to the Eri system.

"I almost believed I'd lost you," he said, close to her ear.

"I did, too. But this isn't over yet. They probably want to kill me for what I've done."

"What *have* you done?" he asked, ending the hug and stepping just far enough back to hold her face in his hands and look her in the eyes. "You're hurt. Demora, what did they do to you?"

"The usual. Assault, capture, incarceration, mindrape, stuff like that," she said, trying to sound nonchalant about it. "Oh, and the poisonous animals."

Judging from the look in his eyes, her father didn't buy her levity for one second. She should've known better; he never had. He was Dad, after all.

"Come with me. I want to hear what T'Pau has to say about this."

They'd started to walk over to the Minsharans, but the name stopped her dead in her tracks. "T'Pau?"

"Yes." He frowned. "Do you know her?"

She only nodded. She hadn't stumbled on just some faction, but the one she'd been looking for! *I have to say, you're a decent guide, S'task.*

Thank you, Demora. Remember, however, that crossing the mountains was the easiest part. I think it would be best for us both if you let me address T'Pau. I will need to convince her that killing your friends and us will serve no purpose.

You want to do the talking? How's that supposed to work?

If you are willing, I shall access your brain's speech center. You will not be shut out. If you want to interject, feel free to do so. However, it may be confusing to our listeners.

Didn't S'oval tell me that this wasn't possible before? I had to meld with him to talk to you. Was he lying?

He said no such thing. There was no lie, only an . . . omission.

Ah, semantics at its best. But given everything that had happened, she just couldn't summon the energy to be angry at S'task and his crony, not now. *Okay, then. Let's do this.*

Ahead of her, Dad had turned around, lines of worry in his face making him look older than he was. "Is something the matter, Demora?"

"No, it's all right, Dad. Just do me a favor, okay?"

"Anything." He resumed the walk back toward the Minsharans.

"Don't let anything I say confuse you. It'll become clear in the end."

He obviously had no idea what she was talking about, but he knew better than to press her for more information and so said nothing.

The ranks of the Minsharans were full of eager, young faces, but one of them was at least as old as S'oval, her face wrinkled, her long hair graying and thin. This could only be T'Pau, the leader of these fanatics. Ever since Demora's stumble on the hill, the Minsharans had had their weapons drawn and pointed directly at her. She hoped that S'task was up to the job of calming this volatile situation.

Demora walked up to the woman, but made sure to stay out of arm's reach of her. Her father stood just behind her. All three of them were in the middle of the small plain, halfway between the two opposing forces. As she observed the natives in their drab-colored desert tunics, she felt S'task shifting in her mind as he took control of part of her brain.

"Members of Clan Hgrtcha, do not fear us. This woman's

name is Demora Sulu, and she carries my *katra*. I, S'task of ta'Valsh, speak to you in the hope of achieving peace between your clan and these aliens. You may now question me to ascertain my identity."

That was all? Somehow she'd expected more from somebody who called himself a soldier-poet.

T'Pau seemed similarly unimpressed, but after some time, she finally spoke. "You know our name, but you are unfamiliar to us—if you really are who you claim to be. Are you not the alien who killed one of our loyal clansmen and maimed another?"

"Demora was forced to defend herself. If she had not, she would be dead—and thus I would be as well."

"You speak of yourself as a third party. Why is that?" asked T'Pau.

"As I said, she carries my *katra*. Without her willingness to meld, it would have been lost, despite surviving the centuries since the Conflagration."

T'Pau nodded in what Demora thought was surprised respect. "You know about *katraveh* and our history. But is this proof?"

"Certainly not," Demora said—or rather, S'task. "That is why I offer myself to you to examine me." *Hey, easy! That's not what we talked about before!* "Ask me questions only a T'Khasian can know."

"So that you can recite what you learned during your clandestine observations? I think not."

"These people have been here since the middle of Ahhar. Do you really believe they found out everything there is to know?"

"You are very resourceful. Those that can spend months among us, nearly undetected, can also retrieve information from our secret stores. I believe I can ask you any question I like, and you will answer it as though you had rightfully come by the knowledge."

"Then ask me something that is not stored anywhere. Ask me something that I could not know if I were not of T'Khasi."

"We prefer to call it Minshara," said T'Pau archly. " 'T'Khasi' is a name that belongs to the argot of priests and mystics. Where is the place you stated as your origin? I know of no ta'Valsh."

My, that woman was a hard sell, wasn't she? Despite their situation, Demora was beginning to respect the leader; she was as sharp and quick as a woman a third of her apparent age. "I am appalled. Have you forgotten your heritage? My city's foundations may no longer stand, but it did not disappear entirely. At the time of my birth, ta'Valsh was as old as I am now, and it withstood raids, sandstorms, fires, and floods, only to be reduced to dust in one night."

"Somebody told you about this, I have no doubt." T'Pau's unwillingness to believe was painfully evident.

From the corner of her eye, Demora saw her father move toward her. "What is this?" he said, ignoring the weapons that were quickly being pointed at him. "What are you doing to my daughter? I'll have no more of your mental trickery!"

"Trickery?" T'Pau repeated. "This is no trick that I would play. I would suggest, you mere *tvee'okh*, that you rein yourself in; otherwise it might end badly for you."

It was time for Demora to do something, so she pushed S'task aside. "It's me again, Dad." She turned to face him. "Please be reasonable. There is a chance for this to end well for everyone, but you have to trust me." Hikaru merely grunted at this; he was certainly used to being scolded by his daughter.

"And you," Demora addressed T'Pau, "would do well to mind your language. Racial epithets are not going to improve matters. If, that is, you actually are interested in improving matters. Frankly, I have my doubts."

"Have you decided to stop the make-believe? A wise decision. It was not very effective." T'Pau actually sneered at her, a grimace made even worse by the wrinkly folds of her skin.

Time was running out, Demora knew. Pretty soon, the situation would deteriorate, somebody would fire the first shot, and few of them would survive the coming slaughter. She needed to do something, but what?

The hell with it. Only a few steps separated her from T'Pau. Before anyone could react, she crossed the distance and put her hand to the surprised leader's face.

★ ★ ★

S'task, help me out here, will you?

What are you doing, Demora? For a disembodied spirit, he sounded very astonished.

Help me meld with her! I can't do it on my own. She wasn't going to believe anything you said to her. This is the only way.

I do not agree, but I have few alternatives. As long as we are joined with T'Pau, they will not risk killing us, for fear of her falling into the abyss with us.

Okay. So get cracking.

I will do my best, he projected, but he didn't exactly sound confident. **T'Pau, hear my words. In search of wisdom and truth we join our minds together. Our thoughts are merging . . . our thoughts are one.**

The old woman's reaction was predictably negative. <u>What have you done? Break the meld at once!</u>

I will release you, but only if you listen to what I have to say. I am indeed S'task of ta'Valsh, come here to teach and instruct those willing to learn in the principles of a new society.

<u>My people will kill you if you do not let me go this instant!</u>

I do not think so. They would not dare harm you. Why are you so defensive? We are merely trying to convince you of our honesty. Nothing we have said is a lie.

<u>Does that include the black-clad aliens?</u>

I cannot speak for them. However, Demora is their leader's daughter. She knows him best.

I was hoping you wouldn't drag me into this.

Demora, this was your suggestion.

Oh, right. Anyway, what we're trying to do is simple: leave this planet and go home. We'll remove every trace of our presence here and will conduct further interactions between our people on an open and honest basis.

<u>I care little what you do, so long as Clan Hgrtcha gets what it needs—the weapons necessary to finally master Minshara.</u>

Demora tried to hide her revulsion at the idea of the bloodthirsty Minsharans having access to antimatter weaponry, but didn't succeed.

I realize you are fighting because you feel you must, T'Pau-*hel*. Let me offer an alternative.

On what basis? I know nothing about you.

I have difficulty believing this. Are you not familiar with *The First Song*?

I am. However, what do the teachings of Zakal have to do with you?

Zakal!? That deluded mystic couldn't rhyme a couplet to save his life. My name removed from my greatest work—I am appalled!

As you should be, *T'Kehr*.

You confuse me.

A mere test; I apologize. One cannot be too careful. Rest assured that I am not ignorant of our past and your role in it.

I thank you. It is a great relief that my efforts have not been entirely forgotten. However, what shall we do about the present situation?

Good question, Demora interjected. She'd been tempted to call this experiment a failure, but now they seemed to be getting somewhere. *Tell your people to lower their weapons. I will ask my father to do the same. Then the two of you should probably sit down and have a fruitful discussion about all this. You seem like reasonable people, so I expect the talks to be successful.*

I will overlook your impertinence because you are young and ignorant, alien. A Minsharan would know better than to speak out so rudely in the presence of her elders.

Really? Fascinating. Now, why don't we end this small talk for the time being and get to work? I promise, both of you will have more than enough time later to pick your brains once we end this crisis.

Agreed. T'Pau-*hel*?

I see no reason not to concur.

How encouraging.

★ ★ ★

Demora opened her eyes to see T'Pau and herself surrounded by grim-faced Minsharan fighters and one old man who seemed somewhat out of place amidst them. Bald and almost as ancient as their leader, he wore ornate jeweled clothing that showed him to be a high-ranking monk.

T'Pau held up a hand to preempt any untoward movements of her people, and Demora used that moment to look around for her father. He was standing as close to her as possible, his arms folded across his chest. His troops, most of whom were Andorians and thus had little tolerance for high temperatures, looked weary and, in some cases, dangerously close to a heatstroke. They had to get things moving, to let these people return to their cool ship.

"Are you all right, Demora?" he asked, even as the adept inspected her and T'Pau, who simply waved him away.

"I'm fine, Dad. They've agreed to talk, so you'd better organize some place to sit down and chat."

He wasn't entirely convinced, but he didn't press the issue of her health. Instead, he said, "Remind me later to force you to tell me everything."

"I will." She grinned at him, despite her injuries. "Be reasonable to them; they'll try to do the same."

"I'm always reasonable."

"Now *that* I wouldn't—"

"Demora, now's not the time. What was that about you killing Eridanians?"

"Self-defense. Details later. Now you get going; have your guys beam down a tent or something similar. You wouldn't want to get roasted, would you?"

"Certainly not. I would be glad, though, if you could let *me* be the commander, at least this once. Will you let Chirurgeon M'Benga examine you, or do I need to order you?"

"I'll go voluntarily, thank you."

As she walked over to the chirurgeon, she took a quick look back and saw her father in conversation with T'Pau and the monk, preparing for the continuation of the talks, once Demora's wounds had been seen to. Because of the mind she carried, she needed to take part in the negotiations. Hopefully they would be able to reach an agreement. The situation needed to resolve positively—they owed that to Doctor Grayson and all the others who had died.

She'd never met M'Benga before, but only one of the IG personnel had blue piping on his uniform, and so she approached him, putting on her best smile. "Chirurgeon? My father tells me you're the best bone-mender in the fleet."

Less than two hours later, a tent had been set up out in the Forge, in a (relatively) radiation-free zone where the transporter could function. While Lieutenant th'Rellvonda and his men had toiled away in the scorching heat down below, Demora had enjoyed the care of Jabilo M'Benga above.

Now she had just beamed back down, together with Subcommander Yudrin, who she'd met a couple times before, but not since she'd become Dad's XO. She struck Demora as the ideal person to rein in her father's whims. What he needed was a first officer who told him exactly what she thought of his decisions, plans, and orders.

They'd materialized next to the standard-issue tent that was open to all sides to let in whatever cooling wind there was and to allow everybody outside to hear what was being discussed. Inside stood a metal table and six metal chairs, three on each side. Demora would sit there with her father and Yudrin, opposite them T'Pau, Mystic Lateth, and another Minsharan whose name she'd already forgotten. An earthen jug containing a dark, steaming liquid and six cups had been placed in the center of the table. Everything was ready.

Where was Dad? She cast a searching look around and eventually found him in the distance, speaking to the tallest Andorian she'd ever seen. Trying to catch his attention, she waved, and eventually he looked up, ended his conversation with the man, and came over to her. The big Andorian followed at a distance.

Her father nodded at Yudrin. "Subcommander."

"Commander."

"Now, dear, shouldn't you be still in bed? I'm sure I told M'Benga to—"

"To keep me on the ship while you were having fun down here? Really, Dad, you should know me better. I'd have come even if I didn't have a Minsharan philosopher in my brain."

"I've been meaning to ask about that. Isn't it uncomfortable?" Dad asked, full of parental concern. Though he'd never said it, she'd always suspected he still suffered a lot of guilt from when his assignment to *Kumari* had forced him to leave her behind on Andor.

"Not particularly. If he keeps himself in check, that is. He can be pretty pretentious."

I disagree with that assessment.

Demora ignored him and went on. "What's the holdup? Shouldn't we have begun already?"

"There's been a delay on the side of the Eridanians," explained Yudrin. "Something to do with T'Pau's health, I believe."

"Well, she isn't as young as she was, I'm told," said Dad.

"Aren't we all? Especially you."

"Easy, Ensign, or I'll have you assigned to waste reclamation. Poor Crewman th'Clane deserves some company."

Visibly uncomfortable with the familiar talk between the two, the giant Andorian was fingering the collar of his uniform shirt. "Commander," he said, "if there's nothing else . . . I'd like to give the area another sweep."

"By all means, Lan. Better safe than sorry."

They watched the security chief walk off toward the hills, where two teams of *Kumari* troopers were watching the surroundings.

"Are you ready for this?" asked Demora.

"I think so," Dad said. "I'm not giving these people advanced weaponry, no matter what Shras says." M'Benga had explained the general's orders to her while she was in his sickbay. "And I'm not going to try to get the telepathic weaponry. Eridani's been at war for millennia because of it; we don't need that in the IU." He grinned, despite being fully aware of what to expect when he showed up at HQ empty-handed. Shras wouldn't be happy, to put it mildly. "Fortunately, my senior staff agrees with me on this one."

"They do? Ah." She stopped herself, unsure how to interpret the look he gave her. "You gave them an order, didn't you? Good to know they follow you, and not the nutjobs back home." Yudrin, Lan, M'Benga, and the others certainly made a formidable lot, and it relieved her to know that they were on Dad's side. "Oh, look, over there!" Figures were approaching in the distance. "Looks like the report of T'Pau's death has been exaggerated."

"Now we can finally get started," said Yudrin.

Dad sighed. "Do I have a choice?"

Demora and Yudrin looked at each other. Smiling, the first officer said, "Not really, no." The more she saw of the woman, the happier Demora became. Demora had performed the duty of keeping him in check back in the day, but now she had her own life, and so she was glad that Yudrin didn't give in to his whims easily.

"Well, let's do this, then. Subcommander?"

"Yes, sir?"

"Tell me when I get too diplomatic, will you?"

"Certainly, sir. I'll immediately hand you my blaster."

They walked over to the table and positioned themselves behind the chairs, her father in the middle. They had a good view of the northern part of the Forge, from where T'Pau's entourage was approaching.

After long minutes that the heat made unpleasant despite the tent's shade, the Minsharans finally arrived. As clan matriarch, T'Pau was the first to take a seat.

Mystic Lateth then took the jug and poured the dark liquid

into six cups. Demora knew how much her father liked tea, so she hoped he'd enjoy this.

Lateth, whose clothes incorporated intricate designs that reminded her of ancient art created by humans from the Meso-american region of Earth, placed one cup in front of everyone and then spoke, no doubt part of some arcane ritual.

"This *mah'ta* tea is an offering to our ancestors," he said. "We drink it to calm mind and body, in order to be most effective at our chosen task. May these talks be fruitful. I wish us all—"

The echoing sound of metal hitting metal interrupted him. All heads turned to find the source. It was Yudrin who first spotted it: "Over there, near that rock!"

Demora saw it, but she was too late. Everyone was. Near the rock stood Lan, the big security chief, dark blue blood on his uniform glistening in the sun, two Minsharans wielding blades before him. As Yudrin began to move, Lan fired two shots, dropping each of them to the ground. Demora couldn't see if they were dead.

Lan's chest had been slashed from sternum to left hip, and just as a pair of troopers reached him he wavered, then fell to his knees. They were just in time to keep him from collapsing entirely.

Yudrin was next to make it to Lan. She seemed not to care about the armed Minsharans who had hurried over to see if their fellow fighters were still alive.

What could possibly have caused this at the very moment that talks were supposed to begin? Who was to blame? And why?

There was no chance of discussing a cease fire now. She only hoped that this disastrous incident hadn't made a return to the discussion table impossible. History was full of examples that showed just how little it took to bury all hope of diplomatic success.

A throng of people, both Minsharan and IG personnel, had formed around the injured—or dead?—but her father and T'Pau carried enough weight to at least create a narrow corridor. Demora's greatest fear was that more fights would break out, now that the fuse had been lit again. Quite a few on either side were likely to oppose an end to hostilities. *Kanlee* was a problem, always had been since the early days of Andor's interspecies relations. Among Andorians, it was perfectly acceptable, but taking blood for blood wasn't exactly a universal tenet, nor was it conducive to peace.

"Get me a chirurgeon!" her father shouted. Yudrin spoke into her communicator, giving orders to whoever was at the other end. Then she ordered the troopers to form a circle around the wounded men, to avoid them getting trampled by dozens of excited, angry people.

Without warning, Jabilo M'Benga materialized in the crowded area, dangerously close to a Minsharan, who gave a shout of surprise. "What happened?" he asked, as he bent down to inspect Lan's wounds.

"We're trying to find out," said Dad. "We don't know who acted first. Is Big Lan okay? Can he talk?"

"Let's deal with keeping him alive, first. He's lost a lot of blood, and I would like to get him back to *Kumari*. His wounds are grave, and he needs better care than I can give him here."

"Okay, take him back up. I'll deal with this . . . Great Bird knows how." Her father's face bore a grim expression, and as a security expert herself, she knew just how bad this situation was.

It is T'Pau's turn now, Demora. Only she can prevent her people from making a mistake. However, she herself must *want* to avoid that mistake. If she does not keep her people under control, everybody's life is in danger.

Thanks for that analysis. I reached the same conclusion. The last thing she needed right now was useless advice from a dead poet.

Dad was ordering troopers around. But the Minsharan leader had disappeared in the crowd—and her absence made Demora fear the worst. Had all this been planned? Had they been duped into thinking that a cessation of hostilities was an actual possibility, while at the same time T'Pau had planned their deaths?

The two Minsharan fighters shot by Lan were being inspected

by Lateth and his two aides. Didn't these people have doctors? Or was healing part of a mystic's job description? She hoped they would survive—if they weren't dead already.

She forced her way past the crowd of Minsharans to get her own look at the injured men. Both had been shot where it would have been fatal for an Andorian, but they were alive. Their anatomy truly was different, from their ears to their blood, as green as a pine tree.

What was that? One of the wounded men was partially covering something with his body; no doubt he'd fallen on top of it. Ignoring the suspicious looks from Lateth, she bent down to grab the object. She'd barely closed her fingers around to pull it out from under the man when she experienced a sensation similar to her voluntary meld with S'oval, but of an almost unbearable magnitude.

What have you done? What is this?

How the hell should I know? You tell me! She moved away from the crowd, trying to find some space to recover and to think.

I have not seen a Stone for two thousand years! I had hoped they were no more.

Calm down, will you? You know this thing? What does it do?

A Stone is a weapon, but not like the crude explosives that ravaged T'Khasi during the Conflagration. A Stone works by amplifying the telepathic powers of its bearer. Whoever used it could eradicate their opponents with virtually no effort. It works especially well with negative emotions, of which there is an overabundance on our world. It amplifies those of the target and reflects them back. I have heard of entire armies reduced to nothing more than mindless creatures by a lone user of such a weapon.

You people are making us look like saints, you know that? And I thought Andorians had a violent history. As she thought about what she should do with this telepathic amplifier, a thought struck her. *Say, can I use it to establish a connection to everybody here?*

I do not know. You are not of T'Khasi, and I have never operated a Stone myself.

So much for that. We'll just have to find something else.

However, he continued, **I *have* read a great many books about them.**

Are you going to recite some poetry?

I believe I know what I need to do. Answer me this, however: What would you have me do to them? I cannot believe you want to kill everyone present.

No! I want to talk to them, all at once.

Talk? I doubt that in twelve millennia anyone has ever picked up a Stone with the intention of talking. Let us hope it is even possible.

Hurry up, please!

I must say, I find your youthful impatience somewhat jarring. Now, then, I need to focus my thoughts. Do not disturb me; my concentration must be perfect. I—

He did not finish. An inexplicable surge rushed through Demora, but whether it was just a psychological or a physical effect, she couldn't say. It was over as soon as it had begun, but immediately she noticed something amiss.

S'task was gone. The corner of her mind that he'd occupied before was her own once more. Where had he gone?

Her connection with the Stone was broken as well. Had it malfunctioned? Had she killed S'task by making him do this?

She refused to believe it. There had to be some explanation for his disappearance, and she'd find it. Looking around, she realized with a shock that a great many people of both sides were no longer standing. They were lying on the ground. The others were wavering, and as she watched, a few of them collapsed.

One of them was Dad.

Oh no. No!

She'd killed her father.

She'd killed them all.

It had been a couple months since she'd communicated with him. Of course, they couldn't do it in real time, given the circumstances, but she'd sent him only one message, just after they'd made it to Eri. She wasn't sure why. They'd always been good about keeping in regular contact, ever since he'd been forcibly assigned to Kumari and she'd been left behind on Andor, even through her years at the Institute.

But since actually getting her first assignment, she hadn't wanted to talk to him. It wasn't anything malicious—it just hadn't occurred to her. She wondered why. He hadn't messaged her either, though. She wondered if he was trying to prove something. If she was.

Well, she decided she wasn't. She wanted to know what her dad was doing, out there in space, and he'd probably be excited to hear about the strange old Eridanians. He'd always bemoaned that Kumari never got to go on contact missions.

She checked the security system readouts—everything was fine. As usual. The Eridanians didn't exactly have the technology to take the IG unawares. So she opened up a message window and began to type.

She didn't get very far before the explosion caused the entire base to rumble. Alarms began to ring. She looked down at her console. All of a sudden, there were Eridanian lifesigns right outside. Where had they come from?

No time for that now. She had to coordinate a defense. She clipped her blaster to her belt, flipped open her communicator to call Vrani, and headed out into the corridor to figure out what was going on.

She'd finish the letter another time.

KUMARI: SIX

"The look on your face was priceless!"

Demora shot him one of those looks he remembered all too well from her mother. "Shut up, Dad."

"You were absolutely mortified!" Hikaru continued to chuckle.

"Dad, I *thought you were dead!*"

Hikaru straightened up. "Sorry, Demora, but it was fairly amusing to wake up to you frantically trying to decipher a medical kit. Don't they teach you how to use those things?"

She tried to cover up a sigh by keeping her mouth shut, but it only came out of her nose. "I'm out of practice."

Hikaru removed the infuser from the teapot on his desk, setting it aside, and then poured the contents of the pot into two teacups. He handed Demora one of the cups. She grimaced. "Dad, you know I don't like tea."

"You'll like this," he said. He took a sip. Oh, that was fantastic. There might not be a lot to like about the Eridanians—sorry, Minsharans—but they did make a fantastic cup of tea. *Finally*, he thought. The package of tea leaves had been a parting gift from T'Pau. He suspected it hadn't been so much an act of generosity as a desperate attempt to stop his ravings about the quality of the tea.

That said, though the Minsharan leader was more than pleased to see Sulu and *Kumari* go, she had seemed slightly less hostile than before. Obviously the influence of S'task had done some good already. Or maybe that was just wishful thinking on Hikaru's part.

The comm unit in his desk chimed. Hikaru flipped it on. "Sulu here."

It was Yudrin. *"Commander, the last of the hostages are aboard. Chirurgeon M'Benga's looking them over now."*

"Everyone's accounted for?" he asked.

"Everyone who survived. . . ."

"Good," he said. "I'll be on the command deck in a moment." He switched the communicator off and turned to face Demora again. She was just standing there, her cup of tea halfway to her mouth. "Is it that bad?"

"What?" Her eyes suddenly focused in on him. "Oh. No. Well, yes, but that's not my problem." She sat the cup of tea down on the desk and moved across the room to look out the small viewport, down at the turning planet below. "Seven dead," she said. "Seven people whose protection was my responsibility."

Hikaru went and joined her. "You know, as soon as Gav told me what had happened, I did everything I could to get *Kumari* this assignment. I manipulated a member of the General Staff. I needed to protect my daughter. And then I got here and—"

She removed his hand from her shoulder and turned around. Her hair glowed faintly red in the reflected light of the planet. "—and then you found me, persevering against all odds. Spare me, Dad. I rescued myself and that was all."

He shook his head. "That's not where I was going. During our battle with Sybok's forces, I tried to generate a lot of negative emotions to jam the Eridanians' mind powers. So I thought of you, helpless and vulnerable." He smiled. "But I couldn't do it. Because what I ended up thinking of was what a strong person you are. You always have been. You don't need protecting—you protect me."

And she had, down on Eridani. The telepathic device she'd

scooped up had indeed knocked everyone unconscious, but when they'd woken up, they'd all had a piece of S'task floating around inside their minds. Not his whole consciousness, like Demora had had, but just a little bit of his philosophy, his wisdom niggling at the backs of their minds.

Fortunately, it had been enough to stop the two sides from coming to blows. In fact, it had done a lot more than that.

"And you didn't just save me," he said, "you saved that whole planet." He shrugged. "Well, maybe. Let's get to the bridge."

They made the short walk down to the command deck doors together. Hikaru was impressed by the job M'Benga had done in patching up Demora—she seemed every bit as alert and active as he remembered, taking in the sights and sounds of *Kumari*. Hikaru realized that though she'd been on the ship a couple times as a teenager, this was her first time aboard since she'd received her officer's commission. She was seeing it through an experienced officer's eyes now, not a young girl's.

The door slid open and, of course, Subcommander Phelana Yudrin stood and saluted. "Commander Sulu," she said with a nod. "And Ensign Sulu."

"Good afternoon, Subcommander," replied Hikaru. At least he thought it was. All this bouncing between the ship and the planet had him baffled. "How's it going?"

"We have T'Pau on the line now," she said. "Shall I raise her?"

Hikaru sat down in his command chair; Demora stood at his side. "Go ahead."

Yudrin motioned at Ensign s'Bysh, who pressed some buttons on her console. "Go ahead, sir," the Orion woman said.

"Matriarch T'Pau, this is Commander Sulu. I'm speaking to you from *Kumari,* up—"

"I am not a simpleton, Commander." Well, there was no mistaking that tone of voice. *"We mastered this device quite easily, and I know what it does. I am, however, quite impatient at times, and one of those times is now."*

"We have everyone on board. I trust you found your people all right."

"Sybok and the others have been recovered." After the IG personnel had left the outpost, Hikaru had handed the codes to the detention cells over, allowing her to free Sybok, Tal, and the other Eridanian soldiers. *"So now we must leave this place?"*

Hikaru nodded before remembering she couldn't see him. For all T'Pau's grandstanding, her people *hadn't* figured out how to work the viewers. "My chief engineer removed the fuel from the reactor, so it will be safe for us to drop a torpedo on it, destroying everything we left behind. We can't afford for any of that technology to fall into your hands."

"I understand," said T'Pau. It sounded so strange, coming from a woman who'd ordered the attack on an outpost staffed mainly by scientists. *"S'task and you have given us much to think about. It will be better for all concerned if you left Minshara and her people alone. Having your powerful weapons nearby is too great a temptation. I agree with you, now. With your abilities in our hands, there would be another Conflagration, and I am not so certain we would survive this one."*

"So what do you intend to do now?"

"Clan Hgrtcha shall spread the word of S'task. I had never taken the time to study The First Song *properly before—I had dismissed it as the ramblings of a fool. But he does not propose an abandonment of the ways of the Sons of Vulcanis. We are a violent people, prone to great passions, and he acknowledges that. But they are passions that can be channeled."*

"I understand," said Hikaru. "I think all species reach an understanding like that at some point." According to Demora, the central tenet of *The First Song* was a complex code of honor called *mnhei'sahe.* As she had explained it, it restricted combat and battle to certain times and places, focusing the Eridanian passions into somewhat less . . . violent forms, though it seemed to place a high value on subtle intrigues. "We humans nearly destroyed ourselves as well, but channeled our passions into exploration and learning."

And that was but one of many, of course: for all the trouble it occasionally caused, the rite of *kanlee* ensured that an Andorian could not take a life without equivalent provocation, and it limited how many could be taken. Ensign s'Bysh had on many occasions explained how the highest cultural value of the Orions was staying cool and calm—passions were permitted, but not to excess. Heck, even the Klingons were supposed to have some sort of honor system. He could only hope that S'task's code would serve the Eridanians as well.

"With time, perhaps, Minshara will no longer be a world at war. I am grateful to you—and your impetuous daughter—for allowing me to see a new way."

Hikaru's initial reaction had been that this S'task was using the telepathic amplifier to control T'Pau and the other Eridanians, but Demora had assured him that that was not the case. The ancient Eridanian might have been projected into everyone's mind, but he was a mere fragment of a ghost, nothing more. A new idea, perhaps, but not one they were bidden to obey more than any other idea. Thankfully, just a new idea had been enough.

"Glad to have helped," replied Hikaru. "Now evacuate that outpost before I drop the torpedo on it, anyway. We want to get home."

"Very well, Commander Sulu." She sounded annoyed. *"Live long and prosper."*

"Thiptho lapth, Matriarch T'Pau." It was a traditional Andorian valediction, though its meaning was somewhat obscure. "And good luck."

A squeal indicated that the connection was cut. Not too long later, s'Bysh reported that the outpost and the surrounding area were clear of all life-forms.

"Would you care to do the honors?" Hikaru asked Demora.

His daughter nodded. "Please," she said. She walked over to the weapons console, brushing aside Trooper Vaughn—Big Lan was still in sickbay. She tapped away at the controls for a moment, then looked up. "Torpedo ready. Low-yield charge set." Previously, th'Rellvonda had seen to it that the outpost's fusion reactor was drained of fuel, to prevent the surrounding area from being contaminated.

"Fire," ordered Hikaru. He turned to face the viewer in time to see the blue streak of a photon torpedo curving down to the planet's surface. He could see a brief spark of light once it impacted, but that was all from this distance.

"Sensors confirm direct hit," reported Demora.

S'Bysh checked over her sensors. "All outpost components obliterated," she said after a moment.

"Thank the Great Bird," said Hikaru. "Lieutenant M'Giia."

The helm officer perked up. "Sir?"

"Set a course for Andor. Take us home."

"Aye, sir. I have to say, it's about time there's been something for me to do. I've been—"

"Lieutenant," growled Yudrin. "Most of the excitement in the past couple days has involved people dying."

"Sorry. Course laid in."

"Engage."

Demora left the weapons station to stand at the front of the command deck, leaning over the railing right in front of the viewer. Hikaru went to join her, calling for a reverse angle on the viewer so that they could watch the planet slowly dwindle away as *Kumari* left the 40 Eridani system.

"I guess there won't be any more tears flowing in Eridanus," said Demora suddenly.

"Sorry?" asked Hikaru. What was she talking about?

"The constellation Eridani is named for a mythical river from ancient Earth," said Demora. "Eridanus. There were these five sisters or something, and their brother died. They were turned into trees and they began to cry and they never stopped. Their tears made up the river. I think."

"I didn't know you were interested in mythology," said Hikaru.

"I'm not," said Demora. "I was just remembering something Doctor Grayson told me once. Well, misremembering, more like. But being named after a river of tears did seem quite appropriate for a planet like Eri."

"Or not," said Hikaru, "given that it *is* a desert planet."

She landed a playful punch on his arm. "I was *trying* to be poetic, Dad."

Suddenly the planet disappeared from the viewer in a flash as *Kumari* jumped to warp.

"Estimated time of arrival at Andor is three days," reported M'Giia.

With that, Hikaru's thoughts shifted to what awaited him on Andor, at Interstellar Headquarters. Sure, he was coming back with almost all of the hostages alive—but General Shras would still see him as coming home empty-handed.

"You know why Lan attacked that soldier?" he said to Demora.

"Not the rite of *kanlee*?" She looked quizzical.

"I thought so, but I talked to him a little bit this morning. He was trying to get that telepathic amplifier, to take it back to Andor. He'd realized that I wasn't going to do it." But the Minsharans had read his intentions, and they'd defended themselves before he could get it.

"I thought you said your senior staff agreed that taking the telepathic weaponry would be a mistake."

"So did I," said Hikaru. His security chief had been proven sneakier than he'd given him credit for. He found it hard to be angry at the man: he'd been trying follow the general's orders and save the entire IU, after all. Th'Eneg had been impressed by Lan's idea, if not his execution, saying that if he'd done it himself, he wouldn't have gotten caught. "But there's a war coming, Demora, and we have to win it somehow."

Given th'Eneg's usual utilitarian approach to things, Hikaru had been surprised that he hadn't been in favor of taking the telepathic weaponry. The intelligence officer had laughed when

Hikaru had told him that. "If we could just read the enemy's thoughts," he'd said, "I'd be out of a job."

Big Lan had just wanted to do *his* job—protecting the people of the Interstellar Union. The news out of the other states bordering the Klingons was only getting worse. The Klingon invasion of the IU was inevitable.

In a way, though, Hikaru could take hope from it. Just over a hundred years ago, the Andorian Imperial Guard had bombed the Xindi into near-extinction. Now, the Interstellar Guard was considered the easiest target in the galaxy. Obviously a bad thing in some respects, but it also said something about how easy it was to change and make peace if you really wanted to. The Andorians had done it, the humans had done it. Maybe the Eridanians could. Maybe even the Klingons could, someday.

For now, though, he had to report to General Shras.

"You're in big trouble, Dad."

"I know, Demora, I know. But it was worth it."

He turned and touched her lightly on the shoulder. She surprised him—and herself—by pulling him toward her in the biggest hug she could manage. Whatever was waiting for them back home didn't matter. They had found each other again. If a planet full of telepaths couldn't stop them, then the Interstellar Guard didn't stand a chance.

Honor in the Night

Scott Pearson

Prologue

Nice, France, 2366

Nilz Baris, his white hair bright against the dark blue pillow like clouds in the night sky, rolled over in his deathbed, all elbows and knees and other stiff joints, a careless collection of fragile bones shifting under the light covers.

The rustling of fabric, even from across the room, was enough to wake Leonard McCoy, who had nodded off in the window seat overlooking the *Alée du Palais* toward the Mediterranean Sea. Awakening at the slightest sound was a doctor's talent he had perfected decades ago, back when he was still practicing, and somehow, against all common sense, the ability hadn't faded as much as his hearing. He shifted toward Baris with careful turns, swiveling his whole torso to avoid aggravating his neck, which had grown stiff while he dozed. There were no lights on in the room, and it must have been well past midnight, but enough light spilled in through the open window for him to see the bed. With a squint he saw the covers rising and falling, just barely, with each shallow breath Baris took.

McCoy sighed deeply, running a hand over his wrinkled face. He felt old tonight, like the ancient willow trees he often saw in cemeteries in Georgia, their trunks gnarled and their branches drooping to the ground. Certainly much of the reason he felt old was simply because he *was* old, ancient even, at 140 years; but it didn't help that Baris would likely not make it until morning, or that he was about the same age as McCoy. It made McCoy long for Tonia back home in Atlanta and then feel worse for Baris, alone these last six years since Sima, his wife of nearly ninety years, had died. Baris had become a bit of a recluse since losing Sima, rarely leaving his chateau except for that ill-fated "goodwill visit" to Bajor the year after her death.

Lowering his hand, McCoy looked back at Baris, who continued sleeping peacefully. The monitor on the night stand would alert McCoy to any serious change in vital signs, but he still struggled onto his feet with a quiet grunt and shuffled across the room to the bedside. Although tempted to wake Baris, to get a last chance to talk, he simply looked down with a sad smile and let his friend sleep. They had said their good-byes earlier that night during a delicious meal Baris knew could be his last. Shortly after McCoy had arrived, Baris told McCoy he'd gone off all his medications two weeks earlier. "You may want to live forever, Len, but I don't. I'm lonely without Sima, and the Federation no longer needs me. The meds made me sleepy and robbed me of my sense of taste. But now I can share my favorite meal with my oldest friend." McCoy felt as though the wind had been knocked out of him, but he'd accepted Baris's decision with a sad smile and a silent nod of the head.

They had dined in a small turret off the bedroom with a perfect view of the golden afternoon light shimmering on the rolling waves of the sea. The chef, Lucienne, had served them Baris's favorite local foods: pizza-like *pissaladière*, with sauteed onions and anchovies, and *pan-bagnat*, sandwiches on crusty white bread with tomatoes, seared tuna, peppers, hard-boiled eggs, shallots, capers, and olive oil. She'd opened a bottle of Château Brane-Cantenac Margaux 2338.

Baris, holding his glass by the stem, had said, "You'll like this. It has a robust mouthfeel, very noticeable black currant up front, and a spicy finish."

"Hmmph," McCoy said, taking a swig. "I never understand a word you say when you talk about wine."

There had been two desserts—vanilla custard with caramel sauce, and warm figs with cream sauce, served with espresso.

McCoy had been uncomfortably full but couldn't stop smiling at how Baris had attacked each course with gusto.

They had sat for hours in the turret sipping their espressos and talking of old times. Their reminiscing had been interrupted briefly when Baris's assistant, Gaspard, had informed Baris of a call, which Baris had taken at a communication screen in his bedroom. McCoy overheard Baris saying, "Ms. Jensen, I'm sorry if you inferred otherwise, but I never had any intention of grant-ing you an interview." Baris came quickly back into the turret, a sour expression on his face, mumbling about ramifications, even after all these years. He refused to elaborate, and McCoy didn't pursue it.

Now, as Baris lay sleeping, cheeks still flushed from the shared bottle of Left Bank Bordeaux, he looked so content that McCoy knew it would have been simple selfishness to disturb him. Maybe, just maybe, McCoy would get another chance to speak with him in the morning.

McCoy slowly turned from Baris and made his way back to the window. Easing down onto the seat, he forced himself to look outside instead of morosely staring toward the bed. The southwest-facing window gave him a beautiful nighttime view of the city of Nice. The houses and other buildings, in off-whites and soft corals from yellow to pink, were mostly stucco, some brick or stone, and had clay tile roofs. Low walls topped with shrubs surrounded yards dotted with palm trees. From this hill-side neighborhood, the city descended to the warm waters of the Mediterranean, the shoreline just over a kilometer away. McCoy watched the gentle swells of the sea, glimmering under the light of a waning moon, until the bright lights of the Promenade des Anglais drew his attention back to the shore. The Jardin Albert park, just this side of the promenade from the beach, appeared to be the center of some late-night gathering, and the sea breeze that occasionally wafted into the room carried within its salty embrace gentle strains of music.

A small shiver ran through him, and McCoy unfolded a

blanket from beside him on the seat and spread it over his lap. At around twenty degrees Celsius, the early September evening was probably only a couple degrees cooler than in Atlanta, but the damp air made McCoy feel the difference that much more. Hugging the blanket closer, he glanced back toward Baris. In the soft reflected light, the years seemed to have fallen away from Baris's face, and McCoy saw him as he was when they had first met nearly a hundred years before. Baris had been a mere undersecretary of agriculture at the time, a year before the events that would thrust him toward becoming a special envoy to the Klingon Empire—a stepping stone that had eventually led to the presidency of the Federation.

McCoy entered the bar on Deep Space Station K-7, pausing on the threshold to look to his left and survey the scene. It was a well-lit room and large for the number of tables, but the strange angles of its bulkheads were not inviting to McCoy's tastes, and it had the sparse decor of most stations at the far reaches of Federation space. But at least it didn't have the claustrophobic feel of many of the other frontier bars that McCoy had had the pleasure—or displeasure—to patronize, and the staff seemed pleasant enough, especially some of the attractively attired waitstaff. Earlier in the day, however, Scotty, Chekov, and some other *Enterprise* crewmen had gotten into an old-fashioned barroom brawl here with some Klingons.

Since official business had brought McCoy to the station, he figured Kirk wouldn't mind if he stopped off for a nightcap on his way back to the ship. After convincing himself that the Klingons were honoring Jim's decision that they stay off the station, McCoy stepped all the way inside, allowing the door to slide shut behind him, and made his way to the bar. Business was slow, but McCoy supposed that was to be expected given the brawl and the earlier accident that had claimed two lives. There was a couple at a corner table, the most secluded spot in the bar, and McCoy glanced at them briefly, wishing he weren't here alone. Then he moved on past a small group of civilians at another table, probably colonists of some sort, all rather subdued.

Only one person stood at the bar, holding a broad pear-shaped wineglass by the stem and inhaling the bouquet of the red wine within. McCoy watched, amused, as the man swirled the dark red liquid around, took another long inhalation of the wine, then sipped. As he let the wine flow over his tongue, he drew in another breath through slightly parted lips. Finally he closed his mouth, almost chewing the wine, then swallowed. He sighed with pleasure. McCoy didn't want to interrupt the man's "date," so he turned toward the bartender, a tall slender man with a receding hairline.

"What can I get you?" the bartender said, looking somber but pleased to have another customer.

"Can you make a mint julep?"

"I most certainly can." The bartender turned toward a console on the wall and started pushing buttons.

"I don't mean to sound rude, sir," McCoy drawled, allowing his Southern accent full rein. "But I didn't ask if your machine could make a mint julep, I asked if *you* could." He smiled widely to take the challenge off his statement. "Georgia-style, if you please."

The bartender gave him a sharp look, but he was smiling as he did so. "A man of discriminating tastes." He leaned in conspiratorially. "I don't get much of that out here. Most of my clientele want their liquor quick and cheap." The bartender straightened and tugged on his short jacket. "Present company excluded, of course," he added with a nod toward the other man. He then turned his back on them as he started searching for ingredients.

McCoy glanced to his right at the wine drinker. The man had short brown hair and a fancy-looking suit. He didn't appear very sociable, but McCoy extended his hand anyway. "Doctor Leonard McCoy."

The man turned to face the doctor, giving McCoy's uniform a dismissive glance. He looked tired and drawn but forced a civil expression onto his thin face and shook McCoy's hand. "Nilz Baris."

McCoy's eyebrows raised at the man's name. He'd already gotten an earful from Kirk about the undersecretary who had issued the Priority One alert that brought the *Enterprise* to K-7.

"I can tell by your reaction that your captain has been telling stories about me." Baris turned to face the backbar as he took another slow sip from his glass.

"Well, he may have mentioned a . . . difference of opinion."

Baris quickly turned to face McCoy. "Difference of opinion? I didn't get the impression that Kirk acknowledges any opinions other than his own."

McCoy's diplomatic approach faded fast. "You only just met the man. You don't know him at all."

"But you do, I assume." Baris leveled a piercing gaze at the doctor. "So you've never had a problem getting him to see things from your point of view?"

Even through his anger, McCoy had to stifle a burst of laughter. "Well, he is the captain, after all. In his position—"

"In his position I imagine he relies on specialist crew members to give him advice about subjects he may not be familiar with." McCoy opened his mouth to respond, but Baris didn't give him the chance. "But he comes onto this station, without any knowledge of quadrotriticale grain and its key role in the Sherman's Planet colonies, and he immediately belittles my professional opinion and my authority. He has no understanding of Klingon influence in this—"

"Now wait just a damn minute." McCoy pointed a finger at the undersecretary. "You may be an expert on grain and your colony, but you have no idea what Captain Kirk knows about Klingons. He went toe-to-toe with them on Organia, and he's ready to do so now if necessary, treaty or not."

"That time is past." Baris put his glass down so hard McCoy was surprised he didn't break the stem. "What Kirk fails to understand is that since the treaty, people like me are on the front lines with the Klingons. The war didn't end, it's just being fought through colonial expansion. But the playing field isn't level, because the Federation maintains standards of behavior that the Klingons and their intelligence community do not. I'm just supposed to be making agricultural policy for the betterment of Federation citizens, but instead I'm fighting a cold war against the entire Klingon Empire. Engaging in brinkmanship with the Klingons is not what I signed up for, but that's the situation I'm in! Now, your captain can support my efforts or he can make jokes about my grain. But understand this: that grain is a weapon against the Klingons as surely as are the *Enterprise*'s phasers. And it's the only weapon I've got!" Baris took a deep breath, then a large swallow of his wine. He glared at McCoy as if daring him to respond.

McCoy's jaw clenched in anger, but he had to admit he saw Baris's point. And thinking back on what Jim had told him, he had to wonder if the captain's knee-jerk response to bureaucrats of any sort had gotten in the way of him realizing the full significance of the quadrotriticale. Before they could discuss it any further, however, a man in a light gray suit walked up to Baris's side. He gave McCoy a brief glance, then focused his attention on Baris.

"Sir, Admiral Fitzpatrick has requested an update."

"My assistant, Arne Darvin." Baris gestured toward McCoy. "This is Doctor Leonard McCoy."

Darvin looked at McCoy and blinked his dark eyes nervously before barely nodding in acknowledgment of the introduction. "We should get back to the admiral right away, sir."

"You'll have to forgive him." Baris looked down at his assistant, who was shorter than Baris by several centimeters. "If I've learned anything in the two years I've worked with Darvin, it's that he's even more focused on work than I am, and he's afraid of doctors. Excuse us." Baris and Darvin hurried off without waiting for a reply.

"Is that an example of your bedside manner, Doc?"

McCoy turned to the grinning bartender, who was holding out a glass for him. The ice in the drink made a pleasant sound, and even in the dry air of the space station a dew was gathering on the outside of the chilled glass. "As a matter of fact, it is." He grabbed the glass and took a sip.

"I had to make a few substitutions," the bartender said. "Saurian brandy. And mint flavoring right in the cocktail. I didn't have a fresh mint sprig for a proper garnish, obviously."

McCoy swallowed and smacked his lips in surprise. "Actually, this is exactly what the doctor ordered." With a nod at the bartender, he put the annoying run-in with Baris and Darvin behind him and took another sip.

McCoy smirked at the memories of his inauspicious introduction to Baris. Certainly neither of them would have guessed that they would eventually develop a friendship that would last for several decades. McCoy shook his head as his brief amusement faded. The year following their meeting had brought the tragedy at Sherman's Planet, including the death of Arne Darvin. Out of that tragedy, however, had come the beginning of Baris's rise to fame and power.

Turning from Baris's sleeping form, McCoy again looked out the window, this time at the narrow street below as a woman walked slowly past, humming to herself. She was dressed in white, a chef, McCoy guessed, heading to her *pâtisserie* to start the morning's pastries and brioche. *Does she even know,* McCoy wondered, *that she's walking by the house of Nilz Baris, former president of the Federation, former ambassador to the Klingon Empire?*

Baris had always worn his fame uneasily, almost guiltily. McCoy had long assumed it was because of Sherman's Planet;

from his greatest failure he had led an inspiring retreat, but he remained haunted by the deaths of thousands of colonists. And the failure at Bajor had been a disappointing coda to his ambassadorial career.

The beeping of the medical monitor ended McCoy's pondering. He rose from the window seat, the blanket falling to the floor from his lap. As McCoy made it to the bedside, taking his friend's right hand in his own, Baris took a couple of deep breaths, then released a long sigh. With his last breath, he whispered, "Arne Darvin." The monitor went quiet.

1

Nuevos Angeles Colony, Sherman's Planet, 2267

McCoy rubbed the sleeve of his uniform across his forehead to keep the sweat from running into his eyes. "Remind me, exactly . . . why am I here?"

Sulu looked up from where he knelt on the ground and paused in his extraction of a native flower, a Sherman's Orchid, into a sample container. "You said something about breathing real air instead of the filtered, stale atmosphere that passes for air on the ship." He pointed at McCoy with his small shovel. "You also mentioned not getting roped into any of the diplomatic—"

"All right, all right." He waved his right hand at Sulu. "It was a rhetorical question." He turned away from the helsman and looked back down the hill they had climbed to reach the flowers. It was a warm day, just a month or so after they'd been at K-7, and Baris had arranged a public relations event to celebrate a successful fall planting season. Sulu had provided McCoy a handy excuse for getting down to the planet without having to put on his dress uniform.

The hill was steep enough to raise a sweat while walking up it, and it was deceptively rocky. A greenish purple lichen grew over the whole surface, giving the appearance of a plush carpet, but as you tried to walk across the stuff the rocks beneath shifted unexpectedly. If you stumbled to the ground, as McCoy had done on more than one occasion during the climb, the rocks tore through the lichen and scraped at your shins. A couple kilometers down the hill, the colony of Nuevos Angeles spread out along Leander

Bay. The buildings were mostly prefab, just a story or two in height, in a variety of colors. Colonists could be seen bustling this way and that with the enthusiasm common among people making their way on the frontier.

McCoy turned back as Sulu straightened up, holding the small container at eye level to check on the plant before placing it in the case hanging from a strap on his shoulder. Inside were several more empty containers for Sulu to fill, and McCoy was starting to wonder how long this was going to take. "So, can we get going?"

Sulu gave him an odd look. "Aren't you forgetting something?"

McCoy shrugged. "Like what?"

With a growing grin, Sulu said, "I assume you told the captain you were conducting important biomedical research on our hike?"

"I may have *implied* that, but . . ." McCoy stopped and, after a moment, smirked back. "Of course, thanks for reminding me." He lifted his tricorder and took some scans. With an authoritative nod, he said, "There, that should do it. Now we better get moving."

A sharp voice came from behind them. "You'll do nothing of the kind."

They spun around, startled by the unexpected intrusion. McCoy and the man standing there rather indignantly in a meticulous brown suit exchanged brief looks before saying at the same time, "You!"

Sulu looked back and forth between them. "Doctor?"

With a frown, McCoy said, "This is—"

"Undersecretary of Agriculture Nilz Baris," the frowning man said, looking between the two of them like a schoolteacher with his worst truants. "This is an environmentally sensitive area you are trespassing in, and I will see to it that—"

"Now don't go getting your cravat all in an uproar," McCoy

said. "This is Lieutenant Hikaru Sulu, and he's quite the amateur botanist. He arranged for our nature hike with the colony's agriculturalist."

Baris turned his hard stare toward Sulu. "As undersecretary of agriculture, I'm sure you might guess that an amateur botanist has little sway with me."

The lieutenant exchanged an uncertain look with McCoy, who nodded in encouragement. "Well, Mr. Baris, my posting on the *Enterprise* gives me the chance to study many exotic forms of plant life that most botanists at universities can only dream of. I have published papers on the sensitivity of Weeper plants and the life cycle of Omicron pod plants in accredited journals."

The bureaucrat was already waving a dismissive hand as Sulu started speaking, but stopped as Sulu mentioned his papers. "Omicron pod plants? How do you know about those?"

"The *Enterprise* was at Omicron Ceti III." Sulu glanced at McCoy. "Both of us were under the spores' influence for a time."

Baris looked back and forth between them again, this time with curiosity and without his earlier hostility. "I find that most interesting." He briefly glanced over his shoulder, toward the colony. "I'd like to hear more about extraterrestrial plants you've studied. Do you mind if I join you? I could guide you to some really rare specimens. Did you know there's a carnivorous plant here large enough to catch small rodents?"

Sulu looked to McCoy like an eager child. The doctor scowled, giving a quick shake of his head but stopped as soon as Baris turned toward him.

"Well," said McCoy. "I mean, don't you have to attend the ceremonies or whatever back at the colony?"

Baris's usual scowl came back. "There's no reason for my presence to overshadow Governor Zaman."

McCoy grinned lopsidedly. "And it has nothing to do with Captain Kirk being there?"

"When I arranged this celebration, I specifically requested that someone other than Kirk represent Starfleet. For some reason I was ignored." Baris pointed a finger at McCoy. "Let me assure you, Doctor, if Kirk so much as—" Baris abruptly halted and stared closely at McCoy as he lowered his arm. "You're deliberately baiting me, aren't you?"

"He's got a knack for that," Sulu said. "Just ask Mr. Spock."

McCoy smiled innocently. Baris shook his head. "Well, I'm not falling for it again. Besides, Darvin is there to represent the Ag department." He looked over at Sulu, his expression brightening. "You want to see those carnivorous plants? They're called Sherman's Eaters."

Sulu patted his sample case. "I'm all ready to go."

The undersecretary made off at a brisk pace, with Sulu following closely. McCoy pursed his lips as he ran his arm across his forehead again. "Is everything on this damn planet named after Sherman?" With a shake of his head, he hurried along to catch up.

McCoy beamed into a corridor in the lower level of station K-7. He began coughing as soon as the materialization process was complete. Waving an arm in front of his face to clear away the smoke, which carried the odor of burned circuits and various overheated composites, he started moving in the direction of the noise. Emergency workers in orange coveralls ran back and forth, yelling directions and encouragement at each other over the sound of alarms.

"We're airtight and pressure's rising!" someone shouted nearby. "Crack those doors!"

As McCoy jogged around a bend in the corridor, he nearly collided with a woman about his age, dressed in baggy blue scrubs and carrying a medkit over her shoulder. Her graying hair was pulled into a bun on the back of her head.

She grabbed him by the arms. "Slow down, hotshot, we got a situation going on here." She then did a double take as she looked him up and down, apparently noticing his uniform for the first time. "Wait, are you Doctor McCoy?"

"At your service."

"Doctor Gaetane Lotte," she said, releasing one of his arms and pulling him along by the other. "There was an explosion on hangar deck two, apparently an engine malfunction on a small merchant ship. Damage from the explosion kept the bay doors from closing after the containment field failed. It went hard vacuum in there."

At the end of the corridor two engineers were using a large pry bar to open the doors onto the hangar deck. Various crew stood by waiting. McCoy and Lotte joined the small group, with nothing to do but stand vigil with them.

McCoy realized this was the first moment he had stood still in quite a while. Back on the *Enterprise* it had started with Uhura's voice, professional but urgent, over the intercom. *"This is a red alert. Man your battle stations. All hands . . ."*

He and Christine Chapel had hurried through their battle-stations prep, just finishing when the intercom whistled. *"Kirk to sickbay."*

McCoy hurried over and tabbed the button. "McCoy here. We're all set, Jim. What's going on?"

"There's been an explosion on K-7. I want you to beam straight over." The captain sounded angry, but there was something else in his tone that confused McCoy.

"Did the Klingons attack?" Treaty or no treaty, it was the easiest assumption, given the station's proximity to the Empire. Still, McCoy had hoped Organia's intervention into the war would spare them any more shooting matches.

"No. I'm going to stand down from red alert. I'll update you after I meet with the station manager. Kirk out."

McCoy had opened his mouth for a follow-up question and was left hanging. Instead, he turned to Nurse Chapel with a confused furrow to his brow.

Chapel shrugged. "At least it's not the Klingons." She held out his medkit, which he had grabbed and thrown over his shoulder as he headed out the door for the transporter room.

Now, he adjusted the medkit as the engineers finally pried the doors apart with a loud, grating shriek of metal on metal. As soon as the doors were open just enough, people were squeezing through the gap, even as the engineers continued opening them further.

Lotte hurried forward, and McCoy followed right behind her. There was a deep chill in the hangar, having been open to space just minutes ago, and the smoke was gone. It was dark, with only some of the emergency lights functioning and severed power conduits sparking here and there. The fresh air being cycled into the hangar was quickly filling with the smells of the recent fire, the sharp tang of toxic byproducts.

"Why aren't we using the transporter for evac?" McCoy said as they approached the merchant ship, which looked at least twice the size of a standard *Enterprise* shuttlecraft. The stern was petaled open like a duranium flower, still giving off waves of heat and occasional gouts of energy that flared toward the ceiling. A couple of engineers moved in with equipment in an attempt to contain it.

Lotte glanced over her shoulder without slowing. "The engine overload kicked up a squall of hard rad all through here, throwing off transporter locks. Did you inoculate before beaming over?"

"I wasn't informed of that little detail."

"Sorry." Lotte came to a stop and reached into her medkit, drawing out a hypospray which she quickly pressed to McCoy's neck. "That should do it." She dropped the hypo back into her medkit and drew out a tricorder.

McCoy had already started scanning with his own. "I'm getting a life sign in the merchant ship," he said, surprised.

"Take it," Lotte said as she jogged away toward some mangled wreckage piled against a Starfleet shuttle at the other end of the hangar. "I think there's some of our crew over here."

McCoy hurried to the ship. "I need some help here with a hatch!" he called out to no one in particular, but just seconds later a pair of K-7 crew members ran up to assist, a technician and one of the engineers who had pried the last door open.

"I'll take the tech, you take the wreck," the technician said, a diminutive human with an inordinate number of tools in his belt. He started working on the hatch's controls while the engineer, a woman built like a Capellan, brought up the large pry bar and started forcing it into the seam of the hatch.

McCoy watched in silence, bouncing on his feet with frustration. He looked back down at his tricorder. The life signs were weakening. "We're losing him, I've got to get in there."

"Almost there," said the man at the controls. He had opened an access panel and pulled out a circuit board which he had attached to some gadget he'd pulled from his belt. The technician slapped the board back into its slot and the hatch creaked open a tiny bit. That was all the engineer needed. She rammed the pry bar into the space and with one loud growl and a yank on the bar the hatch opened wide. A cloud of smoke billowed out.

The gangway didn't extend as it should have, so McCoy climbed up through the hatch, scrambling on hands and knees as he tumbled into the ship. He headed toward the bow without glancing at his tricorder; if the pilot had been aft there wouldn't have been a life sign. McCoy started coughing again. The forward compartment had maintained hull integrity, and hadn't vented along with the hangar. That had kept alive the man McCoy now spotted on the deck in the darkened corridor.

Quickly kneeling by the heavyset man, McCoy ran a Feinberger scanner over him. He grimaced as he glanced at the readings. The man's internal injuries were extensive. The explosion must have given off a powerful compression wave. Maybe if McCoy had gotten him into sickbay immediately after the explosion there might have been a chance to save him, but precious minutes had passed following the accident. There was nothing McCoy could do but keep the patient comfortable for the last minutes of his life. He administered a hypo and took the man's hand, although the doctor doubted he was aware of his surroundings.

But then McCoy was surprised by the man's eyes fluttering open beneath his bushy eyebrows. "Are they all right?" A trickle of blood ran out of his mouth as he spoke. His voice was surprisingly robust under the circumstances.

"Who?" McCoy leaned in closer to the man's face. "How many more were aboard?" He hadn't noticed any other life signs or indications of crew or passengers.

The man gave a small shake of his head, trying to smile. "Not 'who,' my friend. The tribbles."

"Tribbles?" McCoy didn't recognize the word.

"Back in the galley. If you could please check on them . . ." His voice faded as his eyes lost their focus. "Kind sir . . ." The man's gregarious smile faded, his face going slack. His grip tightened on McCoy's hand for a last second, then released.

McCoy sighed, which turned into a rack of coughs in the smoky corridor. Turning, he made his way on hands and knees, below the worst of the smoke, back toward the galley. It seemed hopeless for whatever these tribbles were, but McCoy didn't take a dying patient's last request lightly. He found the small galley just past the hatch. This close to the stern, with the explosion of the engine, structural damage was significant.

Slowly getting to his feet, McCoy stepped into the galley, stumbling over a twisted chunk of bulkhead lodged across the threshold. Regaining his balance by bracing himself against the wall with one hand, he glanced around the room. On the deck opposite a small stasis chamber, which was blasted open, the doctor spotted the shattered remains of a transparent container about a meter square and half a meter high. The bottom of it was covered with some sort of mulch, which led McCoy to guess that tribbles were a kind of animal, and this had been their habitat. He reached for his tricorder and scanned the container. There was biological material other than the mulch.

McCoy leaned over, looking closely while continuing to scan, squinting through the smoke. The results were gruesome. The concussion wave that had killed the merchant had also killed the tribbles, pulping their small furry bodies. Grimacing, McCoy straightened up and left the galley.

Climbing out of the hatch, McCoy emerged into a brighter hangar deck. The techs had gotten the lights back on while he had been in the merchant ship. The statuesque engineer was waiting and helped him down to the deck. He looked up and saw her face was smudged with soot and sweat. She looked sad but hopeful. McCoy just shook his head.

Her shoulders slumped. "We found one dead, pinned beneath that wreckage by the shuttle. Three survivors were inside. They've been taken to the infirmary."

McCoy rushed out of the hangar to the nearest turbolift, grumbling, "Come on, come on," while the lift made its way to the infirmary.

He practically ran into the operating theater, finding Lotte and her nurses treating the survivors for the effects of ebullism and rapid decompression. McCoy jumped in to assist. It was touch and go, especially for Gaal besh Vok, a Tellarite who had suffered the longest exposure to vacuum before his crewmates, donning oxygen masks, had been able to drag him into the shuttle. Vok had been in hard vacuum for almost eighty seconds, but he was going to pull through. McCoy leaned back against the wall, took a deep breath, and released it.

"Thanks," said Lotte as the readings displayed above Vok's biobed continued to stabilize. "But we're not finished yet."

They moved into another ward where secondary casualties had been triaged; the crew that had responded to the emergency and been injured in the course of their damage-control and rescue efforts. Smoke inhalation, random bumps and bruises, some first- and second-degree burns, one broken arm, and an Andorian's lacerated antenna awaited treatment. Lotte and the rest of the K-7 medical staff, with McCoy's help, made their way through the patients. Three hours rushed by, and finally McCoy was with his last patient, the Andorian, who had insisted everyone else be treated first.

"You're good to go, Ensign." He gave her a smile. "Keep off that antenna for at least a week."

With a blank stare and a "Thank you, Doctor," she got up and left the ward.

"Tough crowd," McCoy groused. He walked into Lotte's office and found her filling out some paperwork. "So can we breathe now?"

Lotte looked up from her desk. "Permission granted," she said with a smirk.

Before McCoy could respond, his communicator beeped. Lotte shrugged at McCoy as he pulled the device from his waist and flipped it open.

"McCoy here."

"Bones, how's it going over there?"

"We just finished up. Two fatalities, including the civilian merchant. It could have been much worse. How are things on your end?"

"Don't ask. Not only do I have an overzealous Federation undersecretary who issued a Priority One distress call because he thinks this accident was a terrorist attack on some sort of wheat—"

"Quadrotriticale?" McCoy interjected.

"I'm going to pretend you didn't know that. Not only am I dealing with this Nilz Baris, but there's a shipful of Klingons looking for shore leave, and—"

"There are Klingons on the station?" McCoy hadn't bumped into any, but he'd been busy.

"Are you going to keep interrupting me, Doctor?"

McCoy rolled his eyes at Lotte. "Sorry, Captain, sir, please go ahead."

"No, there aren't any Klingons on the station anymore. I had to kick them all off, as well as our crew, because Scotty and Chekov got into a brawl with them at the bar. You, Spock, and a security detail guarding the wheat are the only Enterprise *crew still aboard K-7. So now I have two ships of cranky people who aren't getting shore leave. And Klingons are cranky enough as it is."*

"Why is Spock still here?"

"Because he has to confirm that the explosion was an accident to help get Baris off my back. If Fitzpatrick hadn't called to put pressure on me, I'd have just locked Baris in with his wheat and been done with the whole thing."

"You have my sympathies. I'll be back aboard soon."

"All right. Kirk out."

McCoy closed the communicator and tucked it back under his shirt. He looked over at Lotte, who was shrugging out of her scrubs. She wore civilian clothes underneath, and after she reached back and released her hair from its bun to tumble in a wave down her back, McCoy didn't know if he would have recognized her if he hadn't seen the transformation himself.

McCoy cleared his throat and said, "Well, I don't know about you, but I could use a drink. Care to join me?"

Lotte ran her hands through her long hair, shaking it out after its time in the bun. She looked back at McCoy. "That's tempting, but I just pulled a double shift. I really need to get some sleep. Maybe some other time before *Enterprise* leaves?"

McCoy nodded. "Sure. Nice working with you, Doctor." They shook hands, and McCoy headed off to find the bar.

Silently cursing, McCoy tripped, *again,* on the roots that grew over the so-called trail that Baris had been leading them along for the last hour. The environment was more deciduous than tropical, but the plant growth was thick, and the still air close and warm. A few meters ahead of him Baris and Sulu chatted amiably about horticulture. McCoy wouldn't have guessed the inflexible undersecretary could be so relaxed. As they rounded a corner and moved through some overhanging foliage, McCoy had to brush away another Sherman's Bug, and this time he was able to do so without flinching, jumping, or, as Sulu had put it, screaming like a schoolgirl.

The ungainly creatures could get as big as a human hand and looked haphazardly assembled from equal parts tarantula, praying mantis, and squid. They were deep red and a bit slimy. For some reason, they behaved almost with affection for humanoids, an affection which went mostly unrequited due to their appearance, straight out of a particularly bad nightmare.

"Are we there yet?" McCoy called out as the Sherman's Bug plopped to the ground and scuttled off. He shivered a bit as he watched the glistening trail of slime it left behind on the moss and dead leaves that covered the forest floor.

"Be quiet," hissed Baris. "We don't want to scare away any prey. I'd like Mr. Sulu to get a chance to see the Eater feed."

"Yeah, wouldn't want to miss a plant eating a rat," McCoy said to himself. He followed Baris and Sulu up a small rise. They stopped at the top, looking down into a glade surrounding a small, scum-covered pond. Sunlight glinted off the greenish water, refracting in different ways as a light breeze disturbed the surface. A large worm undulated across the surface of the pond, sending more ripples through the green scum until a bird swooped down, grabbed the worm in its talons, and disappeared into the underbrush. A light perfume of flowers wafted in the breeze, which McCoy assumed was from the rainbow-colored petals growing on vines hanging down from the trees surrounding the pond.

"Follow the vines down to the water's edge," Baris whispered. He crouched down and motioned at the *Enterprise* crew members to follow his lead. "See what looks like a rotted log?"

McCoy squatted down on his haunches and squinted in the bright light. He did see a brown moss-covered shape on the ground near the shore of the pond. It was about the length of his forearm, but bigger around.

"I see it," Sulu whispered from where he knelt down on the other side of Baris from McCoy.

"That is the stomach of a Sherman's Eater. An animal looking for shelter goes inside and then the 'log' clenches tight around its victim."

"Ain't nature grand?" McCoy mumbled.

"Look." Sulu pointed across to one of the Eaters. An animal that looked a bit like a hairless ferret had appeared out of the underbrush on the far side of the pond, hopping toward the Eater.

Baris hunched down a little more. "That's a Sherman's Weasel."

"All right," McCoy said. "Who the hell was this Sherman, anyway?"

But the weasel turned and ran off at a loud rustling sound from some nearby underbrush. The three men looked toward the disturbance to see the branches part and reveal a Klingon officer, who stepped out next to the pond about a dozen meters away from them. McCoy grabbed his communicator as the Klingon looked around the glade and spotted them on the rise over the pond. The Klingon, who had shaggy brown hair and a not-so-neatly trimmed goatee, smiled broadly and started walking up the slope toward them, his gold uniform vest glinting in the sun.

"Well, well, what an interesting coincidence," he said in a loud, somewhat gravelly voice.

Noticing the scanner at the Klingon's waist, McCoy doubted there was any coincidence in their meeting. He also saw the large disruptor the Klingon carried. McCoy was unarmed, but assumed Sulu was wearing a type-1 phaser under his shirt. The three humans all got to their feet, turning their backs to the pond as the Klingon swaggered around them. McCoy flipped his communicator open, but was greeted by static as the Klingon put his hands on his hips and looked them up and down.

"Here we have the Federation official in charge of stealing SermanyuQ from the Empire and two lackeys from Starfleet's finest garbage scow."

Glancing toward Sulu, McCoy saw him tense at the insult and the threatening tone. The doctor gave Sulu a warning shake of the head. The way the Klingon ignored McCoy's nonresponsive communicator made it clear that he had not expected the communicator to work; he must have had a jamming device on him. Then McCoy's eyebrows raised as Baris took a step forward, thrusting an indignant finger at the Klingon.

"You're a long way from the nearest Klingon colony, Korax," Baris said. "Rest assured I will report this. Trespassing on Federation colonial land is a breach of the Treaty of Organia."

The name rang a bell with McCoy, and it took him only a moment to remember that this was Captain Koloth's executive officer, who had instigated the bar brawl with Scotty back on K-7. *Great, a Klingon with a grudge,* McCoy thought. *That's my favorite kind.*

Korax slipped his scanner off his belt and activated it. "Actually, I believe the official border of *your* closest colony is nearly a *qelI'qam* behind you." He waved the scanner's screen at them. "I guess we're all in . . . what's that Earther expression? 'No-man's-land.' Just about anything can happen in no-man's-land." With a self-satisfied smirk, Korax replaced the scanner at his waist. His hand hovered near the grip of his disruptor.

"Is that so?" Baris said, crossing his arms across his chest. "And just what do you think would happen to your Empire's claim on SermanyuQ if Federation citizens went missing in an area with traces of disruptor fire?"

Korax's smugness turned to a scowl as he lowered his hand from the disruptor. McCoy didn't know what to be more surprised about, Baris's effective arguing or his Klingon pronunciation.

"Earthers," Korax spat. "Hiding behind the Organians, like infants behind the legs of their wet nurse."

Sulu subtly adjusted his stance. McCoy could see the lieutenant was preparing to use his considerable martial arts skills if necessary. Korax's attention was drawn by the sparse movement, and his smile returned. "I see you have some spirit, like your scow's engineer. Luckily, a little competitive hand-to-hand combat doesn't seem to bother the Organians."

"I'd be happy to give a demonstration," Sulu said, his voice a deep, threatening rumble. "If only there was someone available who could provide competition, that is."

Korax bared his teeth and lunged forward. Sulu calmly grabbed Korax's outstretched right arm with his left hand, swung his right hand up under Korax's left armpit, and pivoted to his left. The Klingon found himself flipping over Sulu's outstretched right leg, his feet over his head. He slammed onto his back at the edge of the rise, which crumbled away under the impact, sending him sliding down the muddy slope and into the brackish pond with a splash.

McCoy couldn't help but guffaw as he looked between Baris's open-mouthed expression and Korax jumping to his feet, sputtering, his wet hair plastered to his head, his uniform covered with green slime. Sulu was smiling widely and made a production out of dusting off his hands. With a growl, Korax went for his disruptor but the weapon was gone, presumably somewhere beneath the water, which was now covered with startled worms undulating away from the enraged Klingon standing up to his knees in the pond.

Baris turned on Sulu. "What did you do that for? This is escalating to a full-scale incident. Reports will have to be filed with the governor, Lieutenant, and I shall have to take this up with your captain."

Sulu looked stunned, and McCoy grabbed Baris by the arm. "You've got to be kidding me. We're standing here in the

woods with a Klingon soldier, and you're going to tell me—"
He stopped as he noticed a small smirk appear on Baris's usually
stern face. "Wait . . . you really are kidding."

Baris laughed and clapped Sulu on the shoulder. "Well, I have
to go through the official motions, but that was a beautiful sight.
I've wanted to see something like that since Koloth and his crew
turned up on K-7."

The three of them looked back down at Korax, who had
been forced onto his hands and knees, sloshing through the increasingly muddy water, to try to recover his sidearm. All three
laughed so hard, they didn't hear the singsong whine of a transporter beam behind them.

"Sir, are you all right?"

They turned to see Arne Darvin, staring at the three laughing
men with a confused look on his face, which only grew more
confused as he looked past them to Korax still wallowing in the
pond, cursing at the top of his lungs in Klingon.

2

Atlanta, Georgia, 2366

arvin didn't like not knowing where Baris was every waking
moment," McCoy drawled. "So as soon as the ceremonies
were finished, he'd done a scan and beamed over. We stayed until
Korax found his disruptor and stomped away into the forest, then
we walked back." He cleared his throat, then took a long sip of
ice-cold mint lemonade. Setting the glass back down on the table
beside him, the doctor pulled his blanket tighter over his legs and
frowned. "This is one of the many things I hate about being as old
as the hills. I still love a nice, cold drink, but I'm always as cold as
all get-out, myself."

Marta Jensen, a field reporter for the Federation News Service, tucked a rebellious strand of her curly brown hair behind
her ear and gave the elderly admiral a smile. It was a lovely mid-
September afternoon outside Atlanta, and she was comfortably
warm in a short-sleeved blouse and navy blue pants. Her blazer
was draped over the back of her chair. They sat on a homey
veranda, complete with wicker furniture and ornamental vines
growing along the railings. McCoy's wife, Tonia Barrows, was
inside preparing dinner, and the mouth-watering aromas that
wafted through the open windows sometimes overpowered the
gentle floral smells that dominated the backyard.

"Of course I make the meals," Barrows had said with a wink
to Jensen when she arrived for her scheduled interview with
McCoy. Leading Jensen out to the veranda, Barrows added, "An
old space doctor like him, you don't want to know where his
hands have been over the years."

Leonard McCoy certainly lived up to his reputation: curmudgeonly, irreverent, and full of behind-the-scenes stories of famous events in Federation and Starfleet history. Although Jensen had only just begun this assignment, she had a feeling that it could be a turning point in her career. It had come about just days after the death of former Federation President Nilz Baris.

The flags over Starfleet Headquarters in San Francisco flew at half-mast. Jensen sat on a bench on the Presidio grounds, looking out over the bay, enjoying a cool breeze off the water, although the damp air made her hair frizzy. Nearby a couple of Starfleet cadets, a Denobulan and a human, thought she hadn't noticed them following her around. She didn't know if they'd recognized her from her occasional FNS broadcasts or if one of them was trying to get up the courage to ask her on a date. Perhaps it was a combination of the two.

A gentle tone from her handbag drew her attention away from her admirers. She took out her padd and activated the communication function. Her boss at the New York offices of FNS appeared on the small screen. She could never figure out how he maintained such a consistent gray stubble. He never had a beard or appeared clean shaven.

"Jensen?" Mr. Gardner, who had no first name as far as Jensen knew, had the ability to ask myriad questions solely by inflection of her name.

"Not so good," she replied, knowing he was wondering if she'd made a breakthrough on her current assignment. "I've confirmed that Tam Elbrun was reassigned from Chandra Five to the *Enterprise,* so there was obviously some sort of priority first-contact situation requiring a telepath, but beyond that no one is talking. I think his relatives on Betazoid have been notified by Starfleet, but they're keeping the details to themselves."

"Let's put that aside for now."

Jensen frowned. "Listen, I know I can get to the bottom of this."

Gardner was waving a hand at her. *"Settle down, I'm not pulling you off that. But I've got a tip that needs to be acted on. You know who Leonard McCoy is?"*

"Of course. Retired admiral, former Federation surgeon general—"

"That's the guy. Well, I've heard that McCoy was with Nilz Baris when he died. Heard his last words and everything."

Jensen's frown faded as her eyebrows lifted. "That's a pretty high-profile piece of information," she said, trying to act nonchalant. She'd tried to get an interview with Baris for years, had even spoken with him briefly the night of his death. She'd always thought that interviewing the reclusive former president could provide the boost her career needed, but Federation presidents and living legends were a notch or two above the stories Gardner had given her so far.

"It sure is." Gardner leaned in, as if to keep from being overheard. *"And I have reason to believe that McCoy is on Starfleet grounds right now. If you think you're up to it, perhaps there could be a 'chance' meeting between you two?"*

Jensen kept her expression even as she answered, "No problem. I can make that happen." She'd done enough on-air work to have developed her perfect reporter's face, which also served her well when she played poker with friends. At least the few who would still play with her. But up to now her work as a journalist had been one of press passes, official news conferences, and scheduled interviews. Her presence on Starfleet grounds today was under an official pass to see Admiral Margaret Blackwell specifically about Tam Elbrun. She'd never done any undercover investigative reporting. Granted, bumping into the old doctor wasn't exactly cloak-and-dagger work, but she'd have to wander around trying to find him, long after she'd already finished her official interviews. If anyone asked to see her pass, there could be a minor situation.

"Good. Keep me posted." Gardner signed off before Jensen had a chance to respond.

She slipped her padd back into her bag, only now allowing doubt to show on her face. The Starfleet grounds were extensive, on both ends of the Golden Gate, so finding someone surreptitiously was no small task. If only she knew someone on the inside . . . and that thought turned her mind toward her shadows, the cadets who'd been following her like puppies for the last half hour. If they would escort her around the grounds, she wouldn't be stopped by security. Smiling, Jensen turned to them, squinting into the afternoon sun, only to find she no longer had their attention. They had their backs to her and were standing as ramrod straight as an honor guard. It looked like they were talking to Boothby, the Academy groundskeeper she'd gotten to know after a few visits to Starfleet HQ. Woe to anyone who stepped off a path even just near one of Boothby's prized plantings. She knew that from personal experience.

"Listen, missy," Boothby had said to her at their first meeting. He was kneeling on the ground, pointing up at her with a pair of pruning shears. "You may be on the newsvid, but on my grounds you're just another kid about to step on my Talosian singing plants. You have any idea how rare those are? From the Betazoid expedition of 2355. Can't just go down to Genovese's Flowers for some new cuttings."

Jensen lifted a hand to shade her eyes, hoping to get an idea of what sort of infraction the cadets had committed. Perhaps she could put in a good word for them, further incentive for them to help her. Getting to her feet, she smoothed out her clothes and headed toward the three men. She had no idea what she was going to say. She just walked along the path that would take her right past them, and she would see what happened. As she approached, Boothby turned from the cadets toward her—and she realized it wasn't the groundskeeper. It was McCoy himself. As the doctor's bright blue eyes focused on her, she hoped that he wouldn't recognize her.

But now the cadets had turned to see whom the doctor was

looking at. "I *told* you it was Marta Jensen," the human said. He was tall and his blond hair, although neatly combed, seemed a bit long for a cadet.

The dark-haired Denobulan, shorter than the human, held out his hand. "It's a pleasure to meet you." He gave her the broad smile Denobulans were famous for. "We're in the journalism program at the Academy." They didn't look much younger than she, herself, and probably were third- or fourth-year students.

Jensen smiled politely, although frustrated by the loss of controlling her introduction as a reporter to McCoy. Out of the corner of her eye she noticed a mildly suspicious look on his lined face.

"Let me ask you this," the Denobulan said, stepping closer to her. "As Starfleet reporters, we'll be working within regulations, but what's it like for you, outside of the service, trying to cover the fleet?"

"Come on, boys," McCoy said. "No need to put her on the spot with shop talk. Besides, you really think she's going to tell you her secrets for getting information out of a bunch of tight-lipped uniforms? You need to figure that out for yourselves."

The cadets exchanged looks and glanced back at her disappointedly.

"Now don't you two need to get back to the quad or the replimat or whatever it is cadets do these days?" McCoy gave them a piercing stare. "Go on, give an old doctor his privacy. I just wanted to sit in the park, not get grilled by reporters." He gave a quick glance at Jensen, with a twinkle in his eye.

The cadets nodded at McCoy and Jensen and went on their way. McCoy watched them until they were out of sight, then turned to Jensen. He gestured for her to walk with him as he headed for the nearest bench. As they sat down, he said, "All right, what do you want from me, young lady?"

Jensen shook her head. "Nothing, sir. I just interviewed Admiral Blackwell and then stopped to enjoy the view before I left the grounds." She shrugged. "But as long as I've bumped into you, perhaps I could ask you some questions about President Baris."

McCoy snorted dismissively. "I've been around the block one or two million times, you know. You're not fooling me."

Jensen couldn't help but smile at his surliness, which was an obvious put on. "All right, I admit it. I really did see Blackwell, but then I was looking for you. My sources tell me you were with the president when he died."

The doctor nodded, his angry look softening. "Yes, I was there with Nilz."

"You knew him well?"

"I was just about his best friend, I think." Sadness filled his face, and McCoy blinked rapidly as he turned away from her toward the bay.

"I'm sorry," she said. "I know this is soon, but . . ." She trailed off, afraid any further explanation would seem callous. Truth was, this was news right now, and the more time passed, the less public interest there would be in the story.

McCoy continued staring over the water. "Tell you what, Miss Jensen, why don't you come around to the house, meet Tonia, have dinner with us. I'll give you a nice long interview about Nilz. Get in touch with me through Starfleet later this week, and we'll arrange a time."

"Thank you. I appreciate it."

He looked back at her with a small grin. "By the way, Gaspard told me all about you."

Jensen froze for a second. She hadn't seen that one coming. "You knew I'd been trying to interview President Baris?"

He nodded. "I also know that Nilz deserves far more recognition than he ever allowed for himself." As he got stiffly to his feet, Jensen also stood, giving the doctor a little boost at the elbow. He smiled at her. "And don't worry, Gaspard said nice things. I think he has a little crush on you." He winked at her and then shuffled off down the path.

★ ★ ★

"So, why do you think President Baris mentioned Darvin with his last breath?" Jensen couldn't help leaning forward, hoping for some insight from Baris's best friend.

McCoy shrugged. "Well, Darvin did save his life all those years ago. But Nilz never talked about it. If anything, he seemed to hold it against Darvin. I always got the impression that Nilz never really liked Darvin all that much." He looked up with a smile as Barrows came onto the veranda. She moved a bit more smoothly than McCoy did, but she placed a hand on her hip as she eased into a chair next to him.

"You're not exactly unbiased, though," Barrows said with a playful slap on her husband's knee. "After all, Darvin didn't like you."

McCoy rolled his eyes. "Listen, as a doctor you accept that some people are going to have phobias about you, and you develop strategies for dealing with frightened patients. But Darvin didn't even like being near me socially. To be fair, I only met the man a few times, but still. People think Nilz was a hard guy to get to know. Darvin made Nilz look like an empath."

"Did you see Darvin again on K-7?" Jensen took a sip of her mint lemonade.

"Just once. I stayed on the *Enterprise* most of the time, although I did help Gaetane—"

"You mean Doctor Lotte," Barrows interrupted with a smirk. She winked at Jensen. "You see, I've heard about how the second time he asked her, she *did* go to the bar with him."

McCoy coughed. "Yes, well, I helped Doctor Lotte with rounds once or twice. Spock was on the station more often, investigating the explosion of the merchant ship, but I don't remember him mentioning anything more about Darvin."

"And what were Mr. Spock's conclusions about the explosion?"

"It was a malfunction, simple as that. The trader—Cyrano Jones, I later found out was his name—was killed by the explosion, obviously, as I knew firsthand. I had to brief Nilz about that, as part of Spock's report on the incident, and Darvin was there, in the station manager's office."

Jensen checked her research notes on her padd. "That was Mr. Lurry, Walter K. Lurry?"

"Yes, that's right."

"So how did Darvin act during the briefing?"

McCoy smiled and looked at Barrows a bit sheepishly. "I have to admit I did something that might seem a little childish."

"Wasn't the first time, won't be the last," Barrows said, shaking her head and giving Jensen a quick smile.

Ignoring his wife's comment, McCoy continued. "When I got to the office, there were a few chairs left, but I sat down right next to Darvin. The man squirmed like he had a Denebian slime devil down his shorts." The doctor smiled at the memory, then his expression got serious again. "He was very suspicious of Jones, claiming he'd gotten a tip that the trader had visited the Klingon Empire recently. He implied that Jones had planned the explosion, but that it went off by accident while the trader was still aboard. Spock would have none of it and really got his logic up. He demonstrated conclusively that it was an accidental overload due to some faulty whatsamajigger in the impulse drive. All squirming aside, Darvin had to admit there was no evidence of anything suspicious about the explosion, no matter how paranoid Nilz was being."

"But the quadrotriticale crop *did* fail the following year," Barrows said. "Nilz was right to be paranoid."

McCoy nodded. "But there were still a lot of unanswered questions after the fall of Sherman's Planet. We could never prove that the Klingons were involved."

Even before McCoy and Chapel had finished rematerializing in the Nuevos Angeles hospital, he swore he could hear Baris yelling at him.

"Mark my words, McCoy, the Klingons are behind this."

McCoy glanced around what he could see of the facility, down white corridors and out the large windows of the room they had beamed into. He could tell the hospital had been significantly expanded and updated since the *Enterprise* had been to the colony the previous year. Whether that had been part of the original settlement plan or was in response to the continuing and worsening medical conditions in all the Federation colony cities on Sherman's Planet, he didn't know.

"The crop failure? Or the outbreaks?"

"All of it." Baris turned and walked briskly from the room. McCoy, after exchanging a grim look with Chapel, followed him. "Here in Nuevos Angeles, across the bay in Port Emily, in all our colonies, it's the same. Food shortages, rampant illness. We're barely keeping up."

"But the relief effort—" Chapel started to say.

"People get skittish enough coming to a planet with an epidemic, let alone a half-dozen epidemics, close to the Empire, with Klingons right here on the planet, and their ships in orbit." The undersecretary spun around and pointed a finger at them. "I thought the *Enterprise* was supposed to help us by patrolling the border, making sure the colonies were secure. But I suppose I should have expected this from Kirk, after the way he treated me at K-7. That man does not—"

"All right, dammit, can we skip the speech this time?" McCoy blurted. As Baris started to respond, McCoy raised his voice to drown him out. "We've got bigger problems right now than your personal issues with the captain. Okay, he hates bureaucrats and you hate people who challenge your authority. You're both just trying to do your jobs as best you can, and you're never going to see eye to eye. Let's just accept that as a given and move on to what we *can* do, like trying to cure the patients in this hospital."

Baris stood staring at McCoy, his finger still pointing. Chapel glanced back and forth between the men. McCoy's lips were pursed, and he was almost bouncing on his feet, a level of anger he usually reserved for Spock. Baris's thin face was clenched, but he lowered his arm and took a deep breath.

"Fair enough, Doctor. I will admit I'm used to getting my way, and certainly Darvin never tells me if my demands exceed reason."

McCoy nodded. "All right, then." He looked at Chapel, as if seeking confirmation that he had won the argument, then fixed Baris with a thoughtful stare. "I've read all the reports. No one has established a definitive link between the quadrotriticale and the various outbreaks."

"No, but the pattern is the same. The crops fail, and then disease runs rampant through the affected colony."

"But with different symptoms," Chapel added. "Every outbreak is different."

"It's hard to imagine a more effective way to destroy our claim to the planet," said Baris.

"But the Klingons are falling ill too," McCoy said. "This is affecting both sides."

"Only in those colonies in close proximity, and at a much lower rate among the Klingons. And don't forget, they have a wider range of crops suitable for their consumption that are able to grow here. Not to mention the amount of meat they eat, much of it native. They're not as reliant on plants as we are." Baris shook his head. "We can't grow crops, and we're getting sick. Even those who survive have such a slow recovery that essential services are compromised. We're losing the infrastructure needed to support the colonies.

"I've instituted a number of policies to strengthen Nuevos Angeles. I've established strict quarantine zones throughout the colonies. People who haven't gotten sick or seem to show resistance to the various epidemics are being moved here to maintain the colony as the others prepare for evacuation, if necessary. Nuevos Angeles will be our last stand, since it has the best medical facilities."

McCoy hesitated for a moment, glancing at Chapel then back to Baris. "No offense, but where's Governor Zaman in all this? It sounds like you've taken over."

"I *have* taken over. Governor Zaman died this morning in Port Emily. I've informally stepped in, with the cooperation of her staff, at least those still on their feet. But I may soon have to declare martial law." His face was grimmer than ever as he led them out of the room. Turning left into the corridor, Baris nearly collided with a Klingon sporting a neatly trimmed goatee. Darvin was close behind.

"My dear Undersecretary," Captain Koloth said in his ingratiating tone, adding a short bow which did nothing to convince McCoy of his sincerity.

"What is the meaning of this?" Baris sputtered, staring at Darvin. "What is he doing here?"

"I told him you were busy, sir, but he was very demanding." Darvin waved his hands nervously.

"Demanding?" Koloth made a broad gesture of confusion. "Is it demanding to offer aid to those in need?" He frowned. "For all your Federation's talk of cooperation, I would expect more appreciation for the Empire's help in your present tragic circumstances."

Baris went red in the face. "I'm quite certain our present circumstances are being *caused* by the Empire."

Koloth shook his head. "Really, such accusations don't become you." He turned his attention to McCoy and Chapel. "Ahhh, Doctor McCoy, I haven't seen you since our stay on Station K-7. Tell me, has Starfleet found any connection between these terrible plagues and the Klingon Empire?"

McCoy frowned. "No."

"I thought not." Koloth smiled again. "So why do you think Mr. Baris is so reluctant to hear about my offer to help in the evacuation of the ailing colonists?"

"Evacuation!" Baris took a step closer to Koloth. "Of course you offer to evacuate us, that would only help your claim on the planet." He turned toward Darvin. "Please escort Captain Koloth to the nearest transporter station."

Darvin looked at Koloth uncertainly. The Klingon maintained his smile but the forced warmth of it faded away.

"Very well, Undersecretary, but a Klingon does not offer aid twice. If you reconsider, you're welcome to come to me. But I may not be in a generous mood." He spun on his boot heels and stalked down the corridor. After a moment's hesitation, Darvin hurried after him.

"That was the last time I saw Darvin."

They had moved inside for dinner, sitting in a formal dining room, lit by the candles on the table. The ravioli con zucca was stuffed with pumpkin and mascarpone and tossed with sage brown butter, topped with a generous layer of grated Parmigiano-Reggiano. The rich aroma of the butter and cheese filled the room, along with the smell of fresh-baked bread. Only crumbs remained of the appetizer, garlic-rubbed bruschetta with prosciutto and shaved Parmigiano-Reggiano. When McCoy had invited Jensen to dinner, she had no idea that Barrows had pursued international cuisine as a hobby after retiring from Starfleet.

"Most of it's handmade and fresh, but I cheat a little with the replicator these days," Barrows had confessed. "I don't get around as easily as I used to."

Jensen had just put her last forkful of Caesar salad in her mouth as McCoy finished his story. While chewing, she glanced at her padd to make sure it was still functioning properly. In addition to recording the audio, it was also transcribing. She would take out the incidental "Pass the bread, please," interjections later. Jensen swallowed her salad and had a sip of Cabernet before responding.

"But you stayed on Sherman's Planet for several days doing medical research, right?"

McCoy nodded. "Well, we stayed in orbit. Christine and I

minimized our stay on the planet, following contagion protocols. I never trusted the transporter's biofilters. That confounded mix master of a device just isn't meant for—"

Barrows patted him on the hand. "Please, not the transporter tirade again, dear."

Taking a deep breath, McCoy nodded. "Oh, all right, I'll let it go this time. Now where was I? Yes, the contagion. The *Enterprise* had to leave for other missions, but we kept up our research. It took months to tease all those tangled threads apart and weave them back together in a recognizable pattern. By then it was too late for Sherman's Planet. We were back there at the very end, though."

McCoy, medkit over his shoulder, jogged toward the transporter room, weaving through a stream of evacuees on their way to the hangar deck, which had been filled with cots and stocked with emergency rations. Knowing that M'Benga and Chapel were handling the evacuees, McCoy's thoughts were focused elsewhere. A red alert had sounded with news of some sort of explosion on the surface of Sherman's Planet, eliciting echoes of K-7. But this had been at one of the Klingon compounds, while Baris was meeting with Koloth, and no one knew what had happened. How Kirk had talked the Klingons into letting him send down a security detail, McCoy couldn't guess. He did know that two D7 cruisers were close by.

A weary-looking Kyle, with dark circles under his eyes, stood at the transporter controls as the doctor rushed into the room. McCoy wondered how long the lieutenant had been at his station. Before he could ask, the whine and sparkling of the beaming process drew his attention to the transporter dais, where three figures were materializing: Baris and two security guards. The undersecretary, usually so prim and fastidious, was disheveled and covered with fine debris. He was missing his coat, and what remained of his suit was torn and dirty. A large smear down the front of his shirt was clearly blood. There was some bruising around his neck, his left eye was blackened and swelling, and his nose was bloodied. He staggered down off the stage. The guards moved forward to help, but Baris regained his balance and waved them off.

McCoy stepped forward, waving a hand scanner over Baris's chest. That nose hadn't produced this much blood, so there must be another wound. Baris pushed him away as well.

"It's not my blood." Brusque as ever, Baris looked around and added, "Where's Kirk? I expected him to be here gloating over my failure."

"Don't make me dress you down again," McCoy said, thinking of their last argument a few months ago. "The captain's on the bridge, where he should be when trigger-happy Klingons are within spitting distance." McCoy turned his attention to the lead guard. "What happened down there, Leslie?"

"A bombing, sir." He handed McCoy a tricorder. "Apparently Koloth was the target, but the undersecretary was in there too."

McCoy considered the information for a moment, raising an eyebrow. He turned back toward Baris, who didn't interfere this time when McCoy ran the Feinberger over him.

Baris shook his head and let out a long sigh. "It's Darvin's blood."

"So, back to why Nilz would bring up Darvin now." McCoy put a large spoonful of crème brûlée into his mouth. "Since, for whatever reason, Nilz didn't seem to feel personal gratitude for what Darvin did, it could be guilt. Guilt for never acknowledging Darvin's sacrifice. Or, maybe, guilt for all the colonists who died, with Darvin being representative of that. Maybe Nilz wasn't really thinking of just Darvin."

"Obviously, it was a terrible time for him," Barrows said. "I assisted him while he was aboard the *Enterprise* after the evacuation. He was a wreck. The colonies had come crashing down, thousands were dead, Darvin had been killed, and Nilz was taking the blame, although none of it was his fault. He even got medals of honor from both the Federation Council and Starfleet. Most of the colonists felt they owed their lives to his leadership after the death of Governor Zaman. Everyone spoke of how he had stood up to the Klingons, but he was simply overcome with guilt. Still, he never said a word about Darvin to me."

"To me either," McCoy said. "We brought the evacuees back to Earth, and I don't recall if he spoke to me again outside of the exam I gave him. That's when I told him we'd figured out what had happened. The quadrotriticale had been poisoned with a mutagenic virus. The virus caused the crops to fail, and it also infected people. It was designed to mutate based on its environment, so every outbreak was different. If the grain from K-7 had been eaten directly instead of being planted, if would have had yet a different effect.

"Nilz blamed the Klingons, and they had the obvious motive, but there was no direct evidence. The Klingons were quick to point out that they'd had fatalities as well. He was enraged, calling them every name in the book. Of course, he included the captain in his tirade, since he and Jim had clashed on K-7, and it turned out that Nilz had been right to worry about the safety of the grain. I tried to calm him down. I told him about an encounter the *Enterprise* had with a Klingon captain named Kang, and how we'd all been able to cooperate against a common threat. Nilz didn't want to hear it. He said Jim was a warp-speed Captain Bligh and Klingons were all devious killers then stormed out of sickbay. I thought that was the end of our acquaintance. Not long after, I heard he'd resigned. Now, Nilz Baris could be like a sharp stick in the eye, but he didn't deserve the blame that was heaped on his shoulders.

"A couple years later, after our five-year mission was over, I retired from Starfleet. I took on some patients, like an old-fashioned country doctor. One day Baris showed up out of the

blue and apologized. Said he'd decided to try to work with the
Klingons again. I had to surgically reattach my jaw from where it
had fallen on the floor."

Jensen smirked as she sipped her coffee. "What caused the
about-face?"

"Same old story as with many an angry man." McCoy winked
at his wife beside him.

"Her name is Sima Mishra." Baris paused, a faraway look in his
eyes and an equally longing smile on his thin face.

McCoy stared back at his surprise guest, eyebrows far up his
forehead, and leaned back in his chair. He glanced around his
office, noticing that for all its homeyness—the dark woodwork,
the antiquarian books, the framed newspaper advertisements for
nineteenth-century elixirs, the glass case of antique stethoscopes,
sphygmomanometers, and otoscopes—there were no pictures of
anyone who made him look like Baris did now.

"She sounds wonderful."

Baris shook his head and focused back on McCoy. "What do
you mean? We have a professional relationship."

"Professional relationships do not give people the dreamy eyes
you just had." With a growing smirk, McCoy added, "And it
looks like a pretty serious case. Trust me, I'm a doctor."

"She's a colleague, a peer, came to me for advice," Baris stam-
mered while sitting up straighter and adjusting his severely cut
suit. "I would never—" He stopped, mouth still open, then
slumped in his chair. "Oh, who am I kidding? I've fallen for her
like a teenager."

McCoy smiled warmly. He had never seen anyone look so
uncomfortable while slouching in a stuffed chair. He leaned forward with his elbows on his desk. "Tell me all about her."

Baris looked across the desk uncertainly, then made a scoffing
sound. His expression softened. "I've made such a habit of being
brusque and, believe me, in the Federation bureaucracy it served
me well for many years."

"I never got the impression you had to put all that much effort into it."

Baris's eyes widened for a second before he let out a loud guffaw. McCoy nodded, then reached into a bottom desk drawer, pulled out two glasses and a bottle of Saurian brandy, and poured a couple fingers into each glass. He slid one glass toward Baris.

With a self-conscious grin, Baris took the glass. "Sima's the Federation Special Envoy to the Tellun Protectorate."

McCoy nearly spilled his brandy. "Good god, man, she's not Elasian is she?" He'd seen firsthand the effects of the biochemicals in the tears of Elasian women, which gave them great emotional power over affected men. Elaan, the frightfully demanding Dohlman of Elas, had even infected Kirk before her arranged marriage to the ruler of Troyius to unite the Tellun system. The captain had gotten through it, but the mission had taken an emotional toll on him.

"No, no, she's human. She's trying to get the Tellun system back in the Federation, but the Klingons have been making strong overtures to them to acquire their dilithium resources. That's why Sima approached me." His voice turned bitter when mentioning the Klingons. "If my experience with the Empire could help, I could make the Klingons pay for what they did to Sherman's Planet."

McCoy could see the rage boiling up within Baris and decided to see if he could defuse it. "And if you could, along the way, help Sima?"

The fire in Baris's eyes softened, and he took a sip of brandy before smiling. "She's just so beautiful, so smart, so ambitious . . . and seems not to mind putting up with me."

"So what are you waiting for?" McCoy looked out his window at the warm Atlanta afternoon. "It's easy to make excuses not to, but before you know it your only chance may have slipped away."

"You're absolutely right. But first I'll get the professional obligations out of the way. The Dohlman is planning a meeting with the Klingons, and I intend to be there to expose them for what they are." Baris got a wicked smile on his face. "At the Dohlman's insistence, I've called in some favors to arrange for Admiral Kirk to personally escort her to the meeting as Starfleet's representative."

McCoy rolled his eyes. Baris was obviously plotting two revenges; even falling in love hadn't completely changed him. "Well," McCoy said, raising his glass. "Here's to putting up with you."

"Mind you, at the time I was in no position to give romantic advice—"

"You can say that again," Barrows interrupted.

"All right, no heckling." McCoy winked at Jensen this time. "But I must have said something right, because a year later I was best man at his wedding, not to mention that Tellun rebuffed the Klingons. Then I went back to the *Enterprise,* and, eventually, Nilz was appointed as a special envoy to the Klingon Empire. Even though we often went months, even years, without seeing each other in person, we stayed close."

"That's when he began his rise to real power," Jensen said.

"You have to remember the politics back then. After the Klingons took control of Sherman's Planet, they pulled out of Nimbus III—"

"The Planet of Galactic Peace," Barrows interjected. "That was the grandiose title someone on the Federation Council came up with."

"That name jinxed it, if you ask me," McCoy continued with a smirk. "So the Empire focused on the Sherman's Planet region. Boundaries in space are very nebulous, if you'll pardon the pun, and every colony they won within the terms of the Organian treaty expanded their sphere of influence. For twenty years Nilz went head-to-head with the Klingons, first as envoy, then as president, then as ambassador, building inroads alongside every setback. By the time Praxis exploded, there was a lot of overlapping territory in the Alpha Quadrant. When Baris and Gorkon signed the Praxis Accords, it was largely because the Federation was worried that if we didn't give the Klingons what they needed they would be in a position to take it. But Baris made a mutual defense pact part of the agreement. He was certain that the UFP and the Empire could work together, he was insistent about it. He was self-important, demanding, loud, and aggressive. So, you can see why he and the Klingons got along great!"

Jensen laughed as she pushed back from the table. "Now, that's a quote. But I really should be going, it's late. Thank you for your time and the amazing dinner." Everyone stood and shook hands, then they walked her to the door. She paused on the threshold. "I do have one last question. You seemed uncertain about some of the tricorder scans after the bombing that killed Darvin."

McCoy frowned. "Yes. I haven't thought about that in decades." He folded his arms, and his eyes focused elsewhere. "There were some anomalies in the blood work. Darvin's blood on Nilz's shirt. Any number of reasonable explanations: contamination at the scene, environmental exposure over the years, some sort of metabolic abnormality. Nothing serious, but certainly something that would have been cleared up by a proper postmortem. Under the circumstances, however, that wasn't possible. We couldn't even recover the body. We just broke orbit and headed home. Arne Darvin was dead, and there was nothing more I could do."

3

Klingon Capital City Hochbutlh, Sherman's Planet, 2273

I have returned, Governor."
Koloth looked up from his large desk, a slab of native stone, roughly hewn and polished, and stared into the thin face of Nilz Baris. "My dear Undersecretary, how many years has it been?"

"Nearly five Earth years."

"Yes, that sounds correct." Koloth smiled widely. He enjoyed smiling at non-Klingons, who generally found it unsettling. They found it even more so since he had been part of a test group the previous year that had received an experimental cure for the Augment virus; all tainted DNA had been purged from the group, restoring their true Klingon appearance. Koloth now had full Klingon ridges, as well as teeth that could properly chew into the heart of a *targ*. Interestingly, Baris showed no reaction to Koloth's changed appearance. Starfleet Intelligence must have briefed him. Koloth dismissed his disappointment at this and moved to assert his control of the meeting in other ways.

"Five years since you fled from your failed colonies, ceding SermanyuQ to the Empire. The Federation knows well how to retreat." He leaned back in his chair, folding his arms across his chest. "I must admit that I'm a little confused about why you asked for this meeting. Federation presence in this sector is minimal. I was under the impression that you have no jurisdiction here."

"You are correct that the agricultural department is no longer tasked with colonial developments in this region." Baris took a seat without being offered one, and made a show of getting comfortable.

Koloth narrowed his eyes as he watched Baris. Humans were rarely comfortable on Klingon furniture and, unaccountably, Baris was smiling back at him. Allowing a glimpse of his frustration in his tone, but maintaining his smile, Koloth said, "You have something more to say?"

"You may want to consider getting a new assistant, Governor. Your intelligence is out of date. I am now Federation Special Envoy to the Klingon Empire. I have a wide range of issues under my jurisdiction, but—" Baris leaned forward, his elbows on Koloth's desk. "—as you might imagine, Klingon colonial policies in the Alpha Quadrant are of particular interest to me."

Koloth frowned. The miserable little *bekk* who handled his paperwork and appointments was going to have a long career of waste reclamation ahead of him, on the most backwater Klingon world Koloth could find. He should have kept Korax at his side instead of allowing him to rise to the rank of captain.

"I see I have your attention, my dear Koloth." Baris leaned back in the chair, folding his arms to mirror the Klingon. "We humans have an expression, one that I'm sure a Klingon could understand. 'Lose the battle, but win the war.' I may have lost Sherman's Planet, but I'm going to be watching very closely now. The Empire thinks they can get around the Treaty of Organia, and they certainly got away with it on Sherman's Planet, but that road is going to be closed now."

Koloth put his smile back in place. "Congratulations, Envoy Baris." Koloth vowed to see to it that Kor conquered a planet expressly for the purpose of providing the worst possible environment for that *bekk*. "But I have no knowledge of what you refer to. The Empire needs no tricks to beat the Federation. Our superiority as a race is all we need to outperform you Earthers and your allies."

Baris didn't rise to the bait. He just stared smugly back at Koloth. "That's a nice little story you can tell yourself, while you use desperate tricks to cause our colonies to fail so that you can claim additional planets. It's sad, really, that the once mighty Empire is forced to such underhandedness by the Organians. It's almost as if the Empire is afraid to beat the Federation in a fair fight."

Koloth leaned forward on his desk and stared, unblinking, at the human. Like Kor with the Organians, this new Baris had a grudge: with Koloth. Just as Kor's grudge made him a ruthless governor, eager to exert his control over his subjects, Koloth would have to make sure to never again underestimate Baris. The human, curse him, was right: it was sad that the Empire had been forced to wage war with words instead of the *bat'leth*. But like the *bat'leth*, words could be an edged weapon, and Koloth was skilled in wielding them. He had actually enjoyed the war of words he'd conducted with the undersecretary over Sherman's Planet, as the Federation called it. In fact, Koloth reflected, he still had one verbal knife left to twist into the envoy. All of his previous battles with Baris—memories of many of them were filling his head, competing for his attention, one leading to another—had progressed to one final confrontation in this very room, the scene of Baris's brutal and humiliating defeat five years ago.

The explosion shattered the double doors to Koloth's office, and a piece of one of them the size of a carving plate glanced off Koloth's head. He had just half-turned back toward the door in the instant before detonation, so he caught a glimpse of the debris coming his way and was able to duck, although not quite quickly enough. He let out a growl as his head was snapped back by the impact and the shock wave lifted him from his feet. Landing on his back, he skidded along the polished floor of the corridor until colliding painfully with an overturned chair. Flaming pieces of his office decor rained down around him as his vision faded.

"Are you okay?"

Koloth forced his eyes back open as someone shook his arm. Through the smoke-filled air, Baris leaned over him, a look of apparent concern on his soot-smudged face. Koloth, his usual jovial nature—for a Klingon—falling away, grabbed the human by the throat with his right hand. "Federation *petaQ*. What treachery did you bring with you?" His voice sounded odd, and he realized his ears were ringing from the explosion. Alarms, also sounding strangely muffled, jangled in the background.

Baris's eyes bulged in pain and surprise. He grabbed at Koloth's tight grip on his throat with both of his hands. Luckily for the human, Koloth's left arm seemed unable to move at the moment. Baris managed an incoherent coughing reply, spittle flying from his lips. Koloth sat up, left arm hanging dislocated and limp at his side. The human had been crawling on his hands and knees, but Koloth's movements forced Baris up onto his knees and then back into a sitting position. Now they both sat there in the chaos after the explosion, staring at each other as Koloth tightened his grip.

Out of the corner of his eye, Koloth saw a *bekk* approaching as if to assist. One glance froze the enlisted woman in her tracks. He wondered where she had been earlier, when Baris had barged into his office unannounced. But that would be settled later. Turning back to Baris, Koloth was surprised to see the look of fear on his face had transformed into anger. The human raised a foot, planted it on Koloth's chest, and with a solid push broke Koloth's grip on his throat. Baris fell onto his back, gasping for breath.

As Koloth staggered to his feet, Korax rushed to his side. The Klingon first officer glanced down with a sneer at Baris before saying, "I have put all the colonies on alert, and ordered the cruisers to converge on *Enterprise*."

"Well done." Koloth realized he was still shouting over the ringing in his ears. The alarms had been stopped, although there were still small fires burning in the corridor and back in his office, judging from the smoke. "Fix this," he snapped, gesturing at his limp arm.

"Yes, sir." Korax grabbed Koloth's left arm firmly in both hands and, with a practiced pull, twist, and shove, popped it back into place.

Koloth flexed his left fist as he stared back down at Baris, who had stopped coughing. The bureaucrat's assistant had saved both their lives, a situation Koloth found disgusting. He had never liked Arne Darvin. From the moment he had first met the subservient *to'ba* on the Federation station K-7, there had been something about the human that just didn't seem quite right. It was a feeling that did not change when Koloth had met him again on SermanyuQ.

"What is the meaning of this invasion?" Baris blurted, leaping to his feet, as Koloth and Korax entered his office in Nuevos Angeles.

"My dear Undersecretary," Koloth said with a smile. "Klingon military power is unquestionable, but even I might consider it an exaggeration to label the two of us an invasion."

Korax laughed derisively at Baris. "Not to mention, it is not an invasion to be on your own planet."

"It is not your planet, Korax, and it never will be. The Federation will convince the Organians to award us sole colonization rights."

"That remains to be seen," said Koloth. "Which is why we are having this meeting. I have been appointed by the High Council to oversee the Klingon colonies here, and I intend to ensure the treaty, loathsome as it is, is followed to the letter. No Federation or Starfleet tricks."

Darvin burst through the door just as Koloth finished speaking. "Unlike the Empire, the Federation doesn't use tricks," he said, his voice a little louder than necessary. His nervous eyes shifted between Koloth, Korax, and Baris, and he took a further step away from the Klingons.

"Where have you been?" Baris said, turning his sharp stare on his assistant.

"Sorry, sir, I . . . I had a personal issue I was attending to. I came as soon as I was notified."

Koloth looked Darvin up and down, the convivial air he generally had around non-Klingons turning sour. Korax had his problems, but if he ever behaved in such a way as this *shuVak*, Koloth would cuff him like a misbehaving targ. By the look on Baris's face, Koloth guessed he was considering something similar, at least in weakling human terms.

Korax laughed loudly. "Personal issue?" He took a step closer to Darvin. Darvin moved back a little, looking at the floor. "Were you at your tailor, getting some nice soft Earther clothes, something comfortable to be frightened of your own shadow in?"

At first allowing himself his own quiet chuckle at Korax's playful cruelty, Koloth stopped short when he glanced at Darvin. For a moment, a passing second at most, he thought he saw a fiery anger in the human's eyes, but before he could be certain the look was gone. Something about the human made his skin crawl, something false, unnatural. But his thoughts were disrupted by Baris.

"Is this what you've come for, Koloth, to abuse Darvin? You're certainly not going to find any of your alleged Federation tricks up his sleeve, and I have better things to do with my time. I would think that you would too, if you're as serious about colonizing this planet as I am."

Koloth turned his eyes away from the disturbing assistant. "I'm serious, the Empire is serious. SermanyuQ promises to be a Klingon foothold, a stepping stone to the Alpha Quadrant. It will be mine by the merits of my leadership and the loyalty of the colonists. There is no doubt. We are Klingons."

"What is wrong with you? Are you not a Klingon?" Koloth wrinkled his face in disgust as he looked Korax up and down. His first officer, standing at rigid attention, was covered in mud and green filth, his hair had dried into a grotesque mess of slime, and his wet uniform smelled like the inside of a *targ*. An unhealthy *targ*.

"Captain, the Earther—"

Koloth silenced him with an upraised hand. "There is no shame in being bested in combat by a superior foe."

"He is *not* superior!"

"Then you *were* shamed."

Korax opened his mouth to reply, hesitated, and closed his mouth.

"Ahh, so you are capable of thinking before acting." Koloth moved behind his desk. "You were told not to approach the Federation colonies. You were told not to engage the Federation colonists. You were told to avoid any Starfleet personnel you might see." Leaning forward, hands on his desk, Koloth sneered. "You did all of these! You threatened the highest-ranking Federation official in the region, and did so in front of officers from the *Enterprise,* one of whom mounted your *jornub* on a painstik."

Korax was visibly shuddering with anger. "Captain, I—"

"I did not give you permission to speak!"

Clamping his mouth shut, Korax returned his stare straight ahead. He did not submit by casting his look downward, but he also did not challenge by looking directly at his commanding officer.

Koloth sighed. "Sit down, Korax." As Korax moved to the nearest chair, Koloth said, "Not on the chair, you'll ruin the leather." Korax froze, then sank down onto his haunches. Koloth sat down behind his desk, forcing Korax to stretch upward to be visible, teetering on the balls of his feet. Suppressing a grin, Koloth continued speaking. "As you know, I expect to be appointed governor when the Empire wins this planet. Someone will need to command the *Gr'oth* while I'm on the surface. Perhaps you should keep that in mind while you make future decisions."

"Yes, Captain."

"Get out of here, you're leaving puddles on the floor."

"Yes, Captain." Korax stood, saluted, and hurried from the room, his boots making squishing sounds as he left. Koloth swore he could still hear the squishing of boots when the communication panel built into the desk signaled. He hit the response button. "What do you want?"

"*Sir,*" said the *bekk* on comm duty. "*Undersecretary Baris is demanding to speak with you.*"

"I'm sure he is. Make him demand for as long as you can, then put him through."

The *bekk* handled the six-wheeled ground vehicle like a drunk handled his tankard of bloodwine—carelessly, with much unnecessary bobbing and weaving and the ever-present threat of the insides being spilled out. Since Koloth was a passenger, he held on tight to the duranium roll bar above his head.

"Tell me, young warrior," he said, shouting to be heard over the noise of the vehicle's engine and much-abused gears. "Do you exact revenge on all forms of transport, or just this vehicle?"

The *bekk* looked about to answer when he realized what Koloth was getting at. With a slight shrug of his shoulders he slowed down. "It's not much further, Captain."

Koloth nodded. He would have preferred simply beaming to their destination, but transporting into the neutral areas between Klingon and Federation colonies was forbidden. Not that it wasn't done; during Korax's shameful adventure the year before, Baris's repugnant assistant, Darvin, had done so, which had given Koloth the leverage to minimize the amount of whining Baris was able to do about Korax's own transgression.

"Speak of the *Qatlh,*" said Koloth as they came over a rise and approached a crowd of about sixty people, twenty Klingons facing off against Federation colonists. Darvin stood at the head of the Federation contingent, mostly Earthers, but some of the other mongrel aliens in the Federation were represented as well.

Nearby, Korax stood, hands on his hips, glaring at Darvin, clearly ready for any excuse to attack, even against superior numbers.

The *bekk* didn't slow as he neared the crowd, instead he drove the vehicle like a wedge between the opposing sides, forcing Darvin to leap backward with a yelp as he finally applied the brakes and skidded to a loud, gravelly stop.

"I enjoyed that," Koloth said as he tabbed the door control. The *bekk* just nodded with a feral grin as the door swung up and out and a cloud of dust settled inside the vehicle. Koloth jumped down to the ground and slapped at his dark uniform, raising a small cloud of the dust. It was warm and dry this time of year, and dust was an annoyance Koloth could not get used to.

Korax walked quickly toward Koloth. "Captain, a routine patrol found this illegal encampment and called in a control unit."

Koloth, as he rounded the vehicle, was now able to see down the other side of the crest they had just driven up. Thirty or so tents were arranged around a central fire pit with a thin dark pillar of smoke slowly rising and drifting away on the wind. A creek flowed nearby, the sound of the water filtered though a copse of trees encircling the clearing. A Klingon camp would have been on the crest, defensible high ground, not hidden in a low spot, but these were humans. He looked away from the camp as Darvin came around the vehicle, a look of outrage on his nervous face.

"You have no right to be sending such large patrols through neutral territory," he snapped, speaking loudly. He waved a hand at the people behind him, and they held back.

"My—" Koloth halted his customary greeting. "Mr. Darvin. If we were to compare violations, I think it's clear that this settlement is the more serious."

"This is *not* a settlement. It's nothing more than a . . . a camping trip."

Koloth smiled and took a step closer. Darvin's dark eyes darted left and right, avoiding Koloth's piercing look. The human had a real problem with people "getting in his face" as the Earthers said. Koloth loved that phrase, as Klingons loved getting into people's faces. "A camping trip?" Koloth chuckled, glancing back down at the tents and then looking at Korax.

Korax's brooding look brightened. "A camping trip?" he echoed. "Earthers camp like Klingon children at play." He gestured grandly at the tents, smiling broadly. "But even for Earthers, this is more than a weekend furlough. I can see your poorly stacked firewood and smell your poorly tended latrine. Your fire is smoking like a beacon. Any enemy would know your presence from a *qell'qam* away."

"We aren't soldiers," a man behind Darvin growled. He was big for a human, and his green jumpsuit seemed just a little too small for him. His name, "McAllen," was stitched above the left breast pocket of the suit. McAllen tried to step in front of Darvin, but the smaller man put out a hand to stop him.

Korax laughed as he walked closer to the two humans. "You don't need to tell me that, Earther. A Klingon would never mistake you for a soldier." Stepping past Darvin as if he didn't exist, Korax went eye-to-eye with McAllen. "Some sort of mewling, suckling herd animal, perhaps."

He looked around at the patrol, who laughed and raucously punched each other in agreement. Korax turned back to McAllen, who had gone red in the face. "No, wait, I must apologize for that. It's not really a fair description, is it?" He prowled around the big human, forcing Darvin to step back out of his way. "Even a herd animal has a spine. Isn't that right, warriors?"

The crowd of Klingons laughed and cheered Korax on. "But the mud worms of Noch'tuQ Prime . . . they are able to feign standing on their own by allowing mud to dry like a shell around their pale, defenseless bodies. But come a light rain, or even the slightest push—" Korax poked McAllen in the chest. "—and the spineless worms tip right over."

Korax glanced back at his audience, who roared in pleasure.

As Korax turned his smiling face back to the human and met the colonist's large fist crashing into his nose, the roar of the Klingons got even louder.

"My dear Governor Zaman," Koloth said, gesturing at the wide floor-to-ceiling windows which gave a panoramic view of Port Emily nestled next to Leander Bay. Pleasure boats, both powered and under sail, were traversing the dark blue bay under the bright summer sun. "I must compliment you on your view. It really is rather attractive, in a soft, human way—no offense."

"None taken, Captain." Elizabeth Zaman leaned back on a couch facing the window. The streaming sunlight brought the deep greens and reds of her office to life. The soft carpet, warmed by the sun, was loved by her orange tabby cat, Kashmir, who sprawled by the window.

"Can we get to the point, Koloth?" Baris stood in a corner of the office, squinting in the sunlight, arms folded tightly across his chest. Darvin hovered nearby, a step back from his boss, in the shadows. Korax stood on the other side of the office, staring at Darvin.

"Undersecretary," Zaman said, her voice full and inviting, but with a hidden edge, like a Klingon wife. "With all due respect, I believe Koloth requested this meeting with me."

Baris shrugged and remained quiet, his jaw clenched. Koloth stared at him until the human looked way, turning toward the shelves on the wall beside him. They held a sitar, wood carvings representing the spiral horns of a Markhor goat, a holoimage of K2, and other heirlooms of Zaman's ancient Pakistani heritage, all of which the governor had painstakingly pointed out to Koloth.

"Please," she said, gesturing for Koloth to sit on the couch.

He looked down at the human woman, uncertain what to think of her. She was clearly in a position of power, and she had made Baris keep quiet, not an easy task. But her clothing—all yellow and orange, the baggy trousers and loose-fitting tunic hiding her feminine form—looked weak, nonthreatening. She watched him, a curious expression on her face.

"I'm sure the Klingon colonies, if ever I was invited to them, would also have their appeal . . . in a brutal, Klingon way. No offense."

Koloth felt his smile grow a bit more genuine. He gave her a slight bow as he sat on the couch. "I am surprised that your people can go for a boat ride under the circumstances." He turned away from her to watch the bay. "Especially when their fellow colonists are living hand-to-mouth in the outlands in violation of—"

Baris spoke up. "That is a misrepresentation of the circumstances."

Koloth glanced over the back of the couch at Baris, but before he could respond he was distracted by the governor's cat jumping into his lap. Koloth snapped his head around to look down at the creature, which stared back at him with unblinking eyes. He wrinkled his nose and drew his face back from the orange-furred vermin.

Zaman stood up and walked to the windows, arms clasped behind her back. "I don't know about Klingons, but humans, and many others in the Federation, look to recreation for relief in troubled times." Zaman kept her back to the room. "I was also under the impression that the problem had been taken care of since the unfortunate incident last month."

"It was a simple misunderstanding," Baris said. "It only became an incident because Korax has to incite riots wherever he goes. Koloth, you are responsible for his actions."

"I do not deny that," Koloth said. He put one hand on the cat and pushed it. The beast pushed back. Koloth respected its determination and decided it could remain in his lap. "And surely you are equally responsible for Mr. Darvin's support of the illegal settlements."

"They are not settlements. The colonists—"

"Stop," Zaman said sharply as she turned to face the room. "Mr. Baris, what does he mean by Darvin's support?"

"It's simple Klingon propaganda, Governor."

Zaman looked at Darvin, who seemed to have receded further into the shadows. "Mr. Darvin?"

Darvin's eyes shifted between Zaman and Baris, Koloth and Korax. Korax bared his teeth at the human. As the pause grew longer, Baris turned toward his assistant.

"Don't tell me there's any truth to this."

"Sir, I . . ." Darvin gave Korax a fierce stare as the Klingon started laughing. "Sir, you would never get anything done if I bothered you with every development. I simply let some of the colonists know that temporary summer camps away from the colonies hardest hit by the—"

"Darvin!" Baris looked shocked. "You had no authority to do such a thing. I trusted you to implement my directives, not go off on your own."

Koloth waved his right hand dismissively and addressed Zaman. "Don't worry, Governor, it's not as if we weren't already aware that you've had some difficulties with your crops. And some public health concerns. Nothing too serious, I hope?" Zaman watched him with an unchanging expression. "The Empire stands ready to offer you any assistance you need."

"Governor, he's trying to trick you." Baris paused to glare at Koloth. "Any knowledge they have of our situation is because of their spies, masquerading as patrols, threatening anyone they meet in the neutral territories. And if you take their assistance, the treaty states—"

"Mr. Undersecretary, I am the governor of the Sherman's Planet colonies, not some naive schoolgirl, I see what's going on here." She folded her arms. "Clearly, the Klingon patrols are using their right to monitor neutral territories as a pretense for intelligence gathering and harassing Federation colonists—

colonists who are, at best, exploiting a gray area in the treaty language."

Before Koloth could protest her clearly biased portrayal of events—and out of the corner of his eye he saw Baris about to take issue as well—she added, "It's obvious that both of your assistants need to be kept on shorter leashes, gentlemen."

"Governor Zaman," Baris said. "I had no idea Darvin had encouraged the colonists."

"I don't care right now." Zaman turned away to look out across Leander Bay. "I know that you outrank me, but I do not appreciate you or your assistant making decisions without my input, decisions which affect me and my colonists. This meeting is over."

"But Governor," Baris started, but they all turned as the door burst open and Zaman's receptionist, a Bolian named Halin, rushed in. At the same time, Koloth's communicator began chiming. The sound startled the cat, which jumped to the floor and ran away.

Halin had a frightened look on his face. "There's been another incident in the outlands. There are casualties."

Even years later, the memories were all still clear. Koloth sat in the same office, which had, of course, been repaired after the bomb, and then expanded when he had become governor of the Klingon Empire's newest colony. And here was Baris again, still ranting about the Empire. It was all so similar. But Koloth had seen things the night of the explosion that still made him wonder.

At first, when Darvin had started screaming like a frightened child that there was a bomb in Koloth's office, the words had not even registered. While Baris had been yelling accusations of sabotage against the Empire, Koloth had been squinting at Darvin, reflecting on his intensifying dislike for the Earther. Baris, a self-important bureaucrat, could be troublesome, but he was not that different from his Klingon counterparts. And he always said what was on his mind, thrusting a finger in the air, declaiming whatever triviality he thought was most important at the moment.

Koloth had determined a strategy for dealing with him within moments of meeting him on K-7. But Darvin . . . there was something about him that Koloth had never trusted. Koloth immediately found it hard to believe that Darvin could have even recognized an explosive device, and he certainly was not going to flee his own office the way Baris had after Darvin had repeated his claim. He was a Klingon warrior, and he strode toward danger. But when Darvin, usually as skittish as a pregnant *s'tarahk,* rushed at Koloth, pushing with surprising strength, Koloth had begun to suspect there might be something to the Earther's panic.

"Out of my way," Koloth said with a growl, shoving Darvin aside and looking under the edge of his desk. He raised his eyebrows in surprise when he actually saw a small box affixed to the wood. A single small red light blinked off and on, as if indicating the device had activated. *"QI'yaH,"* he said quietly. He had not believed any of the Federation colonists capable of such an attack, even in their current desperate state.

But then Darvin had grabbed him by the arm, yanking him away from the desk, almost flinging him toward the door. Koloth stomped into the corridor, shouting for a technician, hoping to defuse the device if indeed it was a bomb. When he realized that Darvin was not right beside him, he started turning to look for him. That's when the bomb had gone off, throwing Koloth to the floor.

After Baris had caught his breath from the firm choking Koloth had given him, the human got unsteadily to his feet.

"Where's Darvin?" he had asked. It had sounded routine.

"He did not leave the room," Koloth had answered, wiping at the blood streaming from his smooth and fragile forehead. He watched Baris think that over, and then begin to walk slowly toward the ruins of Koloth's office. Koloth followed, his shoulder still throbbing. It was difficult, edging through the splintered doors, stepping around burning debris, breathing shallowly in the billowing smoke. Ahead of him, Baris stumbled, fell to the floor. The smell of burned flesh was suddenly strong.

Koloth grabbed Baris with his good arm and hauled the human upright. Beneath Baris had been the remains of Darvin. Taking off his coat, Baris dropped it over the body, apparently a human custom. He turned to face Koloth, the front of his shirt now covered in blood. He hadn't said a word, just walked from the room.

Now, Baris had returned to the same room, pacing back and forth, challenging Koloth to be honest about the Empire's strategies for expansion. All of these memories had rushed through Koloth's mind like a scream in the night. He smiled, a wicked one born of his weariness of Baris and his hatred for the odious assistant who had saved his life. "I will be honest with you, if you will be honest with me. Why do you think Darvin stayed behind? Was he frozen in fear? Or did he not want to face your failure, and preferred to die, even in his enemy's territory, than live while so many colonists had died, and for what? You still lost Sherman's Planet."

Baris froze in place and glared at Koloth. He waited for Baris's outburst, his typical Federation self-righteousness. Instead, the envoy said, "I don't know and I don't care." He turned and stalked from the room, so much like he had done years ago, but this time there was a door he could slam behind him as he left.

Koloth glared at the door long after Baris had gone, knowing that he was not the only one who had changed over the years.

4

Paris, France, 2366

The wise warrior fights for the victory he wants; he does not waste time trying to predict the victory he will achieve." *Dahar* Master Koloth, Klingon Special Envoy to the Federation, gave Jensen a small smile that, on just about any other humanoid, she would have described without hesitation as "whimsical." Looking Koloth up and down, at his wild mane of wavy gray hair cascading to his shoulders, the white scimitars of his mustache scything down from his upper lip, the Klingon crest of his ridged forehead, his dark gray and black clothing, all leather and chain mail and accessories that were part decoration, part edged weapons, she was reluctant to ascribe any whimsy to him at all—out of fear of repercussions.

The reporter sat there, uncertain how to respond even after all the time she had spent with him this morning, filling the nervous silence by glancing around his office. It was common for embassies to be decorated in the style of their homeworlds; never had Jensen seen it taken to the extreme of this room. Koloth's office in the Klingon Embassy was positively dingy, lit only by simulated torches. The air was damp, even chill, as if they were in a castle, and the floors looked more like rough-hewn stone than the ceramic tiles of a building in the heart of Paris. The Eiffel Tower should have been visible through the window that Koloth paced in front of, his leathers creaking, the metal clinking, but instead a holographic overlay transformed the view into nighttime in the Old Quarter of the First City on Qo'noS. Dark, greenish clouds hung low over the towers and spires, dim lights shown in the dusk, diffuse in the drizzle that fell, making the walkways glisten. If Jensen squinted into the simulated distance, she could even see the infrequent lone figure moving through the darkness, hunched down in the weather.

Jensen had listened intently to Koloth's recollections of Baris, their growing personal enmity over the years in which they had, if not fought, then certainly competed over territory desired by both Federation and Empire. When Mr. Gardner had succeeded in making this appointment for her to follow-up on some of the implications of McCoy's stories, she had not known what to expect. Koloth himself was certainly a conundrum, at times dark, even vindictive, then, just seconds later, lighthearted, verging on the unthinkable in Jensen's experience, a whimsical Klingon. But the details he had added to the Darvin story were almost shocking. Clearly there had been some sort of falling out between Baris and his assistant, but if Baris had truly no longer cared what had happened to Darvin all those years ago, why had he mentioned Darvin on his deathbed?

McCoy had thought Darvin could have been a symbol for Baris's guilt about the fall of Sherman's Planet. But listening to Koloth's story, it seemed more personal. Unlike Koloth, who seemed to resent being saved by a human he despised, perhaps Baris felt guilty that Darvin had died saving him while they were having some rather serious professional disagreements. Or, it still could have been simple belated gratitude toward the man responsible for allowing Baris to have the rest of his life, which had turned out to be full and rewarding.

As Jensen mulled that over, she became aware that it was quiet in the office, only the subtle crackle of the torches in the background; the clumping of Koloth's boots and the sounds of his elaborate clothing had stopped. Turning toward him, she found Koloth staring back at her, a hint of a smile haunting his mouth.

"My dear Ms. Jensen," he said. "I was beginning to think you had entered some kind of catatonia."

"Oh, no, I'm sorry, I just . . ." she trailed off as he laughed robustly.

"No apologies necessary, the room often has that effect on humans. The gloom and the torch light seem to hypnotize them. But it makes me comfortable." He dropped down into the chair behind his desk. "If we're going to continue this interview, however, let's make some adjustments."

As Koloth tapped at a control panel on his desk, the lights came up, losing their flickering, flamelike quality. The floors became more polished, the sparse furniture less worn; most likely this was the real nature of the room, the rest a holographic overlay. Lastly, the First City faded out of existence, replaced by a sunny fall day in Paris, the Eiffel Tower perfectly framed in the window. Jensen blinked in the sudden brightness.

"There." Koloth turned to glance out the window. "I do like that tower. It would fit right into the Old Quarter back home." Then he returned his gaze to Jensen. "Now, shall we continue?"

Jensen almost laughed at the transformation, and she caught a twinkle in Koloth's eyes as he watched her, waiting for an answer. "You *are* a whimsical Klingon," she suddenly blurted, then felt horrified, putting her hand over her mouth. Certainly, Klingons had killed for lesser affronts to their honor; and this was a *Dahar* Master, a living legend among warriors.

But Koloth rocked back in his chair and his laughter fairly echoed in the room, reverberating off the cavernlike walls. "Whimsical!" he repeated. He smiled widely at her, his vicious teeth bright in the now well-lighted room. "Never before, I'm certain, has that word been used on a Klingon." He leaned forward, his arms on his desk. "But the way we stomp about, butting heads and drinking bloodwine and singing songs of honor . . . it is somewhat fanciful at times, I must admit." He made a show of turning his smile into a stern frown. "Nevertheless, I forbid you to ever repeat such an accusation in public."

Jensen, feeling immensely relieved, quickly said, "Of course not."

"Good. I trust you to your honor." He adjusted various accoutrements of his wardrobe that had been disarranged by his laughter. "Now, back to the point I was making . . . I had quoted Kahless. If I had tried to imagine how events would play out between our governments, I would have been mired in confusion as circumstances twisted and turned like a mad *targ*. For instance, here I am, a special envoy, the same title Baris challenged me with on SermanyuQ. The Empire and the Federation are allies. Surely not the victory I was fighting for, but it is a good victory, and arrived at, in no small part, because of what I did fight for. If I had tried to guess this outcome and fight toward it, perhaps the outcome would have been something entirely different. Perhaps it would have been an end for both our governments. This is why Kahless tells us we must be true to our own honor and actively make our choices. One should not live in 'bad faith,' to use the words of this city's most famous philosopher."

Jensen tilted her head as she considered that. "I wouldn't have guessed that Klingons read Jean-Paul Sartre." Koloth gave a small shrug and a hint of a smile. Jensen returned the smile and leaned forward. "Darvin's name was the last thing spoken by President Baris. Do you think Baris was remembering the man who saved his life?"

Koloth scoffed. "He could just as well have spoken my name."

Koloth did not favor the empty shell of Darvin's body with another glance before following Baris out of his ruined office. He edged his way through the broken doors just in time to see Korax's fist collide with Baris's head. The human staggered backward under the force of the blow. A cheer went up among the crowd drawn by the explosion and now eager to see a fight. Korax advanced on the undersecretary.

"Hold!" Koloth walked briskly into the semicircle of Klingons.

"But the Earther tried to kill you, sir," Korax said, pointing at Baris, who leaned against the wall, silent, a hand to his eye.

"He was in the room with me until the other one warned us. What sort of plot is that?" Koloth glared at all of them. "This human is no warrior. What honor can come of fighting him, or of watching the fight?"

The female *bekk,* the one who had been away from her post, stepped forward. "But you accused him yourself." Before Koloth could respond, she gave Baris a backhanded cuff across the face. Blood ran freely from Baris's nose as he cried out. A few of the spectators shouted their approval.

Koloth rushed toward her. She was obviously trying to impress him, knowing she had failed him earlier. He extended an outstretched open hand to her forehead, snapping her head back and bouncing it off the wall with an audible crack. She kept on her feet, but her eyes lost their focus.

"You defy my direct orders to my face, *bekk?*" His face nearly touched hers as he continued yelling. "I spoke with him leader to leader, a position you will most likely never find yourself in." Turning away from her, he glared at the rest of his warriors. "It is a good thing the Federation colonies failed on their own, because the future success of our colonies is doubtful, given your performance here today. You stand in a burning building and cheer a pointless fight instead of putting out the fire or checking for more explosives?"

Another *bekk* approached Koloth from the side. He spun on the young warrior, grabbing him by his uniform. "What do you want?"

To his credit the *bekk* did not flinch as Koloth shook him, but held up a communicator in one hand. "It's the Earther captain, sir. Kirk wants to speak with you."

Koloth took the communicator and shoved the *bekk* aside. He looked down at the device in his hand with all the hatred he felt for the Federation at this moment. "If there was any doubt left about who is getting this planet, Kirk, it vanished today in an explosion. Your so-called peaceful colonists just tried to kill me."

"This was no sanctioned action on the part of the Federation, Koloth. I will personally see to it that the guilty parties are found. I'm sending down a security detail to help in the investigation."

Before Kirk had finished his sentence, the annoying high-pitched whine of Starfleet transporters filled the corridor, and two red-shirted crewmen materialized in front of Koloth's office. Smoke from the room swirled around them. One started taking tricorder scans as the other hurried to Baris. The nearby Klingons stood stiffly, jaws and fists clenched, clearly torn between Koloth's orders to leave Baris alone and wanting to engage the *Enterprise* crewmen.

"As if justice would be done by whatever token punishment the Federation might impose on its coddled and cowardly citizens."

"Let's skip the debate about jurisprudence. Is Undersecretary Baris all right?"

"He is. Only because I personally intervened on his behalf. My people would have his head on a pike for today's attack. I'm beginning to regret my decision. I demand, under the terms of the Treaty of Organia, that all Federation citizens be removed from this planet at once."

"We'll start with Baris," Kirk said, and cut the connection.

Koloth looked up to see that both security guards now flanked Baris, and the three of them disappeared in the flurry of the transporter effect. Koloth stared at the empty space for a moment, then looked around for Korax, who was talking into his communicator.

"Is it asking so much that Starfleet should not be able to beam in and out of my compound at will?"

"That's what I was looking into, Captain," Korax said, lowering his communicator. "The explosion disrupted a power conduit that runs beneath your office, and the transporter scrambler went down. It's running on auxiliary power now."

Koloth nodded and turned on the *bekk* he had smacked in the forehead. She came to attention under his glare. "You! Get that carcass out of my office and dump it in a swamp somewhere. Then get back here and stand guard. If you feel like walking away again I will have you nailed to the door. The rest of you try to remember your training and do your duty."

He stormed back into his office, kicking still-burning pieces of debris out of his way. Sitting behind his ruined desk, he watched the *bekk* as she stooped and hoisted Darvis's corpse onto her shoulders. She swayed for a second, shifted the weight, then stood to her full height. With a nod at Koloth, she left the room.

Koloth stared at the stain Darvin had left behind on his floor and thought about the last time he saw the odious human before today.

"Unbelievable," Koloth murmured as he looked through the viewers at the human settlement in the woods. The Earthers kept right on making these camps even as more skirmishes broke out between them and his warriors. "How far outside the colony are they?"

Korax was huddled down beside Koloth. "Two and a half *qelI'qammey*."

"If Baris knows about this—"

"I did see Darvin here yesterday when we discovered the camp."

Koloth bristled at the mention of Baris's assistant. He jumped to his feet. "Follow." He didn't wait for Korax's response. As he advanced toward the Earthers, quietly winding through the trees, ignoring small animals he sent scurrying for new cover, he knew Korax was coordinating the rest of the warriors. Bursting into the small clearing, he bellowed, "Attention."

The humans jumped at the sound of his voice and his sudden appearance. Koloth hesitated for a moment, taken aback at how ragged and emaciated the aliens appeared up close. But they were still in violation of the treaty. "This is an illegal settlement. You will disperse to your assigned colonies. A complaint will be filed with Governor Zaman."

"You can't send us back there," a human pleaded, approaching Koloth. "The plague is killing everyone."

"That is the Federation's problem, not the Empire's."

Another human came forward from the gathering crowd. He was larger than the rest and looked familiar. "It *is* the Empire's problem. You're making us sick." There were yells of agreement, and, as a group, the colonists took a step toward Koloth. They froze again as more Klingons appeared out of the woods behind him, but the big human continued. "You're poisoning our crops."

Then it came back to Koloth—this was McAllen, the colonist who had punched Korax months ago, the first time Korax had shown him one of these camps. He shook his head. Further evidence that the Earthers were blatantly disregarding the treaty. "I have offered assistance before. I'll offer it to you now. You can stay in your encampment if you accept medical assistance from the Empire."

"Liar!" someone shouted.

McAllen said, "He's trying to trick us. He'll make traitors of us all, and we'll lose Sherman's Planet."

Koloth stared directly at his main challenger. "You will lose SermanyuQ because of the failure of your colonies and your treaty violations, violations repeatedly committed by people like you at the urging of Arne Darvin. If he is here now—"

Koloth stopped as a rock flew at him from the crowd. He ducked, but the *bekk* behind him didn't and was knocked to the ground. Koloth glanced back to see if the *bekk* was all right, and when he turned back to the colonists the big human was almost upon him. The air was already full of the battle cries of Klingon warriors, who waded into the humans, eager for the satisfaction of embracing an enemy hand to hand. Koloth himself bared his teeth and lunged forward to meet McAllen, whose momentum took both of them to the ground.

As they rolled along the forest floor trading blows, Koloth realized it was lucky for the humans that energy weapons were banned in the outlands. The colonists would survive this skirmish battered and bruised, with some broken bones thrown in as well, but they would finally learn a lesson without things getting too serious. That's when the sound of a disruptor screeched through the air and a nearby Federation ground vehicle burst into flames. McAllen froze for a moment, and Koloth took advantage of the opening to render him unconscious with a solid right cross to the jaw.

"Korax!" Koloth yelled without being able to see his executive officer. "Control the warriors. No more shots are to be fired."

Jumping to his feet, Koloth rushed in the direction the shot had come from. Fistfights were one thing, but energy weapons, even handheld ones, might draw the attention of the Organian *petaQpu'* who had imposed these ridiculous contests on the Empire, instead of allowing them to conquer planets the way they had always done. It was difficult to thread his way through the clearing as panicked colonists ran around crazily searching for cover, many with Klingons in pursuit. Another disruptor shot, coming from a different direction, set a row of tents on fire and made it clear that more than one of the patrol was armed.

Hurrying toward the second shooter, Koloth saw Korax himself fire a disruptor at a wooden lean-to filled with kindling, which burst into flames, sending burning bits of wood in every direction, setting off smaller fires on the dry forest floor. He ran through a sudden break in the crowd and rapidly approached Korax.

"Korax, you idiot, holster that weapon."

"But, Captain—" Korax shut up as Koloth grabbed the weapon from his hand, raising it as if to club him with it.

"I swear on my ancestors, I'm going to promote you just to get you out of my sight."

Any further exchange was stopped by the sound of a ground vehicle rapidly approaching. The vehicle, a match to the one rapidly becoming a burned-out hulk, slid to a stop, sending up a spray of dirt clumps. Baris climbed awkwardly out of the slowly opening hatch on the passenger side.

"What the hell is going on here? Koloth, I demand an explanation for this flagrant violation of the weapons ban."

Slapping Korax on the chest with the disruptor so that he took it back, Koloth walked forward to meet Baris. "I admit my warriors got a little . . . overzealous, but these illegal settlements have already been discussed. Not to mention it was your colonists that started this altercation—"

"That's a lie!" Darvin yelled, appearing from the driver's side of the vehicle. "You can't trust a Klingon to tell the truth."

"Darvin," Baris said, looking over his shoulder. "That may be, but we weren't even here when this happened. And if you've still been encouraging these camps, Governor Zaman is going to want you fired. So keep quiet."

Koloth smiled in satisfaction at the assistant being put in his place, but the smile soon disappeared as Baris turned back. Behind his boss, Darvin was giving Koloth a look of pure hatred that bordered on madness.

"You really think he was crazy?" Jensen asked.

Koloth paused thoughtfully, a stern frown on his face as he looked over Jensen's shoulder, focused on the past. "I do not know. Certainly I could not understand his behavior. On K-7 he seemed weak, even for a human, and his obsequious nature with Baris was repulsive to me. But on SermanyuQ he began to defy Baris and openly antagonize Klingons."

Angling his gaze at Jensen, Koloth continued. "I did not like Baris. From the moment I met him on K-7, his self-important moralizing grated on me. But I understood him and eventually developed a grudging respect for him. I had dismissed him as not being a warrior, but I learned that was not true. Granted, he was no physical warrior, but with words he had the heart of a warrior. He said what he felt, demanded what he wanted, avenged what he lost. Although fear showed on his face, he would not back down from an argument." Pausing, Koloth gave a very human-like smile and shook his head. "*Hu'tegh,* but I actually miss the troublesome old man.

"But Darvin . . . he was always in the shadows, showing one face to Baris and another face to me while he followed his own counsel, causing tension between Baris and Zaman. His loyalty blew in the wind." Koloth clenched his jaw. "Then his final act . . . even Baris did not count it as heroic or redemptive. Why is that? That is the one thing about Baris I never understood. He redoubled his efforts on behalf of the Federation after Darvin's death, but it was not revenge for Darvin. For the loss of Serma-nyuQ, perhaps, and the death of the colonists, but something had already happened to change him before Darvin died."

Koloth looked up from his desk as Baris barged into his office. "My dear Undersecretary, I'm surprised to see you. I thought you would have beamed up to *Enterprise* long ago." He wondered where the *bekk* was that should have stopped Baris outside his doors. Probably sneaking a tankard of bloodwine.

"I am not through here yet, Koloth. No thanks to your marauding thugs, I'm still working to evacuate without further bloodshed between Federation and empire."

"Marauding thugs? As you are withdrawing, we have every right to send patrols into our new territories."

"Your patrols are intimidating the colonists, forcing them out of their homes before they finish packing. They outnumber the Starfleet security forces, so they are doing whatever they want."

"Just another demonstration of how the Federation wasn't prepared for settling this planet. That's why we Klingons perse-vered."

Baris suddenly leaned forward, banging his fists on Koloth's desk. "Klingons do not persevere, they lie and cheat and manipulate!" His face was red with anger, his arms, still on the desk, trembled. He raised one arm to point shakily into Koloth's face. "And they murder in cold blood while hiding behind the Organians."

Koloth jumped to his feet so quickly his chair tipped over with a loud crash. Without thinking he had already drawn his blade and was holding it toward Baris's face. "You dare accuse me of such cowardice! I should gut you where you stand, Earther, but it is you who hide behind the *HosDo' jay'*. Were I to kill you, the Organians might give SermanyuQ to the Federation."

Baris laughed, an empty, cruel sound even to Koloth. He rubbed his face with both hands, smothering the outburst. When he moved his hands away, spreading his arms wide, his expression was drained of all emotion. "Try it, Koloth. Perhaps you would be pleasantly surprised at how much the Organians will allow us to get away with. Or maybe you already know."

"No!" Darvin shouted as he rushed into the room. "Sir, the colonists—"

"What are you doing here?" Baris said, spinning toward his assistant. "I told you to leave. I don't want your help."

Koloth squinted at the human, confused. With a growl he stabbed his blade into the surface of his desk. "You will both leave now, and I will never have to see either of you again on my planet." He rounded the desk to chase them from his office. Baris stood his ground, as if daring Koloth to attack, but Darvin scurried away, keeping the desk between himself and Koloth. The miserable human now stood behind Koloth's desk as if it belonged to him. Koloth and Baris stared at one another for long, tense seconds.

"There's a bomb under the desk!" Darvin screamed.

Koloth and Baris turned toward him.

"Run, sir! There's a bomb right here."

Baris shook his head and hurried from the room. Koloth growled again and headed for Darvin.

"Baris left without looking back." Koloth shook his head. "He didn't ask about Darvin until afterward, even after asking if I was all right. When he left the room, it was as if he didn't care if both of us were killed in the explosion."

Jensen sat with her chin propped in her hands. "And afterward, when Baris was special envoy, you never figured out why he acted that way?"

"I didn't often deal with him directly after that." Koloth stood, stretched, and began to pace the room. "I was governor of SermanyuQ, and that was where I stayed for many years. The Empire's success there gave us more leeway under the Treaty of Organia. We focused primarily on colonies that were above or below the galactic plane, outside of territory the Federation claimed, so that we could expand toward and into the Alpha Quadrant without causing conflict that would give the Organians a reason to step in. We were growing past our traditional boundary with the Federation, without firing a single disruptor. It was a territorial war without being a shooting war, something no Klingon had ever imagined. We chafed a bit under its limitations, but we knew it was gaining us resources and strategic systems that would serve us well if a shooting war broke out.

"*Dahar* Master Kang, back then a well-respected captain who had tangled with Kirk, was the commander of our Alpha Quadrant initiative, and he was a strong enforcer of the Empire's policies. It was he who had to deal with Special Envoy Baris. I briefed him on Baris shortly after he accepted his assignment, and when I was through, Kang said, 'This human has grown a spine to match his bluster.' I thought that the most fitting description of Baris. And Kang had learned to never underestimate a human."

5

Zenith Colony, Benecia, Alpha Quadrant, 2275

Ensign Vella Shaden suppressed a shiver as she stood waiting by the shuttlepad. A chill spring breeze off Zenith Lake seemed to move right through her gray Starfleet uniform. The largest lake on Benecia, at nearly six hundred kilometers long and up to three hundred wide, Zenith Lake had a considerable effect on the weather of the city. It was always colder by the lake in the summer months, and this early in the morning the cold damp air was especially unforgiving.

Shaden recognized she was oversensitive to the cold, having grown up in the controlled environment of Stratos as a coddled member of the city-dwelling caste on her homeworld of Ardana. Taking advantage of the much-needed cultural reforms of 2269, she had gratefully escaped the caste system, which could be just as limiting, if not as dangerous, for the city dwellers as the ground dwellers. It had seemed fitting to enter Starfleet, as Captain Kirk and his crew had been instrumental in bringing about the reforms that gained her the freedom to pursue something other than a life of philosophy. Thoughtful reflection and intellectual debate were important, but they had become empty, unproductive pursuits in Stratos. Although that had changed in the wake of the elimination of the castes, she had never regretted pursuing the more active life of a Starfleet officer. Except maybe this morning, as she was unable to keep from shivering as another damp gust of wind blew around her. She was tempted to check the life-support monitor built into her uniform's belt buckle to see if she was becoming hypothermic, but she knew that would be an exaggeration.

She raised her left arm in front of her and, with her right hand, activated her wrist communicator. "Ensign Shaden to shuttlecraft *Franklin*. What's your ETA?" The shuttlecraft from Starbase 11 was overdue by only a few minutes, but it was her job to worry about its passenger.

"This is Franklin," a woman's voice answered. *"We took a little detour up here, but everything's fine. Be there in a couple minutes."*

"Acknowledged." Shaden stared out across Carlton Bay, once a thriving aquafarm which had drawn colonists to establish Zenith just five years earlier. A couple different native species of seaweed had proven to be a tasty and nutritious food source for many humanoids, as were the fish and crustaceans that were part of the ecosystem of the bay. Careful harvesting had demonstrated the easy renewability of the resource, and Zenith had prospered, soon surpassing Benecia City, the original settlement, in population. The Federation Colonial Authority had been eager to invest in Zenith since Benecia had, in 2273, fallen under the terms of the Treaty of Organia, and they wanted to ensure that the fate of Sherman's Planet was not repeated here.

There were now three Klingon colonies on Benecia, all located on Talso, the southern continent in the western hemisphere, or QeHDeb, as the Klingons called it, the "Angry Desert." It had not seemed to express anger at the Klingons, however. By all accounts the Klingon colonies were thriving. The same could not be said for Zenith. Last fall the chayla fish, an integral native of the bay, had had a below average spawning season. This spring, the knulech crab, which fed on the eggs of the chayla, were starving. In turn, the thinning numbers of knulech were not pruning enough red spiral plants as they searched for chayla eggs, and the excess red spirals were choking out the eggpod weeds. Carlton Bay was dying, and the harder people tried not to mention Sherman's Planet, the more everyone thought about it. The mood in Zenith was somber at best, but still determined.

Benecia's youngest city, Dunwich, was having its own problems, a series of technological failures and industrial accidents
that had many whispering accusations of sabotage against the
Klingons. But here, unlike on Sherman's Planet, the competing
sides were on opposite sides of the planet, an attempt to avoid the
desperate clashes that had erupted before the fall of that colony.
Luckily, Benecia City had been free of any problems. The continued stability of the capital city helped anchor the Federation
colonists, and so far relations with the Klingons had remained
cautiously neutral. Nevertheless, some colonists whispered about
the Empire scheming to steal Benecia, and Shaden thought of the
planet as a dry forest just waiting for a lightning strike to ignite the
long-standing suspicions between the Federation and the Empire.

The ensign was distracted from her gloomy thoughts by a
flash of movement over the lake. Finally the shuttlecraft had
come into view, taking a wide arc over the water on its way to the
pad, affording its passenger an overhead view of the entire city
spread along Zenith Lake, as well as a glimpse of Carlton Bay.
She had not seen the bay from the air herself, but had heard it
had a grayish hue now, not the more mottled red-blue color of
its healthier days.

Ducking her head as the descending shuttle kicked up sand,
she turned to the side to let things settle, then scurried toward
the shuttle after it touched down. She came to attention as the
hatch opened, folding out and down to create a step.

A thin figure appeared in the hatch, hesitating only a second
before stepping out into the chill morning air as he turned the
collar of his jacket up. "There is a Klingon cruiser in orbit."

"Welcome to Zenith, Mr. Baris," Shaden said with a nod,
not knowing what he expected her to say to his nonquestion.
She stepped forward with her hand extended. "I'm Ensign Vella
Shaden."

Baris shook her hand perfunctorily, a slightly confused look
on his face. "Ensign, there is a Klingon cruiser in orbit without
Starfleet escort."

Shaden nodded. "Yes, sir, the *Klolode*. It comes and goes, as does the *Exeter*. Here in the outreaches—"

"That is unacceptable." Baris stared upward for a moment, as if sending his anger into space at the Klingons. Then he leveled his gaze back on Shaden. "Who are you again?"

"Ensign Shaden," she repeated. Behind Baris, Shaden noticed the pilot taking some luggage out of the *Franklin*. "I'll be assisting you here on Benecia."

Baris was shaking his head before she finished speaking. "I didn't request any assistant. There must be some mistake."

"I don't think so, sir." Shaden was trying hard not to let his indignant attitude get on her nerves. She'd seen enough arrogance back in Stratos to last a lifetime; High Adviser Plasus had made an art form of it. "My orders were very clear."

"Your orders are not my concern, Ensign. I'm perfectly capable of carrying out my assignment here without Starfleet interference. I am a Federation special envoy."

"That may be, sir, but as such you are not in my direct chain of command, and until someone in that chain of command gives me new orders, I am your assistant whether you like it or not."

The pilot had come up next to them, clearly eager to get going, and now she stood there, eyebrows raised, looking back and forth between Baris and Shaden as they stared at each other. Shaden knew that she had, ironically, made a rather arrogant response to the self-important envoy. It was all too easy to fall back into a holier-than-thou attitude when you'd been raised a cloud minder.

But now, if she was not mistaken, she saw a hint of a grin move fleetingly across Baris's face. "Well, Ensign, only two other people talk to me that way—among people I like, that is—my wife and my doctor. So since you put it that way, I guess I'll accept your assistance. Perhaps you could start by helping me with my luggage?"

"Certainly, sir." Shaden grabbed a suitcase in each hand as Baris picked up a duffel bag and a briefcase. "I have ground transportation to take us to Benecia City. Governor Traylith is expecting you."

"I'm sure he is. But I need to talk to the Klingons as soon as possible."

"What do you want?" Kang shouted at the door of his quarters as the entrance chime sounded. He had left orders with his executive officer that he was not to be disturbed, but he had barely begun filling out the reports—reports he was weeks behind on—before this interruption.

The door slid open to reveal his wife, and science officer, Mara. She and Kang still retained the smooth foreheads of their *QuchHa'* heritage; the experimental treatment that had returned Koloth's full Klingon appearance had not worked on them, Kor, or many other Klingons, leaving the Empire increasingly divided into castes by their physical differences. Kang was even required to have a *HemQuch* liaison in the QeHDeb colonies instead of speaking directly with Governor Krell. It undermined his authority in the Alpha Quadrant initiative, a command he had earned through years of exemplary service to the Empire. Making the insult more personal, Krell himself was also *QuchHa'*, but one who had been transformed by the test treatment. With a shake of his head, Kang pushed those troubles out his mind and focused back on Mara. She stood at attention like a proper officer and warrior, but the look on her face was that of his wife. It made his blood boil. With a growl he grabbed a data reader and threw it across the room.

"This paperwork will be the death of me."

Stepping inside so that the door slid shut behind her, Mara made her way slowly across the room. "It will take more than bureaucratic *baqtagh* to kill my husband."

"You're right." Kang stood. "Something like endlessly orbiting this planet waiting for the Federation to leave instead of just taking it for the Empire."

"Bridge to Captain Kang."

Kang grimaced. "What?"

"Federation Special Envoy Baris is demanding to speak with you, sir."

"So?"

There was a pause. Mara gave Kang a small grin at the communication officer's discomfort. *"Sir, he says that the Treaty of Organia states you must meet with any newly arrived Federation representative. He also demands that we leave orbit since there is no equivalent Starfleet ship in system. He threatens sanctions if—"*

"Enough. Arrange the meeting. Kang out." He frowned at Mara. "More diplomacy. I will end up in *Gre'thor,* with all this talking we do to appease the Organians."

"You have earned your place in *Sto-vo-Kor* many times over." Mara tilted her head. "Perhaps Baris is here to announce their withdrawal from Benecia."

Kang's frown did not lessen. "I am certain that would only entail more forms."

"He what?" Governor Stez Traylith, his green eyes wide, spun his head toward Shaden. His perfectly coifed red hair stayed in place. It matched the color of his shirt. The dark blue suit he wore was just as immaculate. There were rumors that Traylith never sat unless absolutely necessary, avoiding anything that might compromise the lines of his fashionable clothing.

"He's already arranged to meet with Captain Kang." Shaden smiled. "Although I assume you understood that."

Traylith stomped over to a pitcher of water on a small table in an alcove of his well-furnished office. "But Baris hasn't met *me* yet. He hasn't even spoken with me. And I'm hearing this from you, instead of him. I'm the governor!"

"He needed to rest after his voyage here from Starbase 11. I don't think he meant any of this as a slight toward you, Governor. That's why he requested quarters in Zenith, to avoid the appearance of coming into Benecia City and taking over."

Traylith looked up, spilling a bit of water down the side of his glass before slamming the pitcher down. "I don't care about appearances, I care about reality."

Shaden had to stifle a laugh. The governor's attention to his personal style was so well known, it was hard to accept his dismissal of appearances.

"And for Baris to drop in and set up headquarters in Zenith and start meeting with Klingons before even acknowledging me is—"

Traylith stopped speaking as a deep rumble shook through the office. A tall vase skittered off a shelf and crashed to the floor before he could grab it.

Shaden forced down a surge of panic; the rumble brought back memories of safety drills on Stratos. Although the city was the most advanced piece of antigravity technology known in the Federation, when you lived in a city in the sky unexpected rumblings inspired fearful thoughts.

They both stood there, glancing about the room. If not for the shattered vase, it was as though nothing had happened. But then a deeper, more prolonged rumble gripped the room. Traylith's imported mahogany desk vibrated across the floor as the water pitcher fell and shattered.

"Earthquake?" Traylith said, speaking loudly over the rumbling and various alarms and sirens that could now be heard from every direction. The communication panel in the desk began chirping in a variety of tones.

Traylith stumbled toward Shaden, and she caught the governor's arm, stabilizing both of them. She shook her head, confused, as the shaking faded. "Starfleet tested for tectonic stability before choosing this location. There shouldn't be any earthquakes."

Then the floor seemed to drop a meter before undulating back up like a rug being shaken out. Thrown off their feet, they tumbled along the floor and crashed into the wall near the door, which popped open with a sound of splintering wood as the frame was deformed by a twist in the building. A potted plant tipped over, rolling across the floor and leaving a trail of dirt. The window behind Traylith's desk shattered, shards of glass cascading inward. The shaking stopped again, but this time Shaden didn't find the stillness a relief, but instead was filled with the fear of the quake returning.

"Let's get out of here," she said, getting uneasily to her feet. Traylith was slow getting up, holding his left arm, which appeared broken. With a wary look at the crooked doorway, they hurried through, joining a throng of frightened people moving through the corridor. The floor was uneven, broken through entirely in spots and showing glimpses of the basement level below. Pieces of the ceiling littered the corridor, and sparks issued from an exposed energy conduit in the wall. A maintenance worker sprayed it with foam. Dust filled the air, causing many of the escaping personnel to cough and wipe at their eyes.

Moving through the front door of the government building and into the square outside, Shaden was stunned at the devastation before her. Debris from damaged buildings was everywhere. The surface of Government Square and Greenbush Street were cracked open. Trees lay on the ground. Several buildings along the street had collapsed completely. Cries for help started to fill the air, and emergency shuttles were buzzing by overhead as emergency teams responded to the disaster.

"We need to contact the other colonies for help," Traylith said as he surveyed the damage. He winced as he adjusted his hold on his broken arm. "We'll need to evacuate as many as possible, set up emergency shelters, search for people trapped in the rubble." He started to sit down, and Shaden helped ease him to the ground. "Starbase 11 will send aid, but we'll be on our own for nearly a week unless there happens to be any starships closer." He glanced up at her. "If the *Exeter* is at the far end of her patrol route, we may have to contact Governor Krell. The Klingon ship's transporter could be a big help in getting through these collapsed buildings."

Shaden was impressed by the governor's reaction. Gone was the immaculately groomed politician, replaced by a level-headed responder to a terrible emergency. Before she could reply, her communicator chirped. Raising her left wrist, she opened the channel. "Shaden here."

"Are you all right, Ensign?"

It was Baris; Shaden had forgotten all about him. "Yes, sir. I'm here with Governor Traylith."

"Good. Tell him I'll get to the bottom of this."

Shaden and Traylith exchanged glances. "I don't understand, sir. I assumed you heard about the earthquake."

"Yes, and I intend to take it up with Kang when I meet with him. I'm certain the Klingons are behind all of this."

"This is some sort of human joke." Kang exchanged looks with Mara, who sat beside him at the briefing table, then turned his intense eyes back on Baris. They were in a conference room in a Starfleet compound in Zenith; Baris had refused to meet with Kang on his ship. Baris sat across the table from Kang with his assistant, who was doing an admirable job of supporting her superior, but Kang could see the doubt in her eyes.

Baris turned his attention on Mara. "Do you deny the possibility of a technological cause for a quake?"

Mara frowned and looked at Kang, who gave a small nod. "It is not impossible, but we did nothing to affect the tectonic stability of Benecia City."

"It would be a violation of the treaty," Kang said. He leaned forward, once again fixing his steely gaze on the Federation envoy. "More importantly, it would be dishonorable. This may not be a proper battle for colonies, but I fight honorably whether I'm able to draw blade or not."

Baris folded his arms across his chest and leaned back in his chair. "And why should I take you at your word?"

Kang's expression hardened. "You dare question my honor?" His voice had dropped in volume, but the warning in his tone reverberated through the small conference room. For a moment he considered leaping at the sanctimonious envoy. But before Baris responded, the door to the room opened. Everyone at the table turned at the interruption. Kang growled in frustration at the appearance of Kamuk, his *HemQuch* liaison with Krell.

Kamuk stood on the threshold, looking around the room, his long, dark hair wild and uncombed. A single braid hung behind his right ear and down the front of his tunic. He wore an elaborate leather and mail uniform, a style of a hundred years ago that was popular among the *HemQuch* to further differentiate themselves from the simple uniform worn by most *QuchHa'* warriors for more than the last decade. Behind him hovered a nervous Starfleet ensign, casting an apologetic glance toward Baris and Shaden. Kamuk acted as though the ensign didn't exist. Kang couldn't help but glance with a frown at the elaborate crest on Kamuk's forehead. Increasingly the *HemQuch* were taking control of the Empire, relegating *QuchHa'* to secondary status. Only his exemplary status as a warrior had kept Kang in his position of power. Kang refused to do as some *QuchHa'* had done, to resort to surgical alterations to regain the appearance of Klingons untainted by the Augment virus.

"Captain Kang," Kamuk said, glancing over at the humans. "As your colonial liaison I'm surprised I wasn't included in this meeting."

Kang kept from sighing at the politician. "You'll notice that neither Governor Traylith nor Governor Krell is present. This meeting is between myself and Mr. Baris at his insistence."

"Yes, the special envoy." Kamuk stepped further into the room. Shaden motioned at the ensign to close the door, which he did with a look of relief on his face. "You were in charge of the Federation colonies on SermanyuQ."

Baris looked back at Kamuk for a moment before replying. "Technically, I was only overseeing the quadrotriticale, but as the ranking Federation official on the planet, it was necessary for me to exercise more control as the crops and the colonies failed. My experience there has led me to a new role in opposing the imperial expansion of the Klingons."

Kamuk bared his teeth. "I see. Your settlements on Benecia are just colonies, but ours are 'imperial expansion,' is that what you're saying?"

"Yes. When the Empire resorts to sabotage and subterfuge as they did on Sherman's Planet, then this is no longer about colonies. This is about conquering territory just as much as a straightforward military invasion."

Kang laughed darkly until Kamuk looked at him and said, "What do you say to these accusations?"

Narrowing his eyes, Kang said, "I say they are typical human paranoia. Koloth has told me all about the envoy. He covers up Federation weakness by blaming Klingon conspiracies for the failure of their colonies. There was no evidence that Klingons were behind the poisoned crops on SermanyuQ. Now, we are to blame even for nature's whims. The very ground shakes for the Empire."

Kamuk did not hesitate, nor did his expression waver from seriousness. "Prove him wrong."

Kang did not respond for long moments. The attention of everyone in the room was on him. On Mara and Shaden's faces he saw looks of surprise, almost amusing in similarity. Baris, of course, wore the smug smile that Koloth had often complained of. Kamuk was as though carved of stone, unreadable, unblinking.

"And if he claimed tiny winged Klingons flew around his bed at night, would you ask that I disprove that as well? Even if you wanted to, you do not have the authority to have me pursue such a waste of time."

"I do not have the authority, but the people who assigned me do." Kamuk took a step forward. "So far, I have given them favorable reports on your performance. If that were to change, they may have to reassess your assignment."

Kang felt his body course with a warrior's energy, the thrill before the attack. Then he felt Mara's hand on his arm. He had learned to trust her instincts about when to fight—and when not to. He forced himself to acknowledge the attack on his authority had not been open and direct enough for the immediate use of a *d'k tahg* on this bureaucrat's neck. Kamuk was wrapping himself in politics and blatant anti-*QuchHa'* propaganda. And it would probably work in the current state of the Empire. Kang had come too far to risk his entire career over one *HemQuch petaQ*.

He stood quickly and was amused to see Kamuk take a step back. Clearly the liaison knew he would be no match for Kang in combat, however bold his words. Kang said, "If you are certain about this course of action, we will need to return to the *Klolode* immediately."

"Yes." Kamuk looked pleased at his victory, but also just a little suspicious.

Kang knew he had given in too quickly, but he could not stand being in the room with these people anymore. He strode out immediately, without looking back. Mara was right behind him as they walked briskly down the corridor toward the exit.

"We are not actually going to investigate these outrageous claims, are we?"

Kang did not answer until they were out of the building, walking across an open square toward their beam out point. "We will go through the motions to appease Kamuk. And while we do so, we will prepare the troops to render emergency assistance for the Federation colonies. All three of their weak and failing cities will be put under martial law for their own protection. By the Treaty of Organia, Benecia will soon belong to the Empire."

"What the hell just happened?" Shaden paced around the room, waving her arms, while Baris remained sitting at the conference table, a thoughtful expression on his thin face. She had contained herself until after Kamuk had left. After Kang and his science officer had stormed out, Kamuk had remained behind to offer emergency supplies from the Klingon colonies to Benecia City.

"That, Ensign, is called *winning.*"

"Are you so sure?" She stopped her pacing and leaned forward with both palms flat on the table, staring down at Baris. "You should have asked Kang for help instead of antagonizing him."

"Kamuk and Krell will get us all the help we need."

"And you don't think there will be strings attached? I thought Federation policy was to refuse any aid to avoid the appearance of the colonies not being self sufficient."

Baris's expression turned dark. "I've tried that before. It didn't work." But then his face brightened. "Besides, Kamuk acknowledged this was an emergency. Any planet can have an emergency that outpaces its ability to respond. That doesn't necessarily disqualify us under the terms of the treaty. And Kamuk understands the treaty. Why do you think he wants Kang to prove there has been no clandestine interference against our colonies? He's making sure the Empire doesn't lose this system."

"I think he was taking advantage of a situation to pull the rug out from under Kang. In case you aren't aware, there's a bit of a culture war going on within the Empire. We see these two races going at each other all the time here in the outlands. It's the caste system of Ardana all over again, and Kang's group is being forced into the role of the ground dwellers."

"I'm completely aware of that situation." Baris stood and straightened his jacket. "We can use it to our advantage. Regarding our situation, it's Traylith's responsibility to assess the needs of the colonies and ask Krell for assistance. I've got to stay focused on the bigger picture of Klingon expansion in the Alpha Quadrant, and that's Kang's purview."

Shaden stood straight. "Bigger picture? How about the picture of hundreds, maybe thousands of casualties from the earthquake?"

"And how many casualties will there be if the Klingons sweep through this whole sector, sabotaging Federation colonies as they go, gobbling up every planet they can?" Baris shook his head, his jaw clenched. "I've seen their work up close, Ensign, don't forget that. I was on Sherman's Planet to the bitter end. I promised myself I would not let that happen to another colony if it was within my power. Benecia will not fall to the Empire under my watch."

Folding her arms, Shaden took a deep breath then let it out as she studied Baris. "I hope you're right, sir. But ask yourself why Kamuk was here bargaining with us instead of Governor Krell. He has his own agenda if you ask me. I don't trust him."

"Don't worry," Baris said, an edgy look on his face. "I trust no Klingon."

6

FNS Center, New York City, 2366

The day after the earthquake, troops from the Klolode *and from the* QeHDeb *colonies moved into key points throughout all three of the Federation colonies.*" Although Kang was on a screen, his severe gaze made Jensen feel as though he was in the room with her. The *Dahar* Master was currently a guest lecturer on Klingon military tactics at the Beta Aquilae II Starfleet Academy annex, and Mr. Gardner had arranged for the interview before she had returned from Paris, reserving FNS's own state-of-the-art communications center for the occasion.

Jensen was glad she had interviewed Koloth first. He was downright personable for a Klingon, and had proven to be the shallow end of the pool before wading into Kang's more intense personality, which seemed to radiate out of the monitor as she looked at him. His hair was darker than Koloth's, and pulled back into a ponytail, but his neatly trimmed (for a Klingon) goatee had gone a bit gray. He had a crested forehead, having finally received the perfected treatment for the Augment virus in 2290. Unlike Koloth, he had appeared just as intense in his old, more humanlike form, which she had seen in archival images provided by Starfleet.

Jensen had been surprised by what she had learned about the *QuchHa'* caste of Klingons during her interviews; although the Federation and the Klingon Empire had been more or less at peace for eighty years, there was not a lot of contact between the two peoples. Jensen had assumed that there were different races of Klingons, some more human in appearance. She had no idea that their ancestors had been physically altered by some mysterious virus or that the descendants had eventually all been cured. Klingons continued to avoid discussing the subject if at all possible, but those who had lived through the cure could not deny the fact that they had been transformed, even if they still kept secret the exact nature of the disease of their forefathers.

"How did Baris react?" She eased back into the comfortable chair and resisted glancing around at all the tech surrounding her. The room was equipped for holographic communication, but Kang had preferred an old-fashioned flat-panel connection.

Kang made a scoffing sound. *"I was surprised that his head did not explode. He thought he had outmaneuvered me by cooperating with Kamuk, but I was still within my authority under the treaty."*

"And he had come to Benecia to negotiate with you because of the Empire's aggressive advances." Jensen knew that the word "aggressive" would have been too suggestive with most interviewees, but her growing understanding of Klingon culture led her to believe Kang would not take it as an accusation. "That hadn't changed."

Kang thought a moment. *"No. In retrospect, I played into his hands, because one cannot bargain with an enemy without open conflict. But there was always something more to it than that. For a human, Baris had an almost Klingon hunger for revenge. He was no warrior, but he was still ruthless in his own way. Sharp like a bat'leth. Kamuk saw something in him, that much was clear."* Kang shook his head. *"But I never understood Kamuk. His motives were his own."*

Kang, with Mara at his side, beamed into the ruined streets of Benecia City in the first wave of troops. The humans and other Federation species were busy in the rubble, pulling out survivors and the dead, trying to get their city functioning. They had been rushing forward, cheering, as he materialized, clearly expecting Starfleet rescue workers. As the beaming process completed, they skidded to a halt. Cries of joy died on their lips, fading in the dusty air. Although some ran away in a disgustingly open display of fear, others stood their ground. As supplies and equipment beamed in nearby, the humans looked uncertain.

Kang stepped forward a few paces from his soldiers, drawing the attention of all the colonists. "We come to give aid in the name of the Klingon Empire. Please direct all inquiries to me, Captain Kang. Do not interfere with the duties of my soldiers."

The troops were already spreading out, setting up checkpoints to control the crowds and organize the dispensing of rations and emergency shelters. Other were already fanning out over the ruined buildings, scanning for bodies, living or otherwise. Kang had instructed the men to act as though the corpses were of worth, in acknowledgment of Federation customs. He also knew that similar units were moving through Zenith and Dunwich. He had to move quickly to outmaneuver any possible Federation assistance on its way.

Kang began to walk down the street. Although many of the Federation colonists gave him wary glances as he passed, they did not turn away the assistance of the strong Klingon soldiers. Mara followed, taking scanner readings. She mumbled something to herself.

"What is it?" Kang said. He kept his eyes on the nervous humans.

"My scans confirm that there are no major tectonic faults in this region." Mara looked up at him, confused. "There is no obvious cause for this earthquake."

Kang stopped and turned toward her, lowering his voice. "How can that be?"

Mara shook her head. "I don't know. Maybe there was an external cause."

"What do you mean?" Kang looked around to make sure no one could overhear them, but everyone he could see appeared to be focused on the relief efforts. "Are you saying that Federation envoy's rants could have some truth to them?"

"All I'm saying is that given the lack of geophysical explanations, there must be some other cause," she said with a scowl. "It could be a microsingularity, a quantum string fragment—"

Kang held up a hand, impatient with the scientific terminology. "But could this quake have been caused artificially?"

"Of course, I acknowledged that when the human first accused us."

Taking a deep breath, Kang again surveyed their surroundings. This time he noticed a small group of humanoids heading in their direction. He thought he recognized Baris among them. "Return to the ship. Devote all your energy to this. Let no one else know. I don't want Baris or Kamuk to know of this. They would use the information to their own ends."

"Yes, Captain." She stepped aside and drew a communicator from her belt. She disappeared in the transporter effect before the approaching group arrived with Baris, his assistant, and the Federation governor, Traylith, dressed in clothes too fine for the situation and with one arm in a sling. Kang was surprised to see both Kamuk and Governor Krell trailing along with them.

"What is the meaning of this invasion?" Baris yelled. His face was flushed with anger.

"You needed assistance, and the Empire is providing it." Kang looked only at Baris, ignoring the other Klingons.

"I had an agreement with Kamuk for emergency supplies, nothing else."

As Kang glanced at Kamuk, he noticed the disdainful look Krell gave him, as if getting the Augment treatment first had really made the governor more of a Klingon. Kang turned back to Baris. "Perhaps Kamuk has forgotten that he is my liaison to Krell, not yours."

"I agreed with Kamuk," Krell said, glowering at Kang. With a small tip of his head he turned his back on the group and moved several paces away, clearly expecting Kang to follow.

Kang frowned and joined the governor, who started walking again when Kang was at his side, giving them more privacy from the others. They had to pick their way around rubble from the quake and avoid the occasional Federation colonist.

"You risk the ire of the Organians," Krell said quietly, but laced with anger. "If we are to win this planet, we must tread softly, as though tracking a *cob'lat*."

"You mean slink about in dark alleys as you did on Neural, handing out firearms to primitives? That did not win Neural for the Empire."

Krell drew a deep breath, turning toward Kang as though about to attack, but he only grabbed Kang's arm. "Neural was not lost because of the Organians, it was lost to the interference of Kirk *jay'*. Here the Federation is *asking* for our supplies. That will turn the judgment against them, unless you make the Organians think we are trying to take their colonies by force."

Jerking his arm away from Krell's grasp, Kang took two steps away and then spun to face the governor, in better position to fight if need be. "You spend too much time pondering your own plans and not enough on the enemy's. Do you think Baris learned nothing when he lost SermanyuQ? He refused Koloth's offers of assistance and lost the planet. Here they have talked you into offering minor aid. They sacrifice this battle to regain their strength with your help, and then they will be in a position to come back to fight for Benecia and perhaps win the metaphorical war."

A slight doubt seemed to wash over Krell's face, like a cloud passing overhead. Then the pompous certainty of a full Klingon looking down on a *QuchHa'* returned. "I could as easily say you think too much of the large moves in your war plan and forget the details needed to win a single planet. By the time the Federation colonies get through their current difficulties they will be dependent on our help and the planet will be mine. Do not interfere with my leadership again. You need me to win Benecia before you can move further into the Alpha Quadrant."

Kang's steely gaze did not waver from Krell, and he continually raised his voice as the governor tried to interrupt. "Interference?

I have not kept your personnel from distributing the supplies you promised, Governor. You're free to do what you want, within your colonial authority. But you have not won Benecia yet. I remind you that my approach is what turned Beta XII-A from an unclaimed planet nominally within Federation space into the Empire's Voh'tahk system, and I did so after the loss of most of my crew and my ship. So regardless of the path you take on this planet, I will do what is within my authority in this *quadrant.* If you want to be considered for the position of planetary governor once Benecia is ours, you would be wise not to interfere with *my* leadership." He tore his communicator from his belt and called for transport.

"I watched Kang beam back to his ship and knew the Klingon soldiers were going to stay in the colonies." Retired Starfleet Captain Vella Shaden paused, taking a deep breath which she held for a long time before exhaling. Her white hair was cropped close, her skin pale. Every so often a slight tremor ran through her body.

Jensen suppressed a grimace. Even over the monitor she could sense Shaden's pain as a sufferer of Droxine's Syndrome. Decades after the desegregation of Ardana's society, it had been discovered that some of the city dwellers had a genetic condition that, over time, made them hypersensitive to conditions on the ground. The syndrome developed slowly, eventually manifesting a number of symptoms including difficulty breathing, but generally not becoming evident until the sufferer reached ninety to one hundred years old. So far, the syndrome had stubbornly resisted a variety of treatments, including returning to Stratos. The Central Hospital of Altair IV led the research effort on Droxine's Syndrome and had become home to a small community of former residents of the skies of Ardana.

"Are you sure you want to do this, Captain?" Jensen leaned forward, a concerned look on her face. "I'd really be happy to simply submit written questions."

"Please, call me 'Vella.' And this is the most interesting thing that's happened to me since I retired. Don't worry, I'll perk up as my morning meds kick in."

Given Shaden's condition, Jensen had been reluctant to contact her at all, but the then-ensign had been present at many key moments in Baris's career. Jensen's initial contact by text had been answered with a vehement request for vid communication. Jensen figured if Shaden wanted to go through the discomfort of a prolonged interview over subspace, she could endure the inconvenience of getting up at three in the morning New York time to make the connection. Of course, it had worked out that it would be the same night that she had spoken late with Kang. After arranging his next interview for the following morning, she'd taken a quick nap, gotten a bite to eat, tried to run a brush through her hair, and was ready to contact Altair IV. She'd never left FNS Center.

"So, back to that morning so long ago, the mood was quite sour, as you can imagine," Shaden continued. *"I had assumed the Klingons were acting as one in the name of the Empire, but that's when it became clear to me that their personal agendas could have serious consequences for us."*

"That can't be good," Shaden said. Kang had beamed away, obviously angry, and Krell was left standing there alone, waving his arms and yelling as if he might reach Kang in orbit with the power of his lungs alone. Nearby Federation colonists and Klingons alike had stopped their recovery work to look at the commotion. As Krell glanced around and stalked back toward the group, bystanders quickly turned away and got back to work.

Shaden glanced at Baris and Traylith, then swept her gaze around the ruined city. A haze of smoke and dust hung in the air. The sad cries for help that had filled the streets immediately after the quake were no longer heard, but they still haunted the streets. The clatter and crash of digging and occasional cave-ins now dominated Benecia City, punctuated by sirens as survivors were found. Shaden knew that many survivors were being beamed out directly, located by biosigns, but somehow the presence of the sirens had been reassuring; now they were sounding less and less frequently. Her eyes met Traylith's for a moment, and he gave her a reassuring nod.

Kamuk, watching Krell stomping toward them, started laughing, Baris turned on him. "There is nothing amusing about this. Our colonies are overrun with soldiers! You promised that we would get supplies only."

"I promised no such thing. I *offered* only supplies, I did not vouch for what Kang would do." He held up a hand as Baris pointed a finger at him in obvious preparation for more yelling. "This is what I expected would happen." He leaned closer as Krell approached. "Kang is a reasonable man, a man of honor, not like Krell. And it is Kang who has the real power here, not Krell and his connections."

Baris lowered his finger and his voice. "What about your connections?"

Shaden was surprised at how quickly Baris had transformed from enraged to conspiratorial as the situation altered, but figured that was what someone in Baris's line of work had to be able to do.

Before Kamuk could respond, Governor Krell was upon them. "That insolent *QuchHa'*. He does not deserve a position of authority over me. A curse on his miserable house!"

"Careful of such curses, Governor," Kamuk said. "It could spill over onto your own *QuchHa'* heritage."

Krell had a *kut'luch* in his hand before Shaden saw where it came from, its serrations glinting in the sun. She took a step back, pushing Baris behind her, and drew her phaser.

"And how do you come by your crest?" Krell said in a deep, quiet tone. He waved the *kut'luch* closer to Kamuk's face. "Under a similar blade, perhaps?"

Shaden could sense that was a horrible insult, although she

didn't have a full understanding of the Klingon castes. She held Baris back as the envoy tried to step around her outstretched arm.

"Gentlemen—" he started, before they were all surprised by Traylith suddenly pushing himself between the two Klingons.

"Stop!" Traylith shouldered Kamuk aside as he thrust his good arm out to push Krell on the chest. "You're fighting like dogs over table scraps while my colonists suffer."

Krell's eyes flashed with rage at Traylith, but it was obvious that the Empire would lose Benecia for certain if he harmed the Federation governor. With a growling sneer at Kumak he sheathed his blade. "Remember your place, liaison. You are here to handle Kang, nothing more. I expect you to see that these troops are withdrawn as soon as possible." He turned on his heel and stalked off.

Traylith moved to a piece of rubble that provided a convenient place to sit. "I grow to hate that man. I never knew I could get so angry."

Shaden turned toward Kamuk, her phaser lowered but not holstered. He had an amused but wolfish Klingon smile on his face. "You won't need that phaser for me, Ensign."

Baris had stepped out from behind her now. "What are you playing at, Kamuk? Whose side are you on?"

Kamuk watched Baris for several seconds, then seemed to come to a decision. "Those answers are rather . . . sensitive in nature. For the ears of a Federation envoy alone."

Baris glanced at Shaden. "Don't worry, we'll stay in plain sight." Without further hesitation he turned toward Kamuk and motioned for him to follow. The two set off up Martin Street, which had been cleared of rubble. Soon they were in a heated discussion.

"What do you think that's about?" Traylith said.

She shook her head. "Klingons and diplomats. Who can tell?"

★ ★ ★

"And so we watched them. At one point I thought they were going to come to blows. When they came back, Baris was pale, shaken, as if some vast Klingon conspiracy had been revealed to him. Shortly after that the second quake hit." Shaden shrugged at the decades-old emergency and winced at the movement. *"Things moved very quickly after that, and I never found out what they had discussed."*

"That's understandable under the circumstances," Jensen said with a yawn. "Sorry, but I'm very tired. Could we talk again tomorrow?"

"Sure. But you don't have to pretend to be tired to give me a break. I can tell when my condition is catching up on me."

Jensen laughed self-consciously. "Actually, I was so caught up in the story I didn't notice. I really am tired, and now I also feel like an inconsiderate jerk."

Shaden laughed, then coughed, a look of pain crossing her face. *"Oh, don't make me laugh."* She caught her breath with some effort. *"We'll talk again soon. Get some sleep."*

"Thank you. Good night." Shaden faded from the screen. Jensen shook her head at having said good night; it was early morning for her and nearly noon where Shaden was on Altair IV. She really needed sleep, but now she had to prepare for Kang's next interview.

Since his return to the *Klolode*, Kang had noticed the crew avoiding him as much as possible. He knew he was slamming around, yelling at miserable *bekkpu'* for minor infractions, but he could not completely contain his outrage. Now, in his quarters away from the eyes of his crew, he could let out the anger that had been building up for hours. He swept his arm across his desk, scattering memory cards and data readers to the floor. "Curse politicians and bureaucrats! They are two sides of the same worthless coin."

Mara gathered up her memory cards, pointedly leaving Kang's on the deck. "Then go smash *their* work," she said with a soft growl.

Kang's expression brightened as he laughed loud and long. "Thank you, my wife. If not—" He stopped as an alarm rang out from Mara's computer station. "What is that?"

Mara's eyes had widened as she moved to the computer. "There's been another quake in Benecia City." She tapped at the keys, watching complicated data stream across the monitor. "I've been researching this since you sent me back to the ship. I've locked out access to any seismic data at the bridge station and have done everything from here. No one knows about this but me. This data is coming in on a secure subspace channel from ground stations. I doubt the Federation personnel are in any position to review the data at this level of detail." She looked at him. "It does not look good."

"A strong quake? I would not want to lose soldiers to this. They deserve to die in battle."

"They may still get the chance, and sooner than you think." Mara changed the display to show a schematic of the city. "Look at this plot of the first quake." She placed her finger on the monitor, moving it along a narrow shaded band running through the center of the city. "Seismic data seem to indicate a series of epicenters along this line during the duration of the quake."

Kang found the idea suspect, but did not doubt his wife. "A moving epicenter."

"In effect." Mara tapped some keys. "Now I add the new data." Another band appeared, slightly shifted from, but parallel to, the first.

Kang's eyebrows raised up his forehead. "This is not a natural phenomenon."

"No." Mara looked away from the monitor, deep into Kang's eyes. "Our geosynchronous orbit keeps the Federation colonies on the opposite side of the planet. These lines correspond to the trajectory of a polar orbit."

"Which is no coincidence. A ship passing over their colonies caused these quakes."

"It would have to be cloaked."

"Yes." Kang bared his teeth. "And even cloaked no Romulan ship would come this far from home."

Jensen rocked back in her chair, stunned at this revelation. "There is nothing like this in the official records."

"*No.*" Kang leaned forward, as if to compensate for Jensen leaning back. "*And I promised Baris I would not reveal it. But now . . . the Federation should know how tirelessly he pursued his ideals, even at great personal cost.*"

"Baris knew?" Jensen sat back up. "But those who caused the quake were responsible for killing hundreds of Federation citizens. They deserved to be brought to justice."

"*They received justice from my forward torpedo tube. And Imperial Intelligence made a substantial anonymous 'donation' to the recovery efforts.*" Kang smiled grimly at the memory. "*Baris convinced me of the need for keeping this terrible secret. In doing so, he single-handedly turned the course of history between Federation and Empire. He was a man of honor. I will say no more.*"

"*I guess I should have expected this,*" Shaden said quietly. The comm system had automatically compensated and boosted the volume, so Jensen had no difficulty hearing her. The old retired officer looked nervous. "*I'm not so sure it should be exposed even now. We still have our disagreements with the Empire—Bajoran independence comes to mind—and who's to say they wouldn't flare up more often, or burn hotter, if we expose the compromises the peace was built on?*"

Jensen rubbed at her eyes. She'd slept only about four hours in the last two days. Even her hair felt tired, and she needed a shower. Between her last, truncated interview with Kang and this interview with Shaden, Jensen had tried to do some additional background research, but her mind was reeling with the scoop that had fallen into her lap, and sleep-deprivation had made it difficult for her to concentrate. When she'd dropped into Mr.

Gardner's office to give him a quick update—there had been more going on at Benecia than recorded in the standard histories, but nothing related to the late Arne Darvin—she'd barely been able to string together a coherent sentence. Now she was back in the FNS comm center, where she'd spent too much time lately. Food containers littered the desk.

After yawning, Jensen said, "I tried to tell myself that Kang couldn't be telling the truth, that Baris couldn't have gone along with this. But even you knew?"

Shaden sighed, but at the same time sat up straighter, got a little more spark in her eyes. *"It may seem simple now, looking back, judging what we did was wrong. You know what they say about hindsight."*

Jensen nodded. "I know. I'm sorry, I didn't mean to sound so holier than thou. Please, tell me how it happened."

Shaden looked thoughtful for a long time. If Jensen hadn't been so tired, she might have demanded an answer, but she was content to wait. Finally Shaden nodded. *"All right, I'll tell you what I know. But you have to understand that Organians or not, we felt like we were balanced on the edge of a knife back then."*

"I knew it! I knew it all along." Baris paced back and forth in the secure conference room they had set up in an office building in Zenith. Traylith, Kang, and Kamuk all sat around the one long table in the middle of the room, while Shaden stood off to the side, near the door. She had to resist the urge to tell Baris to sit down or at least stand still. "This proves Imperial Intelligence was behind the fall of Sherman's Planet."

"You have no evidence of that," Krell shouted. "I demand that you make no such accusations. We are only here to discuss the alleged treaty violations on Benecia."

"Alleged?" Traylith said, his voice rising in disbelief. "You were caught red-handed."

"All we really know is Kang claims to have destroyed a ship."

Krell glared at his human counterpart, using his fierce Klingon appearance to his full advantage.

Kamuk, his hands resting calmly on the table, laughed. "Kang exposed an I.I. Bird-of-Prey. His science officer has scans of the bioweapon they used on Zenith Lake. The *Klolode* recovered the graviton emitter they used to cause the quakes. These are more than claims. And it's not difficult to imagine that intelligence agents were behind the troubles in Dunwich."

"Perhaps." Krell glared at Kang. "But we are left with much to imagine, since the emitter is only the largest piece left among the wreckage. You are finished Kang. You have the blood of Imperial Intelligence on your hands."

Kang felt no need to raise his voice. He knew his white-hot anger would carry just as easily if he whispered. "Yes, but I spilled it with honor as I avenged those of my crew killed in the second quake, securing their entrance to the halls of Sto-vo-Kor." He leveled his finger at Krell. "If you were aware of I.I.'s presence, *you* are finished, Krell. I will see to that."

"We are all finished." Krell shifted his hateful gaze from Kang to Kamuk. "The two of you have lost Benecia. May you rot in *Gre'thor*. Although I'm certain you will do so in the dungeons of Imperial Intelligence first." Krell stormed from the room. Shaden had to jump back out of his way.

Traylith frowned at the remaining Klingons before turning toward Baris. "I want a full investigation and reparations. It's clear that Benecia will be awarded to the Federation."

"No," Baris said. "Benecia will be jointly held by the Federation and the Klingon Empire."

The room fell completely silent. Everyone but Kamuk gaped at Baris as if he'd transformed into a Gorn.

"What the hell are you talking about?" Traylith said when he finally regained his voice.

"Exposing this illegal and botched covert action would embarrass the Empire and call into question all the previous systems gained under the treaty. Federation-Empire relations would be set back by a decade."

Shaden shook her head. "All due respect, sir, but isn't this what you've been after all along?"

"Yes." Baris finally took a seat. "I wanted—needed—proof of Klingon treachery. To help ease the burden of all those deaths."

"And now we have it," said Traylith. He turned to glare at Kang and Kamuk. "So forget diplomatic relations. We can make them pay for what they've done, and the Organians will have our backs."

"You know this for a fact?" Baris said. He looked at Kang. "I have my proof of the blood on Klingon hands. But that blood cannot be unspilled. I have to think about the deaths I can prevent. We all behave as though the Organians are looking over our shoulders, about to dispense their justice if we violate the treaty. But obviously we can't afford to count on that. The Organians have their own inscrutable motives."

Kang frowned for a moment before responding. "You think that if we expose what has happened here, the Empire will challenge the treaty openly. If it were found to be a fiction, there could be all-out war. Both sides would suffer billions of dead."

Baris nodded. "But if we compromise, and keep the appearance of the treaty intact, you can use your influence to stop Imperial Intelligence from interfering. They wouldn't have to, since you would have gained this foothold not because of their actions but in spite of them."

Traylith shook his head. "But if we share the system, the Empire will continue its expansion into the Alpha Quadrant."

"The competition will be fierce, but the treaty will prevent violent military intervention. The Klingons will have to satisfy their urge for battle by celebrating bloodless victories in the colonies. And they will also have to accept their losses. I'm sure that Kang sees the honor in that. And he also sees that his improbable victory here will serve him well in the eyes of the *HemQuch*." Baris turned toward Kang and actually smiled.

Kang stared at Baris, his brow furrowed, a grim frown on his face. Finally his expression softened, and a dismissive scoffing sound almost became laughter. The hint of a smile appeared on his face. "You seem to have gained a deep insight into the Klingon mind over the years, human. Krell will owe you his deepest gratitude. Without you, I would have seen to it that the only colony he governed was an asteroid housing a waste reclamation facility."

"That was it?" Jensen said. She shook her head in surprise. "With those few words he eased tensions across two quadrants. That agreement won him the presidency."

"Yes, it did . . . nine years later. At the time, the success of the gamble wasn't so obvious. Even the Klingons looked at each other doubtfully before leaving the room. I don't think they liked each other.

"Then Traylith stood up and said, 'I sure hope you know what you're doing. Because now I have to stay here and work with Klingons on my planet. May the Fates help me.'

"After the governor left, we sat at the table, just the two of us, for a very long time. Finally I looked over at Baris and said, 'Sir, how did you come up with that stuff about honor and the HemQuch? *That turned everything around.'*

"He turned toward me and made me promise to never reveal what I'm about to tell you. But if Kang has judged within his honor that we can reveal our old secrets, who am I to argue? After I promised, he simply said, 'Kamuk told me.'"

7

Deep Space Station K-7, 2288

Lieutenant Commander Shaden kept a close eye on the curving corridor ahead as she walked alongside President Baris and his wife, Sima, on their way to the banquet hall. The susurration of multiple overlapping conversations reverberated off the walls. Her imagination transformed the sibilant sounds into warnings and threats, and she glanced sharply from side to side, expecting the glimmer of an obsidian blade, the polymer barrel of a projectile weapon, the clever tools of assassins circumventing security scans.

Echoes from the past filled her thoughts: Klingon shouts, her own cry of warning, the spark of metal on metal. With a shake of her head, she tuned out the soft conversations between Baris and his entourage; getting caught up in what someone was saying could cause a lapse in concentration. Instead she focused on extraneous sounds, listening, watching, and even smelling for anything out of the ordinary. Was someone talking too slow, too fast, too quiet, too loud? Was someone running, trying to hide their face, giving a signal? Did the lights just flicker, gravity fluctuate, the temperature change? Space stations like this were all about uniformity and conformity, and anything that stood out from the background was an anomaly, and an anomaly was a potential threat.

There, the asymmetric footfalls of someone positioning themselves for attack, someone tensing and spinning around at just the right instant—no, gentle laughter at someone who had scuffed their shoe on the deck, stumbled into the wall, tripped up the next person. The regular rhythm of a group of people walking together returned, the laughter faded away. Shaden exhaled, forced herself to breathe normally. She knew that Starfleet security teams were all over the station, and the place was being scanned so intensively she was certain the color of her underwear was a topic of discussion in a situation room aboard the *Enterprise*-A, which was monitoring the security op from nearby. But back in Stratos there was a saying: you can't trust someone else to keep you away from the ledge.

Some thought she was overprotective, even paranoid. But none of the people who voiced such opinions had been with Baris for over a dozen years to see firsthand the opposition he stirred up, the dangerous situations he walked into, unflinching, taking for granted that she would get him out, just as she had during that second quake back on Benecia. They had been arguing about Kamuk back then—and now, as she led the way through the parting doors into the banquet hall, suddenly here was Kamuk standing right in front of her. She came to a rapid stop, bouncing awkwardly to keep her balance, finding herself overwhelmed by memories of when she had last seen him four years before.

Lieutenant Shaden swallowed nervously and, without moving her head, shifted her eyes back and forth, trying to take in as many of the Klingons as possible. The High Council chamber was crowded, drearily lit by torches, and dense with gruff Klingon voices as they awaited the arrival of Chancellor Kesh. Risking drawing attention to herself, she turned slightly at the waist to steal a glance at President Baris. He'd been in office for all of three months, and he was already presenting a treaty to Kesh and the High Council, a formal nonaggression pact between Federation and Empire.

Relations between the two powers had reached detente since

the Benecia Compromise, as Baris's decision to share the planet with the Klingons had come to be referred to. Hostilities continued to flare up now and again, but so far, such expressions of the age-old enmity between the powers had been limited to localized skirmishes in the vicinity of the growing Klingon presence in the Alpha Quadrant. The more they happened without Organian intervention, however, the more likely larger battles or full-scale war became. Under the circumstances, one would expect the President to be feeling nervous, even threatened, in a room full of Klingons arguing among themselves and occasionally coming to blows.

But Baris stood quietly, his expression forceful, his gaze unblinking when met by Klingon eyes. Sima stood beside him clad head to toe in black, including leather jacket and boots, a sharp contrast to Baris's conservative gray suit. She called the ensemble her "Klingon clothes," something she'd come up with while winning the Tellun Protectorate back from the Empire. The look did catch the Klingon eye—perhaps more than Baris liked—but the couple, both hard-line negotiators, had long ago learned how to use their differences to complement each other in productive ways. Standing by themselves, presidential security ordered back to appear strong before Kesh, they were a force to be reckoned with. Neither of them seemed to react at all as one voice suddenly rose above the others.

"No one more than I hates the collar forced on us by the Organians." Captain Kor paced around to gain space as he talked, and the crowd parted almost reverentially. "Yes, I have fought the Federation when necessary, and found in them worthy opponents. I am sure there will be times in the future when I may feel the urge to best Starfleet in battle." He paused, letting a cheer go around the room. Shaden found it disconcerting, but Baris's expression did not change. Sima stole a glance at Shaden, her dark eyes unreadable. "But I have also fought the Romulans." A hush fell on the room. Shaden remembered that Kor had won a pivotal battle against the Romulans near the Briar Patch several years ago, which had erased whatever burdens he had carried as a *QuchHa'*. "And I say any time spent fighting the Federation is time I'd rather spend teaching lessons to the honorless Romulans!"

Another cheer echoed through the chamber, but Shaden did not think it was quite as loud as the one that had followed Kor's mention of fighting Starfleet. Still, Baris allowed a small smile onto his face as he looked down at Sima beside him. Shaden had been with Baris for nine years now, and she recognized that look. He felt that he had already won. Shaden was not so sure about the treaty or Baris. After being assigned to him on Benecia simply because she was next up on the duty roster, he'd kept her at his side, in one capacity or another, ever since. Attaché, liaison, security, advisor . . . she'd had a number of titles over the years. He used his growing power to always find a way for her to work for him. But she'd never known whether it was because he liked her, because she did a good job, or because she was one of the few who knew the ugly secret behind the Benecia Compromise.

"You would be willing, then, to trade one collar for another?"

Shaden looked in the direction of the mocking voice to see who had spoken. She spotted a *HemQuch* Klingon as he forced himself out of the crowd to face Kor. He had large bushy eyebrows above intense, piercing eyes, and his mustache and goatee seemed to enhance the sneer on his face.

Kor gave him a passing glance. "If you have an argument with me, do me the honor of stating it openly. That way I will know what I speak of when I tell you you're wrong." Kor smiled at the appreciative laughter he received.

The newcomer narrowed his eyes. "Do not mistake me for one of these *toDSaH* who still bow and scrape before the victor of *Klach D'Kel Brakt.* I am Lord Kruge."

Turning away, showing Kruge his back, Kor said, "I know who you are, *Commander*." He spun around, facing Kruge again, his voice raising. "A petty little warlord always trying to inflate his power. I may frequently boast of my victories, but I have many of them, and they always serve the Empire first and my ego second."

Kruge nodded slowly, a wicked grin on his face. Shaden glanced at Baris. The president had a look of concern now, but Sima appeared unshaken. "You are known for having a mouth as clever as your battle plans," Kruge said, pacing around the circle the crowd had formed around him and Kor. "But perhaps your eyes are not as sharp as your tongue."

"I could take a whelp such as you with my eyes closed," Kor said, ignoring Kruge's insulting tone, but matching his circling movements. Shaden could see excitement for a fight building in the crowd of Klingons. She stepped forward a bit, ready to keep Baris and Sima out of the way if the argument turned violent. "But I shall let you live for now, because I'm curious if you'll ever get around to explaining what you're mewling about."

"The 'pact' this Earther brings before us." Kruge shifted his eyes toward Baris. "It's little more than an excuse to steal our military secrets."

"That is an outright fabrication," Baris shouted, stepping forward, pointing at Kruge. Shaden put an arm on his chest, pushing him back. He pushed her arm down, out of his way. Out of the corners of her eyes she could see the rest of the Federation delegation tensing.

Sima folded her arms across her chest. "The agreement clearly states *both* sides will share nonmilitary technologies which *could be* weaponized. Actual weapons development is already covered under a number of existing agreements among the major powers."

"He understands that," Kor said with a nod to Sima. "He's only baiting your husband so that he can boast of facing down the leader of the Federation. That his accusations are empty means nothing to someone who thinks honor, like a shield, is something you raise only when you need to hide behind it."

"That will be your last insult of me or anyone." Kruge drew his *d'k tahg* and approached Kor. The Klingon crowd roared in approval while the Federation contingent backed up. Baris stayed where he was as his security guard moved forward to shield him from the altercation, but they were jostled aside by the increasingly enthusiastic crowd of Klingons spoiling for blood.

Kor laughed, his arms spread wide. "Do your best, my *lord*."

One soldier slapped Shaden on the back, nearly knocking her off her feet. "Now you will see how real warriors fight, Earther."

"I'm Ardanan," she mumbled as Kruge lunged forward, egged on by the chants of the crowd. But then he dodged to the side, and a look of surprise crossed Kor's face as Kruge darted between Baris's guards as they struggled to get in place.

"Watch out!" Shaden dived toward Baris, trying to get between him and Kruge. But she was coming from the side opposite of Kruge's knife hand; as he swung the blade in an arc toward the president, he would have a clear target even as she began to get between them. Baris did nothing to protect himself, instead pushing Sima back even though he was obviously the target.

But then another blade swung into view, parrying Kruge's with a flash of sparks and forcing it downward. Kamuk emerged from behind Baris, pushing a cursing Kruge backward. Shaden recognized him from nearly ten years earlier on Benecia; she'd heard he was now a minor staff member for Gorkon, a member of the High Council, but they had yet to see Kamuk on Qo'noS until now. With Kruge being handled by Kamuk, Shaden plowed into Baris, forcing him further away from the assassin, the two of them stumbling into Sima. Shaden glanced over her shoulder to see Kruge's blade slicing up Kamuk's side, leaving a trail of blood as he raised his arm high. A round of encouraging cheers went up in the Klingon audience. As Kruge jabbed back down, going for Kamuk's neck, Kamuk brought his *mek'leth* up.

Kruge grabbed for the flashing blade with a gloved hand but missed, and it plunged through his leather uniform beneath his ribs. More cheers, and the crowd chose sides, shouting out the names of the opponents. Kruge grabbed Kamuk's wrist with a yell and held tight so the blade could not be withdrawn. Kamuk fell back, pivoting away from Kruge's downward stab, but Kruge came forward, overbalancing them both. They fell to the floor, Kruge's *d'k tahg* biting deeply into Kamuk's shoulder, but Kamuk used their momentum to flip Kruge over him, driving his blade even deeper into Kruge's gut.

As Kruge tumbled over him, Kamuk pulled his *mek'leth* free. Kruge landed hard on his back, his momentum sliding him across the floor. Kamuk scrambled to his feet, his weapon hand in front of him, his other arm hugged to his injured side. Blood flowed freely from where Kruge's *d'k tahg* remained in his shoulder. The crowd was chanting Kamuk's name, sensing a winner.

Kruge was growling, struggling to get to his feet, but he slipped in his own blood as it poured from him. It was clear that Kamuk had done serious internal damage. Kruge finally stood, one hand gripping the wound to pinch it shut. He took a few unsteady steps forward, reaching out with his good hand as if to reclaim his blade from Kamuk's shoulder and continue the fight. He received some shouts of support, but they were not enough. His eyes lost their focus and he fell, crashing to the stone floor face-first without trying to break his fall. He was already dead. Although some of the Klingons seemed disappointed the fight was over so quickly, most of the crowd cheered Kamuk's victory.

Satisfied the violence was over, Shaden backed off Baris as he unself-consciously hugged Sima close before turning back to face the Klingons. The security guards were now close beside them, phasers drawn. They were surrounded by shouting, foot-stamping, back-slapping Klingons. In the middle of this bedlam, Kor stepped up to Kamuk, grinning widely as he grabbed the victor by the shoulders. "Even a short fight can have great spoils." Then without hesitation he grabbed the *d'k tahg* and yanked it free of Kamuk's shoulder. Kamuk clenched his teeth and growled at the pain.

"Your *d'k tahg*, Captain Kamuk," Kor said as he held the

blade out hilt first. "Although the crew of *bocmoHwI'pu'* and *Ha'DIbaHpu'* Kruge fills his ship with are no prize. They will stab you in the back if they get the chance."

Kamuk accepted the *d'k tahg* and stuck it in his belt. "I will keep that in mind." He moved to the body of Kruge and knelt to the floor. He rolled the body onto its back.

Baris pulled Shaden close. "What's he doing?" he whispered.

Shaden gave a little shake of her head as she watched Kamuk open Kruge's eyes and stare into them. "I don't know." Then Kamuk leaned back, stared upward, and let out a roar at the ceiling. All the Klingons followed his lead, and the full-throated bellowing of dozens of warriors rattled the swords that hung on the walls.

"Yell," Sima said.

"What?" Shaden looked around Baris at her.

With a nod at his wife, Baris said, "When in Qo'noS." He leaned back and yelled at the top of his lungs. Shaden, Sima, and the guards followed suit, but suddenly the room went quiet, and they were the only ones yelling. They looked around and found the Klingons eyeing them with respect as they stepped back, clearing the floor. Kamuk got to his feet and also stepped away.

Shaden was confused by the parting of the Klingons for only a moment before she realized Chancellor Kesh had entered the chamber. He made his way straight to the corpse. Looking down at it, he said, "The entertainment has finished even before I arrived. I should have liked to have seen that performance." He fastened his eyes on Kamuk, who, standing nearby with his bleeding shoulder, was the obvious winner. Kesh inclined his head slightly to Kamuk then, with a nudge of one boot into the ribs of Kruge's corpse, said, "Someone clean up this *targ* food." Finally the chancellor turned toward Baris. "Well, Mr. President, I imagine the next time you visit Qo'noS, you will know enough to wear a blade."

★ ★ ★

"Mr. President," Kamuk said. "It is good to see you. Chancellor Gorkon looks forward to meeting you again."

Shaden had regained her footing, and now she watched Baris closely. Four years ago she had been surprised at Baris's reaction to having his life saved by Kamuk; although clearly happy to be alive, he had expressed no gratitude to his savior. It was as if Baris thought of it only as a growing debt to Kamuk, a debt he would rather not owe to a Klingon. Even when Kamuk had spoken for the nonaggression pact, Baris had seemed to resent the support. Especially when that support helped to change the mind of the principled Gorkon, who had in turn been able to sway Chancellor Kesh, always suspicious of the Federation's goals, in favor of the treaty. Shaden had tried to discuss it with Baris, without success.

And now Gorkon was the new chancellor, Kamuk his chief of staff, and Baris seemed well connected to the Empire, an enviable position. For the first time, the majority of people in the Federation were hopeful for real progress with the Klingons, for a chance to ease tensions further and move toward a true and lasting peace. But Shaden could see the distrust on Baris's face. He'd been on edge ever since arriving on the station, which wasn't surprising, considering the events that had transpired here and on nearby Sherman's Planet twenty years earlier. When Gorkon had invited Baris to a summit on Qo'noS upon becoming chancellor, Baris had made it clear that he was not ready to return to the Klingon homeworld. Luckily, Gorkon had taken this in stride and suggested K-7, now a Federation oasis surrounded by Klingon colony planets. Baris had grudgingly agreed.

"What are you doing here?" Baris blurted.

Kamuk looked confused. "I am Chancellor Gorkon's—"

"I understand that. I mean what are you doing here *now*? Since the Federation is hosting this summit, we were meant to arrive first."

"The chancellor is not here yet, as you can see." Kamuk gestured around the room. "And while you are hosting, the summit was at Chancellor Gorkon's suggestion. So I was checking on the hall before he arrives to ensure everything is satisfactory."

Shaden looked around herself. A large table was filled with foods representative of both sides, presented in such a way that would force people to mingle as they filled their plates. Murals decorated the walls, depicting various historically and culturally important incidents from both the Federation and Klingon viewpoint, but carefully avoiding conflicts between the two. One depicted a cooperative levee project from Benecia.

Baris shrugged his shoulders. "I'm surprised to find you still on Gorkon's staff. I thought you were going to captain that ship you won by killing Kruge."

Kamuk shook his head. "My skills serve the Empire better in a political role. Kruge's first officer took the ship, and I stayed at Gorkon's side. So now, as on Benecia, you and I again have the chance to advance peace between our governments."

"It is Chancellor Gorkon and I who will be working together."

Shaden's eyes widened at Baris's continuing rudeness. Although accurate, Baris's last blunt comment was clearly intended as a slight toward Kamuk, minimizing his role. Glancing toward Sima, the lieutenant saw an expression of surprise which quickly disappeared from the practiced diplomat's face. Sima lowered her perfectly arched eyebrows and her usual brilliant smile returned to her dark-complected face. She smoothed her gown, although it still looked as carefully arranged around her trim figure as it had when she first put it on.

"Kamuk," she said. "Years ago on Qo'noS I never got a chance to thank you. I am in your debt for saving my husband's life." She extended her hand. Baris looked as though he wanted to slap her hand down, but he pursed his lips and did nothing. On some level he must have recognized that she was getting the situation back on track.

Kamuk took her hand, shaking it firmly. "It was my duty to stop such a cowardly attack on an unarmed man. Besides," he added, with a glance at Baris, "I find your husband to be almost Klingon in his ability to anger and annoy those around him. To lose a Federation president my people can understand would be a serious blow to relations between our governments."

Shaden was duty bound to stifle her response, but Sima laughed richly at her husband's expense. Sima was Baris's opposite in so many ways. Her singsong, Hindi-influenced accent and rich voice were miles away from Baris's frequently harsh inflections. He was uptight while she was relaxed, serious while she joked, angry while she was philosophical. Doctor McCoy, Baris's oldest—and perhaps only—friend often said that Sima had mellowed Baris. Shaden was almost afraid to imagine him without her. Certainly she couldn't understand his continuing friction with Kamuk. But she also knew that he was not the only man against whom President Baris held a grudge. Captain Kirk certainly understood that.

"Admiral Kirk." Baris glared down at Kirk from the podium of the Federation Council chamber. Lieutenant Shaden stood off to his right, embarrassed that this was one of the first meetings Baris had scheduled when power returned after the so-called whale probe left the system. The mysterious object that had nearly destroyed Earth had left only because of the actions of Kirk and his crew, including Spock, rescued in resurrected form from the Genesis planet. The saucer section of the *Enterprise* now lay at the bottom of San Francisco Bay, but the whales they had brought back from the twentieth century had saved the planet. Looking around the room at myriad faces both extraterrestrial and human, most seemed to mirror her distaste for the proceedings. Certainly, Carol and David Marcus made no effort to put on diplomatic expressions. She feared Baris was harming his reputation by pursuing this trial so openly.

Kirk and his shipmates Spock, McCoy, Scotty, Uhura, Sulu, and Chekov, already at full attention, somehow straightened up even more. Baris had wanted only Kirk to stand before the council; Shaden suspected this had been as much to spare his friend McCoy as to focus on his nemesis Kirk, but certain protocols had to be followed. Baris was nothing if not a stickler for protocol.

Kirk said, "Mr. President."

Baris scowled as though the acknowledgment was somehow an affront. "It certainly comes as no surprise to me that you are in your current position. When I first met you eighteen years ago, I was immediately exposed to your flagrant disrespect for authority, your almost complete disregard for the chain of command, your haphazard way of following orders, and the whimsical decrees of your own command.

"In short, the very kind of behavior which has led to the charges you now face: conspiracy, assault on Starfleet officers, theft of the *U.S.S. Enterprise,* sabotage of the *U.S.S. Excelsior,* negligent destruction of the *U.S.S. Enterprise,* and, finally, disobeying direct orders of the Starfleet commander-in-chief. Although I believe you think you have the right to do whatever you want to do, I am required to ask you how you plead."

"On behalf of all of us, Mr. President," Kirk said, "I am authorized to plead guilty."

Baris paused a moment, appearing surprised. "I am glad to see you finally take some responsibility for your rogue behavior, although I am disappointed that you have taken so many fine officers along with you." Shaden noticed that Baris couldn't help but glance at McCoy as he said this. McCoy's expression made it obvious the two of them would be having quite the debate the next time they met as friends. "Along those lines," Baris continued, somewhat hastily, "the council recognizes there were mitigating circumstances and strongly recommends the dismissal of all but one charge, disobeying a superior officer. That charge is levied against Admiral Kirk alone." Baris paused, a look of distaste crossing his face. "Against my better judgment, I have decided to follow the will of the council and restrict your punishment to a mere reduction in rank to captain, which, regrettably, will also put you back in command of a starship."

The audience reacted with cheers and applause as Kirk and his crew looked at each other in astonishment. Shaden also found herself smiling widely in surprise; the last time she'd spoken with Baris he'd planned to pressure Kirk into resigning in exchange for dropping the charges against the rest of the crew. When Baris glanced her way she did her best to wipe the smile from her face, but not before the president saw it and frowned. She shrugged her shoulders at him.

With a shake of his head, Baris said, "This council session is adjourned." He turned from the podium and walked briskly from the room as council members left their seats to congratulate Kirk and his crew. Shaden followed quickly after Baris, leaving the celebration behind. Sima was waiting for them in the hallway, and the three of them walked along with Baris in the middle.

"That was quite the change of heart, Mr. President," Shaden said, giving Baris a sidelong glance.

"I still think Kirk is a menace," Baris said sharply. He kept walking quickly away from the council chamber as if to distance himself from the whole affair. "It was only sheer luck that his loose-cannon behavior paid off."

Shaden shook her head. "Then, with all due respect, why didn't you discharge him from the service? Why give him back a ship?"

He gave her a brief sideways glance, then looked straight ahead again, his jaw clenched tight.

Sima leaned forward to look over at Shaden as they walked. With a wink she said, "I made him do it."

Shaden smirked and nodded knowingly. "You won't regret it, Mr. President."

"I already do. Who knows how much more chaos Kirk will spread now that he can gallivant around the cosmos freely again.

It was better to have him contained in Starfleet Command. But even that never worked very well."

Although Baris appeared frustrated by the smirk she had on her face, Shaden counted herself lucky that she was able to keep from laughing. Especially since Sima was giggling like a schoolgirl.

"Mr. President," said Shaden with a nod of her head toward the banquet hall's far entrance. Baris gave Kamuk a last disapproving look, then turned in the direction of her nod. Gorkon swept into the hall with his daughter Azetbur, General Chang, Brigadier Kerla, and the rest of his entourage. Shaden again wished they had Kirk and Spock in the room to help Baris represent the Federation.

Baris had begrudgingly allowed himself to be ferried to K-7 on the *Enterprise*-A after the Federation Council and Starfleet had insisted Kirk and his crew were the best ones for the job. He had studiously avoided the captain, and ordered that the ship and crew function only as monitors and backup, isolating Kirk from the Klingons and himself. Shaden felt their absence was a bit conspicuous when dealing with an Empire that placed so much emphasis on their warriors, but Baris would not be persuaded, even by Sima.

If the president felt any intimidation from the martial appearance of the Klingons, he did not show it. He straightened up to his full height, took Sima's hand, and strode forward to meet them. Shaden followed at his side, his entourage falling in behind them. The two sides met in the middle of the hall. Kamuk positioned himself somewhere at the edge of the groups, fading into the background.

"Mr. President," Gorkon said. "We meet on equal terms this time, both as leaders. I hope we can use that to our advantage."

"Chancellor." Baris gave a small nod of his head. "I don't seek advantages, only fairness."

Gorkon's brow furrowed. He appeared to Shaden to be a very thoughtful man, and he was trying to decipher Baris's somewhat adversarial and cryptic response. "I simply meant that I serve my own honor now. I am not so restrained by the prejudices of certain members of the High Council who disagree with the growing . . . well, if not peace, then certainly lack of hostility between our peoples."

"I understand what you're saying." Baris's expression remained stern. "And I do seek peace between our governments and for our peoples. But know this: I don't seek peace *with* you, so much as peace *from* you. I don't think that we see eye to eye on much other than the idea that war between us would be devastating and serve as an invitation for the Romulans to sweep across us all. If the High Council is concerned that we are approaching some sort of society where Federation and Klingon citizens work together hand in hand . . . Chancellor, I neither wish that nor imagine it possible."

The Federation representatives seemed stunned into silence. These were not the platitudes expected in opening remarks, much less in an exchange of greetings. Baris had jumped right into a negotiating stance, even though no formal proposals had been made by Gorkon when he called for this summit. Shaden stole a glance at Sima, who looked as confused as Shaden felt.

An awkward silence stretched out while Baris gazed unblinkingly at Gorkon. The chancellor had maintained a neutral look on his face as he listened, and now the barest narrowing of his eyes hinted at displeasure. Chang laughed suddenly, a startling sound that seemed to reverberate off the walls in the quiet room. He had a twinkle in his lone eye; the other, presumably lost in battle, was covered by a patch that appeared to be physically riveted to his head. He was bald and had a gray mustache just at the corners of his mouth.

Still laughing, Chang stepped forward, causing the presidential guards to move up as well. Baris waved them back. Chang glanced at them with his bright eye, then stared back at Baris. "Do your advisors tell you not to speak so bluntly? 'A wretched soul, bruised with adversity/We bid be quiet when we hear it cry/But were we burdened with like weight of pain/As much or more we should ourselves complain.' Yes, that is true, is it not, Mr. President?" Chang laughed again and then turned away toward the buffet table. "Ah! 'I prithee go and get me some repast; I care not what, so it be wholesome food.' Let us eat."

Gorkon leaned toward Baris, who looked shaken by Chang's performance, perhaps even a little pale. Shaden could not remember when she last saw him so troubled by something. Out of the corner of her eye she noticed that Kamuk seemed to relax as Chang moved away.

"It is true what I have heard, Mr. President," Gorkon said quietly, drawing back Shaden's attention. "You have a tongue like a *bat'leth* that cuts to the bone of an issue." With a grim smile, he added, "This reminds me of a Klingon saying: 'Though you long to break the bone, you may not like the marrow.' Not as poetic as General Chang's Shakespeare, perhaps, but relevant. We have a long road ahead of us."

Baris blinked a few times as the color returned to his face. Again he and the chancellor shared a long look. The president's expression finally softened just the tiniest bit. "Then, Chancellor, we should try not to break too many bones."

8

Klingon Deep Space Station *Dugh naHjej*, 2366

Jensen couldn't believe that she had come all the way out to Dugh naHjej in the Bajor system to get the runaround from the rather stoic Klingon who sat across the table from her. Gardner would be angry, even though the quickly improvised, and admittedly chancy, trip had been his idea. He had come up with his scheme right after they'd had an argument back in her office at FNS Center.

"You do realize who Kamuk is, right?" he had said to her. She had been updating him on all that she had learned so far, and the more she said the more he had looked at her like she was pulling his leg about something. Finally he had blurted out his question while she was still talking.

"What?" she said, annoyed at being interrupted. Her interviews with Kang and Shaden had left her sleep deprived and cranky. "What do you mean?" She had just told Gardner about Kamuk, so why was he asking her if she knew who he was?

"I don't believe it." Gardner shook his head. He wore his wavy gray hair long, and it flopped around his shoulders. "How can you not have heard of him? He's the governor of Bajor."

She felt as though a black hole suddenly yawned open somewhere beneath her feet. "That's the same Kamuk?"

"Of course he's the same." Gardner threw his hands in the air. "You uncover these back-room secrets, connected to a powerful political figure *who's still alive*, but you sit there talking about him like he's just some character in a holonovel!"

"I've been focused on events from a hundred years ago, so give me a break," she snapped back at her boss. Kang and Shaden had both probably assumed that she knew who they were talking about, but she simply hadn't made the connection. Jensen wasn't sure what was worse, her embarrassment at missing the obvious or her anger that Gardner was acting like she didn't know who the governor of Bajor was. "Besides, you thought this was just some little human-interest piece about Baris's last words, you never guessed it would turn into this kind of political intrigue. I've got a scoop that rewrites history and you're nagging me about something I would have eventually remembered anyway."

They sat there glaring at each other. Finally Gardner sighed, running his hands back through his hair and holding it behind his head. "You're right." He leaned back and looked at the ceiling. "To tell you the truth, I've been freaking out a little. Baris is a hero for standing up to the Empire while keeping the peace. Hearing that he made these kinds of compromises to build that peace is a shock. It's the kind of thing that might have been better left unknown."

Jensen nodded, although she thought the truth, however distasteful, was always preferable.

"You've got to see him," Gardner said.

"Who?" she said, even though she had known whom Gardner meant.

"Kamuk. Face-to-face. He's not going to discuss something this delicate over a comm channel. We were lucky with Kang, but Kamuk is still in a powerful government position. Obviously, our approach will be the Baris retrospective. Don't let on that we already know about the cover-up of Klingon sabotage."

Gardner had called in a favor with a friend in the Federation Merchant Service and Jensen found herself hustled onto the *F.M.S. Geldonero,* which happened to be leaving for Bajor on a cargo run in just a few hours. She'd barely had enough time to pack and get a proper meal. Gardner had figured he had the length of the journey to set up the interview, and he was convinced Governor Kamuk would agree to make a few nice remarks about Baris. That left it to Jensen to finesse her way into the deep waters of old secrets without Kamuk simply walking out of the room. To prepare for that, she had used the time en route to do additional background research and another interview with Shaden, where she had learned more about Kamuk's rise to power after Benecia, and his continued, and quite fortuitous for Baris, crossing of paths with the Federation president.

Upon arrival at the former Cardassian station, hanging like a giant spider in orbit of Bajor, Jensen had found herself ushered straight from the *Geldonero* to a briefing room by two huge and silent Klingon guards. They had left her alone in the room with a brusque "Wait here."

After a few minutes staring out a floor-to-ceiling port, past the docking ring and pylons to Bajor below, she had heard the door open. Turning, she had found the serious countenance of Kamuk's aide-de-camp, Lieutenant Worf. She had researched him as well. His father, Mogh, formerly of Imperial Intelligence, held a seat on the High Council and was a vocal supporter of Kamuk. His mother, Kassin, was a *mok'bara* master and trainer of the martial arts. Kurn, his brother, was a sergeant in the Klingon Defense Force. Interestingly, Worf's family owed their lives to Starfleet, which had stopped a Romulan invasion fleet from attacking Khitomer. Starfleet had intervened under the mutual defense pact the Federation and Empire had signed shortly after the explosion of Praxis. This was the same treaty the Empire had used as a pretense to conquer the Cardassian Union in 2358, after which Kamuk had become governor of Bajor.

"What do you want?" Worf had said, standing opposite the briefing table from Jensen.

Jensen tilted her head slightly in confusion. Gardner had confirmed the interview just yesterday, and the guards who had escorted her from the docking ring had obviously been expecting her. "I'd like to see Governor Kamuk. The meeting was arranged by Mr. Gardner of the Federation News Service."

"I am aware of the arrangements." Worf gestured to a chair and had waited for Jensen to sit down before he did so. "However, the governor is busy."

"When do you think he'll be free?"

"It is hard to say. The governor is very busy."

"I can wait."

"As you wish." Worf had then leaned back in his chair and folded his arms across his chest, with a quiet creaking of leather and clinking of armor from his elaborate uniform.

And that was where Jensen still found herself, staring across the table at Worf. She was certain that he had not blinked for several minutes. He just looked at her with a noncommittal expression, content to wait her out. Maybe Kamuk was having second thoughts about their meeting and had sent Worf to wear her down. And Worf was savvy enough to use a more human approach, not go all Klingon on her. Which only made Jensen all the more determined to get through to Kamuk.

Hoping to catch Worf off guard after the prolonged silence, she slapped her hand down hard on the table and shouted, "So?"

"So what?" he said without hesitating. His deep voice was perfectly even. Jensen thought that he was a perfect combination of an annoying politician and an even more annoying big brother.

"Is the governor going to honor the appointment he made with me or not?"

"Do you question the governor's honor?" Jensen's careful choice of words had gotten through, and Worf's voice rumbled threateningly. But she thought she also caught a glint of enjoyment in his eye at her confrontational question. She didn't want him to enjoy any of this, so she backed off.

"I just want to ask him about President Baris. As I'm sure my boss explained."

If Worf was disappointed by her conciliatory response, he

didn't show it. Instead, he went right along with it. "You can ask me any questions you have. I am authorized to give statements to the media on the governor's behalf."

"But I'm looking for personal reminiscences. Governor Kamuk worked with Baris. You did not."

"Then we will have to wait." He folded his hands together on the table and went back to his waiting expression.

Jensen knew she had to wrong-foot Worf somehow, zig when he expected her to zag. "Listen, Worf, I like you, I really do." She reached across the table to pat his big hands. "I'm flattered you want to spend time with me, but I just don't think of you that way."

Worf squinted at her, clearly confused. "I did not mean to imply that—"

"It's all right. I just think it would be better if we kept our relationship professional." She gave his hands a squeeze, then folded her hands together mirroring his. "Don't you, Lieutenant?"

His brow was furrowed. "Yes, but . . . I never—"

"Good, that's settled. Now if you could just check on the governor?" She leaned forward. "Or did you still want to sit there gazing across the table at me?"

Worf frowned. "I was not 'gazing.' A warrior . . . glowers."

"Whatever you say." Jensen shrugged and leaned back in her chair giving him a sympathetic smile.

His frown deepened, and he seemed to growl a little. After a moment he stood. "I have other duties to attend to. Feel free to tour the public areas of the station while you wait. I will contact you if I have an update on the governor." He turned and stomped out of the briefing room.

Jensen smiled after the door closed behind him, savoring the small victory before sighing disappointedly. She was certain she would not see the governor. But as long as she had come all this way, she might as well tour the station. It wasn't often you got the chance to immerse yourself in Klingons.

★ ★ ★

Jensen allowed herself to be swept along by the crowd through the broad main corridor in the central core of the station. The boisterous Klingons and the more introspective Bajorans that made up most of the station's population seemed to get along well enough. The Bajorans had had eight years to get used to their liberators and protectors, and in that time the former Terok Nor had been transformed from a forced labor camp to a center for interplanetary commerce as well as home to the colonial offices of the Klingon Empire. The current relatively peaceful relations between the Empire and the Federation allowed Governor Kamuk to encourage trade between the Federation and the many systems of the former Cardassian Union under his influence, which reached far beyond the Bajoran system. His strategy had turned Dugh naHjej into a central hub for traffic throughout the quadrant.

The result was a wildly varied cornucopia of shops along the thoroughfare, with Klingon armorers wedged between Bajoran tea and clothing shops, along with various restaurants and stores catering to beings spanning both the Empire and the Federation. The sights, sounds, and smells of the hustle and bustle were almost overwhelming, and Jensen started looking for a restaurant to duck into for a meal, someplace she could relax.

But as she walked past a bar, a chorus of excited shouts within drew her attention. She saw a crowd huddled around some sort of gaming table. A few scantily clad Bajoran women appeared to be bar employees, and the rest of the crowd was mostly Klingons. One Klingon roared something unintelligible and head-butted the Klingon next to him, who took out a table and the humans sitting around it as he tumbled over backward. As frequently happened with Klingons, Jensen was unable to tell if this altercation was in anger or celebration, but she found herself entering the establishment anyway, moving to a nearby unoccupied table for two.

She had only just sat down when a voice from behind her said, "What's a beautiful woman like you—"

"Doing in a place like this?" she finished, turning to look toward the voice.

A Ferengi in a loud jacket stood behind her with a hurt look on his face. "This place is Quark's. I'm Quark."

"Oh." She shook her head. "I didn't mean anything by that. It's just an old line."

"The old line I was *trying* to say was 'What's a beautiful woman like you doing all alone?'" He looked her up and down as if he was imagining her in one of his employees' revealing outfits.

Jensen rolled her eyes. "I can see you're really hurt."

He shrugged as he sat down, uninvited, in the other chair. Of course, it was his bar. "Well, there's only so much you can do with Cardassian architecture." He glanced around, then gazed back into her eyes. "Can't really start tearing down walls on a space station. No matter how much you yell at your idiot brother to do so." He glanced over at the gaming tables. "Thank the Blessed Exchequer for the replicator. Klingons drink more than Bajorans, but they also break a lot more things while doing so." He turned back to her with the ingratiating smile of a salesman. "Speaking of drinks, what can I get you?"

Something occurred to Jensen, and she looked at Quark with a thoughtful expression. "How long have you been on the station?"

She could see that he understood she wanted something from him, peaking his Ferengi interest in commerce. "I asked you first."

Jensen leaned forward. "Get me something expensive. And then answer my question."

"Oh," Quark said, putting a hand over his heart. "I think I'm falling in love."

Baris, seemingly undistracted by the noise of the dabo tables or the general buzz of conversation, looked out across the small crowd he had gathered in Quark's. "Governor Kamuk knows what I have done for the Empire. From the beginning of my administration I worked for a real peace. Shortly after my election Chancellor Kesh signed the nonaggression pact I brought to the High Council. Within a year of that treaty, when experimental colonizing technology proved unstable, but easily weaponized, we shared the Genesis device with the Empire. I was committed to avoiding any new arms race with the Klingons, and we of the Federation always held up our end." He paused, catching the eyes of Bajorans in the crowd, trying to gain the attention of those eating their lunches. It was a captive audience.

Quark came out from behind the bar to listen to the feisty former Federation ambassador to the Empire. He found the human annoying, but Baris had been attracting attention and pulling people in to see what he was talking about. And those people were buying drinks. When Baris had arrived on the station a week or so earlier, he'd spent his time in the Promenade outside Quark's. Although his official work for the Federation had ended decades ago, he was enough of a celebrity to draw a crowd once someone recognized him and word spread. He'd start talking about Bajoran independence and such and would soon have both supporters and hecklers. Station security didn't appreciate the crowds clogging up the corridor, or the anti-Klingon subtext of his speeches. Quark was surprised at how gently he was treated, however, and suspected Kamuk had to be behind it. So when Baris had moved into Quark's, and after sales picked up, he let the ambassador entertain the clientele with his idealistic Federation nonsense.

Baris folded his arms across his chest and looked over the crowd, frowning. "So why does Kamuk dig his heels in here, in only this system? During the last few years, the Empire has let other former Cardassian conquests go—"

"Those systems had few resources," a Lissepian trader said, stepping closer to Baris. "And no strategic value. They served no purpose for the Empire."

"Nevertheless, it shows that the Empire, if not Kamuk, is capable of letting systems go. All I want to do is ask Kamuk, 'Why not Bajor?' But he refuses to meet with me."

An old Bajoran man shrugged. "Maybe because you are not an official Federation representative. Why *should* he meet with you?"

"I have known him for decades. I set in motion the events that led to this. But the mutual defense pact of the Praxis Accords was not supposed to be used as pretext for conquest." Baris hesitated for a moment, looking past the Bajoran and the Lissepian to two security guards striding briskly toward him. The crowd parted for the frowning Klingons, but Baris did not back down. "And certainly not as a justification for Kamuk to maintain his grip on Bajor."

The guards came to a halt in front of the ambassador. The taller of the two growled, "Few Bajorans would say Kamuk has a 'grip on Bajor.' They have freedoms unheard-of on most Imperial worlds." He glanced around and saw people nodding in agreement.

The shorter, a woman, added, "How dare you accuse the governor. Neither the Empire nor Governor Kamuk have broken any treaties."

"The Empire has honored the letter but not the spirit of what I set out to accomplish. True honor is not in the parsing of treaties."

"This is not about honor." The tall one frowned. "If it were, you would be in a border system that wanted independence. I want to know the real reason you have focused on Bajor."

"Well?" Jensen held out both hands palm up, frustrated that her surprise new source had stopped talking. "What did Baris say?"

Quark shook his head. "I didn't hear."

"With ears like that?"

"That's just the point, they're very sensitive." He rubbed a hand along one large ear, looking at her with a strange smirk.

"So?"

"So when the governor's aide suddenly picks you up by them, it's painful. Very, very painful." He frowned at the memory and covered both ears with his hands as if he expected it could happen again. After looking around to make sure no one was listening, he lowered his hands and leaned forward. "Worf accused me of supporting Baris's views by allowing him to speak in Quark's. When I pointed out I did it for the drink sales, he didn't see the humor."

Jensen couldn't help laughing at that. "He is a bit of a stick in the mud."

"Tell me about it." Quark surveyed his establishment, his sharp eyes darting between employees and patrons. "He makes it hard for an honest barkeep to make a living."

Jensen followed his gaze around the bar. It was all an overwhelming jumble of flashing lights and a cacophony of voices to her. She doubted that honesty was integral to making a profit at Quark's. "So how did the rest of his visit go?"

He turned back to her. "At first I though it was going well, but it turned into a disaster. I thought Kamuk was going to kick me off the station. Literally, right out an airlock. I barely broke even."

Rolling her eyes, Jensen shook her head. "I meant how did it go politically speaking."

"It's the same thing. You know what they say, 'What's good for business is good for politics.'"

"And by 'they,' I assume you mean the Ferengi?"

"Of course." He straightened his jacket. "The Rules of Acquisition tell you everything you need to know, even if you Federation do-gooder types don't want to admit it."

Jensen chuckled and lifted her empty glass. "Okay, well, why don't you make this do-gooder another one of these and tell me about it."

"Your wish is my profit," Quark said dreamily, staring into her cyes. His gaze still lingered on her face when he suddenly bellowed, "Rom!"

Another Ferengi rushed to the table, fumbling to a stop and glancing nervously toward Jensen. "Yes, brother?"

"Another Mutaran Meltdown for the lady, and keep them coming."

As Rom scampered off toward the bar, Quark shook his head. "You know how it is with family . . . can't live with them, can't sell them for a decent markup."

Before Jensen could ask if that was a joke or not, Quark said, "I told Baris he had two choices: go back to making speeches in the Promenade or rent a private conference room where he could control who attended."

"Let me guess. You just happened to have a room available for just such a purpose."

Quark gave a big smile of his crooked and sharpened teeth. "It's like you've known me for years."

From the rear of a large conference room, Quark kept a close eye on the help while Baris, standing behind a podium, gave a long, insistent speech. Every time one of the attendees stirred restlessly, a server quietly approached to see if a complimentary drink or snack was needed. Compliments of the ambassador, that is. Quark would bill Baris later. Presenting the invoice would require some finesse, as it was safe to assume that Baris had not read the fine print which stated that food or beverages served by Quark outside of Quark's proper carried an additional surcharge.

Quark knew he deserved every bit of latinum he could get. Not only was he forced to listen to Baris discussing quadrant politics in self-important and all-knowing tones, it had been necessary to hire temporary workers, and they needed constant supervision to maintain the proper level of service. Especially Nerys, a fiery Bajoran from planetside who had practically demanded the job. He'd hired her only because he was desperate for Bajorans willing to work on the former Cardassian station and she had offered to work for reduced pay. Glancing around for the young redhead, he spotted her close to the podium, watching Baris speak.

He glared at her, as if he could get her attention with the power of his eyes boring into the back of her head. She was just standing there, staring at Baris, not paying attention to any thirsty attendees—and with Governor Kamuk sitting right there in the first row! When Kamuk had unexpectedly joined the audience shortly before Baris asked everyone to take their seats, the former Federation president for once had looked speechless. Now Nerys was almost in Kamuk's line of sight to Baris. Quark started walking toward her, acting nonchalant, giving a smile and a nod of the head to anyone who noticed him. Baris seemed to be winding down, but he did have a surprising amount of energy for a hew-mon his age. Quark had learned that firsthand during the negotiation for the fees.

"I know the Klingon Empire as well as anyone," Baris was saying. "I have struggled against and worked with the Empire for a hundred years. As undersecretary of agriculture I faced the challenges of the Treaty of Organia. As a special envoy I negotiated the first joint Federation-Klingon colony on Benecia. As Federation president I negotiated a nonaggression pact with the Empire. Following the explosion of Praxis, I negotiated a mutual defense pact. After President Ra-ghoretreii appointed me ambassador to the Klingon Empire, I worked with Chancellor Gorkon and Chancellor Kaarg, although it was a time of increasing friction between the Federation and Empire. Throughout all this, Governor Kamuk, in a variety of roles, reached across the divide between our governments and the difficult history of our peoples to support my work toward peace. And that is why I urge Governor Kamuk to finish what the Klingon Empire started three years ago when they conquered the Cardassian Union and liberated Bajor from its terrible occupation." Baris nodded toward

Minister Jaro Essa, the Bajoran liaison to the governor, seated in the first row near the governor. He then turned toward Kamuk, speaking directly to the governor, who maintained a neutral expression. "Give Bajor the freedom it deserves, Governor. Let Bajor go."

Baris stepped back from the podium just as Quark stopped alongside Nerys. Quark was reaching toward her when she blurted out, "And then what, Ambassador?"

Quark froze in place, his hand still outstretched to tap on Nerys shoulder, as all the attendees turned to stare in surprise at the young Bajoran. Jaro, however, maintained a neutral expression. Quark couldn't help but suspect something devious was going on. If he had learned anything during his year in the system, it was that Bajoran politics and religion were very complicated.

Baris stepped back to the podium with a cross expression. "What was that, young lady?"

Kamuk glanced toward Nerys and Quark looking slightly amused. By then Baris's angry scowl had gotten Quark moving again; although the interruption didn't seem to really bother Kamuk, it was Baris who was paying him. He grabbed Nerys by the elbow. "Sorry, everyone, it's so hard to find good help these days, I'm sure you understand."

Nerys yanked her arm away from Quark and gave him an icy glare. "You touch me again, Ferengi, I'll break your fingers."

Quark flinched and jammed his hands in his pockets. Baris frowned as Nerys took a step closer to the podium. "What happens after the Klingons leave? The Federation did nothing to help us for thirty years while Cardassia robbed us of nearly everything we had. Why do you care so much about us now?"

"I disagreed with Federation policy toward the Cardassian Union at the time." Baris gave a sympathetic look to Jaro. "But I had been retired for over five years when Cardassia occupied this system." He turned back toward Nerys. "It is because I disagreed with that policy that I decided to take advantage of my history with the Empire to work on your behalf now."

"But that's just the problem," Nerys said sharply. "You simply appointed yourself to come here. The Federation sat by while we were enslaved, but now that the Klingons are here you want them out. This isn't about Bajor at all. This is about the Federation wanting to tell everyone what to do."

"That's not true." Baris gripped the podium. "I'm not even here in an official capacity. This is a personal mission—"

"That's even worse!" Nerys pointed at the old human. "This is all between you and Kamuk. You don't care about Bajor at all."

"That's enough," Jaro said softly as Baris bristled at the accusation. Quark suspected Jaro had used Nerys so that he could stay on Baris's good side while also scoring points with the governor. Quark found himself nodding appreciatively at the ploy, if that's what it was. Meanwhile, Nerys spun around, glared at Quark until he stepped aside, and then stormed from the room.

"That was the end of Baris's goodwill visit," Quark said. "The strange thing is, even though everything worked out fine for Kamuk, the governor was furious with me. He forbade me to charge Baris for the food and drink provided in the conference room." Quark shivered. "It's like I gave it away for free! Disgusting."

"What do you think the governor was so mad about?"

"Well, if you ask me . . ." Quark leaned closer to Jensen.

"Yes?" she said, having decided early in the interview to overlook his flirting.

"If you ask me, you need another Mutaran Meltdown, then I'll tell you all I know about Kamuk."

A deep voice rumbled, "I do not think that will happen."

Quark squealed in fear and clamped his hands over his ears as Lieutenant Worf stepped up to the table. Jensen turned to see the tall, broad Klingon looming over her.

"Why are you talking to the Ferengi?" He folded his arms across his chest and stared back at her.

"That's simple," she said, smiling up at him. "Because he's talking to me."

A small twitch at the corner of his mouth was Worf's only reaction. "Point taken." He glared down at Quark, who still had his hands on his ears.

"I shouldn't be threatened in my own bar!" Quark yelped.

"He isn't threatening," Jensen said, looking Worf up and down. "He's just . . . menacing."

"She is correct," Worf said while he continued staring at Quark. Finally, the Ferengi slowly lowered his hands from his ears. Worf then turned back to Jensen. "Governor Kamuk will see you now."

Worf led Jensen back to the same nondescript briefing room where she'd first met him. He didn't speak, ignoring her questions about what Kamuk was like to work with. Once she stepped over the threshold into the room, he turned and started back down the corridor.

"Wait, you're just going to leave me here all alone?" she said.

Worf glanced back, a taciturn look his face, but she thought she spotted a twinkle in his eyes as he said, "Yes." Then he turned and was gone before the door slid shut.

Jensen chuckled as sat down behind the table, but then grew somber as she thought about Kamuk, a man who had made history. Not only had he conspired with Baris to change the course of Federation and Empire, he'd saved the recently elected president from an assassin. What did that do to a person, to live in a world you had made? Baris had seemed to be worn down by it over the years, but Kamuk still held an influential position in the Empire. Before she could reflect more on that, the door slid aside and Kamuk stepped into the room. Jensen stood.

Kamuk was not an imposing presence, at least not physically; he was shorter than Worf, and his warrior leathers were less ornate than most Klingons wore. While the crest on his forehead was prominent, his dark gray hair was pulled back into a long braid tied with a simple leather thong at the end. His dark eyes seemed blank at first, then became quite piercing as he looked across the table at her.

"Governor." Jensen reached out a hand. She actually felt a little nervous. There was something about his unassuming calm that had its own power. He had worked with presidents and chancellors, ambassadors and captains, and reshaped two quadrants.

With a nod he shook her hand firmly. "The death of Nilz Baris is a great loss," he said, a note of sadness in his voice that softened his dark eyes. "He inspired me to do great things."

"Yes, he is mourned throughout the Federation." She meant that, but she also had to gently lead Kamuk along until she could demand answers about the schemes he and Baris had perpetrated.

Kamuk motioned for her to sit down, moved to a corner of the room to get them each some *raktajino* from a replicator, and then seated himself. "I first met Nilz in the Federation year 2275." He slid a steaming mug across the table to her. "He had no love for Klingons, but Klingons have always been an acquired taste for humans. Unlike *raktajino*." He took a sip of the dark brew. "Of course, Nilz never touched *raktajino*." Another sip. "We met next in 2284 . . ." And Kamuk worked his way through his history with Baris. It was all quite dry, a censored recap of everything she had already learned on her own, right through Baris's years as an ambassador until Kamuk moved on to other responsibilities after Kaarg became chancellor.

"Excuse me, Governor," she said, interrupting a recitation of initiatives Baris had made as ambassador. "I'm sorry, but you've said nothing that isn't in the public record."

He gave her a blank stare. "We were public figures. Everything we did went into the public record."

"Well, no it didn't, actually." His gaze again turned piercing, like the point of a knife. She let him worry on that for a moment, then threw him a curveball to keep him guessing. "For example, Admiral McCoy heard Ambassador Baris's last words: *Arne Darvin*." She expected another blank stare, but instead the governor's eyes widened.

He stood up abruptly and walked around the table to gaze out the port, his back to her. Jensen raised her eyebrows in confusion. She'd only been trying to throw him off guard before she brought up what had really happened on Benecia. By then Darvin had been dead for seven years; but maybe Baris had mentioned his late assistant to Kamuk. Could Kamuk actually know what the last words meant? She'd given up on finding out. "Governor?"

Kamuk turned back around slowly. It was station night, and the lighting in the room was subdued. The governor's face was lit by the reflected light of Bajor's Okana Desert streaming through the port. For a time Kamuk stared in her direction without looking at her. Then his eyes focused on her face. "I will tell you what I know of Arne Darvin."

9

Sherman's Planet, 2268

"Something is wrong, Kamuk," Darvin said in Klingon, leaning close to the small screen on the table. Speaking his native tongue almost seemed awkward to him; he feared that by now he spoke it with a Federation Standard accent. If so, the Klingon looking back at him did him the honor of not reacting to it. The face on the screen, like his own, looked much like an Earther, the curse of the *QuchHa'*.

Kamuk frowned. *"Are you suspected?"*

"No. After all this time I have practically become one of them. They would never suspect." Darvin curled a lip in disgust. "I am more Earther than Klingon now."

"Then what is it?"

Darvin glanced at a tricorder next to his communication screen. It was set to mask the comm signal and alert him to anyone nearby. Everything seemed clear. "The quadrotriticale is coming up. The farmers are saying it looks like it could be a 'bumper crop.' That means it is larger than expected."

Kamuk laughed deeply and looked at Darvin like he was a dim-witted child. *"You truly do not understand what is happening?"*

Grinding his teeth together kept Darvin from saying something to threaten his career. He relied on Kamuk to extract him from this mission, something he hoped was finally approaching. Darvin had been living as a human for nearly his entire adult life after being recruited by Imperial Intelligence for his extremely humanlike appearance, even among the *QuchHa'*. It minimized the need for surgical alterations, especially compared to Klingons altered to replace specific humans. Taking advantage of a hole in computer security, a false identity and background were entered into a Federation database on a colony in the Ramatis system. Starting as a low-level colonial functionary, Darvin had penetrated the Federation's large bureaucracy with hopes of making an important breakthrough for the Empire. When he had gotten shifted over to the agricultural department to work as Baris's assistant, his mission had appeared to hit a wall until the Treaty of Organia upended the nature of the conflict with the Federation.

Suddenly Baris's influence over colonial development gave Darvin easy access to intelligence that could serve the Empire's need to compete for territory nonviolently. But his increasing responsibilities as an agent didn't stop there. Kamuk came up with a more active assignment, going beyond mere intelligence gathering. Darvin was in a position to shape certain aspects of Federation colonial development. He could subtly sabotage the Earther colonies by setting them up against the strengths of the Klingons. It had been a short step from there to Kamuk's next, less subtle, mission: the destruction of a colony by poisoning their chief food source.

Darvin had gone along with it grudgingly. It had not seemed honorable; gathering intelligence was one thing, but this, this seemed like stabbing an unarmed enemy in the back. But Kamuk assured him the directive had come from the upper circles of Imperial Intelligence, which would also be pursuing more aggressive covert operations elsewhere. It was clear that Kamuk was fully behind it. Darvin had had little choice while still in the middle of a deep cover mission.

"I understand that I risked my cover to contaminate the quadrotriticale seeds on K-7," Darvin said once he trusted himself to be able to fake an appropriately respectful tone of voice. "And now the crops are sprouting up as though nothing happened."

Kamuk continued to chuckle. *"A simple crop failure may not have been enough to force the Earthers off the planet. I will give the humans that. They are tougher than you would expect from their incessant babbling about nonviolence."* Kamuk paused and reached off screen to grab a tankard of bloodwine, taking a deep, sloppy drink. It was a ritual for him, eating and drinking in front of Darvin during their communications, taunting Darvin with food he had not tasted for years.

Darvin furrowed his brow. "Then what is going to happen to the grain?"

"To tell you the truth, even I do not know the exact outcome." Kamuk put the bloodwine aside and wiped his mouth with his sleeve. *"But I do know it is the humans you will want to watch. That is where the entertainment will be."*

"What is going to happen?" Darvin said, enunciating each word sharply. It was the most angry demonstration he had allowed himself in front of his controller.

"The crops will mutate differently depending on their immediate environment. As they begin to fail, their colonies will be overrun by multiple plagues." Kamuk shook his head, but he bared his teeth with pleasure. *"They will lose SermanyuQ."*

Darvin stood next to Baris as they looked out across one of the many fields near the Nuevos Angeles colony. The early morning sun gave the ripe quadrotriticale a golden glow as it waved gently in a soft breeze, the dew on the wheat glinting like the edge of a blade. Harvesting would begin soon, within a week at most. Darvin turned away from the field and looked past the colony to the soft waves of Leander Bay.

"Beautiful, isn't it?" Baris said, still looking across the field. He rubbed his hands together in the cool morning air.

"Yes, sir." Darvin put on a smile. He had been undercover for too many years to allow his inner thoughts to affect his expression. Although he did have one unfortunate weakness, an overpowering revulsion for the various small furry creatures the humans found "cute." He shuddered as he thought of Governor Zaman's cat.

"It grew so fast. It'll probably all be harvested before the delegates arrive for the spring conference." Baris's face took on a grim expression. "Starfleet will probably send that self-involved Kirk again. At least I'll be able to show him how well the colonies are doing. People other than starship captains can make important contributions to the Federation."

Baris looked at him expectantly. Darvin nodded. "Yes, sir, that's true."

"Of course." Baris shivered. "I'm a little chill. Let's head back. The walk will warm me up."

"You go on ahead. I feel like taking a hike." He tilted his head at the steep lichen-covered hill that rose up above Nuevos Angeles.

"Suit yourself. I'll see you back at the office." Baris headed off without further comment.

Darvin shook his head as he watched his self-assured boss walk briskly toward the colorful buildings just a few kilometers away. Soon Baris's world would come crashing down as the colonies struggled with the results of a disastrous harvest. With a frown Darvin turned toward the purplish hill and started walking. Soon he left the gentle fields behind, stumbling occasionally on the steepening rocky slope. By the time he reached the top, and could see the entire colony spread out below him, his anger had burned away, leaving him with a dull feeling that had become all too common.

The idea that warriors should poison enemy civilians sickened him. What was happening to the Empire? To think he had worried that his time undercover as a human had affected his Klingon nature. He was still more of a Klingon than his controller could ever be—if Kamuk did indeed support this mission. But it was possible that Kamuk, like himself, was simply in a position where saying no to his superior officer was not an option.

Darvin gazed down the steep, lichen-carpeted slope toward the city on the bay and its surrounding fields. Except for the extravagant colors of the prefab buildings, it could be any Klingon colony, although with more emphasis on grains than on livestock. If he squinted he could just make out Port Emily on the far side of Leander Bay, shrouded with a light morning fog. A handful of other Federation colonies were spread along the coast, but they all had quadrotriticale crops, like multiple time bombs nestled around them. As harvest time grew near, Darvin spent more and more of his free time hiking in the forest. It wasn't that he feared the coming plague. He assumed that Klingons would be relatively safe, although given the mutation factor that had been engineered into the virus, nothing was certain. He hiked in the forest because he couldn't bear to look at the colonists knowing they would soon be exposed to such dishonorable deaths, with no chance to fight their real enemy. Humans weren't so different in that regard.

Just as he was about to turn and head into the forest, a suspicious movement drew his attention back to the field below. A large tractor—not an automated croptender, but a relatively old-fashioned operator-driven vehicle—was crossing the field. What had caught his eyes was its odd angle as it cut across the crop. The driver had left the carefully planted rows and was plowing through the wheat, leaving an obvious track of crushed plants. Finally the tractor came to a stop. Darvin had started down the hill toward the field without really thinking about it, but he came to a halt as the door to the tractor's cab opened and the driver tumbled out, disappearing into the wheat.

Darvin waited, but the driver did not reappear. It could have been a rare heart attack or stroke, but deep down Darvin knew the plagues had begun.

"Sir?" Darvin looked in through the open door of Baris's office, where the human sat with his face buried in his hands.

"What?" The question was muffled from behind his hands.

"Governor Zaman has informed us of another outbreak. A new one, in Cape Winston."

"Another unknown disease?"

Darvin ground his teeth together. "Yes, sir." Each new outbreak felt like a jab with a painstik from the Second Rite of Ascension, a test of his will and endurance as a warrior. "The governor has updated Starfleet Medical."

Baris let his hands fall to his desk and looked at Darvin with bloodshot eyes. "You should go."

Darvin hesitated. "I'm not sure what you mean."

"You should evacuate. There's no need for both of us to risk our lives. Leave with the relief ships after the next food shipment."

The suggestion enraged Darvin but he was careful to manage his expression. He was finding it harder and harder not to show his true emotions. "I won't leave you or the colonies. My duties are here." There were so many layers of meaning to that, and Darvin found that he couldn't really separate them anymore. His cover role, his true Klingon self, his misgivings about this mission. His feelings for the Federation enemy and his cowardly controller. It had all melted together into one misshapen mass. When he spoke he no longer knew whose motives he was serving.

The comm unit on Baris's desk chimed softly. When Baris didn't react, Darvin stepped forward to answer it.

"Don't," Baris said, holding up his hand. "It's that engineer again, Ray McAllen. He's hounding me about doing something, but Zaman and I are doing everything we can to respond to these outbreaks and crop failures."

Darvin hesitated, but let the chime go unanswered until it stopped. It was then that he decided that it was time he started serving his own motives. He would start with a visit to McAllen.

★ ★ ★

Darvin stomped back and forth across his quarters. He and Baris had just come back from one of the outland encampments that McAllen had organized with Darvin's help. They'd gotten there in time to discover a firefight going on between Klingons and the unarmed colonists.

"*Hu'tegh* Korax, that *petaQ*," he mumbled. "He would shoot an Earther in a sickbed if it served him."

He stopped and looked out his window, which faced Leander Bay. There were no sails visible, although the weather was perfect. At the beginning of the outbreaks the colonists had kept up their pastimes, but as more and more fell to the plagues sweeping the cities, everyday routines fell away, leaving only a desperate day-to-day struggle. Finding a way to retain some personal honor during this cowardly mission was becoming increasingly difficult.

"What *yIntagh* in Intelligence came up with this? Kamuk said the directive came from above, but I think the specific mission parameters were his. There must be some other way I could get around his *baQa'* orders, *pel'aQDaj ghorpa'*."

Darvin had spun away from the window and started toward the door when he realized how he had lapsed into Klingon and, worse yet, while talking to himself. He came to a halt. He was letting the situation get to him too deeply, endangering his cover. Outside of his communications with Kamuk, which took place under very controlled conditions, Darvin had not spoken Klingon in years. He didn't even think in it anymore, and his dreams were populated by humans speaking Federation Standard. For the first time he considered asking for an early extraction.

Going back to the window, he looked across the bay to Port Emily. Baris was meeting with Governor Zaman right now, trying to smooth over the incident in the outlands. He could go over there right now and demand to go home—

Darvin grabbed his head in his hands. What was he thinking? He had to go to Kamuk for extraction. Yes, he would have to get

Baris's approval, but Baris had tried to get him to evacuate early on in the crisis, that should be no problem. It was Kamuk who would be difficult. If only Darvin could simply think straight under all this pressure . . .

A chime sounded from his desk. He turned toward it, wide-eyed. That was his secure link to Kamuk. They were not supposed to talk until next week. He'd never had an unscheduled call from his controller. Hurrying to his desk, he took out the vid communicator and his tricorder. Only after establishing without a doubt that he was in no danger of being detected, Darvin activated the communicator.

Kamuk appeared on the small screen. His expression was grim, as usual, and difficult to read beyond that. *"What is going on out there?"*

"Everything is proceeding according to plan." Although Darvin answered immediately and in an even tone, for the first time he was concerned that his distaste for his controller might have shown on his face. Certainly the odd reaction on Kamuk's face didn't bode well.

"Do not joke with me. Speak in Klingon."

Darvin froze for a moment. Hadn't he spoken in Klingon? He wasn't sure. But Kamuk had no reason to lie about such a thing. He must have slipped. "Yes, of course," he said, perhaps speaking a little too loudly. "You caught me by surprise with this unplanned communication."

Kamuk bared his teeth. *"I am sure I did, from what I hear through other channels."*

Other channels? This was more serious than Darvin had suspected. Koloth must have filed an official report about the outland colonies. That was his duty, to report possible treaty violations to the Empire. Kamuk knew that Darvin had been trying to save the lives of Federation citizens, an action that could brand him a traitor to the Empire.

"I can explain, Kamuk. I needed to maintain my cover. As the plagues worsen, it is expected for humans to commit acts of desperation. I felt that—"

"Enough!" Kamuk shook his head. *"You would think that after all these years I would have some understanding of you, but you remain inscrutable to me. I contacted you to congratulate you on your initiative."*

Darvin knew that he looked openly surprised now. "Sir?" He had not foreseen any positive outcome to his rebellion against Kamuk's mission, not from Intelligence's point of view. He had been in open defiance of his controller.

"These camps you got the colonists to set up in violation of the treaty. That took advantage of the outbreaks in a creative way and adds another strike against the Federation. You may have sealed the fate of SermanyuQ. The planet will soon belong to the Empire. I will recommend you for a commendation for this."

"Thank you, sir." Darvin cast around for something else to say to cover the roiling, conflicted emotions rising in him. He really could not think clearly through all the tangled duties he carried, his duty to the Empire, to Imperial Intelligence, to Kamuk, to his own honor, as well as the duties his cover demanded, to the Federation, to Baris, to the colonies. "I do what I can to serve the Empire," he added.

Kamuk nodded. *"Indeed, and you have served well under difficult circumstances for many years now. I think you have earned much more than a simple commendation. I think we shall bring you home to Qo'noS at the completion of this mission."*

There it was, the extraction he had been hoping for all these years, increasingly so as his mission had changed into the current travesty. "I do miss Qo'noS, I must admit. What goals do I have yet to meet to conclude this assignment?" He had to be cautious. If he appeared to be too eager, Kamuk might take it as a personal insult and postpone the extraction. If he didn't appear eager enough, Kamuk could interpret his conflicted honor with torn loyalties. Controllers always had to be on the lookout for deep-cover agents gaining sympathy for the enemy. That risk was part of the job.

"Not much remains. Continue monitoring all Federation communication with the colonies. Continue your initiative with the illegal outland colonies. Most importantly, keep a close watch on Baris. Obviously, as the ranking Federation official, he will be a focus of the Organians when we invoke our treaty rights to the planet. It will not be long before you are walking through the First City again." With a small nod, Kamuk terminated the signal.

Darvin released a deep breath. He was so close to home. And he had maintained his own honor as much as was possible. Soon he would be able to leave this behind and get on with his life as a true Klingon.

Darvin could not keep up with the distress calls flooding in from the colonies. The government had broken down; Governor Zaman had been dead for weeks now, and Baris had stepped in to administrate the colonies. They were trying to manage the evacuation, but the Klingons were complicating matters by moving into the colonies prematurely.

"Listen to me," Darvin said, leaning closer to the small communication screen. The woman on the screen kept talking, gesturing in panic, so he raised his voice. "I understand you want your family together. But you have to get them all to a single evac center. The transport ships have to do mass beaming to keep on schedule, there's no other way." He closed the channel. The desperate woman would have talked in circles for another hour if he'd let her.

From his own office down the hall, Baris's voice rose to a point that Darvin could hear it clearly. "What are you talking about? I know what I've said about Kirk, but this is an emergency. We need every available ship, I wouldn't care if every crewman was Kirk."

Darvin couldn't help but laugh, even under the circumstances. Or maybe because of the circumstances, the stress and the dishonor he'd been living with for the last several months as the plagues spread through the starving colonies, he needed release.

He couldn't stop laughing, even though it felt like he was out of control, a state an agent in his situation couldn't allow. Even with the growing fear that he was bordering on some sort of break-down—behavior so human—he kept laughing. Until he looked up and saw Ray McAllen filling the doorway of his office.

The big engineer, although his frame was as broad as ever, didn't fill his jumpsuit until bursting anymore. Gaunt and pale, he looked like an animated skeleton, the dingy and torn jump-suit hanging limply over his bony shoulders. His eyes appeared sunken and hollow, as if they were drying up in their sockets.

"You're killing us, Darvin." McAllen's voice was low and soft, matter of fact instead of angry.

Darvin's laughter, immediately stopped after seeing McAllen, seemed to haunt the office around him as he opened his mouth to speak. Nothing came at first, then on the second try he said, "I don't . . . what do you mean?"

"You've left us behind. We're not going to make it."

Darvin relaxed. For a moment there he had thought McAllen somehow knew who he really was. "The ships are here, Ray. We're getting everyone off."

"Everyone?" McAllen took an unsteady step forward. His face was white except for dark shadows under his eyes and what looked like a trace of blood at the corner of his mouth. "Only those still left alive. Not the people already buried. Not the ones lost in the woods."

Standing and making his way slowly around his desk, Darvin held out a hand to steady McAllen. "I'm sorry, but we're doing all we can. If—"

"Not enough!" McAllen lashed out at Darvin, hitting him in the chest, but the blow was weak, barely noticeable. "Why did you send us into the outlands? We're lost out there."

"I don't understand. The camps were supposed to be cleared weeks ago."

"We can't get back. Not enough vehicles. And now transport-ing is forbidden because of all the mass beaming for the evac ships. You're evacuating the cities, but there are people trapped in the camps." McAllen started coughing, deep, racking coughs that wrenched his entire body.

"We'll get them. The evac ships—" Darvin stopped talking and grabbed McAllen as he doubled over, keeping him on his feet. Baris appeared in the doorway, a look of concern blended with frustration on his narrow face.

"You might want to stay back, sir." Darvin grimaced as McAllen's coughs brought up bloody phlegm and spattered it across the floor. Some Klingons had become sick during the outbreaks, but so far Darvin had seemed immune to everything. But he knew Baris had survived only on luck and quarantine laws.

"He needs a doctor." Baris hurried away as if to make contact emergency services.

"No one will be able to get here," Darvin called out after him, realizing immediately how callous that must have sounded to McAllen. He looked back down at the human, whose coughing had quieted. McAllen glanced up, still doubled over from the coughing fit. Pink spittle covered his lips, and a dark fluid ran from his nose.

McAllen stood up, pushing Darvin away. "Let go of me. I don't need your help." He swayed, his arms flailing around. His eyes rolled back and then he fell forward, vomiting blood as Darvin caught him and eased him to the floor. McAllen was completely limp but so terribly light.

"No!" Darvin rolled McAllen onto his back, turning his head to the side to clear his airway. "Did you find a doctor?" Darvin yelled, hoping Baris would hear. He looked back down at McAllen. "Ray!" He felt for a pulse, found none, and started CPR. Darvin cried out in frustration as he heard McAllen's ribs crack under the pressure, but he kept going. "I was trying to save you. The camps were the only way." He leaned in and forced air into McAllen's lungs, then went back to chest compressions. "I did what I could. Between Kamuk and Baris—"

Darvin froze. Had he just said the name of his controller out loud? Shaking his head, he went back to CPR. He had to focus on this, not think about everything else that was pushing him toward the dark edge of madness he felt he had been struggling against for months. After he gave McAllen another several breaths, however, he found himself leaning back, overwhelmed with the futility of it all. He ran his sleeve across his face, wiping away McAllen's blood. He leaned forward and spread McAllen's eyes wide open, staring into them deeply before leaning back to howl a warning to the warriors in Sto-vo-Kor . . . he would have done so without another thought if, as he straightened up, Baris had not been in the doorway staring at him, his mouth open in surprise, the color drained from his face.

Darvin stared back at his boss, realizing what he had been doing. He could think of no way of explaining his behavior, he could only hope that Baris had not seen him start the death ritual, that he was reacting to McAllen's gruesome death. He had to get ahold of himself, had to maintain his cover for only a little while longer, Kamuk had all but promised him extraction after the fall of Sherman's Planet.

"He's gone, Nilz." Darvin thought that was probably the first time he had ever used Baris's first name outside of making introductions. He stood up slowly, trying to keep his gaze away from the bloody body at his feet. "I'll try to contact his family, but it will be difficult to find them. They may still be . . ." Darvin stopped talking as he glanced at Baris, the look in his eyes. Was it fear?

Baris's expression changed to a grimace, his skin flushed red. "What are you saying?" He stepped forward, trembling. Darvin wondered if Baris was sick too, then realized that it wasn't weakness but anger that made the human shake so. He had seen Baris this enraged before but only when—

"Klingon!" Baris shouted. "You're speaking Klingon." Baris's fists were clenched at his sides. He didn't seem to notice the body on the floor between them.

Darvin felt as though all the energy suddenly drained from his body, leaving him numb, paralyzed. He wanted to deny it, accuse Baris of hallucinating, but he had to admit it was possible that he had slipped into his native tongue. All the stress of this mission had come to a head.

"Darvin!" Baris yelled, taking another step closer. He was not a violent man, but he was taller than Darvin, and he glared down at his assistant as he grabbed his jacket and shook him. "Explain yourself."

The physical confrontation snapped Darvin back to his senses. He grabbed Baris's wrists and wrenched loose the human's grip with his Klingon strength.

"I am Klingon," Darvin said.

10

Klingon Deep Space Station *Dugh naHjej*, 2366

Jensen's stomach roiled with nervousness, but she did not break eye contact with Kamuk seated across the table from her. After all but giving up on discovering the significance of Baris's last words, Kamuk's revelations about himself and Darvin and their roles in Imperial Intelligence had shocked her. When he finished speaking, she had no trouble keeping her eyes focused on the perplexing Klingon. "Governor, I don't fully understand what you're telling me. Your actions on Benecia ran counter to the wishes of Imperial Intelligence."

"I did what I thought was right for the Empire."

Jensen took a moment to think that over. "Then it seems you had a change of heart about how best to serve the Empire after Sherman's Planet."

Kamuk stood and again looked out the portal behind him, gazing down at Bajor with his hands clasped behind his back. "Yes. That changed everything."

"Darvin's second thoughts about poisoning the grain must have eventually gotten through to you." When Kamuk's lack of response seemed to imply agreement, Jensen continued. "You knew Darvin while he worked with Baris, right up until his death. Do you have a guess why Baris's last thoughts were of Darvin?"

Kamuk shrugged in a very human way, then turned back toward Jensen. "No one can really know. Was it his own guilt at never exposing Darvin? The compromises, the complicity, upon which he built his career, and how it all led back to Darvin?" He shook his head. "We all feared the Empire and the Federation could destroy each other if the proper balance wasn't struck. Those of us who thought beyond blind faith in our own governments were willing to sacrifice what was easy for what was right. The burdens we had to carry as a result seemed a small price for what we accomplished."

"Like Darvin did in the end. Trying to help the colonists escape the plagues. And giving his life to save Baris and Koloth." She leaned forward on Kamuk's desk. "But what happened after Darvin admitted to Baris that he was Klingon? He must have contacted you again."

Kamuk sat back down and looked Jensen in the eye. She held his gaze until he seemed to make a decision. He nodded slightly, and a brief smile played across his lips. "Darvin contacted me two more times after admitting who he was to Baris. By that time, he was no longer torn about what he had to do."

Baris pulled his arms from Darvin's grasp and staggered back, the color draining from his face. Then his eyes widened. "You did this, didn't you?" His voice was a whisper. "You did something to the grain."

"I'm sorry. I was only told the crops would fail. I didn't know that—"

Baris's color had come back, and he stood up straight. "Don't try to excuse what you've done, it's monstrous." He gestured down at McAllen. "Look at him! The way he died, the way they've all died. Klingons, you're all animals . . . worse than animals."

Darvin shook his head. "No. Not all of us. There is no honor in this, it stains the Empire with stolen blood, blood that should have been earned in open battle. Once I found out it was too late. But I've done what I could."

"We both know what you've done." Baris moved toward the door. "I'm informing Starfleet."

Darvin had to step over McAllen's body to grab Baris by the arm. "Don't you understand? If all that I've done to help during the plagues is exposed, I will be a traitor to the Empire in the eyes of many Klingons. I have given you advice based on my knowledge as a member of Imperial Intelligence. I've become a double agent, trying to maintain my cover while trying to make up for my part in this."

"Trying to save your own skin, you mean. While those you poisoned died horrible, painful deaths. Where's your honor in that?"

Darvin released his hold on Baris and slumped against the wall, staring at the floor. "You're right. Perhaps my honor is beyond saving. But think of this." He looked up at Baris. "Think of how tenuous relations are now. Think of how even this evacuation hangs on a worn thread. To expose me, to expose I.I.'s involvement now, would only pull that thread tighter, from both ends. Koloth knows nothing of me, of how his own honor has been compromised by my actions. Kirk and the *Enterprise* are approaching the system, already suspicious." Standing up straighter he reached toward Baris again, not to grab him, but to put a hand on Baris's shoulder as though he was still an employee talking to his boss.

"Don't think of me, of how I would be arrested by Starfleet or killed by the Empire. I deserve whatever comes to me and more. But think of the fuel you would add to the fire in this system right now. Don't jeopardize the evacuation. At least wait until this emergency is over before starting another."

Baris stared at him long and hard with his cold, sharp eyes. "It's true the Klingons are interfering with the evacuation as it is." He looked sickened by having to admit it. "I'm going to see Koloth and make sure we get all Federation personnel out of this system. Beyond that, I don't know what I'll do." He started down the corridor, then looked back over his shoulder. "I do know, no matter what, I will carry their deaths with me for the rest of my life."

Baris disappeared around a corner in the corridor on his way outside. Darvin looked back at McAllen. He still wanted to perform the death ritual, but no longer had the drive to do so. Instead he made his way back to his desk and reached into the center drawer to take out his vid communicator and tricorder. After ensuring the security of the signal, more out of habit than feeling any compelling need to do so, he opened a channel to Kamuk. Like Baris, he felt like he didn't know what he was going to do.

"What do you want?" Kamuk said, appearing after only the slightest of delays. *"I thought you would be on a Federation ship by now."*

"The evacuation is not going smoothly."

"I guess that is to be expected. Earthers are not as disciplined as Klingons."

"It is the Klingons who are making the evacuation difficult!" Darvin snapped. Kamuk looked stunned at his outburst, but Darvin was beyond feeling surprise at his own behavior. He acted like a Klingon in front of humans and a human in front of Klingons. He had no control over who he was anymore. "I need extraction now. Baris . . . suspects. I could end up in a Starfleet brig if I evacuate with him."

"That was not the plan. We do not want Koloth to know how we have used him. You must leave with the Earthers and then make your way to a neutral planet."

Darvin slammed his fist down on his desk. He heard a cracking sound that could have been either the wood surface or the bones in his hand. "No, Kamuk. You told me I would be extracted after this mission. You told me I would see Qo'noS soon."

"You will see Qo'noS when it serves the needs of Imperial Intelligence and no sooner," shouted Kamuk. *"And from what you tell me, this mission is not yet over."*

"I have achieved all primary mission objectives—"

"That is my judgment to make." Kamuk spoke quietly again, which was all the more threatening. *"It seems the parameters of the mission have evolved. I have new orders for you."*

Kamuk stood by a floor-to-ceiling window gazing out across his country estate on Qo'noS, deep in the Mekro'vak region. It was late in the evening, but the bright light of Praxis shone on the grounds and bathed Kamuk in an eerie pale glow. The only other illumination was from a large bed of glowing coals in a sunken pit in the center of the room, all that remained of a roaring fire earlier in the evening. The room was designed to evoke the feeling of a cave. The furniture was sparse and made from unfinished logs. Trophy heads decorated the rough-hewn walls, and the matching furs were spread about on the stone floor. On the far end of the room hung a variety of edged weapons. The only exception was the technology demanded by his profession, but they were kept hidden until needed.

Kamuk often stood here, staring out the window. The grounds had been minimally landscaped, allowing a longer line of sight without losing the natural feel of the wilderness surrounding the estate. Sabre bears and wild *targs* often roamed across his land, and he liked to tell people of the time he brought down a *lingta* by simply opening a window and throwing a *mek'leth* at the nearby beast.

A quiet buzzing drew his attention away from the window and he glanced around the room. Finally he located the source of the noise, a vid communicator on a shelf, tucked behind statuettes of battling Klingons. He stood staring at it for a minute before he walked over and picked it up, tilting his head as he looked at it in the dim red light of the fire pit. This had been the communicator dedicated to Darvin while he served on SermanyuQ and had not been used since shortly before the agent's death the previous year. Curious, Kamuk activated the device, his eyes widening at the appearance of Darvin on the small monitor.

"You are surprised to see me."

"Yes," Kamuk said, recovering his composure quickly. "I must admit I underestimated you. I wouldn't have guessed you capable of this."

"We are all trained to have contingency plans."

As Kamuk nodded at the screen he moved slowly across the room toward his desk. "True. Just as I had ways of getting you out of the Federation . . . if you had given me the chance." Sitting down, he reached for the communication panel in the desk.

"But you did not seem inclined to use those plans." Darvin frowned. *"You cannot signal for help. I have jammed all frequencies other than ours."*

Kamuk froze, his hand poised over the emergency button on the companel. "I see I have underestimated you yet again. Clearly I did not make full use of you on SermanyuQ." He turned his chair around to face the window, squinting out at the moonlit trees gently swaying in an increasing wind. There was a storm coming. He held up the comm device in his left hand, looking at Darvin even as he watched the grounds outside. "You should come back to Intelligence. People with your abilities are well rewarded." Reaching behind with his right hand, he slid open a desk drawer and withdrew a disruptor, making sure to keep the movement out of the line of sight of the comm device.

"I served Intelligence for years and have nothing to show for it. My life as a dead man has been more satisfying than my service as an agent."

"I understand." Kamuk stood up, disruptor behind his back, and walked toward the window. "The life of a deep cover agent is much like that of a prisoner. But you are free now. I would not send you back into deep cover, you have earned that."

Outside the gathering clouds had muted the light of Praxis, and the increasing wind caused distracting movements in the grasses and brush. Kamuk snapped his head from side to side, trying to pick out anything suspicious in the deepening darkness. The moaning of the wind in the trees and the scraping of a low-hanging branch across the roof were soon joined by the undulating sound of a downpour, the hard spatter of drops against the large window. He turned his attention back to the comm screen, but Darvin was gone.

Kamuk dropped the communicator. Before he could raise the disruptor, his right arm was grabbed and wrenched upward behind his back, threatening dislocation. He lost his grip and the weapon clattered to the floor. With a roar he swung his left arm backward, bent at the elbow, and was rewarded with a solid crack as his elbow met Darvin's head. The agent stumbled back, losing his grip on Kamuk's weapon hand. Kamuk continued spinning around to the left, swinging his right arm in a wide arc at Darvin.

Darvin ducked the roundhouse swing and charged forward, grabbing Kamuk around the chest. They crashed into the transparent-aluminum window, the air rushing out of Kamuk's lungs, and bounced off. Kamuk, trying to catch his breath, grabbed Darvin's neck and jumped forward, overbalancing them. Darvin went over backward, Kamuk landing solidly on top of him. As Darvin's head cracked against the stone floor, his grip around Kamuk loosened.

Kamuk rolled off Darvin, coughing as he drew in a deep breath. Before he could get his bearings and look for the disruptor, Darvin, still on the floor beside him, punched him in the neck and clawed at his throat. He grabbed Darvin's wrist with his left hand and brought up his other arm, wrapping it around Darvin's elbow. Then he thrust his left hand toward his waist while he jerked his right arm farther up, and he heard a bone snap in Darvin's arm.

Darvin cried out and fell back. Kamuk jumped quickly to his feet and looked down at Darvin. He was still lying on the floor, but now he held the disruptor in his good left hand. Darvin bared his teeth in victory and pulled the trigger, but nothing happened. Kamuk leaped at him. Darvin slammed the disruptor forward, catching Kamuk on the side of the head, just missing his eye and tearing a gash across his upper cheek and his ear. Ignoring his broken arm, Darvin grabbed Kamuk and rolled, using Kamuk's momentum to throw him to the floor.

They both scrambled to their feet and faced each other in the dim light of the glowing embers in the fire pit. Darvin held his broken right arm to his stomach. Blood streamed down the left side of Kamuk's head, his ear hanging backward on a flap of skin. They slowly circled each other.

Kamuk nodded. "I never knew you had a warrior's heart. You seemed like a mewling human to me . . . Krek."

Darvin shook his head. "I do not deserve that name. I buried it for far too long. My dishonor has left me a nameless Klingon. "

"What dishonor?" Kamuk feinted left then tried to attack, but Darvin anticipated him and shifted accordingly. Kamuk backed off. "The Organians forced us to seek a new path."

"Honor must be our bedrock. If we let it become shifting sand, we will blow away."

"A noble philosophy. You can stand on that bedrock while an Earther knifes you in the back."

Kamuk suddenly spun around as if to retreat from the room. Darvin rushed forward, but instead of continuing toward the doorway, Kamuk, with a quick grab and twist, was facing Darvin again, swinging in his right hand the antler of a Kolar beast he had snapped off a trophy mounted on the wall. Before Darvin could jump back, the sharp broken end of the antler sliced him across the chest, sending a spray of blood through the air.

As Kamuk completed his swing, his right side was unguarded. Darvin punched Kamuk in the jaw hard enough to snap his head back into the wall. Kamuk's eyes rolled around unevenly from the concussion, but he swung back again with the antler, forcing Darvin to block the blow with his broken arm. Darvin staggered backward and Kamuk lunged at him, bringing the antler in low. Darvin brushed the antler aside, avoiding disembowelment, but Kamuk continued forward, charging into Darvin. The two Klingons went down into the fire pit.

As Darvin landed on his back with Kamuk on top of him, an

explosion of sparks rushed into the air around them, stinging their faces and hands. The smell of smoldering hair filled the air, and the glowing embers rapidly burned through their clothes. Darvin tried rolling to one side, but Kamuk held him down on the coals, a foot braced against the side of the pit. Darvin suddenly rolled the other way, and before Kamuk could adjust they were on their sides, face-to-face, bellowing in rage and pain as they struggled atop the coals. As if in agreement, they both released their holds, rolling away from each other and scrambling to their feet on opposite sides of the pit, their hair and clothing smoking. They began circling the fire, first one way, then the next, keeping the pit between them.

"You are a fool to try to kill me," Kamuk said. He still held the antler in his blistering right hand. "Do you think you'll regain your Klingon self by avenging the deaths of Earthers?"

"Even Earthers can have honor, I have learned. More than a Klingon who has strayed far from Kahless."

Kamuk chuckled cruelly. "Do you think you insult me with legends?"

Darvin backed a little farther away from the pit and stumbled over something on the floor. Kamuk didn't waste a second, leaping toward him over the coals. Before Darvin recovered his balance, he felt the antler plunge into his side. Darvin went down, Kamuk's firm grip on the antler lodged in his ribs pulling Kamuk along with him. They struggled on the floor, rolling back and forth. Kamuk tried to pull the antler out, but it was wedged in too firmly. Instead he snapped off the length of the antler still protruding from the wound, but his burned hand lost its grip. As Kamuk reached for the dropped antler, the hand of Darvin's good left arm landed on the object he had tripped over. He swung it at Kamuk's hand, not immediately realizing in the dark room that it was a small ax for chopping firewood.

He brought the blade down on Kamuk's outstretched fingers as they grabbed the antler. Kamuk yanked his hand away with a howl, leaving the broken antler and three fingers on the floor. He rolled away while holding the bloody stumps of his fingers tightly to staunch the bleeding. Darvin crawled after him, the antler piece stuck in his side making it difficult to stand or breath. Kamuk got to his feet and walked to the wall where his blades were displayed, catching his breath while Darvin wheezed along on hands and knees.

"You fought well, but it is over." Kamuk reached with his left hand toward a *bat'leth*, but then moved to grab a *mek'leth* instead. He looked down at Darvin, a smile on his face. "I will allow you a choice: swear loyalty to me, or I will kill you."

Darvin was on his knees and his good hand, his broken arm curled beneath him. Blood ran freely from the wound in his side, puddling on the floor. He looked up at his old controller. Kamuk held his bleeding hand to his stomach, and blood also ran from his torn ear. But he gripped the *mek'leth* firmly in his good hand. Under Kamuk's angry glare, Darvin slowly sat up, easing back onto his haunches.

"Well?" Kamuk said. He took a step forward, swinging the blade back and forth. It glinted red in the dim light of the fire pit. "Answer me."

Darvin raised his broken arm, which held the disruptor.

Kamuk started laughing. "Did you not learn the lesson of your first try?" He raised the *mek'leth* over his head. "Just when you were starting to impress me."

"I did learn my lesson." Darvin steadied his aim. "That's why it is not my finger pulling the trigger."

Kamuk's eyes widened as he saw that Darvin held one of his severed fingers against the trigger's biosafety, and then the disruptor fired.

Jensen stared wide-eyed and unblinking at Kamuk, who had paused in his story to get a fresh mug of *raktajino* from the replicator. When he turned back to her, breathing deeply over the steaming beverage, he wore an almost sympathetic smile as he regarded Jensen.

"The first year was the trickiest. Luckily, I knew much about Kamuk, more than he realized he had let slip to me over his years as my controller. I knew he was reclusive and had no family to speak of, knew what his general responsibilities were. Taking over from his country estate was easier than you would guess. Very few questioned his increasing isolation, and his various operatives, pleased by his change toward a more—shall I say humane—style of leadership, became great defenders of him.

"After I received the cure for the accursed virus and gained the appearance of a true-blood Klingon, I could move freely again. The transformation was so substantial, no one doubted me. At that point I had truly become Kamuk in the eyes of my fellow Klingons."

Jensen was shaking her head. "I can hardly believe it. You really are Arne Darvin?"

Kamuk shrugged as he sat back down behind his desk. "Part of me is, I guess. But I have now lived far longer as Kamuk than I did as Darvin. Or even as my own youthful self, Krek, a name I have not spoken aloud in over one hundred years."

"But how did you do it? Everyone believed you'd been killed in that explosion."

"I brought the bomb with me to Koloth's office and planted it while he tried to chase us from the room. I transported out as the bomb detonated and beamed in a corpse treated to match the genetic signature in my Federation records." He noticed the look on Jensen's face as she thought it through. "No, I did not kill someone to stand in for me. Sadly, it was not difficult to find an unclaimed body on Sherman's Planet during the plagues. And deep cover agents have a variety of technologies available to them to fool standard scans. I also knew that it was unlikely the body would be closely examined under the circumstances. But as Darvin, I had nowhere to go. Staging my death was risky, and there was a good chance I would accidentally kill myself in the attempt. Truthfully, I did not care much one way or the other at the time."

"But did Baris know?"

"Not then. If he had suspected, I am certain he would have reported me to Starfleet. As it was, he allowed his guilt to overcome his honor, and he kept to himself the shameful secret that he had been working alongside a Klingon agent for years. He blamed himself for inadvertently allowing me to poison the quadrotriticale and cause thousands of deaths. I also was haunted by those deaths, but deservedly so."

Jensen spoke in the same hushed tones as the governor. "You said he didn't know then. When did he realize who you were?"

The governor stared over Jensen's shoulder. "I told him on Benecia."

"Whose side are you on?" Baris glared at the Klingon as they stood in the ruins of the city.

Kamuk thought for several seconds before making his decision. "Those answers are rather . . . sensitive in nature. For the ears of a Federation envoy alone."

Baris glanced at Shaden. "Don't worry, we'll stay in plain sight." He turned toward Kamuk and motioned impatiently before walking briskly up a street that had been cleared of rubble. Kamuk took a deep breath and followed. After they were out of earshot of Shaden and Traylith, Baris came to a halt. "Well?"

Kamuk leaned a little closer, softening his voice, and said, "It's me, sir."

Baris drew back, a confused look on his face. "What? What did you say?" He shook his head slightly.

"It's me, Darvin."

A flock of emotions raced across Baris's face, confusion, suspicion, denial, anger. His eyes narrowed. "No." He had spoken firmly, if a little hesitantly. His voice fell to a whisper as he shook his head. "You can't be."

Kamuk nodded. "It was the only way to save myself. To live so that I could atone for Sherman's Planet."

Baris's breathing became ragged, his hands clenched in hard fists. "Don't you dare mention Sherman's Planet." His whole body shook. "I am not a violent man, Kamuk, but so help me, I will beat you down, I will not play whatever game—"

"Ray McAllen still haunts my dreams," Kamuk whispered. It was something he could admit only to Baris.

At the mention of the colonist, Baris froze. He seemed unable to blink. His face had gone red with rage, but now the color drained from his face as his arms hung limply at his sides. He swayed on his feet as if about to feint. Kamuk reached out a hand to steady his former boss.

"No," Baris snapped, slapping Kamuk's hand away. He took a step back but also leaned forward to look closely at Kamuk's face. "No," he said again, but this time it wasn't disbelief, it was dismay—and recognition. "There's no atonement. Not even the death you deserved then."

"I understand your feelings," Kamuk said, his voice nearly back to normal. "But hear me out. I'm an agent of Imperial Intelligence, although Kang and Krell don't know that. I'm in a position to change the Empire's approach to colonial expansion under the Organian treaty. I swear on my honor, on Kahless, to pay for what I did on Sherman's Planet. However, I believe I can do so in a way that will not harm the Empire. I am a loyal Klingon."

Baris shook his head. "All lies, all games. Just another role for you to play."

"Yes, it is a role, but it's no game." Kamuk took a step closer, a wolfish smile on his face. Baris did not retreat. "The real Kamuk gave the order to poison the quadrotriticale. Killing him was my first step back to honor."

"He still didn't trust me, of course. He hated me." Kamuk finished his *raktajino*, giving the empty mug a disappointed look before continuing. "But he saw that the course I was taking was the right one in the long run. My little civil war within Intelligence forced the changes I'd hoped for, but it also forced me out. Luckily, Gorkon, a very forward thinker, took me on his staff, and I continued to reform certain extreme elements within the Empire, forcing them down a more honorable path. I found myself in a position to help Baris again as he rose in power, and for decades we promoted peace between Federation and Empire. I did so out of a sense of paying my honor debt. Baris, however, did so out of fear that being exposed would cause everything to come crashing down. While I felt that I continued to redeem myself, he felt increasingly guilty and compromised. I did not foresee the effect my becoming governor of Bajor would have on him. It brought everything to the surface."

"So his coming out of retirement for the Bajorans . . . his motive really was just to get back at you."

"That was part of it, but you should not think it was entirely selfish. He truly believed the Bajorans would be better off free from the Empire. My presence just made it all the more personal."

"What about you, Governor? Do you think the Bajorans would be better off free?"

Kamuk paused, taking a long deep breath and releasing it with a sigh. "I do. When they are ready. This issue is exactly what broke Baris."

"You mean at the conference he organized here five years ago?"

"Yes. He was certain he could convince me to move for immediate Bajoran independence."

"Who was that young Bajoran woman?" Baris paced in front of Kamuk's desk. He pointed a pale, wrinkled finger at Kamuk. "Do you know her? I swear, if I find out you orchestrated that little scene, I will lodge a formal complaint with your ambassador."

"Relax, please." Kamuk looked Baris up and down, concerned the old human was going to do himself harm by his own rage as he stomped back and forth in the governor's office. "If anyone staged that, it was Jaro."

"So it was only coincidence that when you finally deigned to see me this is what happened?"

"That is precisely why I avoided seeing you earlier. I knew that you would accuse me of manipulation. I wanted you to see for yourself what the Bajorans would freely say outside of my presence. Did that server say anything that you had not already heard?"

"But why would any Bajoran say those things? They practically give Bajor to the Empire."

"Did you listen to nothing that she said?" Kamuk shouted, startling Baris. "They are not ready to be on their own. Their planet was laid waste by the Cardassians and they resent the Federation for doing nothing about it."

"So you get to be the hero, is that how this works?"

"Nilz, just shut up and sit down!"

They glared at each other across the desk for a long minute, then Baris did ease his ancient frame into one of the chairs facing the desk.

"Just put aside your hatred for me for once. You must understand that I see Bajor as continuing atonement for my past. As governor I can assure that the Empire will do no harm in this system. The Empire has come a long way from Sherman's Planet and Benecia, but it is still an Empire, and its needs come before its subject systems. But I am a voice of moderation. The Empire protects Bajor more than the Federation ever did, and I protect Bajor from the Empire. Bajorans like Jaro understand this, and they honestly appreciate what I have done as governor. I will not abandon them.

"You were not able to protect Sherman's Planet from me, but you no longer need to try. I am doing good here. You can trust me. You have done so for decades. Why are you fighting me now?"

"I haven't trusted you since I heard you speak Klingon. But I was willing to work with you because you were doing the same thing I was . . . protecting the quadrant from violent expansion. But when the Empire used the peace we built to conquer Cardassia and then kept the Union's slave systems within the Empire, we parted paths.

"I could have turned you over to Starfleet the moment I discovered you were Klingon, but I didn't. I could have exposed you on Benecia, but I didn't. After all we've accomplished together, how can you turn your back on me now?"

Kamuk smiled a sad, human smile at Baris. "I don't believe I have, Nilz, don't you see? I have taken Bajor under my wing as protectively and fiercely as you did with Sherman's Planet. If you can't see that, we will have to agree to disagree. But please don't think I've turned my back on you. I'm sure you won't believe this, but I have always thought of you as a friend. I have cheered your successes and grieved your losses. I roared to the sky when I heard about Sima's death. On my honor I tell you this."

Baris's fierce glare finally softened, and the weight of his years seemed to suddenly press down on him as he slumped in his chair. "But how could I ever really trust you?" he said softly.

Kamuk leaned forward. "Think of how I saved your life in the Council chamber all those years ago. That was only a small payment on my debt of honor. When I chose that road I could not turn back. But I started on that path long before I killed Kruge. After you found me out on Sherman's Planet, I received new orders." He paused and shook his head. "My last assignment as Arne Darvin was to kill Nilz Baris."

Jensen sat in her chair, feeling a bit numb from all the revelations. This was the biggest story of her career, probably the rest of her life. But Gardner's doubts rose in her mind; this would change everything. No matter what she did, she would never see anything the same. Was her boss right, that some things were better left unknown? She hated second-guessing herself.

Kamuk had gotten up again to gaze out the port at Bajor. "Nilz went back to Earth, his long and heroic career capped by failure and embarrassment, taken to task by the very people he was trying to help. It was a sad ending, and I told that miserable little Ferengi that he would not profit from it.

"My crimes had weighed heavily on Baris throughout his life. He contacted me a few weeks ago. He praised me for my work on rebuilding Bajor, and I assured him we were nearing independence. I told him I wanted him at the ceremony, but he knew he would not last much longer. He wanted to die with a clear conscience, but he was concerned about the ramifications, especially for me and the Bajorans. I told him to do what his honor dictated." Kamuk turned back toward Jensen. "It is the same thing I tell you."

"But why tell me at all?" Jensen said loudly, suddenly angry at the immensity of what had been laid out before her. "You could have kept this to yourself and no one would ever have known."

"When you told me his last words, then I knew in his final moments he was thinking of what I did. Perhaps it is time to give voice to that. In a way, I have given you Nilz's final interview. And now you must make the same decision Nilz did." Kamuk headed toward the door, which slid open at his approach.

"But I don't know his decision." Jensen stretched her arms wide in confusion. "All he said was your name. It could have just as easily been accusation as absolution."

Kamuk stopped at the threshold, turning back to her, and smiled grimly. "That is why the true warrior must always rely on his own honor, not someone else's. It is a lesson I learned most painfully."

He turned and left, the door sliding shut behind him, leaving Jensen alone with her thoughts. The ramifications were stunning: Relations between Federation and Empire would be shaken. The legacy of the late Nilz Baris, a beloved president and ambassador, would be reassessed. Kamuk would be exposed as—what? His actions over the last hundred years had reshaped the Empire for good or ill, depending on your viewpoint. He had assumed two different identities, bringing death and salvation as he tried to maintain his honor. What would happen to him, to Bajor, if he were exposed?

Shaking herself out of this reverie, Jensen got to her feet. She found herself looking down at Bajor even though she needed to back to the *Geldonero*. Gardner expected to hear from her soon, and she had a deadline.

Acknowledgments

DAVID R. GEORGE III

As has often been the case, I must first thank Marco Palmieri, who offered me the opportunity to pen one of the *Myriad Universes: Shattered Light* stories. When we first discussed the possibility of my writing a what-if *Star Trek* yarn, I told Marco which of the various series I knew best, and so in which framework I could most easily develop an alternate-history tale. Marco immediately suggested that I set my narrative in a different incarnation of *Trek,* in order to present myself a greater challenge. Marco not only understands the artistic process, but passionately supports and encourages it. He is a fine editor, and even more importantly, a good man and a good friend.

Thanks as well to Margaret Clark, who inherited this project from Marco, and who provided both solid guidance and welcome encouragement. Margaret knows her *Star Trek* and she knows how to edit, and she never fails to provide perspective and an opportunity for scholarly debate. Thanks also to Jaime Costas and Emilia Pisani, who helped bring this story home.

I would also like to thank my fellow contributors to this volume, Steve Mollmann and Michael Schuster, and Scott Pearson. It's a pleasure to take this voyage with these three hail-fellows-well-met. A long and winding road, perhaps, but at least we've finally arrived at our mutual destination.

On an extremely personal note, thank you to Marty Nedboy.

I knew Marty for nearly fifteen years before his tragic death, and that decade and a half seem like a cheat now, hardly enough time to enjoy such an uproariously funny, strikingly unique man. He had a powerful zest for life, an incredibly quick and sardonic wit, and an encyclopedic knowledge of both film and musical theater; in fact, in the last years of his life, he cowrote a stage musical, which I hope one day to see on Broadway. I know that I will be retelling his jokes and relating stories of his life for the rest of my days. As his dear niece, Robin Nedboy, once noted, I am a card-carrying (though high-functioning) member of the Cult of Marty.

I also want to thank Walter Ragan, who not only welcomed me into his family, but continues to make me feel at home there. After all these years, I still look up to Walt, a man of high character. His love and support are boundless.

I can never pen acknowledgments without thanking Jennifer George and Anita Smith. These two fine women mean the world to me, not just because they continuously bolster me, but because of who they are. Jen and Anita are simply the best, in absolutely every conceivable way.

Thanks also to Patricia Walenista, without whom I most assuredly would not even be here. Without her warm and loving presence in my life, my journey would have taken a far different form, and I would have been the worse for it. Every day, she sets an example of how to seek fulfillment and happiness, while at the same time contributing to the world in a positive, caring way.

Finally, thank you to Karen Ragan-George, who keeps my heart beating quicker, my brain thinking deeper, and my mouth laughing harder. Each day, each hour, each minute with Karen are fuller than they would be otherwise. She adds a singular quality to my life that continues to enrich me, and though there are not enough words to convey how much I love and appreciate her, in a very real sense, Karen makes all my words possible.

STEVE MOLLMANN & MICHAEL SCHUSTER

Like any work of *Star Trek* fiction, there's a long list of influences that have informed our work—far too many to list here in their entirety. We'll take a stab at the most important ones.

Our portrayal of the Sulu family owes a debt of inspiration to *The Captain's Daughter* by Peter David and *Serpents Among the Ruins* by David R. George III. Not to mention Jacqueline Kim's performance in *Generations* and George Takei's in so many years of *Star Trek*, especially *The Undiscovered Country*.

Our depiction of Vulcan obviously owes a lot to Diane Duane's books, most notably the ones that feature both the poet S'task and an obscure philosopher called Surak (*Spock's World* and *The Romulan Way*). In addition, we used material from various other literary sources, such as *Dwellers in the Crucible* by Margaret Wander Bonanno, the *Vulcan's Soul* trilogy by Josepha Sherman and Susan Shwartz, *The Lost Years* by J. M. Dillard, and *Ishmael* by Barbary Hambly, as well as the RPG sourcebook *The Way of Kolinahr*. If this had been a book about Klingons, we could have used the indispensable *Klingon Dictionary* by Marc Okrand. Unfortunately, no such reference exists for the Vulcans, which is why we would have been free to simply make up all the phrases. However, we stumbled across two remarkable fan-run websites that were exactly what we needed—the Vulcan Language Institute (http://www.stogeek.com/wiki/Category:Vulcan_Language_ Institute) and the Vulcan Language Dictionary (http://www .starbase-10.de/vld/)—so we were able to give our alien phrases some semblance of authenticity.

As you will know if you've already finished this story, Andorians also factored into it a great deal. Foremost among our influences was the work done with the species in the *Deep Space Nine* novels under Marco Palmieri, especially *This Gray Spirit* and *Andor: Paradigm* by Heather Jarman. Also influential were

"Yesteryear" by D. C. Fontana, the *Starfleet Academy* comic series by Chris Cooper, *The Fall of Terok Nor* by Judith and Garfield Reeves-Stevens, and the *Star Trek: Enterprise* episode "The Aenar" by André Bormanis (story by Manny Coto). We also nicked some characters from here and there to staff *Kumari*: our universe's Phelana Yudrin was seen in Michael Jan Friedman's *My Brother's Keeper* trilogy, Vanda M'Giia is from the *Starfleet Academy* computer game, and s'Bysh derives from A. C. Crispin's novel *Sarek*. Other bits and pieces too numerous to lay out here were borrowed from various other sources as well, for which we are thankful to Ian McLean's website, *The Andor Files* (http://www. geocities.com/therinofandor/).

And without those excellent resources Memory Alpha (http:// memory-alpha.org/) and Memory Beta (http://startrek.wikia .com/), we'd have been in a heckuva lot of trouble.

Of course, we are eternally grateful to our editor Marco Palmieri for giving two relative newcomers an opportunity like this. It's not often one gets to carve out one's own universe! His suggestions shaped and improved this story immeasurably. And thanks to Jaime Costas and Emilia Pisani for picking up the ball and running with it.

Special thanks to Brendan Moody and Jonathan Polk for reading the first draft of this manuscript. And double special thanks to Steve's fellow members of the Storrs Eight: Jared Demick, Gordon Fraser, Chantelle Messier, Jessica Petriello, Zara Rix, Christiana Salah, and Jorge Santos, plus Angela Bouchard and Phillip Messier. The Storrs Eight has provided many evenings of commentary, camaraderie, and cuisine, and without them this would be a much weaker work.

Steve also has to thank his family for putting up with him spending his 2008/09 holiday visit writing, especially his ever-patient mother and father. And most of all, Hayley, who didn't seem to mind too much when he ignored her. Which is good, since she'll have to get used to it.

Naturally, Michael wants to thank his family and friends as well, for their love, their unfailing support, and their acceptance of the fact that he's unlikely to write a "normal" novel anytime soon.

SCOTT PEARSON

I'd like to thank my wife, Sandra, and daughter, Ella, for many nights and weekends of patience while I clattered away at the keyboard. Thanks to Gene Roddenberry and all the cast, crew, and writers of the original series. A big thanks to David Gerrold for "The Trouble with Tribbles" (Ella says it's her favorite episode) and to William Schallert (Nilz Baris), Charlie Brill (Arne Darvin), and William Campbell (Koloth). A memorial kudos for Michael Pataki (Korax), who passed away while I was revising the manuscript. Michael Ansara (Kang) and John Colicos (Kor) also receive barbaric yawps.

The episodes "Affliction," "Divergence," "Day of The Dove," "Errand of Mercy," "Trials and Tribble-ations," and "Blood Oath," and movies *The Search for Spock*, *The Voyage Home*, and *The Undiscovered Country* provided important backdrops, and all their writers and actors are much appreciated. Michael Dorn's Worf and *Star Trek: The Next Generation* and *Deep Space Nine* shaped the latter parts of my story.

I drew McCoy material from David R. George III's *Provenance of Shadows*. *Excelsior: Forged in Fire* by Michael A. Martin and Andy Mangels was a significant back story. Marc Okrand's Klingon language books were a great help, with further Klingon goodness from Lawrence Schoen and Keith R. A. DeCandido. I thank all the other writers and actors of episodes and books referenced in asides too many to enumerate. Mike and Denise Okuda's *Star Trek Encyclopedia* and *Chronology* were indispensable, as were Geoffrey Mandel's *Star Charts* (and Tony Morgan's index to the charts, at www.startrekcrossindex.com) and the websites Memory Alpha, Memory Beta, and Chrissie's Transcripts Site (www.chakoteya.net).

Jeff Ayers, Jeff Ford, William Leisner, and Paul Simpson were beta readers extraordinaire. I tip my hat to Bill in particular, my first reader who nailed down a number of loose ends. I wouldn't be here except for editor Marco Palmieri, who gave me the chance to pitch and bought the story. Editors Jaime Costas, Margaret Clark, and Emilia Pisani all helped bring it home during turbulent times. Marian Cordry at CBS made great suggestions.

Regarding my fellow authors, the multitudinous David R. George III and the crime-fighting duo of Steve Mollmann and Michael Schuster: in my *Trek* story "Full Circle" I stole much of Harriman's back story from David's *Serpents Among the Ruins*. In turn, Steve and Michael referenced "Full Circle" in their S.C.E. novella, *The Future Begins*. So it's very satisfying to be in an anthology with these guys.

Tangential thanks to: Inge Heyer and the Shore Leave staff for having me as a writer guest at their fabulous convention. Fans and friends for socializing on Facebook, TrekBBS, and Live Journal. Greg Cox, Kevin Dilmore, Kevin Lauderdale, Dave Mack, and Dayton Ward for emails that are sometimes just not quite right. Lastly, Orson Welles and Herman J. Mankiewicz for their contribution to this alternate life story of Nilz Foster Baris.

About the Authors

DAVID R. GEORGE III has visited the *Star Trek* universe many times in his writing. His novels have appeared on the *New York Times* and *USA Today* bestseller lists, and his *Star Trek: Voyager* episode, "Prime Factors," received a nomination for a *Sci-Fi Universe* award in the category "Best Writing in a Genre Television Show or Telefilm." His most recent *Trek* work, the *Crucible* trilogy, comprises the novels *Provenance of Shadows*, *The Fire and the Rose*, and *The Star to Every Wandering*, which helped celebrate the fortieth anniversary of the original *Star Trek*. Three other novels—*Olympus Descending* (which appears in *Worlds of Deep Space Nine, Volume Three*), *Twilight*, and *The 34th Rule*—take place in the *Deep Space Nine* milieu. Another novel, *Serpents Among the Ruins*, and a novella, *Iron and Sacrifice* (which is contained in the anthology *Tales from the Captain's Table*), are so-called *Lost Era* tales, set in the years between the original *Star Trek* and *The Next Generation*. David also wrote "Deep Into That Darkness Peering," an introduction to the *Twist of Faith* omnibus, and he has also penned nearly a dozen articles for *Star Trek Magazine*. His forthcoming novel, *Rough Beasts of Empire*, returns to the twenty-fourth century to explore a divided Romulan empire and the nascent Typhon Pact, and features the principal characters of Spock and Benjamin Sisko. Outside of *Star Trek*, David's novelette, "Moon Over Luna," appears in the anthology *Thrilling Wonder Stories, Volume 2*.

Born and raised in New York City, David presently makes his home in southern California, where he lives with his delectable wife, Karen. They are both aficionados of the arts—books, theater, museums, film, music, dance—and they can often be found partaking in one or another of them. They also love to travel, and are particularly fond of Paris, Venezia, Roma, Hawai'i, New York City, and the Pacific Northwest. They also enjoying taking cruises, and following their beloved—though frequently heartbreaking—New York Mets.

No animals were harmed in the writing of this author bio.

STEVE MOLLMANN is a Ph.D. student in literature at the University of Connecticut, where he spends his time studying the depiction of science and technology in fiction, especially during the Victorian period of British history. His first publication was co-written with Michael Schuster, a Scotty novella called *The Future Begins*, which was reprinted this summer in *Star Trek: Corps of Engineers: What's Past*. They also wrote two short stories for *Star Trek: The Next Generation: The Sky's the Limit*, and their first full-length novel, *Star Trek: A Choice of Catastrophes*, will be released in 2011. In addition to his fiction publications with Michael, Steve has also written an article on *The War of the Worlds* for *English Literature in Transition*. He resides in Willimantic, Connecticut, with his wife, Hayley, and their two cats, but he will always be a Cincinnatian at heart, even if he technically never has been by geography.

MICHAEL SCHUSTER lives in a picturesque Austrian mountain valley, with half a continent and one entire ocean between him and Steve Mollmann. A bank employee by day, he likes to come up with new (or at least relatively unused) ideas that can be turned into stories with loving care and the occasional nudge. Currently, the two are hard at work building their own universe-sized sandbox to play in. More information about them (as well as background information about their stories, including *The Tears of Eridanus*) can be found at http://www.exploringtheuniverse.net/.

SCOTT PEARSON has published humor, poetry, short stories, reviews, and nonfiction. "Out of the Jacuzzi, Into the Sauna," his not-entirely-serious mystery story, is available in the anthology *Resort to Murder*. "Finders Keepers" resides in *Full Throttle Space Tales #3: Space Grunts*, edited by Dayton Ward. His poetry has appeared in the online magazines *Strange Horizons* and *Down in the Cellar*, as well as in various print magazines and anthologies, most recently in *Paper Crow*. He contributed the discography to *Whole Lotta Led Zeppelin: The Illustrated History of the Heaviest Band of All Time*. He never really knows what he's going to do next.

Scott's first published *Star Trek* story, "Full Circle," appeared in *Strange New Worlds VII*, followed by "Terra Tonight" in *Strange New Worlds 9*. His story "Among the Clouds" is in the *Star Trek: The Next Generation* twentieth anniversary anthology *The Sky's the Limit*. He has also written for the official *Star Trek* magazine. *Honor in the Night* is his first published novel.

Scott works as an editor for Zenith Press, a history publisher in Minneapolis, and X-comm, a regional history publisher in Duluth, Minnesota. Scott lives near the banks of the mighty Mississippi River, fabled in story and song, in personable St. Paul, Minnesota, with his wife, Sandra, and daughter, Ella. Visit him on the web at www.yeahsure.net, www.facebook.com/yeahsure, and http://scottpearson.livejournal.com.